The Postulant

♥ ♥ ♥

A NOVEL

MARIO A. IEZZONI

ISBN 978-0-9789187-4-3

The Postulant

Published by Mario A. Iezzoni

www.thepostulant.com

miezzoni@gmail.com

Dedication

———

To my wife Mary Ann
friend, life partner

~

To my daughter Kate
determined, dedicated, deserving

~

To my daughter Mariel
introspective, worldly, talented, special

~

To my son Christopher
intellectually gifted, wind always in his face

"Go confidently in the direction of your dreams! Live the life you've imagined. As you simplify your life, the laws of the universe will be simpler."

Henry David Thoreau

In Memory of

———

Keith Backlund

1952 – 2012

~ ~ ~

Master Woodworker

Innovator

World Renowned Whitewater Paddle Designer

Simply the Best

Prologue

Before leaving for the Fatima Vocational Retreat in Golfito, Costa Rica, Lucy Dennison wanted to get together with her college girlfriends one last time and complete the dare the threesome had joked about since freshman year in college. A week after their graduation, they met near Lucy's home and drove to Rockport, an isolated river access point nine miles downstream on the banks of the Lehigh River. It was time to execute the dare, to skinny-dip at Devil's Elbow.

Irene and Rachael, Lucy's friends, had always thought she was a bit loony, and her recent decision to enter the convent, just as crazy.

"Lucy's bipolar, I tell ya. She's got a dark side," Rachael told Irene, after Lucy ran ahead of them, excited.

"How do you know that?" Irene questioned.

"Many times I witnessed Lucy's personality shifts," Rachael recalled. "Unexpectedly, she'd shut down, isolate herself, and not talk for days. Her younger sister—in confidence—said Lucy had a psychological disorder. And mentioned her family felt it best that she join the convent."

"Lucy's not cut out for the convent—she's too much a free spirit," Irene said, quickening her pace.

"Sister Lucy, wait, wait for us," Rachael called, trotting along the railroad grade with Irene, racing to catch up with their good friend.

Lucy stopped at a waterfall that tumbled into the Lehigh River, then called to her arriving schoolmates. "Finally, we are here. Time to do the dare and become deliciously sinful. You guys didn't believe me, did you? You thought a future nun wouldn't do this kind of thing. Well, you were wrong."

She slipped off her sneakers and walked down the steep embankment, onto a flat rock that extended into the river.

"Holy shit, Rachael! She's going to do it," Irene said, concerned she'd have to follow.

"Now, guys, just as we bet, for it to be official, you must swim across the river, get out on the other side, then swim back."

Irene and Rachael looked at each other and shook their heads; neither expected Lucy to take the dare seriously.

Thin, small-breasted, and dark-haired, Lucy slipped off her clothes, wadded them, and tossed the bundle to her friends.

"Catch! Who's going in next?"

Stark naked and with a crazy look, Lucy dove headfirst into the current.

Splash.

Lucy's bare body surfaced and bobbed in the swirling river. She flung water from her hair.

"Told you I'd do this—always wanted to. I've dreamed about this all year—my last fling before I head south to Celibate Village."

Rachael turned to Irene. "Maybe it is best she become a nun. I pity the man destined to marry her. Lucy's not right."

"Hey, goofy Lucy," Irene called. "You better start swimming; the current's taking you downstream."

Lucy flipped onto her stomach. Her ivory buttocks turned toward the sky. Snow-white legs flapped and splashed. There was no progress. She flipped over and tried to backstroke.

"Guys, I don't think I can make it. The current's stronger than it looks."

Lucy drifted toward the rapid below.

~ ~ ~

Downstream, surfing his kayak at his favorite spot, was whitewater river guide Mark Weston. He did not see the girls trotting along the railroad grade. He was deep in thought, studying the flow of the river as it raced past. It had been two years since he returned from Costa Rica, two years since he made love to Jane on Pavones Beach.

This afternoon, he was feeling lonely. He missed Jane. So he hopped on the river for a quick whitewater run to clear his head and stopped to surf his favorite wave. Mark missed her reddish, curly hair, her perpetual smile, and innocent expression. He missed the open, intellectual conversations they often enjoyed. And regretted Jane's decision to become a nun.

He did make the effort to talk her out of her decision while in Costa Rica, after he returned from his daring solo descent of the Rio Chirripo. But Jane's close friend, the soon-to-be Sister Elizabeth Florence, told him Jane had affirmed her decision, and had left to start her postulancy.

Florence said Jane wanted to thank him for the painting of Pavones he gave her. And that her decision to enter the convent was final, and please don't come looking for her.

Staring into the river, admiring the hologram that projected from his Ashland paddle blade, Mark looked upriver when he heard cries for help. Directly in front of him was a girl. If he hadn't moved his kayak quickly to the right, the bow would have speared her.

"Where did this babe come from?" he thought. "She's stark naked."

Mark spun his kayak off the wave and caught up with the girl drifting in the current.

"Need some assistance, baby cakes?" the handsome young river guide said, chuckling.

"I don't think so," she said.

"You are not going to make it through this rapid without getting hurt." Mark eyed her. "By the time you get to the bottom, you're going to be black and blue if you don't climb aboard."

"All right, but close your eyes, mister river man."

Lucy had reconsidered her plan because she didn't want to explain to her controlling father where the bruises came from.

Mark closed his eyes.

Lucy crawled onto the front deck of his kayak, sprawled lengthwise, and wrapped her arms and legs around the hull.

"If I can't open my eyes, how am I going to get you through this rapid?" He chuckled.

"I guess you're going to have to peek."

With Lucy clinging to the bow, Mark opened his eyes and started to maneuver around the rocks and through the waves.

"Enjoying the view?" Lucy asked.

"Lovin' it," Mark said. "You're gorgeous."

No man had ever told Lucy she was gorgeous before. In fact, this was the first time she was naked in front of a man.

With a devilish look, Mark brought Lucy to the riverbank.

As she sat on the bow of his kayak, her petite chest bobbed in his face.

Mark turned red.

Lucy spoke candidly.

"I've never done this before. What a way to end a perfect day—rescued, with no bathing suit. I'm sure it's every man's dream."

Lucy bent over and kissed Mark squarely on the lips.

"Thank you, mister river guide."

Lucy crawled off his kayak and scurried up the embankment.

"What's your name?" Mark asked as she hurried away.

"It's baby cakes. I thought you knew that."

Lucy stood proudly on the riverbank and waved goodbye.

Stunned, Mark shook his head in disbelief, then rolled upside down in his kayak to clear his thoughts.

His memory of Jane had suddenly erased.

He'd found a new conquest.

†

Sister Katherine

Chapter 1

"Sister Katherine's death is my fault," thought Keith Ashland while hanging upside down in his kayak. "I killed her." But the river bottom, with its cobbled Appalachian stones, didn't care to listen. Keith's life journey had intersected Katherine's scripted existence and snuffed it out.

"Brrr, this water is always so damn cold," he said, rolling right-side up, looking around to get his bearings. The narrow scars that encircled his wrists, ankles, and neck had drawn tight from the chilly water. Their dull, stretching pain reminded him again of a horror he struggled to forget.

"Good, I'm past Tombstone Rock. The danger is behind me," he said, digging his kayak paddle into the churning river, heading to the takeout.

Over the Maryland state line, on the Upper Youghiogheny River, Keith Ashland had just finished his run of the region's most notorious whitewater. The intense physical exertion, the mayhem, had put him at peace—as it always did. And with the memory of Sister Katherine, his love for her, his heartache, now numbed, he shoved his kayak into the back of his station wagon and headed to the saw mill before it got dark.

Keith often went to the mill to search for discarded lengths of hardwoods to use in the handcrafting of his now famous New World paddles. Building the world's best whitewater paddles was an obsession for him, rivaled only by his love for negotiating the challenging rapids of the Upper Yough.

With no real production schedule, he built paddles when it suited him, or when he foresaw the moment his funds would run dry, denying him his booze and his self-prescribed, mind-numbing herbal medications—fearful a lacking would drop him back into the reality he ran from each day.

His flat gaze rolled about the quiet mill until it fixed upon a stack of hardwoods loosely piled on a pallet next to a 72-inch saw blade licked wet by the settling fog, eager to consent to a nighttime of rust. As his pupils worked to transfer the image to his brain, a grin lifted his weary face. Several of the lengths possessed the tight, resolute, linear grain he sought, but rarely found.

Keith bundled the wood and headed home.

The flathead six of his '64 Chevy Nova station wagon banged away, spewing exhaust each time it traversed another dip in the pitted road. Beneath the seat, an empty bottle of Scotch rolled left and right, atop a greasy hoagie wrapper. A Styrofoam coffee cup, with chewed plastic lid, took flight, racing like a trapped squirrel, escaping out an open window moments before he turned off, heading deeper into the woods to his trailer.

Arriving at the dingy singlewide, he made his way to his woodshop in the converted back bedroom. Letting the unbundling lengths tumble onto the worn workbench littered with wood shavings and hardened resin lumps, Keith pulled the overhead lamp close.

Reaching for a tuning fork and tapping it against a chunk of metal, he touched the stem to the hardwood. He listened . . . The resonance told him the density buried within.

No one knew of the tuning fork technique. It was his most closely guarded secret. And each time he heard *that* perfect note, he placed the special length on a shelf underneath the workbench. This was his private stock. The final lengths he found tonight.

Lifting a full bottle of Scotch that always sat within reach, Keith cracked the cap and chugged. He raised his eyes to an oil painting that hung above him. It was of a Costa Rican beach, with endlessly rolling ocean waves racing onto cobblestones that jutted from the jungle's edge. Above the tropical greenery were towering, smokestack cumulus clouds that lifted into a deep-blue sky.

But it was the lacquer frame, carved from remnants of a bloodstained cross, that was most disturbing. Sculpted within the hard teak were crucifixes, with the nailed body of Jesus and of a woman—each of Jesus' outstretched hands touching the fingertips of the crucified woman.

As his eyes flooded with tears, he lifted the bottle to his lips and turned away.

Chapter 2

The next morning, when Keith arrived in Friendsville, Maryland, his nicotine/caffeine high had fully arrived. The Nova made its way over a bridge into the center of town, the home of Hell and High Water River Outfitters.

He climbed from the car and quickly untied his kayak, strapped to 2x4 roof racks. With his thumb, index, and middle fingers pinching the rope, he pulled until the tension maximized.

The rope end shot over the boat, striking the cinderblock wall on the other side.

"Convenient and efficient," thought Keith, proud of the simple ways he did things, proud of the clean knots that tied down his boats.

Lifting his kayak, Keith lugged it to a green painted school bus that sat outside the Outfitters' building. He opened the emergency door and rammed the kayak up the aisle. Grasping the stern with both hands, he shoved, lodging it between the seat cushions. He crawled in, closed the emergency exit, and stretched along the last seat, placing his lifejacket under his head as a damp pillow.

He chanted, "Boat, paddle, lifejacket, spray skirt, helmet." Making sure he had all the equipment he needed.

Sporting a bad hangover, Keith questioned whether he'd be useful as a river guide today. He lifted his head and peered out the bus window. "Here come the rafters," he said as three thin Vietnamese girls were about to board.

His closest friend, a chiseled, blond-haired, blue-eyed river guide named Mark Weston, followed.

Keith's attention turned to the attractive Asian women coming down the aisle. Chattering in English, the girls crawled over his wedged kayak to get to the only empty seats. Two sat directly in front. The third girl took the seat across the aisle.

In mid-sentence, they switched to their native tongue.

Craving another cigarette and a jolt of caffeine, Keith closed his eyes and listened to their conversation in a language he was once fluent in.

The girls teased their friend in the half-empty seat about how cute Mark was. They chided her, asking what she'd do if he fell in love with her. Then went on to plan her whole life, saying she would become a mountain woman, making many healthy babies. That it was worth it, because the river guide was handsome and strong like a water buffalo.

As the bus rolled forward toward the main highway and started up the long grade that would take them to Sang Run, the put-in, Keith dosed off.

Chapter 3

His flashbacks always came when he slept. They started with him pinned against Tombstone Rock, his kayak folded around his legs, entrapping him; running out of oxygen as his head slipped beneath the surface, losing consciousness.

But this time, perhaps triggered by the sight of the Vietnamese women, his haunting nightmare was much different—more horrific.

~ ~ ~

The brightest kid in his high school graduating class, Keith had joined the Navy, thinking volunteering would avoid a trip to the Vietnam War. To his surprise, the Navy shipped him off to a repair facility on the Vietnam mainland, a naval base on the southern shore of the Quy Nhon seaport.

With not much to do, Keith occupied his free time by carving teak chess pieces with a Swiss Army knife. And for exercise, he ventured to the beach to surf the unusually long, consistent breaks on the south side of the inlet.

Occasionally, a priest flew in to serve mass atop a picnic table overlooking the bay. One day, prior to the outdoor mass, a small boat set off from the village across the bay with a nun to assist the military priest, and to retrieve a few dollars from the soldiers for the upkeep of the village Catholic church.

The narrow, cigar-shaped dugout operated by a bald Vietnamese man arrived. Riding in the bow was the nun, swathed in flowing black garments. The small man maneuvered the craft toward shore, letting the bow slide up the silt bank as far as it could. Adjusting her balance, the nun, holding her head low, gingerly stepped out.

Mud stuck to her tightly laced black shoes. Rosaries draped in her left hand swayed as she gingerly made her way up the embankment.

As she arrived, a tired, sheepish priest opened a weathered leather bag. From it, he lifted a gold crucifix wrapped in fine, decorative, ivory linen. He unfolded his stole and held it in both hands. Pinching the fine fabric, he kissed and lifted it over his head, allowing it to drape his khaki uniform.

As the nun moved behind to adjust his collar, the priest took out his nicked chalice and a small, weathered Bible, swollen from the humidity.

He kissed each then served the mass.

Keith's eyes followed the nun as she came from behind the priest and sent a sweeping glance over the praying troops. She was striking. Her gentle Asian cheeks dissolved toward, large, stunning, almond eyes. Her facial expression held a confident, uncomplicated serenity.

She stood stoic, radiating a peaceful beauty as she softly recited the mass with the priest.

Captivated by her beauty, Keith watched her intently, and deduced she was of mixed heritage, not entirely Vietnamese.

When the short service ended, the priest gave the nun a quick study. Her brown eyes deliberately rolled toward the priest, revealing her sternness. His eyes jerked away. He was no match for the intensity she displayed.

The nun glided around to collect what the soldiers cared to share. When she approached Keith, he produced a twenty-dollar bill and hastily handed it to her. A glow of gratitude lit the eyes that matched his fervent gaze. The money disappeared into a pocket concealed somewhere in the loosely flowing linens.

In a graceful turn, she headed in the direction of the boat.

As she made her way down the slippery bank, Keith rushed to assist the nun, extending his arm for support. With finesse acquired from another culture, the nun placed her delicate hand on his forearm.

Lifting her head, revealing her generous, brown eyes with long, lifting lashes, she smiled.

Keith's entire body quaked as her beauty descended upon him.

Frantic, he wanted to speak with her. He asked in barely understandable Vietnamese, "Is ... is ... there mass in the village?"

The nun answered softly in clear English, "No, but you are welcome to visit and pray if you wish."

Pointing to the steeple across the inlet, she adjusted the pitch of her gentle voice. "But there is no priest."

The nun looked back to see if the priest heard her comment.

~ ~ ~

The next day, Keith crossed the bay to the village. There was a tiny square with a marketplace on the north side. A white clapboard Roman Catholic Church occupied the south side of the square. A sand dune to the east blocked much of the heavy ocean breeze.

Keith entered the modest church with its saintly statues positioned throughout. Wood-framed pictures depicting the Stations of the Cross hung evenly spaced around the impeccably clean church. A marble altar glistened from the sunlight that beamed through stained glass windows.

When Keith saw no one was inside, he exited and wandered around back, toward a rectangular structure. It looked like a classroom, with living facilities in the rear. On the front porch, a slender Vietnamese girl swept sand deposited by the sea breeze. The top half of her broom was broken in a way that forced her to bend a bit too far. Clutching the handle with both hands, she struggled to sweep the steps.

She wore loose-fitting, dark blue shorts with a simple white T-shirt. Graceful olive legs extended from her tiny frame below a waist that was Hepburn thin. Shining brunette hair, cut medium length, seemed too curly for that of an Asian girl.

The nun straightened, emitted a slight wince, and said in a clear, forthright voice, "How are you?"

Keith stumbled to respond. The greeting in English rendered him speechless. Her expressive brown eyes sent a shiver down his spine.

Stammering, he finally uttered, "Hello, what's your name?"

"Sister Katherine," the nun said politely.

"Are you from here?" Keith asked, holding a distance.

"Yes and no, you may say. My mother was born in this village. But my father was a French soldier who met her while on duty here."

She pointed toward the church. "They were married over there and moved to Paris shortly before I was born. So it depends on how you measure, if I am from here or not."

With a glow in her eyes, she went on. "I like to think I am a native." The nun continued, as if she had not spoken to anyone in months. "The church assigned me here after the Viet Cong chased the priest from the village. Also, the bishop, knowing my mother was from the village, needed someone local to look after this property."

She paused, thought for a moment, then, blurted, "Or, it could be as punishment for disrespecting Mother Superior, Sister Bernadine."

Suddenly, she clapped her hands. "Oh! You're the soldier who helped me to the boat. Is there something I can help you with?"

"Yes," Keith said, delighted she recognized him.

"What brings you here, soldier?"

Justifying his presence with an excuse, Keith pointed toward the open inlet.

"I usually surf on the south side and wanted to see if the beach break to the north is just as good." Anxious to keep the encounter alive, he added, "Is there something I can do to help you?"

Katherine motioned toward the broom.

"Get me a broom with a longer handle."

Then suddenly, as quickly as the conversation began, it ended.

She whirled on her heels and scampered off into the building, closing the door behind her, leaving him flat-footed and speechless.

Keith stood in shocked silence. Had he done something inappropriate? Puzzled, he went back to the base.

That night Keith made Sister Katherine a broom handle, giving it a subtle curve for leverage.

After duty the next day, he returned to the church and found Katherine in the back again. He asked for the broken broom and fitted the extension. It fit perfectly, increasing the length so Katherine could stand upright.

"You're a gifted woodworker," she complimented.

Leaning the broom against the wall, she asked, "Would you do the church a favor?"

"What is it?" Keith asked.

"My parents donated a cross that hung over the altar. But the Viet Cong took it to shore up their tunnels. Do you think you could construct another wooden crucifix to replace the stolen one?"

"Sure!" Keith said, pleased she asked.

"And beware," she suddenly warned. "Only come to the church in the daytime. It's not safe at night."

~ ~ ~

Over the next several weeks, Keith stopped by on a regular basis to visit Katherine. He built a workbench on the south side of the rectangular building.

Finding a rusted hatchet, Keith cleaned, oiled, and sharpened it.

Eager to please Katherine with her many, sudden maintenance requests, he repaired and improved just about everything, including some creaking pews, a wobbly kneeler, and broken confessional doors. All with the hatchet he found.

The friendship between them began to blossom. Katherine became comfortable with Keith's nonthreatening presence. She taught him Vietnamese and made lunch, pleased to converse in one of the four languages she spoke fluently. And before it got dark, they strolled on the beach, sharing personal histories.

On one such occasion, Katherine revealed her life story. That her parents were devout Catholics, often expressing in their prayers that she'd honor the family by becoming a nun when she grew up.

"In the sixth grade," Katherine said, as they walked along the ocean, "a heavyset nun named Sister Angeline told me I'd been picked by God for his Calling. Soon, people in church and my relatives concurred. They said I had kind, considerate, caring qualities, and would make the perfect nun."

Keith watched Katherine stare out at the endless gray-blue horizon, as if questioning her calling.

"I constantly heard them say, 'God will reward you when you die, Katherine. You'll go straight to heaven. You're destined to serve as a nun.'"

"As a child, I was so anxious to please everyone. So I went along with the idea." Her brown eyes searched Keith's for understanding.

He gave her a smile and touched her shoulder.

"Besides," she continued in a soft voice, "the nuns always said boys are dirty and bad with no self-control. There is filth about them. Boys are substandard, inferior in every way, not good enough for your virginity. Only God is good enough for you."

"Sister Katherine, what else could you do?" Keith said, sympathetic. "How could a young, impressionable girl doubt those she loves and trusts?"

Katherine continued. "Their influence became a part of me, until their words were me," she confessed with a catch of regret in her voice.

"Not that I always agreed. I remember times when I cried out that I wanted to be a mother—or perhaps a pastry chef. But my parents and the nuns were relentless. They insisted my true calling was as a nun. I was criticized and shamed whenever I balked at the notion, until I learned to keep it within, learned not to trust them."

Keith guided her out of the sun and into the shade of a palm, where they paused. "So you have reason to hold a discontent for the church."

"Yes," Katherine confessed as she glanced about warily. "I hold deep resentment. But the bitterness has brought reason into my life; a mission to change the church from the inside, as a participant."

She moved forward on the path across the dune. "When I'm alone, I dwell on how hopeless it is for me, stuck way out here, unable to change the church. That depresses me," Katherine said, looking back, gesturing him to follow.

"This conversation makes me sad, Keith. I want to think of happy things now. So please take my mind off my problem."

Keith noticed the sudden use of his name in a full sentence. She'd allowed her dialogue to become more familiar, personal.

"I'll do that if you answer a question that plagues me about Catholic nuns."

"Go ahead, ask," Katherine replied.

"I understand a vow of chastity is a pledge all women have to make to enter the sisterhood. But isn't that contrary to human nature?" Keith said, gazing into her eyes.

Sister Katherine nodded.

"How could anyone give up the natural gift that God intended us to use?" Keith fully expected Katherine to pull back from his personal probing.

Instead, she laughed. "Boy, you can certainly change the topic."

She shocked him further with her next words. "It's about time we talked about this."

Keith wondered for a wild moment if he wanted to go here with Katherine. Then he realized with a missed heartbeat that it was too late. She was hooked.

"It's an issue." Katherine blinked those big eyes at him.

Keith furrowed his brow—he'd drawn himself into a conversation that lived only inside his head.

She stomped one foot into the sand.

"The church sweeps issues of sexuality under the rug. The sex thing crouches there like a giant lump. Nobody dares to talk about it. What a shame. Because if we confronted the notion head on, becoming a nun may not be so bad or such a mystery," she said boldly.

"So you asked the right question, Keith. What about our God-given instincts, feelings for pleasure, desires of biology? How can we suppress what is natural? There, I said it for you."

Keith let her talk.

She cut those large almond-shaped eyes at him. "Nuns and priests should not fight what is natural and biological. However, most nuns suppress thoughts of sexual desire. They are scripted through guilt—keeping it deep inside, fearing repercussions from God and Mother Superior. We are told to sacrifice, train ourselves to suppress all sexual urges. It is a sin if we don't. But I do not think I could survive as a nun. So, I cheat a little."

Suddenly shocked, Keith dared hope there was still hope for him.

"Cheat?"

"Yes, cheat. I pleasure myself."

Instantly, Keith became aroused. He shifted his stance so that she would not see.

"It is a good feeling. It's my deepest feeling," she said with a degree of shyness. "It's pleasurable. But I remain committed to the church. I believe others in the church do the same. We just do not talk about it."

"I care deeply for you, Katherine. What if we become physically intimate?" Keith held his breath.

Katherine touched his hand. "I'm sorry, my friend. I cannot. I have decided, just as you decided to join the Navy, to pursue a much greater purpose."

"What purpose could be greater than two people joined together?"

"My purpose is to make directional changes within the church. Devotion to the church is my life. Personal pleasure is secondary at this time."

She shook her head sadly and waved him away. "You should get going before it gets dark."

Chapter 4

Keith finally finished the crucifix he promised Katherine. The heavy cross was magnificent. He'd poured his heart into it, constructing it from teak with grainy shades of caramel. He'd sanded the sturdy cross until it glistened like lacquer.

Several sailors from the base—and a heavy hemp rope—helped Keith hang the cross behind the altar. As the soldiers worked, Katherine prepared lunch for them all. Afterward, the men returned to the base, but Keith remained to clean up and admire his work with Katherine.

The relationship between them had evolved into a close, trusted friendship. Katherine enjoyed how Keith listened intently to her, without challenge or judgment. When she started talking, she could not stop. At the age of twenty-five, she unleashed feelings bottled since childhood. The remoteness of her village, Keith's attentiveness, had allowed her to feel free enough to openly express her opinions.

Grateful for the time-consuming task Keith had finished, Katherine asked if he'd like to see her personal space.

And of course, he did.

Her small room in the rear of the rectangular building was neat. Against the wall, stood a chest-high, dustless dresser topped with a photograph of Katherine's parents. The blanket on the simple cot that served as her bed was perfect. A small crucifix, framed with braided strips of palm fronds, hung above the head of the bed. At the foot, on the exposed wall where Katherine could see it when she woke, hung an unframed painting.

The painting depicted a tropical beach with perfect, collapsing ocean waves. Puffy smokestack cumulus clouds rose high into the powder blue sky. A lingering sun cast a prism of flickering pastels upon a cobblestone shore. In the background, a mountainous peninsula, covered with lush, tropical vegetation, extended from right to left, ending halfway across the painting. A turquoise ocean filled in the rest of the painting.

Immediately drawn, Keith moved closer. Katherine came and touched his shoulder. Slipping her arm around his waist, she whispered, "Those are the Waves of Pavones."

"Incredibly alive!" he said in awe.

"That was painted by a friend of mine while we were on retreat in Costa Rica. The artist, Alex, made me aware that each of us is different. And some of us can't ever change who we are."

"You were on a retreat?" Keith asked, immersed in the splendor of the oils on canvas.

Dropping her arm, Katherine stepped back. "Sister Bernadine's Dungeon," she said boldly.

Still mesmerized by the painting, Keith said, excited, "Look at those waves, perfectly formed left-point beach breaks. I'll bet they break for at least two kilometers. The wave heights look like single overheads. I'd love to surf those. Where are they? Is this beach for real?"

Then Keith put his hand to his face. "What an idiot I am. Please forgive me. What in the world is Sister Bernadine's Dungeon? Sounds cruel."

"Let's go for a walk on the beach," she said, inviting him to leave her bedroom.

Barefoot, they strolled from the building and headed over the dune.

It was getting late. Although it was against Keith's better judgment to hang around the village after dark, he hadn't seen anything to alarm him in recent weeks and decided to risk it.

The soft wind juggled the shimmering curls in Katherine's hair. Her perfectly proportioned, olive-colored toes pitched sand as the couple made their way along a narrow pathway and over the grassy knoll.

It was an atypical night. The sky was clear. The humidity fell off a bit. The full moon had not fully risen as dusk set in. Keith imagined the waves he had seen in the painting breaking on the beach that appeared as they crested the dune.

As the couple strolled toward the lapping waves, Katherine spoke.

"A few weeks ago we talked about why I'm a nun."

She threw some more sand with her toes.

"Let me explain by telling my story.

"The Catholic Church has been misguided in its effort to recruit people to the vocation. Using fear, intimidation, and guilt to falsely hold onto young women and men who are seriously considering joining the sisterhood or priesthood," Katherine explained.

"What gives them the right to be so deceptive?" Keith asked.

She nodded. "Exactly, but intimidation is their weapon which they wield to control, particularly the growing children. A child's creativity, freedom of expression, exuberance are repressed, because the church believes it leads a child toward individuality, away from conformity, which is necessary to deploy the peer pressure it needs.

"The church comes down hard on nonconformists, tries to destroy their spirit, often permanently harming those with personalities that can't conform.

"The character annihilation I have witnessed, for the rationale of keeping an organization adequately staffed, was wrong, Keith. I hate what has come to pass."

Keith spoke. "Children should be permitted the freedom of thought."

Clenching her fingers into a fist, Katherine raised it to the evening sky. "The Vatican has gone way overboard. The only way to change this wrong is from within. That's why I am a nun."

Strolling along the deserted beach, Keith listened intently as a cluster of sandpipers retreated ahead.

"I admire your passion!" he said.

"What happened to Alex, my dearest friend, made me wake up, and see for the first time," Katherine said. "Because of her, I am committed to changing the rather subservient role of women within the church."

Katherine looked directly into Keith's eyes. "I think you need to understand a little more, before I explain where my strongest feelings come from.

"Prior to World War II, the church had little problem finding people throughout the world to serve as priests and nuns. Parishioners, along with parochial teachers, had convinced enough of their adolescents at an early age to pursue the vocation. There wasn't much concern. And during the war, many women who feared they'd never find a husband entered the convent," Katherine told him.

"After the War, though, recruitment changed. Societies progressed, standards of living increased. Young men and women pursued pleasurable, personal enrichments. Families became less nuclear. Adolescents grew skeptical, rebellious, and contested the teachings of the church. The church lost its grip, finding itself incapable of convincing enough young adults to seek the vocation.

"Sisterhood was about committing to vows of sacrifice, obedience, chastity, and poverty. Who would want that, knowing there are better pleasures on earth?" Katherine said with a slight degree of cynicism.

"No matter how the Vatican framed it, they were fighting a losing battle. Fewer men and women joined the vocation, opting out of an eternal promise that seemed debatable."

Katherine became animated.

"Under pressure, the Church, needing nuns to run parishes and schools, appointed a hardhearted nun with a novel approach as to how they should enlist, and keep hold of, those contemplating the sisterhood.

"Her name was Sister Bernadine. They made her Mother Superior."

Katherine sighed, set her hands to her sides, then slapped her thighs.

"I nicknamed her Sister Saint Bernard, because she had these long, labored cheeks, like a Saint Bernard dog. With spiky whiskers that pricked when you greeted her, kissing her on the cheek. There was this tuft of gray hair that grew faster than the rest of the black hair on her head. She was hefty, nervy, pushy— a bully!"

"You hold bitterness," Keith said, attempting to rub a grain of sand from the corner of his eye.

The illuminating moon had risen. The couple allowed the lapping waves to run over their feet. A retreating covey of sandpipers skittered around them and spurted off in the opposite direction.

"I tried to quell my angst, but couldn't," Katherine said. "I prayed for forgiveness. But I also think God saw the harm Bernadine did to hundreds of young girls."

"What did Bernadine do to burn such hard feelings in a wonderful person like you?" Keith asked, concerned.

"It was Alex, the artist who painted the picture in my room."

Katherine bit her lip to hold back tears. In spite of her effort, they released and traced the soft roundness of her chin, dropping to the sand.

"She took her life. Bernadine drove Alex to that choice. And when I think further, many more young girls were tormented to the point their individuality was permanently impaired."

"How could that be?" Keith asked.

"You know what a cult is?"

"Of course."

"Bernadine—with the blessing of the church—planned to indoctrinate young girls by managing their perspectives, as cults do."

Picking up a shell that was in their way, Keith spun it into the ocean.

"The Mother Superior actually carried out her plan while the church stood idly by."

"I can see why you're resentful, Katherine."

"Sister Bernadine had discovered that the church owned abandoned real estate, donated by parishioners throughout the world. She convinced Rome to create retreats for young adults thinking of entering the church . . . And, after attending one of these retreats, they could formally announce their intention—yea or nay.

"The church, Bernadine indicated, would, of course, accept either decision.

"Sister argued her idea would attract greater numbers of young adults, put less pressure on the religious educators burdened with promoting their vocation. Her idea made it easier for a priest, nun, or family member to encourage a child to consider a life with God—an idea everyone embraced, including the kids under considerable pressure from everyone around them.

"Bernadine's first retreat was a banana and date palm plantation in Costa Rica. Alex and I attended that retreat," Katherine said.

Puzzled, Keith asked, "Someone actually gave away a plantation?"

"The plantation was struck with banana blight. Its heiress, whose father owned the United Fruit Company, donated the ruined plantation. They named it Our Lady of Fatima Vocational Center. The center sat tucked against a mountainside, near a town named Golfito in Costa Rica. It was a beautiful, tropical, peaceful place. Perfect for contemplation," Katherine said.

"For Mother Superior, the most important quality of Golfito was its remoteness. The isolation permitted complete control of whatever went on at the retreat. She was able to influence the local population, because they depended upon the needs of the retreat for income.

"There was a cluster of dormitories where the plantation workers once lived. There was a schoolhouse and, of all things, a bowling alley that doubled as one of the dorms," Katherine described.

"Sister Bernadine boasted that the plantation was the perfect place for future postulants to seriously think about their direction in life, away from the pressures and spoils of society."

The full moon reached into the night sky as they walked the endless strand of sand.

"The only problem Sister Bernadine had with the location was the heat and humidity. Sister was portly. It bothered her so much that when she visited, she stayed only a few days. I later learned Sister used the heat to her advantage.

"You see, Keith, I was one of those vibrant kids who received the calling from God," Katherine said. "We wilted under that sun, and were prone to her controlling ways."

Katherine's voice rose over the muffled sounds of the collapsing waves.

"Every time I see a full moon like this one," she said, pointing skyward, "my mind drifts to the night I met Alexandria, onboard the ship sailing to Golfito."

A gentle evening breeze kicked up. Keith watched the locks in Katherine's hair blow back, exposing the length of her tender neck. He wanted to kiss her. It took all of his strength to hold back, contain his desire.

The breeze finally relaxed. Katherine's hair, shimmering in the moonlight, fell back in place as she looked directly at him with her big eyes and honest expression.

"As the boat passed through the Panama Canal, I was walking along the deck, late at night. At the bow, there was this girl about my age, holding a palette—painting. She sat inside a coiled hemp rope with her legs folded with a canvas in her lap.

"I introduced myself and asked where she was from. She told me her name, and that she was from Elliston, South Australia. That she was nocturnal by nature.

"Her hair was like mine, full and curly—but cherry red. She was stocky, the build of an Italian woman. Her cheeks were lifted, like chipmunk cheeks packed full of little nuts. Her face was splattered with an overabundance of red freckles.

"Alex had a cheery disposition, behaving as if the world was created just for her, not the other way around. She smiled at the end of each sentence, like she'd discovered something new and adventurous to look forward to, once she was done talking to you.

"I later learned her family had lost their vineyard in Italy and emigrated to Australia to open a new vineyard with the few grape plants they'd salvaged.

"I asked how she could paint in the dark."

" 'I'm what you call a naturalist painter,'" she told me. 'I paint in the elements with Mother Nature, so my paintings take on that intangible quality the outside environment offers. It's my passion. And when I'm done with this crazy retreat, I can cast myself out into the world to be a famous traveling artist.'

" 'You mean you aren't going to become a nun?' I asked her.

" 'No way,' Alexandria said. 'All the horses in the Queen's army couldn't corral me like that. In thirteen weeks, I'll finally be free.'

"Alex's eyes looked as though she was about to burst into tears when she mentioned the retreat and her determination not to do what everyone expected, to become a nun. That was the first time I came across someone in the program who openly said they would leave."

Katherine stepped onto a sharp seashell and nearly tripped after her leg buckled.

Quickly, Keith grasped her waist and caught her.

She gripped his forearm. "Thank you. Shall I go on? Are you sure you aren't totally bored?"

"Never," Keith said. "She was your friend. I am captivated by your story."

Katherine paused and stared into the stars, thinking about Alex.

" 'I'll soon be liberated,' Alex told me. 'Released from a community that forced me to do this. Free from everyone in the Australian wine region who authenticated my conscription. They told me to make them proud. I'll make them proud of me as a famous painter—not as a celibate.'

"What a boatload of issues, I thought to myself," Katherine said, as Keith listened intently.

"Sounds that way," he responded.

To avoid the sharp shells left by the retreating tide, he took her hand and led her higher on the beach.

As they walked beneath the moonlight, Katherine revealed how for the first time, she realized some people were trapped by the church, held captive, and kept emotionally destabilized. It was not in their nature to be nuns. These women carried an unpurgible yearning that remained vaulted by a guilt that gnawed away their spirit.

"Alex was one of those unfortunate individuals," Katherine said in a matter-of-fact voice.

"As children, we were never permitted to mentally explore contrary perspectives. Becoming a mother, a spouse, or a lover was never mentioned in our households. Such topics were forbidden.

"What we heard was either filtered or controlled. We were told we were better than everyone, for pursuing such a noble, self-sacrificing profession.

"Eventually, this form of early conditioning makes you self-centered."

As she took hold of Keith's hand, goose bumps and a thrill of excitement overcame him.

"Self-centered? I don't get it. Aren't people of the cloth supposed to be humble?" he said.

"I doubt I can provide a clearer answer. Except to say, we grew to believe, what was told us.

"We were told, as God's servants, our sacrifice here on earth would provide for a higher stature in heaven for all eternity. Those who follow the Calling will be better off in the eyes of God than those that don't. So yes, I thought I was superior for the lifelong sacrifice I was about to make.

"Perhaps a better word would be pious," Katherine said, pausing, thinking.

"It was Alex who knocked me off my pedestal. I truly believe God put Alex in my life for that very reason. She opened my mind, unlocked my perspective.

"Alex's introspective nature enabled her to defy the influences that surrounded her. She had an affinity for searching for the sunshine on rainy days. She was a free thinker, as artists often are.

"But she had a dark side," Katherine indicated, continuing about Alex.

"Our ship to Golfito had about one hundred passengers. Half got off in Panama City. After we departed, Alex clued me on the girls that remained onboard. She asked if I noticed anything peculiar.

" 'No,' I replied.

"She said, 'Think again.'

"I shook my head. I had no idea to what she was alluding.

"Alex said, 'Didn't you notice how most of the young girls are very attractive?'

"I said, 'No.' But when I considered her suggestion it was more than apparent.

"That's what was unique about Alex. She revealed the abstract, or, should I say, the contrast in everyday life.

"Alex said, 'It's as if they were selected, just as the grape pickers on my father's vineyard choose the most perfect grapes on the optimum day to make the best wine.

" 'Only young, beautiful women boarded this ship,' Alex said."

Katherine glanced at the full moon that was well on its way into the night.

"I quickly pointed out that there were some plain-looking girls.

"Alex answered my observation by asking me this: 'Did you ever ask what their interests were? Or their majors in school?'

" 'No,' I told her. 'Without a reason, that would be inappropriate.'

" 'They are language majors, journalists, recorders of events—spies,' Alex said.

"I didn't like where the conversation was going. I was not sure how to take her. So I left Alex to her painting, avoiding her for the rest of the trip.

"However, her unusual observations lingered suspiciously in the back of my mind."

As Katherine told her story, the ocean and its gently breaking waves had gone to sleep for the night. The breeze that chased behind them dissipated. Katherine spoke softly, her voice no longer in competition with the ocean. She walked closer to Keith, occasionally running her hand along his forearm.

She continued with her story.

"When we arrived in Golfito I bunked above Alex in the same dormitory. We nicknamed the dorm 'The International House' because many of us were from different countries.

"Alex appeared more normal then. She seemed careful, not wanting me to think her as unusual.

"For several weeks we just hung out, exploring the countryside. I remember some Americans from New York University working a geological dig a kilometer south of the pier, near the edge of a date palm orchard at the outskirts of the town. Occasionally, we were allowed to tour the dig and talk to the students and their professors."

A frown came over Katherine's face.

"But the visits to the dig stopped when one of the retreat girls fell in love with a young archeologist from the university and ran away with him, back to New York.

"We found the Tico villagers to be very friendly. They loved bringing their children to the elementary school we ran at the retreat.

"And during mass, the priest often reminded Golfito residents that we were at an important juncture in our Catholic lives. Encouraging them to pray for us, with the hope we will all enter the convent.

"Our dorm doubled as the bowling alley, where, on Sundays, the bunk beds were pushed aside to form two bowling lanes down the center. We looked forward to Sunday afternoon, because that's when we got together as a group, to laugh, and simply enjoy ourselves.

"Other than bowling and teaching school children, we spent our time attending daily mass and praying for guidance.

"For Alex, the routine quickly became boring. She started to explore deeper into the countryside with her canvas and paints. The villagers came to love her and enjoyed her distinct, often creative demeanor.

"She painted several town structures, including the unusually high pier, sometimes trading her paintings for transportation to the Osa across the bay.

"Many times Alex traveled by boat with merchants who traded with the Indians. She told us Golfito and the surrounding jungle looked a lot different from the sea.

"But one day, Alex did not come back from one of her excursions. I hurried to the municipal dock to locate the ferryboat captain who'd taken her that day.

"He said he dropped Alex off early morning on Pavones, a beach about an hour south. Said she wanted to spend all day painting the waves.

"The man said a south swell blew in and he was unable to make it to the dock at the mouth of the river to pick her up."

" 'I can only go back when the waves calm,' he said. 'The Osa protects us, but not south, where Pavones lies. The shoreline catches the swell. I'll go when the wind is done.'

"It was three days before the captain went for her. We waited anxiously for the ferry to return. As the boat appeared and docked, we saw Alex with an excited smile. She yelled to me. 'Holy cow! You should have seen the beach I was stuck on. I don't think anyone knows it exists.

" 'Look at this!' She held up a painting.

"It's the painting you saw on my wall," Katherine said warmly, recalling her love for her close friend.

"Her three-day absence from the retreat made me realize how important Alex was to me. I'd missed her.

"Oh," Katherine exclaimed. "What a breath of fresh air that crazy girl was. We all came to appreciate and enjoy this unique person.

"But one day, when it was my turn to clean the bathrooms in the back of the International House, I came across notes discarded in the wastepaper basket. Curious, I read them. And realized they were about Alex, her outgoing nature, habits, likes, and other ramblings.

"One note indicated how disruptive and inappropriate she behaved," Katherine said with some sadness.

"Those chronicles of Alex caused me to wonder if someone was tracking my activities.

"So, late that night, when everyone was asleep, I asked Alex how she came about the unusual thoughts she'd expressed on the ship.

"Alex walked me out back and up the hillside. We crouched behind a tree, at an angle that permitted us to look downward into one of the dorm windows.

" 'Look!' she said. 'See for yourself.'

"I saw a candle flickering in a room. One of the not-so-pretty girls was busily writing.

" 'She's documenting us,' Alex said. 'The notes she writes will go off to Sister Bernadine.'

"I was incredulous. 'How do you know this?' I asked her.

" 'Sister Pearl, my sponsor in Australia, I often found her writing at length about me. When she wasn't around, I'd read her notes. They were reports about my behavior, preferences, tendencies, and my personality.

" 'Sister Pearl wrote her observations about whether I was for or against joining the sisterhood.

" 'One day, I confronted Pearl. And after some distress, she confessed, saying if she did not send this information to Mother Superior, Bernadine would reassign her to some remote atoll in Micronesia, far away from her family in Australia.

"You see, Pearl's father had Dementia. Her mother had died. They were poor. Sister needed to remain in Australia to be with her father."

As the bitterness in Katherine's voice grew, she gripped Keith's arm tighter.

"That's when I learned about the evil side of Bernadine.

"Alex said that Sister Pearl was surprisingly honest, saying she hoped one day everything would change. Sister told Alex to follow her dreams and be true to herself.

"Goes to show you how much we misjudge people. Sometimes, people like Sister Pearl are forced into making life choices that are beyond their control," Katherine said, continuing.

"One particularly disturbing piece of information Alex bestowed was her feeling about why Mother Superior was spying. 'Bernadine resented men!' she said.

"Mother Superior was incredibly self-conscious about her lifetime weight problem. This made her bitter. Sister Pearl heard that Sister Bernadine was in love at one time, with a handsome man. She'd left her studies as a nun to marry him. But a year later, she returned and never spoke of him again.

"Rumor had it Bernadine had quite a bit of money, and that her fiancé had stolen her fortune and disappeared. It seems her whole life was now focused upon the vendetta she'd had with men, even after she entered the sisterhood.

"The Mother Superior became a force to reckon with. She'd developed a network of spies who collected information on misbehaving priests. She leveraged this information any time she wanted something from the Bishop.

"Bernadine's retreat in Golfito was the driving force of her vengeance. She placed only beautiful young girls there, whom she programmed in a way that when a man showed an interest, they'd not know how to react—as if the desire part of their personalities had been deleted."

Katherine tugged on Keith's arm to turn them around. They'd walked quite a distance.

"What information did Bernadine collect on you?" Keith asked.

"I never found out," Katherine replied, leaning on his arm while twisting her feet into the sand, unconsciously releasing the growing tension inside her.

"One night, as our time at the retreat came to the moment when we were to announce our desire to enter the convent, I walked into my dorm and found Alex sitting on my bed, holding her painting.

" 'Here!' Alex said. 'I want you to have this as a memory of our time here.' She handed me the painting of Pavones.

" 'Local residents call these the Waves of Pavones. Aren't they spectacular? I have fallen in love with this beach and never want to leave there,' she told me.

"This was our tenth week. I could see the stress building in Alex's eyes. As for myself, I was resigned to joining the church. I had a far greater sense of purpose. I had no other experiences in my life to confuse me.

"But something happened that changed all that.

"On Sunday morning of the eleventh week, husky, brute-like nuns we'd never seen before arrived and awakened us early. They announced Sister Bernadine was coming, and set at the foot of our beds a full complement of garments. The kind nuns wear.

"The nuns spoke in authoritarian voices, almost like drill sergeants. They told us to get dressed, immediately.

"Though surprised, we put on the garments. It was the first time I'd worn them. They were very confining and uncomfortable.

"The nuns came around and inspected us, snapping tight the tiny buttons we missed, adjusting our outfits to fit properly. Then lined us up to be greeted by Mother Superior.

"Alex, who happened to have been up all night, was dragged from bed and kept isolated by two of the sisters. They dressed her. I noticed Alex was delirious from lack of sleep and simply did not know what was going on.

"Sister Bernadine finally appeared and welcomed us to the sisterhood, as if our time to make our decision had passed.

"I think we were so taken and conditioned not to challenge, that no one objected, not even me," Katherine said.

"We were led off to the church and lined in the pews across the front.

"The entire town turned out. A bishop had arrived with Bernadine to say mass.

"Drenched in our own perspiration, we stood the entire time. The clothing was confining. Many of the girls were so uncomfortable they became delirious.

"Each of us had a sponsor. These were older nuns, who'd arrived with Bernadine. They sat directly behind us in church.

"After mass we were quietly escorted off to the elementary school classrooms. They kept us busy listening to lectures late into the night, about things we'd heard many times before. We were sleep-deprived and dehydrated."

Grabbing Keith's arm with her free hand, Katherine held him tighter, as the stress of revealing this personal experience caused her voice to shake and her facial muscles to tighten.

She twisted the balls of her feet, grinding into the soft sand.

"Alex looked stunned. Her eyes held no expression and her body was rigid. I was not able to talk to her because the other nuns had separated her from us. Whenever I made eye contact, she just stared, as if she had been drugged.

"I think Alex may have had some sort of personality disorder that made her react in this extreme manner—possibly a manic depressive disorder. I think Bernadine knew about her illness—the sudden shock flipped her into a state where she couldn't be reached.

"For the next two weeks we were kept busy by our mentors. Consuming most of our time, they coaxed us as to why they needed our absolute commitment. We were encouraged to affirm our decision to enter the sisterhood. And every morning, during each mass, Bernadine would publicly praise the girls that chose to finally commit.

"One night, I felt a sharp pinch in my foot. It was Alex. She had awakened me by jabbing a needle. Apparently, I was so tired she could not wake me by shaking me.

"She said, 'Come with me.'

"We snuck outside, where Alex revealed she's leaving. 'Take care of my painting, Katherine. You've been a terrific friend.'

"I tried to talk her out of her decision, but she could not be dissuaded.

"But the next morning, Alex was still there. What a surprise!

"We did not get a chance to talk because we had to go church. I thought maybe she'd changed her mind.

"At mass, Mother Superior invited three of us to the altar to proclaim our decision. Alex was one of them. The first two girls sheepishly announced they would become nuns.

"Before Alex spoke, Sister Bernadine addressed us. She gushed over what a talented individual Alex was. How children attending Catholic schools in Australia would love to have her as an art teacher. How her family, well known and reputable, with no son to send to the priesthood, sacrificed a daughter, who'd enter the convent without reservation. How proud her family, diocese, and community would be when she returned to Australia, ripened fruit, ready to become the best of wine in all the land.

"I saw that Alex was thrown by Sister's speech. She cowered as Sister poured on the guilt-producing words. Bernadine spoke eloquently for almost an hour. And I watched Alex quickly come undone.

"The smirk on Bernadine's face showed that she enjoyed every bit of her increasing control. Alex was reeled in as each word left Sister's lips.

"But suddenly, Alex started to shake uncontrollably. Abruptly, she darted from the pew, raced down the side aisle, and burst through the church doors.

Katherine choked back tears.

"I guessed Sister Bernadine already knew of Alex's decision not to join the Order. The speech was Sister's last, best effort to seize control of Alex. After all, she knew Alex like a book from all the information she received over the years.

"What amazed me was that no one went after Alex to help her. I think Sister thought Golfito was such an isolated area—where can she go?

"Alex's running away was similar to that of a young child threatening her mother. The mother calls the child's bluff, saying 'go ahead.' A few hours later the child returns, bewildered, hungry, embarrassed, and compliant. Inevitably, the mother gains even greater control over the child."

Slowing her pace as they headed back, Katherine stepped away to walk on her own.

"Alex did not return that night," she said. "We were kept at the church the entire time and asked to pray for her safety. When we left in the evening for a dinner consisting of rice and beans, still no Alex.

"Two days later, someone from town said the water taxi had taken Alex to Pavones. Alex told the captain not to worry about coming back for her.

"The captain said he heard a young girl drowned at Pavones the next day.

"It was Alex!"

Katherine broke into an uncontrollable sob.

Keith came to comfort her, but she pulled away. Gathering herself, she finished the story.

"Her body had washed ashore, partially eaten by the large hermit crabs that roamed the beaches. A caretaker of the retreat boxed what was left of her remains and sent them back to Alex's church in Australia for burial."

Collapsing onto the sand, Katherine put her hands to her face and cried out her anguish.

Keith stood there for a long moment, allowing her the space she needed.

It was very late. The full moon that illuminated the face of the dune cast a lengthening shadow.

He came and sat next to her in the sand. Folding his legs, he lifted her by her narrow waist and placed her inside his lap, then wrapped his arms around her in a tight embrace.

Katherine's weeping slowed until she was quiet.

Lifting her head, she gazed into his eyes with a vulnerable look.

Keith could feel her growing warmth.

Their lips came close and brushed into a kiss. A cresting tide of passion unleashed, as their hearts raced with enticement and affection.

With Katherine cradled in his arms, he lifted to his feet, still passionately locked in the caress of their kiss.

Frantic for a physical affection that overshadowed the sorrow for her dead friend, Katherine stroked every part of him.

He carried her over the dune, back to her room.

They made love, melting into one, falling asleep intertwined in an eternal embrace.

Chapter 5

Keith woke gasping for air. He could not cry out. A wire wrapped his throat, blocking the air passing across his vocal cords. Violently, he struggled as two Vietcong soldiers subdued him, ratcheting the wire tighter.

A gun barrel burrowed his temple, followed with a blow to his face. The men barked orders in a language he barely understood.

For a brief moment, the wire loosened. His lungs filled. But when he resisted his capture, the wire closed tight again. Quickly, he got the message; they weren't ready to kill him—not yet.

They yanked Katherine by her hair from beside him. A stout, bald, brawny man twisted her neck at a torturous angle as he dragged her across the raw wood of the bedroom floor—the instep of her feet squealing as the wood splintered, blistered, and seared her skin.

In horror, Keith rolled his eyes, witnessing Katherine thrash about. Her own eyes, wide open and frightened—the tight wire around her throat, allowing no sound.

The only noise heard in the quiet night was the thumping of her feet on the outside steps. Then the scratching of soil as she was dragged off toward the village church.

Once again, as the wire tightened around Keith's throat, the two men pulled him from bed. Naked, they forced him to kneel and pulled his arms behind his back. They too, were wired so tight the wires cut deep into his skin, dripping blood onto the backside of his calves.

Again, the noose loosened enough for him to breathe, but not enough to speak.

Forced to stand, Keith became nauseous when he saw blood from Katherine's violent extrication smeared across the floor.

A blow hit him dead center in his stomach. Then the butt end of the rifle slammed beneath his chin, breaking three teeth. They shoved him in the same direction as Katherine, blood draining from his mouth, splattering along her bloody trail.

As he fell down the outside steps, the rifle smashed into his face before he could stagger to his feet.

The two soldiers led him to the church and hauled him to the first pew, where they wired his feet together. One of the men crawled into the pew behind and pulled his feet underneath. Another extended the American's bound arms over the back, behind him. In this position, they lashed his tied wrists to his bare feet beneath the pew—a position that forced him to remain motionless.

Behind the marble altar, there was a scurry of activity. A bloody trail clearly indicated Katherine's presence. The two soldiers, finishing with Keith, moved behind the altar to join the bald man.

Katherine was voiceless. Her eyes were big and bulging. There was an expression of terror on her face.

The men untied the hemp rope that hung the cross Keith had carved. Lowering it, they leaned it against the altar. Then the threesome hoisted Katherine to the cross—Keith watching in horror, her beautiful eyes filled with unbearable pain and sadness.

With each twitch of desire to rescue her, his wired skin tore some more. Helplessness and sorrow overwhelmed him. The design of his captors' incapacitation was fashioned to torture him in every way.

They must have known he loved Katherine, deciding killing him was too easy. Instead, their hideous torture would mark him for the rest of his life.

Keith remained motionless, as he watched Katherine's crucifixion unfold.

The fiends easily lifted Katherine to the leaning cross.

First, her hands were tied fast to the crossbeam—again with wire. Next, her waist, and finally her ankles lashed.

The man who'd dragged Katherine to the church produced Keith's razor-sharp hatchet. With his left hand, he pulled a bamboo spike from a pouch that hung on his waist; then, forced the point through the separation in the tendon of her out turned wrist.

Blood pulsed in spurts as the spike sliced an artery.

Pursing his lips, the bald man wielded the back end of the hatchet, driving the bamboo nail through until the other end imbedded the wooden cross.

He repeated the process, affixing the top half of her delicate torso to the cross.

Katherine's feet wriggled epileptically, as the man struggled to position one foot atop the other. After he fixed them into position, he drove another spike through both feet until the bamboo held firm.

Keith heaved, aspirating bile that oozed through his nose.

The three men attempted to hoist the cross with Katherine hanging from it. But it was too heavy. It pitched and swayed as it caught the nun's weight.

The men tried to hoist the cross again. This time, it swung freely, just above the floor. Dark blood flowed like syrup from her wounds, pooling, running along the swales and cracks of the floorboards, searching for its own escape from the horror above.

The short man came and stood inches from Keith's face. In broken English, he said deliberately, "Your nightmare will last forever. You will live to relive this memory for the remainder of your life. Tell your comrades to leave our country. Or we will do the same to them."

The man turned on his heels and headed toward Katherine.

As emotionless as a Samurai warrior, he raised the hatchet so Keith could clearly see as he set its sharp edge at the lowest rib of her chest cavity. The blade separated skin and muscles. Blood flowed freely from the lengthening incision. The small ax cut horizontally along her ribcage, crossed under her sternum, and completed its journey to the other side.

Katherine's quivering body reacted to the trauma.

The short man grimaced with satisfaction. He spat on the floor, as if to deny any guilt from entering his thought.

Resolutely, he lifted the bloody hatchet.

Keith felt his own eyes bulge with the horror of witnessing this mutilation. Sweat drained from every pore as his soul tried to evacuate his body.

The hatchet entered Katherine's chest at the sternum. With both hands, the assassin clasped the handle near the head. Tightening his stomach and facial muscles, he yanked downward. The cold steel parted muscle tissue and adjoining tendons, opening Katherine's bowel. The sharp edge continued to the top of her pubic bone. Blood drained from the edges of the incision as her entrails dropped out.

The murderer turned and glared at Keith—her blood covering the hatchet and every inch of him.

His beloved Katherine was bleeding profusely from the hollow space in her stomach. As the cooler air of the beginning day made contact with the inner wall of her abdomen, steam drifted out.

Horrified, Keith could no longer aspirate through his nose. His body lost its ability to feel pain. He went numb, as the unfolding images burned to the back of his mind.

The Asian frowned as anger filled his face once again. Glaring into Keith's eyes, Katherine's slayer opened his palm and showed his bloody hand. He wiped it on Keith's face then returned to Katherine.

He slid his hand into her abdomen and forced his fingers through her diaphragm. Her throat jumped; her lifeless eyes rolled into her head.

Keith heaved as the assassin's arm shoved higher, until his fingers found Katherine's faintly beating heart.

He pressed closer to her cooling body, his left cheek nestled against her right breast. He positioned his feet. And in one, violent, rapid motion, he squeezed the life giving organ and tore it from inside her chest.

Holding the pulsating heart, he threw it onto Keith's chest. It rolled to his lap. The bloody mass of tissue and muscle sat there beating.

Keith tried to remove it by bouncing his knees. The wires cut deeper.

He looked up at Katherine; she was lifeless.

~ ~ ~

Keith woke in a cold sweat. He was anxious, delirious, his heart racing. His eyes cleared to see people standing on the school bus. The chattering Vietnamese voices terrified him for a moment as his mental state stalled in its transition from nightmare to reality.

When Rodger opened the emergency exit door of the bus, a chilling breeze sucked in and ran Keith's legs, sending a shiver along his spine.

Bewildered, Keith sat straight. He felt clammy, nauseous.

"What a horrifying flashback," he thought.

For a long moment, he thought the tortuous crucifixion was happening, again.

He glanced at his forearms. Scars encircled his wrists. He stared at them. They were real.

Trembling, Keith crawled from the back of the bus and dragged his kayak and equipment into the woods on the other side of the launch area, where he vomited his morning coffee.

He tried to comprehend how he'd lost control. "Was it too much pot, the booze, fumes from the resin?"

"You idiot!" he said, scolding himself for letting the flashback return.

Dragging his boat a little farther downstream, where he could barely see the rafts through the bushes at the staging area, he sat in the cockpit and hung his legs out. He hunched over and collected himself.

"Calm down. Calm down. Calm down," he told his body, as he deliberately went into a meditative state.

† †

Mark Weston

Chapter 6

Kayaking the Upper Youghiogheny was the ultimate in adventure river sport. Negotiating its rapids required tremendous concentration, and absolute focus. This notorious section of Class-V whitewater commanded respect. Though Keith Ashland knew its intricate maze of boulders, chutes, and near waterfalls, one small error, a mental lapse, meant death.

For a few precious hours each day, the bedlam of the Upper Yough freed Keith from his torment. He needed this fix to exist. The Appalachians, with its rivers of wildest whitewater, was the only place for him to endure these days.

Keith drew several deep breaths of the crisp mountain air. "No scent yet," he said, watching Rodger, owner of Hell and High Water River Outfitters, giving the general orientation to anxious rafters.

Mark Weston tied down the trailer that transported their rafts. He distributed paddles, waterproof bags, assigned first-aid kits, and safety ropes. He coiled a long length of yellow polypropylene rope and stuffed it in the stern of his kayak.

Keith watched Mark adjust and set his prusik, another safety rope secured on the shoulder strap of his lifejacket.

Mark gave it a final tug.

Keith scanned the cockpit of his kayak. A four-inch-thick Ethafoam wall ran beneath the deck, from the cockpit rim to the bow. Should his boat become pinned in the current, trapping his legs, the pillar would keep the kayak from completely collapsing and subsequently drowning him.

Cut into the top of the foam, just inside the cockpit, was a three-inch square, four inches deep. Keith pulled the foam plug from the center, revealing a hashish pipe, a small bag of waterproof matches, and several ounces of pot.

He considered getting high, but fought back the nervous urge to take a quick hit. Today might push his limit.

He decided, "No," positioning the lid snugly in place so it would not leak.

The flow of the Upper Yough relied upon periodic releases from a hydroelectric dam, Deep Creek Reservoir, four miles upstream of the launch site. From 8 a.m. until 10 a.m. each weekday, electricity was generated. The riverbed at the put-in trickled until the flow snaked its way, arriving around 10:30.

When the whitewater arrived, the riverbed became a swiftly moving flow. The air temperature dropped fifteen degrees. With it came a heavy mist that lay close to the choppy current.

Keith looked around. Today, eighteen customers occupied six inflatable rafts, with an experienced in-raft guide assigned to each. Mark, Rodger, and Keith would safety-boat in their kayaks. Their job was to retrieve ejected swimmers, getting them back into their raft as quickly as possible.

Sporting a severe hangover, Keith was not thrilled to learn he was the lead boater today, watching out for logs and debris in the rock-congested drops. Mark Weston, the strongest, would take the most difficult positions, where the greatest risks existed. Rodger would control the trip's pace from the back with hand signals, a whistle, or facial expressions that told each guide what he was supposed to do.

Carrying his fiberglass kayak and custom paddle to the river's edge, Keith set the boat atop a familiar laurel bush, where the weight had crushed it, forcing it to grow out sideways. He liked this spot because the bush held the kayak steady while he squeezed into it.

Balancing on his left hand just behind the seat, where the foam pillar supports the stern decking, he transferred his entire weight, lifting, sliding both feet through the manhole-sized cockpit into the narrow hull. He plopped his rump into a seat made of mini-cell foam then slid his legs forward, locking himself in by pressing against a set of thigh and foot braces.

He secured the spray skirt around the cockpit rim, an action that sealed him in, making his craft watertight.

Lurching, the bow cantilevered as his weight pitched forward. Gravity pulled his vessel through the laurel, as the kayak slithered into the river.

Ten minutes previously, the riverbed was nearly dry. Submerged charcoal rocks had been replaced by a swift current that leapt as standing waves.

He gazed upwards, through the low layer of dissolving mist, into a clear sapphire blue sky—not a cloud in sight. The absence of wind had paralyzed the ancient white pines that stood as sentinels, scrutinizing the departing voyagers.

Keith filled his lungs with the fresh Appalachian air. His stomach muscles tightened in preparation of the first few strokes.

Rotating his paddle 90 degrees into a perfect, vertical position, making contact with the current, he torqued his torso, utilizing every muscle in his body, then thrust the face of the blade through the current. The kayak lifted, planed, and glided along.

A first stroke followed a second, third, and fourth, building momentum as he headed downstream into the gorge.

Chapter 7

The blades of Keith's kayak paddle dug deep, one after the other, alternating port and starboard. His handmade, golden kayak paddle was magnificent. Its rippled wood grains shimmered as they caught the sunlight. Expertly crafted blades, set at 60 degrees, not the traditional 90, chugged away. The reduced angle of the offset facilitated a more rapid recovery when connecting successive strokes. It was part of design modification that had significantly improved the paddle's leveraging capabilities—all this came from one small alteration to the Ashland design.

Keith turned his head to locate Mark Weston, who was entering the river.

He smiled, reminding himself he had Mark to thank for the subtle, innovative improvements to his designs. His memory wandered back to the day he first met Mark, who suggested he move his blade offsets from the industry standard of 90 degrees to 60.

~ ~ ~

After leaving Gleason's Diner, famous for its muffin-top dinner rolls and irresistible lemon meringue pie, Keith drove along a county road that paralleled a narrow and very steep creek known as Meadow Run. He was high, of course, his stomach comfortably full. Having heard of a party at the Laurel

Highlands Campground, he decided to drive to Ohiopyle, about nine miles away.

A training thunderstorm that rolled in from the west had dumped five inches of rain in two hours. The Meadow Run was bank full. Keith had never seen this volume of water in the creek before. Craning his head to get a peek of the continuous rapids, he drove along the edge, close to the guardrail. It was tantalizing to think how challenging it would be to kayak it right now.

Near the town of Ohiopyle, the Meadow steeply descends, before it empties into the Lower Youghiogheny, above Cucumber Rapids. Keith encountered several cars, all with kayaks on top, parked at the cutoff. He pulled over, jumped the guardrail, and hurried down the embankment, finding a cluster of people watching a mysterious kayaker size up a notorious drop known as the Slides.

The rapid was essentially a tight waterslide that cut through a horizontal layer of sedimentary rock at a 50-degree angle. The entire creek surged through a deep, V-shaped trough. From top to bottom, the rapid was barely 75 yards in length.

Oddly, the wife of the park superintendent stood there, nervously watching.

At the top of the Slides, on the opposite riverbank, stood a young man in a custom purple lifejacket, nylon shorts, and bare feet. Keith, who knew just about all the local boaters because he regularly partied with them, did not know this person.

The mysterious kayaker paced, busily contemplating how he would run the dangerous drop.

Keith asked one of the local river guides, Johnny Grogan, "Who's the lunatic that's about to meet certain death?"

"I don't know him," Johnny said, fascinated by the notion someone believed the Slides were runnable at this insane level.

The flooded creek raced into the tight, steep drop at an awesome rate. At the top, two enormous cross-curling currents spun like horizontal tornados. Behind the second cross-curl, the steeply angled creek compressed, racing along the right side of a narrowing rock wall. The river's velocity was so fast, the flow lifted away from the stratified surface, forming a pocket, then slammed back, creating a deathtrap known to river guides as an infinite eddy.

It was dusk. The slow, summertime transition toward darkness brought with it the fog. Dripping trees that shrouded the small creek hung low. Bystanders, watching from the limited shoreline, stood silent, the crushing roar of the rapid canceling their murmuring voices.

The state park superintendent's wife, who stumbled upon the crowd, screamed, "Someone, stop him! Stop him! Please!"

There was no response from the spectators, as darkness drew closer and each tense moment ticked off.

"This guy better run the drop soon," Keith said loudly to Johnny, standing next to him.

The mysterious boater paced back and forth. Studying the infinite eddy, he appeared to debate every conceivable option as how to avoid it.

Then finally, his jaw tightened, his face firmed. The intensity of his gaze turned ghostly. And before he could change his mind, he lifted his kayak and trudged upstream through the thick brush.

The superintendent's wife yelled for someone to stop him. "He's going to die!"

She tugged on Keith's T-shirt.

Everyone ignored her.

Running into the small crowd, "Lunatics!" she said. "Isn't anyone going to stop him? You're a bunch of lunatics, wanting to watch him die."

She raced up the embankment, trying to find someone with authority to stop him from killing himself.

The mysterious man perched his boat on top of a laurel bush, the flooded creek angrily splashing in front of him. He climbed into the unstable craft and secured his spray skirt.

The crowd stood emotionally frozen, paralyzed by the delirium. Time seemed to slow and decompress. The screaming lady scrambled back from the road to calmly witness a suicide.

Ten minutes would bring total darkness. At that time, a rescue would be out of the question. The creek flowed entirely too fast. In the blackness of night, a mistake would dictate his death. The watchers understood that.

Keith, who considered himself a wise old owl when measuring such rapids, did not see a plausible route through the Slides. Having been on several first descents with Rodger, he deduced this rapid impassable. But for the moment, he would give this stranger the benefit of the doubt.

Also, Keith knew that rare individuals who etch their names on a first descent commit because they saw something no other person knew. Sometimes, they discover a unique feature, such as a solid flume of water concealed within the boiling whitewater as an escape route. Perhaps an errant pulsation, a timing disguised within the confusion of random waves. Possibly, an invisible eddy that provides safe haven as a necessary pause to recoup and maneuver.

Keith positioned himself where he could observe the entire event.

The mysterious kayaker carried a red shaft kayak paddle with white fiberglass blades, offset at the customary 90 degrees.

Familiar with the paddle's manufacturer, Keith said, "What an ugly design, particularly the fiberglass blades."

He saw the boater make a slight wiggle of his hips. This indicated he was locking himself in—forcing his knees against the deck and legs against the thigh braces, shoving his feet forward, wedging his toes against the side-seams, squashing his heals against the Ethafoam pillar in the center.

Keith held his breath as the kayaker, becoming one with his boat, was about to launch.

The mysterious man lurched forward, entering the churning current. A second shove allowed him to fully set into the creek. Sitting in a tiny eddy, the kayak pitched, lifted, and dropped several inches. Swells pulsated as the current swirled, clawed, and washed over the deck.

Positioning the paddle near the bow, the kayaker wrestled with the erratic movement, aligning for his first stroke. Patiently, he waited, allowing the craft to bob, unbalance, and rebalance, until the correct combination of current and angle occurred, so he could launch into the swift, downstream flow of Slides.

Suddenly, with the thrust of a locomotive piston, the stranger released his energy in a determined rage. He plunged the paddle blade into the violent current, grabbing hold as if it was welded in concrete. Becoming solid, he locked and heaved into the torrent, the hull bursting ahead.

He rotated his chiseled torso like a giant spring, building energy. Gripping the shaft solidly, he adjusted the blade angle, opening the face against the oncoming current. In a fraction of a second, the vessel spun 180 degrees—the blade never leaving the water as the kayak's momentum caught the swiftly moving creek.

A twitch of a singular stomach muscle made for a subtle correction. The bow shifted slightly to realign with the oscillating flow.

"Clearly, this guy knows what he's doing," Keith thought, as the first obstacles, two giant cross-curling waves, loomed. But he was a long way from being convinced this first descent was logical, not suicidal.

The kayak blasted through the cross-curl. Again, the paddle blade intentionally held in the current. The stranger did this for the same reason an insect uses its tentacles. It gave him a feel for the motion beneath him, so he could adjust for stability.

On the backside of the angling wave, a subtle, unseen surge caught the hull, deflecting it right and against the sheer cliff. That slight shift destroyed the entire line. It was unexpected, a miscalculation, requiring a necessary correction . . . But the current was too swift; all the stranger could do was hope for an opportunity that would never come.

The kayak knifed into the second cross-curl too far to the right, slowing its momentum, slamming sideward against an eddy line that stalled its forward progress, losing the momentum required to blast past the infinite eddy.

Keith stood fewer than eight feet away, looking into the meat of the rapid, looking for the expression on the man's face to see if he was alarmed or frightened. What he saw was a concentrated look that said the stranger was thinking through a thousand scenarios for the one that would positively affect the outcome.

Suddenly, the boat flipped completely upside down. The man expertly recovered, rolling up. Again, he flipped. This time he adjusted the angle of the paddle while underneath, using the fast-moving current to force him upright.

The bystanders cheered with enthusiasm. They recognized the excellent execution of a reverse screw roll. It was a new technique, difficult to execute, but designed for such a situation. A mere handful of boaters in the region had the presence of mind to execute that roll in such a difficult spot.

The kayak recklessly raced toward the most serious part of the Slides, a point where the current's speed was so great, it lifted from the rock wall to create a deep pocket known as an infinite eddy—a feared river phenomena caused when water flows at an incredible velocity. Once inside, one cannot escape. Passing this point was critical. It required one stroke at the precise moment, correctly placed, to increase the speed enough to shove the kayak past.

As the kayak accelerated the speed wasn't enough; the man leaned downstream in a desperate attempt to pull through. His paddle knifed in, but the current was too swift for the stroke to be effective. The kayak accepted the reversing direction of the whirlpool and tumbled into the terminal eddy.

Stunned, the small crowd watched in horror.

Trapped, about to be consumed by the violent eddy, the young man tried to salvage his situation—again, by reaching for the faster downstream flow.

As the paddle held fast, he pulled with all his might, as if it did not matter if his boat came with him. But the effort was futile. The mysterious kayaker was sucked into the abyss—a chasm eight feet deep, surrounded on three sides by water shot as if it came from a giant fire hose.

The bystanders stood silent, frozen, as if they'd discovered the end of the universe and no longer knew what to do.

Keith considered reaching for his throw rope but quickly killed the idea, because the current would whisk it away. Instead, he studied the bold stranger, whose demeanor was calm, even though his death seemed imminent.

"This guy looks intent, as if he's solving a Rubik's Cube," Keith said to his friend, observing the mystery kayaker bounce and spin inside the hole, attempting several maneuvers to escape.

They watched as he tried to peel out by spinning the bow into the eddy wall with a powerful stroke on the left to build forward momentum. But the paddle blade scraped against the rock wall, failing miserably, its effectiveness minimized by the lack of space.

Next, he tried on his right by setting the blade, anchoring it in the fastest current. He pulled—the weight of his body angling upward, working against him. The harder he drew, the closer he came to escaping, the steeper the pitch became. Gravity denied his exit.

Sliding back to the bottom of the hole, the kayak continued to bounce violently, smacking the rock wall, deflecting, then nudging the rushing current on the opposite side. There seemed no escape.

The crowd compressed as they edged up, looking downward into the infinite eddy.

The kayaker tried several other aggressive maneuvers to escape. He cartwheeled, paddling head on into the current, getting thrown end over end. Many times, the kayak flipped, landing upside down—quickly rolling, but still stuck in the hole.

Finally, in what seemed to be the only option, he rolled. The top half of the mystery kayaker disappeared, turning his body into an anchor. The friction of the current against his body might drag him out. They watched as he hung there for what seemed an eternity to the onlookers, holding his breath, the creek sounding like a speeding freight train.

And, after what seemed an endless moment, nothing happened.

Though the kayaker was now out of options, Keith saw that he remained poised, measuring his dilemma, still functioning like a slot machine, the tumblers rolling inside his mind.

Keith saw that the stranger was studying the rock wall.

Suddenly, he freed one hand and started running it against the wet surface of the stone, looking for a crack. Then clink, the tumblers matched the same. "Jackpot!"

Lifting the neoprene lip of the spray skirt that sealed the cockpit, the stranger slid from the kayak as it rapidly filled with water. The next two things he did simultaneously. Lifting his knees from the cockpit, he dropped the paddle and grabbed onto the slippery rock face with both hands. The paddle flipped into the muddy creek, caught the main current, and whisked away. Immediately, the kayak sank, and in an instant was gone.

The stranger clung to the rock face on the opposite riverbank.

Moving his right hand higher, finding another handhold, he scaled the face of the cliff and out of danger.

It was now dark. The stranger made his way upstream and disappeared into the woods. On the opposite riverbank, the crowd stared after him, stunned.

Chapter 8

The people who witnessed the event at the Slides milled around in little groups reliving the incident, contemplating what it meant to each of them. Keith was shell-shocked by what he'd seen. The stranger had confidently pushed beyond his personal limit—and the limit of the sport. It lasted fewer than three minutes and ended with an inconceivable outcome.

In the darkness, the fog seemed thicker as Keith climbed the steep bank and headed for the campground.

When he stopped at a barroom at the base of the hillside near the campground, he bought two six-packs of Rolling Rock. The topic inside the tavern, filled with local river guides, was the endless analysis of the attempted run of the Slides, by a man they did not know.

As he ascended the steep road up the mountainside and through the rapidly thinning fog layer, the sky grew clear, the air became crisp. Keith parked in a grassy area in the middle of the campground, near several picnic tables. He observed the stranger who had survived the Slides sitting at one of the tables, cooking on a small stove.

Keith offered him a beer.

Accepting, the stranger pulled the tab and handed it back. The beer was gone in seconds.

Keith handed him another and sat atop the table, so he could be eye to eye with this mysterious person.

"What's your name?" Keith asked.

"Mark Weston," he replied. The man gave him a firm handshake. "Yours?"

"Keith Ashland," he answered.

"I must ask you a question, Mark."

"Go ahead." Mark's eyes were deep blue, his gaze focused.

"From time to time, a guy blows into river country from the mainstream with a suicide wish. Are you one of those? Or was your decision to run the Slides a calculated risk?"

Keith studied the man's expression.

Mark dented the empty can, placed it on the ground, and stomped it flat.

"I'm not so nuts," he indicated.

"There were some really good boaters who have run incredible drops watching you tonight. None thought the Slides at that water level was runnable. I have a lot of respect for them. In fact, they're my friends. We figured you were in over your head," Keith said. "You're lucky to be alive! Did you see something in that drop that would justify you running it cleanly?"

"You don't understand either," Mark said drily, referring to Keith and his paddling buddies. He finished his second beer, accepted a third from Keith.

"Most of you look at the river as if it were rushing by." Mark wiped the moisture from the can onto his jeans. "The river doesn't pass on by, it's stationary. The land moves, not the river."

"Say what? I don't get it," Keith said, confused, questioning his logic.

Mark grinned. "A rapid is actually stationary, it doesn't go anywhere. It doesn't travel downstream, does it?"

"No, it doesn't," Keith responded, with an inclining as to what he was alluding.

"The features of any rapid, such as waves, eddies, pillows, and currents, exist not only near the surface, but, one, two, or even six feet underwater. They're continuously doing the same thing in the same spot, while the river releases its energy.

"Today, I made a mistake, I'm sure you have too. I did not see that tiny surge on the backside of that cross-curl which spoiled my line. I wasn't trying to kill myself."

Keith could feel his own eyes go wide. Was this guy loony-tunes?

"What pisses me off," Mark said, "was ending up in that hole and the way I got out. That wasn't planned! And as you know, there's risk in this sport."

After a few minutes listening to Mark, Keith needed to get high again. The beer provided only a slight buzz.

Mark motioned toward Keith's wooden paddle, tied on top of his Nova. "Who made your paddle?"

"You're looking at him. I'm a lefty," Keith noted. I can't locate anyone who makes left-hand control kayak paddles. So I build my own."

Rolling his blue eyes, Mark said. "Paddle-making technology is in the Stone Age. No one gives enough thought to what's happening with river equipment design these days.

"For example," Mark continued, "kayak paddle blades are offset at 90 degrees, so as not to pick up wind resistance during the recovery phase of each stroke. That concept doesn't jibe on rivers, only in lakes, where the wind can catch the blade. Wind is rarely a factor on whitewater rivers."

Mark's observation made sense. Keith leaned forward and listened intently.

"If you reduce the offsets to 60 degrees, your stroke recovery becomes much quicker. Also, you won't over-rotate your wrist during your offside stroke. The lesser angle not only allows for more leverage, there's less stress involved."

Keith shook his head. He could barely grasp that concept.

"Believe this. If you fabricated a paddle set at 60 degrees instead of 90, your river guide friends would pay you handsomely, once they understood the advantages it poses.

"Also, did you know paddle blades these days are way too big, it's old school. The clumsy paddle I used today bleeds too much energy back into the river. I want to feel the water, not shove it backwards to maneuver. Blades should be smaller with less surface area."

Mark looked directly into Keith's eyes, as if he were inserting the explanation inside Keith's brain.

"Man, you've lost me." Keith cracked his knuckles. "Energy back to the river?"

Without asking, Mark opened another beer.

"Larger blades create an energy imbalance. Too much loads to the shaft. The force has nowhere to go but back to the river. The paddler unknowingly fights with the excess energy not fully consumed in each stroke."

"I've never heard this 'energy' thing talked about before," Keith said, scratching his belly. "I gotta have a beer."

A moment later Keith was downing another.

"Have you ever heard of a thing called waggle?" Mark said.

"Waggle?"

Mark's grin became wider.

"You ever ridden in a motorboat, and while it's moving, stick a canoe paddle into the water?"

"Can't say I have." Keith felt a sense of eeriness set in.

"When you place a paddle into moving water, it interrupts the flow. This interruption transfers energy to the paddle. Can you get your mind around that?" Mark asked.

"Yeah, sort of."

"Once the paddle loads, absorbing all the energy it can hold, the continuing force crams more energy into it. The paddle temporarily loads the excess, but quickly releases it back. This reversal pushes against the oncoming current, neutralizing the energy flow. A pillow of water in front of the blade forms. The paddle twists, flips forward to fill the pillow until it again meets the oncoming current.

"The paddle wags like a dog's tail. Each flip releases just enough energy to bring the retained energy back into balance."

Mark drummed his fingertips on top of the picnic table to emphasize his point.

"Wow, far out. What an incredible revelation," Keith said. "Are you some sort of hydrological engineer or physicist?"

Mark's face closed down and he shook his head. "I just look at things differently. The sport of whitewater is relatively new. There's not much thought put into improving the design dynamics of the sport's propulsion devices.

"There's lots of energy in moving water ready to be harnessed. You can transfer, store, and return it back to its origins, if you know how to manage it. Remember the Duffek stroke?" Mark asked.

"Sure do. The shoulder dislocation move," Keith said, recalling the stroke taught him when he raced kayaks. "Everyone thought that technique was a nifty way to turn faster. That is, until kayakers complained of shoulder sublexation injuries.

"When you flipped your kayak using the Duffek maneuver, it puts your shoulder in an abducted position. Add some resistance while inverted, and pop, out goes your shoulder joint."

Keith jumped up, spied a good spot about fifteen feet away, and relieved himself.

Mark walked in the opposite direction and did the same.

"I can see what you mean," Keith said, refreshed, opening another beer. "You're saying that a paddle serves to transfer energy from the river to you and your boat?"

He threw back half the can, hoping the alcohol would aid his comprehension.

"More than just that," Mark said with a smug smile. "It *stores* energy."

"Stores? Come on, man, you must be on something."

Keith was finally feeling the desired disinhibiting effect of the beers.

Mark honed in on the point he wanted to make. "The basic design of a kayak paddle needs significant improvement."

"You mean the paddle can store a lot more energy," Keith said, acknowledging Mark's seriousness.

Mark leaned forward and stared intently at Keith. "The paddle is a *conduit* that transfers energy between the boater and the river—constantly."

"Holy shit!" Keith set down his beer and stared back. "You're talking about increasing the effectiveness of each paddle stroke by at least a factor of ten."

"Hell, no, brother."

Mark paused a long moment to allow tension to build, then said with conviction, "One hundred, with the right combination of wood and composites, perhaps more."

Keith gulped. He was incapable of speech.

"Wood is the best material made by nature—from energy," Mark said. "They say the wood inside a guitar or piano, when played by the same artist for many years, eventually memorizes the artisan's music. With age, the quality of the music coming from the instrument improves. I believe the same principle applies to paddle building."

Mark again drummed his fingers on the table.

"A kayak paddle built correctly will develop the capacity to draw, sustain, and release energy as needed. The net result is that you will maneuver with greater precision and leveraging capabilities."

"Then what happened tonight in the creek?" Keith asked.

"Inferior equipment," Mark said with finality.

"Damn!"

Keith felt frustrated that he couldn't completely absorb Mark's logic. He needed a few days. Hell, maybe he needed a few weeks for this transfer-of-energy concept to congeal.

Mark continued into the nighttime. He talked about the concepts of energy amplitude, cellulose transfer rates, and the use of tuning forks to study how forces moved inside the blades and through the shaft. How different layers of wood changed the flow of energy, its capability to compress, so more could be harnessed. How reducing the waggle created an internal energy wave that cycled through the cellulose, a wavelength that leveraged its movement.

Keith stretched out on the seat of the picnic table and stared at the stars. That night, the stranger became a friend. Keith asked a thousand questions, discovering that Mark was one of those rare individuals with a distinct perspective. Everything he said was thought out.

Mark continued with what was now a one-way conversation that lasted until the night lifted to witness the dawn. He explained many ideas, formulated new ones, improved old ones, as Keith listened until he fell asleep.

The next day, Ashland Paddles and the New World design was born.

Keith immersed himself in Mark's ideas. He became so consumed his nightmares disappeared. For months he experimented, making minor improvements to his paddle design, but as he continued with different woods, laminates, and applications, his paddles greatly improved.

And when he started making paddles with a 60-degree offset, they were an instant hit.

Keith had turned Mark's concepts into reality. Anybody who owned an Ashland became a superior kayaker, feeling much safer in bigger whitewater. Soon after, other paddle builders followed, but could not replicate the quality of a New World Design.

Chapter 9

Keith was three miles downstream. The first major rapid, Gap Falls, lay just ahead. He was loose. The fresh air and exercise had done its job—as it always did. His muscles were warm and activated. Keith was ready.

The oncoming rafts followed behind, with customers eager and excited. Mark was charging hard toward a setup spot before the first rafts arrived.

Negotiating the descending labyrinth of whitewater that lay ahead would require an extreme effort by all personnel. From this point, none of the guides would waste time talking, unless it was necessary. They'd communicate nonverbally, through glances, nods, hand signals, and facial expressions.

The chilly morning air coming from the canyon ahead arrived as a stiff breeze, making Keith uncomfortable. Preferring to stay dry as long as possible, he decided to sneak past the big wave in the middle of Gap Falls by skirting to the right.

He drifted into the channeling sluice right of center—standard procedure for the lead safety boater. The flow quickened and whisked him down and through the drop. The rolling top of the enormous wave smacked him in the chest. He eddied out so he could watch Mark run the rapid, which was always surprising; no one could guess what he was going to do next, or what innovative move he was trying to perfect.

Mark charged into the drop, his shoulders pinwheeling, paddle blades biting chunks of river like a Mississippi paddleboat. He soared over the ledge and raced down the sluice toward the large standing wave at the bottom. With a full head of steam, Mark slammed into the enormous crest, reached deep into the trough, and accessed the faster current beneath the surface. Quickly, he spun 180 degrees. The stern lifted as the kayak lunged into the oncoming current.

Mark completely disappeared, sucked beneath by the physics of his maneuver.

Keith chuckled as several seconds lapsed.

First to appear was the stern. It emerged like a missile several yards downstream. The red hull exploded upward, vertical, until the bow cleared the peak of the wave. Mark was airborne and continued upward an impressive eleven feet. Then his kayak dropped like a falling arrow. Again, it disappeared, traveling beneath like a submarine.

Keith craned his neck to see Mark's blue helmet become visible, followed by his head, broad shoulders, and finally the kayak. Mark smiled with the joy of having perfectly executed his patented submarine move.

As the rafts approached, Mark ferried to his post inside the large eddy next to the big wave. Each raft blasted through, every customer screaming with excitement. Intermittently, Mark surfed onto the wave to scare the oncoming customers into thinking their raft would run him over. He'd flick cold water like a beaver. The Vietnamese girls chattered like chickens, cursing him for getting their hair wet.

Hearing the familiar, foul Vietnamese curses that Katherine had sometimes used when ranting about Sister Bernadine, Keith laughed. Katherine often used foul language, but when she cursed, it sounded uproariously funny, because the nasty language was unexpected from such a gentle nun.

Rodger glided past in his kayak to catch the lead raft, continuing to the much bigger drops downstream.

Keith was keenly aware that Rodger and Mark had observed his little chicken move at Gap Falls, avoiding the meat of the big wave to stay dry. Though not unusual for Keith to wimp out on a drop, it was important with a trip this size that everyone be on their game. Keith's hesitation meant his friends would pay closer attention to him as they progressed down the gorge, making certain he was up to the task of guiding.

He knew it was time to go to work, to restore his friends' confidence in him.

Keith peeled out of the eddy and dropped backward into the trough of the standing wave. He back surfed and finished with a powerful backstroke that drove the stern into the oncoming current. As he leaned back, the faster current caught and squirted the kayak into the air like a bar of soap. It landed him upside down. Keith quickly executed a reverse screw roll, righting himself.

Mark smiled, aware that Keith knew they were watching.

Rodger looked back in time to see Keith's hull in the air. He smiled, too, then quickly turned and headed to the next difficult rapid.

~ ~ ~

The nearly continuous rapids came fast, back-to-back, seeming to connect, lasting forever. Doglegging drops, six, ten, seven feet, surprised the rafters as the in-raft guides maneuvered around house-size boulders and blasted through walls of boiling whitewater.

The self-bailing rafts filled with water that sloshed about until it drained out the bottom. The only voices heard came from the in-raft guides who barked commands to the compliant guests. The safety boaters waited in eddies, then dropped through slots, positioning in anticipation of a mistake. Each time a rafter tumbled into the river, Mark quickly scooped up the panicked swimmer. Possessing a keen sense of impending danger, it was Mark who was often at the scene before the mishap occurred.

Rapids like Heinzerling, Meat Cleaver, Double Pencil Sharpener, and Lost and Found littered the steepest sections of the gorge. The trip progressed, and each rapid became history.

Having properly executed his guiding responsibilities, Keith was now soaking wet. Though his spray skirt protected him from swamping, water still slopped inside the kayak. His sopping-up sponge floated underneath his thigh. The weight of the water made the craft a bit unstable.

They arrived at the top of the next to last major rapid, National Falls. With the greatest gradient, this rapid afforded a steep, high-velocity adrenaline rush.

Keith powered into the Falls, riding a narrowing tongue of churning water. He blasted through a wall of surging whitewater to catch the largest eddy the Upper Yough had provided since Gap Falls.

One by one, each raft followed and blasted through the bubbling wall. Every raft survived.

Keith gave a sigh of relief; his workday was nearly complete. Soon, he could think about getting high. And would do that soon after the last major rapid, Tombstone Rock.

~ ~ ~

Tombstone Rock is a relatively easy to run, but demanded respect. The rapid was notorious for pinning rafts and kayaks because boaters had let down their guard after successfully navigating National Falls. Tombstone came sooner than expected, due to an odd distortion that made the rapid seem much farther downstream.

Mark often reminded Keith that a continuous Class-V river, such as the Upper Yough, hypnotizes boaters, making them prone to mistakes. He often warned him to remain alert until after Tombstone.

Standard operating procedure for the last rapid required all three hard boaters to place themselves in the rapid before the rafts entered. Rodger took his position where he could jump out of his kayak and scurry upstream to set up a rope rescue should a raft pin. The strongest boater, Mark, would locate within a micro eddy, just below Tombstone Rock. It was nearly impossible to sit in this tiny eddy, but Mark miraculously accomplished the feat each time.

Mark's job was not to chase ejected customers who might fall out if the raft pinned, but to assist with a land-based rope rescue that Rodger directed. Mark would be the closest, and time would be of the essence. His positioning improved the chances of a successful rescue by shortening precious, necessary seconds, thus reducing the magnitude of risk.

Keith was assigned the easiest task. He would lead the rafts past Tombstone, positioning downstream, below Mark. Should there be swimmers Keith would retrieve them.

By the time the trip reached Tombstone Rapid, they were several hundred feet lower in elevation. Keith loved the color of the river at this spot, where the main current had been agitated into a creamy lime green. A warm breeze usually sucked in from the opening valley, generating a misty haze.

But the dampness, his lack of a breakfast, and the awful flashback had caught up with Keith—this was the fatigue he sought. He wanted to be exhausted. He needed dead-dog tired to sleep each night.

Having depleted the reserves in his body, Keith kept telling himself to stay focused a bit longer—one more rapid. Soon, he would administer his mind-numbing concoctions. Tonight, he would be exceptionally tired and incredibly high.

As Keith ferried toward Tombstone Rock, the drenched Vietnamese girls chattered in their native tongue. He heard their voices as he descended into the chute that would lead him safely past. He thought of Katherine for a brief moment—her beautiful smile, the night they made love. His memory suddenly jumped to her crucified figure. In vain, he tried to refocus his thoughts. He needed to align his kayak correctly to carry him past.

He drifted left and missed his mark. Instinctively, an alarm went off. He must correct his line of entry.

Sitting straight, he drew back to force his kayak before the current swept him over the ledge and onto Tombstone Rock.

He pulled on the paddle, but was too far to the left.

It was too late.

~ ~ ~

Certain physical attributes of Disruption live in harmony with the fluid, physical flow of nature. Mayhem exists hidden within the rhythm of routine, often concealed as a dull, lonely, daily interplay, patiently waiting for its moment to arrive. Experienced river guides, working day after day, develop a sixth sense; a closeness with nature that warns them moments before pandemonium awakens.

These warnings, these signals, are apparent in the most minuscule way, such as in the signature of a lapping river wave, the way it spits then rolls, oddly out of sequence with the cadence of the river. Often, an about-to-happen accident throws off a sign as slight as a heart flutter—a beat disharmonious with the natural order of things. A miscue that caught Mark Weston's attention a full second before it occurred.

Keith had allowed his kayak to drift left, merely one foot from where it needed to be. Instantly, Mark charged in reckless abandonment, knowing what happened in ten more seconds would determine if Keith lived.

Keith expected his kayak to slice through the small wave that confirmed the correct line, but it did not. Instead, it deflected left, away from the accelerating flow that was to carry him safely along. He tried to fix his alignment, but the stroke to push clear had been neutralized by the mysterious forces working against the hull.

Before him, a pillow of water rose as it spilled over the ledge and onto Tombstone Rock. Helpless, Keith washed broadside into what was known as the devil's vault. He floated briefly on the bubbling pillow, then solidly pinned.

Instinctively, he leaned into the rock as a way to direct the laminar flow underneath, hoping to get enough lift to sweep him around, where the stronger current would flush him free.

But there was no lift. The laminar current piled against the hull, wedging against the knife-shaped edge of Tombstone Rock. The depths of his instinct screamed that he must do something, "Now!" If he lost his upstream edge, he would flip. The kayak would wrap instantly—the force of the river pinning, trapping him beneath the current.

Lifting his right knee, he drove it into the deck brace to hold the upper edge out of the water. Initially, this positioning worked; the consuming current paused—the laminar flow pulsating, the kayak angling its bow upwards, the Kevlar hull flexing.

Then suddenly, the stern struck the river bottom, wedged fast by the powerful flow that cut through the undercut portion of Tombstone. Water racing over the ledge gathered around Keith's waist as he worked feverishly to free the pinned stern.

As the coldness of the river lapped his shoulder, he released his paddle and scratched at the exposed portion of Tombstone. The surface was slimy. His fingernails struggled to find the tiniest stone nub to grab hold—the force of the current shoving, as though he were inside a panicked crowd, unable to move.

The foam pillars that momentarily kept the kayak from completely collapsing twisted sideways, trapping his legs. The deck vacuumed flat to the contour of his chubby thighs.

He worked frantically, trying to unpin, but the kayak would not budge. The river poured endlessly over his head.

Through open eyes, he watched the churning water flicker like chandelier prisms, casting spiraling rainbows that danced as angelic fireflies. The sunlight that struck air bubbles whipped within the current; swirled as a crystal blizzard, emitting colliding shards of stained-glass color.

He felt an incredible bliss. "The Cathedral Syndrome has arrived," thought Keith, referring to the soothing sensation that comes when your body believes it is about drown.

He felt no panic. "Drowning is not a horrifying experience," he told himself. He was not aware his oxygen supply was cut off. He felt mellow, pleasant—tranquil. The daily gnaw of his infinite stress was gone. The stubborn resistances of his circling scars and the aching tightness in his joints and muscles disappeared. All his physical hurt had evaporated. He felt no urgency, just a melancholy.

Anoxia was upon him. He couldn't see the lower half of his body anymore. And didn't care. A whiteness rose slowly from his waist to his chest, around his neck and over his face until finally crossing his eyes. He saw only a blinding bright white, as if he had stared directly into the sun then quickly closed his eyes.

Katherine's face appeared in the center of the whiteness. Her image grew larger, came closer. She smiled. He felt her love surround him, as if he were her beating heart. Her lips traced out silent words that he heard clearly. "Everything is okay, Keith. I love you!"

Katherine's olive hands extended toward him. They opened to show her wounds.

When he touched her Stigmata, all that was his horror drained through his fingertips. The eternal pain tattooed to his soul flushed free. Reaching, he was ready to go with her. He felt his heart melt into her soul.

Suddenly, Katherine's image and the heavens that surrounded her shook like an earthquake. The brightness blurred and abruptly disappeared. Katherine was gone.

He felt a tug on his left shoulder. He felt it again, but much stronger. His unconsciousness was disturbed. The sound of the rushing river returned. Something had hold of his lifejacket. A hand had grabbed the shoulder strap. A prusik rope slipped underneath and squeezed the rubbery flotation. Keith heard the familiar snap of a carabiner next to his ear. The entire lifejacket tightened like a straitjacket.

A series of sharp, stabbing pains shot through his thigh muscles. A winching pressure maximized until his pinned legs began to slip, at first by a fraction, then an inch, and finally several.

Something pushed on his left shoulder and rolled him away from Tombstone Rock. His hips broke free from the crushed cockpit.

The sound of the rushing water changed, as did the temperature.

Keith floated away, rolling like a ragdoll, tumbling nearly lifeless in the free-flowing current.

~ ~ ~

Mark had seen that Keith was about to be in trouble. By the time Keith dropped over the ledge and onto Tombstone, Mark was charging hard toward him.

So was Rodger!

Keith's lineup for the drop was off. Mark had seen it. Rodger had confirmed it with a hardened stare back to Mark that said their angst-ridden friend was in trouble.

And when Keith dropped over the ledge, Mark was already traveling faster than the momentum of the river toward him, thinking of his limited rescue options as he launched over the ledge at the same moment Keith pinned.

Mark charged for the micro-eddy about five feet below Keith and the turbulences of the ledge. He planted his paddle firmly and spun 180 degrees, solidly parking in the tiny eddy that swirled beneath him. Mark could clearly see Keith struggling to stay upright. With the stern bottom-pinned, the fast-moving water held him down like a press. Mark quickly assessed a shore-based rope rescue would be futile. His only choice was to cut Keith out of his boat. He'd have only one shot at it.

Powerful, confident strokes propelled Mark upstream, against the opposing current. Every muscle in his fit torso contracted and exploded like pistons. The charge ensued. The hull of his kayak lifted as powerful, driving strokes pushed forward. Another stroke more powerful than the last came as the bow of Mark's boat nudged close to Keith's submerged head. Mark studied the positioning of the pin; half of his kayak had sucked beneath the undercut. It was not good.

Mark allowed himself to drift backward to study the pin from a different angle. Then he drifted back into the micro-eddy.

"I must act now, rely on instinct, and find a way," Mark thought.

A bold determination to save his respected friend's life overcame Mark. As he clenched his jaw, the muscles in his face quivered. His deltoids rippled. His stomach muscles became granite. A burst of power that overcame all opposition detonated from inside him. Once again the bow of his kayak confidently charged ahead, into the oncoming current. Two short, punching strokes propelled Mark past Keith's submerged head and into the gap where Tombstone Rock lounged back.

Mark planted a hard, leveraging pry close to the stern. The kayak broadsided the current, the effort so hard, the aluminum shaft of his paddle snapped and sucked into the undercut.

Without hesitation, Mark grabbed hold of the shoulder strap of Keith's lifejacket. He clipped on the carabiner tied to his prusik rope and tethered himself to Keith. As the carabiner shut, Mark's kayak sucked off his body. The boat filled, window-shaded beneath the ledge, then whisked away.

Mark swept downstream, past Keith and alongside Tombstone Rock. The lashed prusik pulled tight and dragged Mark underneath the current. He rolled over onto his stomach, angling to allow the oncoming flow to surf him upward, holding him above the surface.

Grabbing hold of Keith's shoulder strap, he ran his forearm under, locking himself in place. The river pounded at Mark, pushing him side-to-side like a swimming salmon.

Mark reached across his lifejacket and released his knife. He lunged the serrated, stainless-steel edge into the fiberglass deck of the pinned boat. With both hands, he firmly sawed open the deck, puncturing the skin and muscle tissue in Keith's right thigh several times.

The force of the current peeled opened the cavity of Keith's kayak. As it shifted, Mark bear-hugged Keith and freed his hips.

The current swept the tethered pair swiftly downstream. The remaining rapid, although difficult, was not a major concern for Mark. He was very much at home, having effected this kind of swimming rescue many times.

Mark rolled Keith onto his back and began mouth-to-mouth resuscitation. He inflated Keith's lungs with four elevating breaths.

Keith coughed then began to breath.

Chapter 10

Two days later, Keith found himself sober and sitting at his workbench, fabricating a pair of paddle blades. It was early morning, and the first time he didn't go kayaking on the Upper Yough.

Since the accident he had an urge. It was an abstract concept, a design stuck in his head that had to get out.

Using a black marker, he outlined the tip of a woman's nose on the finished face of each blade. Using a small file clutched in his left hand, he scratched off the ink to open the wood pores, then roughened the spot with 80-grit sandpaper, careful not to etch outside of the drawn area. Holding a syringe, he flooded linseed oil onto the prepared surface and rubbed it in with a clean, high-grade cotton cloth. Finally, he dusted the area with industrial-grade, commercial diamond powder, then smiled as he massaged the diamond dust into the wood grain.

He continued, sketching the rounded cheekbones of an Asian woman, her lovely lips lifting into a pleasant smile, her thick eyebrows and almond eyes.

Again, he scratched off the ink, stroked in the oil, and set the diamond powder. He repeated this process, each time adding to the woman's portrait until he had drawn the image of Sister Katherine, with flowing hair and content expression—the expression when she visited him pinned on Tombstone Rock.

To the naked eye, her portrait was invisible until the paddle blades were immersed in the river. The concave curve of each blade behaved like a lens, reflecting refracted sunlight. A three-dimensional hologram of Katherine leapt from the blade and brought her to life.

"This is Mark's paddle," Keith said, dusting it. "It's something special—so Katherine will live and protect him on the river."

Chapter 11

Mark aligned his pelvis perfectly with his spine, so the broad muscles of his torso would maneuver his kayak, not smaller muscles like the deltoids, triceps, and biceps, as commonly believed. The skeletal muscles that wrapped the length of his tall frame were much larger, spanning a greater distance across his body. He could build more power with them. However, it took practice, hours of surfing to study his motion and the physics of it, so he could innovate.

After making one precise, forward stroke, Mark finished it with a slight adjustment, using a combination of muscle groups to ensure the boat didn't spin off, losing the wave. The kayak aligned perfectly, facing directly upstream. He torqued his torso and rotated into a tight coil. The increasing tension drove the kayak forward. The bow sank deep into the oncoming flow. Water raced along the deck, piling onto his neoprene spray skirt. The bow struck a submerged rock and stuck like Velcro. Mark swung his paddle blade across the deck into a crossbow draw. With his left hand firmly gripping the shaft, he rotated his wrist outward. The action changed the knifing position of the concave blade, opening it to the oncoming current. The river transferred its energy through the paddle, up the shaft, through Mark's arms into his torso. The energy loaded like a tense tiger seconds before it pounced on its prey.

An abdominal twitch released the bow from the submerged rock and drew deeper, burying Mark into the trough of the wave. Standing vertical on his foot pegs, he leaned back to keep the kayak from going end over end. It rose into the air, vertically, rotating one and a half times, finally splashing down, upright. The bow and stern had traded positions, perfectly centered on top of the little wave that Mark liked to surf.

He smiled. He had perfected a new move.

~ ~ ~

The late afternoon sun had cast a cool shadow across the rim of the Rockport oxbow. Several hours had passed. Mark had been so focused he did not notice the hikers making their way down the coal embankment to sit on a sandstone outcrop just ten feet from the wave.

Occasionally, Mark looked about to remind himself that he was on earth. On one of those occasions, he saw Keith sitting on the outcrop, watching. In his hands was a new Ashland paddle.

Mark smiled, happy to see his friend was well.

Keith gestured by raising the paddle into the air.

Mark knew what the gesture meant. Keith wanted him to test the kayak paddle, a new design, something Mark looked forward to because each design change brought him closer to the dimension he was seeking.

Mark tossed his old Ashland to Keith. It arched into the air.

Keith confidently snatched it.

Mark surfed a few moments without the paddle, as if to say, "I dare you to chase me out of here, wave."

Keith threw the new paddle high, as if he were celebrating its arrival.

Mark nabbed it.

Immediately, he was excited. The new Ashland was much lighter. Keith's designs were the lightest and strongest around. Any improvement in its featherlight weight was unimaginable.

It took a few moments to adjust to the reduction in weight. He rotated the shaft in his hands to measure the feel.

Setting the freshly lacquered blade into the river for the first time, he made one stroke after another. Right away, the paddle had the ability to force more power with significantly less effort.

"Really cool," Mark said. "How does he do it?"

With a boyish grin, he glanced back at Keith.

Keith nodded, assuring there was more.

To test the upstream attainment, Mark raced forward. The kayak glided against the oncoming current, across the wave's trough, up the lip of the ledge that formed the wave, and into the deep, dark pool of Devil's Elbow.

"Incredible," Mark said. "So easy. Keith has come across an entirely new concept. I wonder what it is?"

Leaving a trailing wake, Mark sprinted upstream to a point where the sun struck the river. The clean shaft glistened as he paddled into the brightness.

"Holy shit, what is that?" exclaimed Mark, looking at the blade as it hit the sunlit water.

"What the frig?" he said, trying to figure out what was going on when it submerged.

"It's an image."

"Huh!"

While looking into the water, Mark drifted along. A hologram of a woman's face jumped from the blade.

Mark was stunned to see it.

Keith sat on the tabletop rock and watched from a distance. He could tell from his reaction Mark saw the hologram of Katherine.

The idea was a good one.

Mark spent considerable time studying Keith's work, constantly dipping the blade in and out of the water.

Turning around, he sprinted back to the wave and surfed a few minutes. His big blue eyes turned to Keith to say, "Here it comes. If I break this damn thing it won't be my fault."

Keith looked back at his old friend with an expression that dared, "Go ahead."

Mark loaded the crossbow draw once again. This time he cranked his torso further, corkscrewing to where his muscles bound so tightly, they wanted to burst through his skin.

Cocking his wrist, he opened the face of the blade, intercepting the flow of the Lehigh River. The energy loaded, and Mark firmly gripped the shaft, defiantly waiting for it to snap in half. He waited for the waggle, a sign the energy was fully absorbed. This time, it didn't occur.

Mark glanced over, smiled, and pulled the trigger.

He forced the boat forward into the deep pocket that created his favorite surfing spot. The kayak exploded upwards, vertical, with more energy than he had ever experienced. It launched into the air, stern first. The bow followed, ejecting completely from the river and continued to rise upwards, clearing the wave top by several feet.

Keith cheered.

The kayak landed deck first into the Lehigh.

Rolling, Mark paddled over.

"Holy shit!" Mark said. "You've done it. What did you do to make it load so much juice?"

"Modified the materials in each of the blades and laid them out differently," Keith said. "To tell you the truth, I didn't expect the changes to make such a big difference. This was the first paddle I made since the accident. It comes from my private stock."

"The hologram?" Mark asked. "What's with that?"

"An idea that came out of my head after my near drowning. Cool, isn't ?" Keith asked.

"Unbelievable!" Mark said, excited. "Let's go eat at the White Haven Diner. I'm hungry for one of their humongous burgers."

Keith scratched his stomach.

Mark flipped the paddle to Keith, released his spray skirt, and jumped onto the rock to greet his friend.

Together, they climbed the steep embankment to the abandoned railroad grade that traced the oxbow.

"What's the rest of the story with your new Ashland?" Mark asked, hoisting his kayak to his shoulder.

"Since the accident, I feel different. That day, I had an out-of-body experience, as if I went to heaven and returned with all these new ideas. I added a carbon fiber layer and laced it between the laminates like you suggested," Keith explained.

"Yeah, I thought you looked different," Mark said, sensing a distinct change in his demeanor. "Lost weight, didn't you?"

Keith rubbed his scars, took a deep breath, and let it out.

"There's an inscription burnt into the laminate at the base of the blade. I've started naming each of my new Ashlands. This one's named Tombstone."

"Eerie name, but thanks, that's some reward." Mark grinned, pleased he was the recipient of this entirely new design.

"Word is you're heading to Costa Rica?" Keith asked.

"Absolutely, to kayak the Rio Chirripo. No one has run it yet, as far as I know. I'm going to put my name on it with a first descent," Mark said.

"While you're there, you should check out a beach named Pavones. Supposedly, there's a left-point beach break that runs for nearly a mile."

"Cool! That's the oil painting you have over your workbench, isn't it?" Mark said as they walked through the coal dirt parking lot to their vehicles.

Keith nodded, "Yes, it is. But I have yet to find someone who can confirm the waves actually exist." Keith opened the door to his Nova. "Tell you what. I have the painting in my car. I was going to leave it with my parents; might as well give it to you. I'll dig it out when we get to the diner," Keith said as he climbed into the car.

"Sounds like a plan. See you at the diner."

A big puff of black smoke blew from Keith's tailpipe. A cloud of oily exhaust drifted into the pine canopy that shaded the isolated river access point.

Mark went to his restored, royal blue '73 International Scout. It had no roof, just a padded roll bar and a windshield that flipped down. Shoving his boat into the back and wedging it between the seats, he got in and turned the key. The powerful rebuilt engine responded immediately.

Chapter 12

Entering the tiny town of White Haven from the south, the Scout crossed the interstate, passed a gas station and a newly constructed Catholic church. Its parochial school was unable to find a nun to act as principal and closed years ago. Two blocks away, he turned right, down a bumpy hill and over a single set of railroad tracks to Main Street. Mark winced as his Scout rumbled over the separations. He'd forgotten to secure his Ashland and didn't like it bouncing around in back.

The diner was famous for its unusually large, plate-size hamburgers. Mark often treated his friends with a visit, laughing hysterically at the amazed expression on their faces when the waitress set the massive burgers in front of them.

Directly across the street stood the oldest building in town, made entirely of hand-laid stones. Several years ago, the big hemlock logs that supported the floors were so dense that they didn't burn when the roof caught fire from a spark thrown from the railroad tracks.

Mark had a close college friend, Danny Dougherty. When Mark brought Dan to the Lehigh to guide river trips with him, Danny stayed and became a permanent resident. He'd ordered one of Keith's paddles almost two years ago and anxiously awaited its arrival.

Danny, who was often penniless, told Mark he was going to buy that old building someday and restore it. He planned to be a chiropractor, often practicing his adjustments on the river guides, particularly the female guides.

With short strides, Danny came around the side of the old stone building, looking for Keith and the New World paddle he said he was bringing him.

"Hey, Keith," Danny said, cautious not to sound too anxious about getting something he paid and waited two years for.

"How goes it?" Keith responded. He dug through the back of his Nova to get the New World.

"Going friggin' bald and my nuts itch," Danny said characteristically, trying to provoke anyone within earshot.

Keith pulled the custom kayak paddle from the tailgate and handed Dan his new stick.

Danny smiled and thanked him, not mentioning the length of time it took.

"I heard Tombstone Rock tried to bury you," Danny said.

"She sure did," Keith replied, his stomach grumbling.

"You have Mark to thank for your sorry ass being here today, don't you?"

Hungry, Keith did not respond.

Danny was excited about finally having possession of his second Ashland. Carrying it over to his Volkswagen bus, a vehicle suited to his personality, he unrolled a felt-lined sheath he made months back and inserted the entire kayak paddle, tying off the top with the drawstring sewn into the end of the sheath.

The young men stood for a while shooting the breeze. Keith relived his experience at Tombstone, adding drama to a story that would be passed along many times, becoming legend. Mark revealed he'd discovered a river no one knew about.

"Now that I'm out of college, it's time for me to check out some new spots," Mark said. He'd majored in geography because he planned to travel the entire world once he graduated.

"Spots?" Danny questioned, inserting his pinky deep into his nose.

"Yeah, you know; cool places like Costa Rica to hang for an indefinite period of time. Until I hear of another good spot," Mark responded.

Danny drew his finger from his nostril and watched Mark and Keith furrow their brows with disgust.

Danny grinned.

"They say there're rivers everywhere in Costa Rica. Many haven't been run yet," Mark explained. "I have a chance to put my name on many of them as first descents."

"For example?" Danny asked.

"Rio Chirripo!" Mark said. "Eighty-five percent of the Chirripo's drainage basin lies in mountains over five thousand feet. No topographic maps exist because there's no satellite imagery. The mountaintops are perpetually in the clouds."

His friends listened intently, fantasizing about the utopian river waiting to be discovered.

"Can you determine the gradient?" Danny asked.

"Based upon the only visible terrain, I figure a volcanic bowl catches the water from the perpetual cloud cover. I am guessing there's not much gradient in a caldera hidden inside the cloud cover. However, all the tributaries meet at the lip to create the Chirripo. From there the river is one continuous rapid with not many pools."

"Sweet!" Danny said.

Keith concurred with a nod.

"Here is the cool part," Mark said, his big blue eyes widening with excitement as he continued his assessment. "The average gradient for the first eighteen miles is one hundred twenty-three feet per mile, and the volume nearly doubles where the tributaries meet."

"Whoa!" Keith said. "A tropical Upper Yough! Warm water and steep drops," he added.

Everyone nodded in agreement.

"Then the gradient increases to more than two hundred feet per mile. It's my guess there may be several waterfall rapids, with the steepest section probably dropping five hundred feet per mile."

"Holy shit," Danny said. "Ya gotta have sex with some Costa Rican woman the night before you run that. Could be the last time."

"That sounds deadly," Keith commented.

"What's deadly, Danny saying having sex for the last time, or the Chirripo?" Mark asked.

Everyone laughed.

Chuckling, Mark continued. "That's what I'm doing this winter, heading to Costa Rica in the dry season to scout the Rio Chirripo and check out the rest of the country while I'm there. Apparently, some great surfing beaches exist on the Pacific Coast. So I'm bringing my surf kayak. And, when I get bored with the rivers, I'll hang at the beaches."

"Let's go eat. I'm starved," Keith said, anxious to eat, but more anxious to ask Mark to check out where the painting came from, perhaps confirming the story behind it, learning a bit more about Sister Katherine.

He didn't want to discuss Golfito and the Fatima Retreat in front of Danny, because he would question him to death about the school for virgins, making lots of crude remarks.

"Let's go," Danny said, noticing the waitress in the diner window stooping to catch a glimpse of the three studs standing in the parking lot.

~ ~ ~

The young men sat at a window booth just inside the entry. All ordered burgers from the chesty waitress, who was in her mid-twenties. She was exceptionally pleasant. Mark and Keith were polite. Danny, as usual, made a suggestive comment about the depth of her cleavage, receiving the expected embarrassing response.

"So, when do you plan to go to Costa Rica?" Keith asked.

"After working the October whitewater releases, I'll drive down in the Scout."

Mark worked off the lid of the catsup bottle.

"Going to be a long drive," Danny added, while glancing back at the waitress, waiting the table next to him.

She saw him checking out her rear and leaned further for him to notice.

"Aren't you concerned about breaking down in Mexico, where if you leave your car it's gone?" Danny asked, a bit distracted, hoping he was going to score tonight with this waitress.

"Can't think that way," Mark replied. "It's bad karma. Might as well do nothing in life if you think like that."

"Can't argue with that," Keith said, agreeing.

"Besides, I spent two years rebuilding the Scout from scratch. I know every inch of it. And didn't skimp. Everything is heavy duty. The engine and transmission are tight. If it breaks down I can find a machine shop and have a part remade.

"All Scout parts are universal," Mark explained, pointing out his vehicle was known around the world for its uniformity in replacement parts.

"Well, guys," Danny said, finishing his meal, "I hate to leave, but I'm applying for chiropractic school. Got to get that application in the mail."

Walking past the waitress, he slapped her on the ass, whispered in her ear, and left.

Mark inhaled the steam from the coffee he ordered. Looking out the diner window, he watched Danny cross the street and disappear behind the stone building.

"Have you ever tried surf kayaking yet?" Mark asked, thinking about the Costa Rican beaches.

"Yes, did some at the Jersey Shore when I got back from Vietnam many moons ago. It's different than what we're used to on rivers. Nice part is, when you wipe out, you wash onto the beach. I call it 'get trashed' practice," Keith said, remembering how the waves always flipped and tumbled him around.

"I tried it for the first time when Hurricane Kate came up the coast last summer. Had a blast," Mark recalled.

"Yes, so I've heard. You got good, real quick, and became a legend. A story floats around about you successfully surfing through the concrete piers underneath the Asbury Park Convention Center," Keith said, smiling at his daredevil friend. "You had a close one, didn't you, Mark?"

"Broke the back end of the Red Rocket III right off, just behind the cockpit," Mark said, liking to identify his boats as Red Rockets and numbering them accordingly when one was destroyed.

"That was a big mistake on my part," he continued. "I was showing off, hoping to get lucky with some college girls staying at the shore for the summer."

The waitress refilled their coffees.

"Damn English dude I was hanging out with told me that's why surfyaks are missing the back end. Said there're easier ways to shorten a boat."

Keith chuckled at Mark's comment, envisioning the conversation between Mark and the Englishman, who may have scolded him about his foolish and nearly impossible act of surfing between concrete piers, where the slightest mistake killed you.

The good friends finished their coffees and paid the waitress, who was having a cigarette.

"Do you want to crash at my trailer?" Mark asked as they left the diner.

"No," Keith answered. "I'm too wired. Got enough caffeine in me to make it to Connecticut to visit my family. But before I leave, I want to give you one last thing," Keith said, opening the side door of the Nova with the hinges barely hanging on.

He pulled out a corrugated box and opened the top. In it was the Pavones painting Katherine gave him.

"Here is that oil painting I told you about earlier. Maybe it can help you locate the beach where these neat waves might exist."

"Cool, they're nearly perfect, almost like someone dreamed them up," Mark said, referring to the barreling crests that seemed to go on forever. "If they're for real, they'll be a terrific ride. I'll check the spot out. You never know!"

He stared at the painting some more. "The artwork around the frame, is that your work?" Mark ran his hand along the lines of the intricately cut crucifixes.

"Yes," Keith said, "Something I did when I was deeply depressed."

"This painting behaves kind of spooky, too. Lately, it never wants to hang on the wall straight. No matter how many times I straighten it, it'd get crooked again—all by itself, as if it were unhappy or unsettled.

"That damn painting hung crooked all the time in my woodshop, except for the day I pinned on Tombstone. It hung level that morning . . . Damnedest thing I'd ever seen," Keith said, puzzled.

He paused, then said, "It might be good to get rid of it and turn over a new leaf. It would be nice if you left it where it was supposedly painted. Here, take it with you and leave it on Pavones for me. I get a feeling that's where it wants to be."

"I'll do that for you," Mark promised. "And thanks for the hologram paddle. I appreciate it."

"Have fun in Costa Rica. Put your name on those first descents, and keep it off a gravestone. Be safe. Don't get killed," Keith said opening the door of the Nova. "And, watch out for those Costa Rican women. Make sure they don't know Danny. You could catch a disease."

"Take care, Keith," Mark said, laughing, envisioning Danny in trouble with some Costa Rican woman.

Mark thumped his fist against the Kevlar hull of the kayak strapped to the roof racks of Keith's Nova. The boat echoed back a familiar sound. The friends patted each other on the shoulder and parted.

Hopping into his Scout, Mark wedged the painting between the seats. He started the engine and quickly made his way out of town.

† † †

Maria Chesters

Chapter 13

~ Twenty-three years later ~

Maria Chesters stood gazing intently at the painting hanging on the wall of her small office. She called it *The Waves of Pavones*, a secret, remote place she'd waited a lifetime to visit.

The day Maria had longed for finally arrived.

At age twenty-two, she stood five feet ten inches, slightly taller than most women. She was slender, but not too thin. Her most notable feature was best admired from the side—a Hepburn waistline with hips tipped ever so slightly to offer a cute, rounded tush. Her face was youthful, unstressed, with freckle-free cheeks. A light complexion, common to her English ancestry, had rarely seen the sun. She had thick brunette hair, but kept it short, because it was appropriate. Her high forehead was a hereditary trait, handed down from her mother. Self-conscious, she kept her bangs low to cover it.

Concentrated, extending eyelashes added to her unique combination of feminine features, but did not dominate her considerable almond-shaped, dark brown eyes.

Conceived under a Virgo's star, Maria was small-chested, as if still waiting for puberty to begin. Her sweet, Princess Diana glance was uniquely hers, owning a vulnerable innocence that cast a blinding spell upon young men who happened to engage her presence.

Though introspective at times, she tended to be an extrovert and was warned by Sister Florence to always keep her outgoing nature under wraps. "It isn't appropriate for postulants to be overly expressive," the nun often reminded her.

The office Maria had worked at was on the second floor of the Psychology Building at New York University at Washington Place. Her workspace was four plaster walls with no windows. The small room contained a simple desk, a telephone, and filing cabinet for her social work files.

Maria had graduated the previous year with a degree in social work. After the 9/11 tragedy, the Sisters of Mercy, overwhelmed by the human need of the event, asked to delay her postulancy, to stay with them for a year to counsel victims recovering from the physiological impact of the World Trade disaster.

As she lifted the painting with its peculiar religious frame from the hook, Maria tossed it a smile before placing it in a heavy-duty postal box confiscated from the post office on 4th Avenue and Blecher Street.

It was time to leave New York and venture forward, to the Fatima Vocational Center in Golfito, Costa Rica.

For her entire life, Sister Elizabeth Florence, Maria's mentor, had told her this day would come. Sister often said how tropical and beautiful Golfito was. "It's a paradise, the perfect place to meditate and contemplate your lifelong calling by God to become a nun. Your trip to Fatima is God's reward to you for your dedication and devotion, Maria."

It was 5 a.m. Maria had forgotten to pack her favorite painting and came from the convent she sometimes stayed to retrieve it. She was fond of the painting and promised her canvas friend she would take it back to visit its native soil.

Whenever Maria felt troubled or demoralized and alone, she longed to be inside the painting, envisioning herself walking the beach with its perfectly breaking waves. The painting was her escape from whatever troubled her.

Sister Florence often remarked that the waves of Pavones did not really exist. That the beach was too steep, rocky, and difficult to walk. That the painting was altered by a creative, bipolar artist who'd added the waves to compensate for the ugliness of the beach.

But Maria's mother, Jane, insisted the waves did in fact exist. That she had walked the beach, and it was as beautiful as the painting revealed.

Leaving her modest office, Maria shut off the light. The freshly waxed floors, worn from generations of students, reflected the dimly lit fluorescents that ran the length of the hallway. Except for the clopping of her leather clogs, the building was dead silent.

Refusing to take the most direct route out and into the quiet streets of New York City, she detoured toward Dr. Jones' office. An archeologist suffering from acute depression, he was one of the few she knew who'd been to Golfito. Maria often stopped by his classroom to listen to his lectures about his archeological hunt for artifacts from the Sir Francis Drake expedition that had landed near Golfito.

If she did not become a nun, she'd become an archeologist, the study of mankind. What a noble profession, she often thought.

A handsome, older professor, Dr. Jones was a world traveler. He was bright, rugged, and a speaker who captivated his listeners with tales of his explorations.

If she were to marry, Maria thought, it would be to an explorer like Dr. Jones—preferably Dr. Jones himself. His age did not matter—much. He was fit, trim, with a much younger look. Although she knew of his depression, Maria felt she could cure him, using her God-given gift of caring to fix this broken man, so he could be hers forever.

Had they the chance, Maria was confident, Dr. Jones would've fallen in love with her.

During those times when her feminine urge reminded her she was womanly, she fantasized about making love to Dr. Jones. And if *The Waves of Pavones* was her daytime escape, Dr. Jones and her fantasy was her nighttime pleasure—both secret places to retreat to, whenever she felt disheartened and misdirected about the scripted life Sister Florence had forced upon her.

Maria walked the weakly lit corridor toward Dr. Jones' office. The light was on. There was no movement through the frosted glass.

Lifting her thin wrist, she contemplated knocking. She desperately wanted to say good-bye, possibly having that fluid conversation that would permit him to open up to her. And if she decided not to become a postulant at the end of her stay at the Fatima Center, she wanted to return to have Dr. Jones as hers.

Maria pulled back her hand, holding off for a few seconds, thinking of Sister Florence, and how she warned her not to think too much of Dr. Jones. Florence said she had it on good authority his disorder was hereditary. "His family had suicidal tendencies. His offspring would be the same," Flo repeatedly reminded Maria.

Sister Florence, in a roundabout way, indicated she knew of his problems and the poor progress of his counseling—because nuns were privy to discuss those matters amongst themselves. Conversations, Maria was permitted to overhear, because she was almost one of them.

Changing her mind, putting her hand down, she set it against the door and whispered, "Good-bye, Doctor Jones."

~ ~ ~

Afraid to sleep, Dr. Jones stayed up all night. Broken-hearted, he didn't want to stay home alone tonight. He fell asleep about ten minutes before Maria came to the doorway.

Dr. Jones had met his wife years ago while at an archeological dig in Golfito. She was a cute, fragile young girl who wandered to the dig from a religious retreat in Golfito. She took an interest in the activity at the dig and started helping. The two became friends.

One day, she arrived frantic, asking Dr. Jones to take her far, far, from here. She revealed to him a secret, describing the retreat as something entirely different than what was told to her.

After Dr. Jones married her, she became pregnant. And with the pregnancy came a change in her demeanor. Dr. Jones tried to get help for her, but there was nothing he could do for his angelic wife.

During her last trimester, Dr. Jones came home one day to find his wife bleeding profusely. She had stabbed herself in the stomach several times, killing his son.

Crushed, Dr. Jones had sought counseling from Sister Florence.

Soon after, the grant money that supported the archeological dig was pulled—the site abandoned.

He later learned his wife was mentally ill. She came from a family with a long history of suicide. In an effort to eradicate the gene from their bloodline, her parents forced her into the church with the hope she would join the convent and purge the family of the curse.

Eventually, Dr. Jones' wife was successful, killing herself in an institution.

Today was the anniversary of the day he first met her in Golfito.

Chapter 14

Carrying the painting, Maria exited the brick building and walked four city blocks to the Christopher Street subway station. Dawn was on its way. As did many city dwellers, she cherished her familiar town, loved its prosperous, gummy surroundings, its rich jungle of ethnic diversity and cultural blend—its smell. New York City was good to her.

Quickly descending the steps into the subway station, she passed fearlessly through the turnstiles and waited within the tiled hollow for the Number 1 train. The wind rushed ahead as the subway hastily arrived with a deafening noise, the brakes squealing and screeching with its multitude of graffiti-scribbled cars. Maria stepped inside, making sure she was no farther back than the seventh car. The doors shut. The train lurched off toward Battery Park.

She settled into her seat, excited about the journey and that it would end in Golfito by sunset.

The train rumbled on, the driver not caring to call the names of the stations—it was too early. Workers ending the nightshift from somewhere in the bowels of the city spilled in as the subway made its way toward the ghostly cavern of the World Trade Center.

Maria sat nearly motionless with her hands on the box as the train approached the World Trade Center station. She studied the expressions of the passengers. The quiet woman sitting across from her suddenly became tense, fidgety, and nervous. Maria wondered what her 9/11 memory was. Was it a friend or relative she knew?

A man, standing, swaying with the rocking railcar, let tears trail the side of his long face.

A Wall Street broker blessed himself.

Maria continued her study. "What an incredible phenomenon," she thought. "It happens on every train that passes through."

Even though she too had experienced the horrific events of 9/11—a witness to its emotional toll—she took it upon herself to absorb everyone's pain by remaining strong and stalwart, as Sister Florence trained her to do. She held the capacity to gather everyone's pain and not give it back, for she truly was blessed with this ability, as told to her by Sister Florence.

Rarely was there an individual who did not show some sort of modification. A black man with traces of gray in his hair nervously rubbed his forearms, perhaps sensing the ghosts around him. A young, red-eyed construction worker twitched his nose, perhaps remembering the odd odor of dust-laden death from the many days he worked as a volunteer at the site. A snoozing homeless lady, on a too small bench, suddenly sat upright, as if she knew exactly where she was, her crazy face, wrinkled and weathered, changing to the sane woman she once was.

The train slowly rolled into the station, the driver clearly, respectfully announcing, "World Trade Center."

This was a special place. The routine of the city had not yet buried its memory. For a moment, the world became entirely different for the people aboard the subway. Each person awakened by an alter ego sleeping within.

As a personal test, Maria restrained her emotion. Surviving the subterranean journey unscathed was her goal. She considered it practice for the day God would call her to the next crisis. She was ready for the ills of the world. Sister Florence taught her well.

The call for Battery Park always started one stop early. The subway driver mumbled, "Battery Park, move to the first seven cars."

Drowsy workers, too tired to count, tried to recall if they were far enough forward. The heavy steel wheels squealed as they bound against the sharply curved rails, the train grudgingly coming to a stop at the Battery Park station.

The driver announced, "Final stop."

With the pace of the crowd, Maria walked along and up the stairwell that opened to the sky. The clear dawn had turned to early morning. She could smell the familiar, hard freshness of the cool ocean air mixing with the brick-warmth that funneled from the corridors of streets and avenues that lined the sentinels of skyscrapers that formed the Manhattan skyline.

People calmly walked the circular walkway that lifted them to the Staten Island Ferry terminal. Inside, the scuffle slowed to form a sober crowd, shuffling forward toward the vessel. Like lemmings, they massed in funneling formation, boarding through suspended gangways.

Breaking from the mass of humanity, Maria circled to the west side of the vessel and sat in her favorite seat, facing the Statue of Liberty. "How incredibly distant and different my tropical destination will be from New York City and the transition I will make to get there today," she thought, as echoing blasts of the ferry's horn let loose.

Massive chattering chains and squealing cables lifted the walkway. Maria rested her head against the riveted metal of the vessel and waited for the thunderous diesel to engage, sending a brawny grumble throughout the ship.

The growl always started deep inside the bowel of the ferry. The brine beneath churned, bubbled, and boiled as the massive propellers turned. There was an immense shudder as a pulsating cadence came to her. She allowed her teeth to chatter by relaxing her jaw. Her body quivered as the reverberations ran through her, rippling her white blouse, wobbling her delicate thighs.

Maria lifted her head from the hull and smiled. The sensation became an itchy tingle, then faded as the momentum generated by the vessel's engine sucked the ferry from its berth.

"It's going to be a long day," she said out loud. "I better get some rest."

Maria set her head against the hull once again. Closed her eyes and listened to the soothing purr and lapping sea. However, the rest wasn't long. Soon, she thought, she must decide if she should become a nun.

Was it the right decision? She wasn't entirely sure. Her body told her something entirely different. She prayed that by the time she left Golfito, the confusion inside would be gone for good.

Maria kept her indecision regarding becoming a nun hidden deep inside, where all her conflicts lived on. Sister Florence told her, "When you make your commitment to God, those pangs will fade until they're asleep forever, my child. With each passing day, you'll grow stronger, capable of controlling your body's wandering nature and the temptation that often consumes the weak."

For a brief moment, Maria wondered what it would be like to have a baby. What it would feel like to coddle, nurture, and sing to her child? What would it feel like to make love to a man?

"Is there a man out there waiting for me to fall in love, to marry?" she often thought. "Dr. Jones would be a good husband."

She dreamt their children would encircle and hang onto her skirt. They'd admire her, and so would her husband, while God smiled upon her good deeds.

Those were the thoughts that contradicted and confused her. And when they came, Maria quickly buried those feelings.

She checked the time. The ferry would arrive at 6:10 a.m. in Staten Island. Leroy, her bus driver friend, would be there on the second run of his loop. Sister Florence was supposed to arrive at her residence at the Merchant Marine Retirement Center and take her to JFK for a 9 a.m. flight.

The time allotted to get to the airport was tight. Flo, no matter how important, struggled to do anything on time. But today was as much a big day for Sister Florence, who'd waited Maria's entire life to see this day come. "Perhaps she'll try a bit harder," Maria thought.

The ferryboat shuddered once again as the reverse thrusters engaged. Maria leaned her head against the ship. This time she let her teeth buzz like a hummingbird. The ferry crushed against the wooden posts and slid along, funneling into its berth. The gangways lowered, the rattling chains argued again, and the tender prepared for the disembarking commuters.

All this time she had the Pavones painting in her lap, protecting it, allowing it to comfort her.

She followed the bunching, then unbunching, passengers through the terminal to the awaiting buses.

Leroy's bus sat three slots away, patiently waiting.

Chapter 15

Leroy Johnson first met Maria when Sister Florence had assigned her to the psychiatric ward at Saint Vincent's Medical Center in Staten Island. Flo wanted Maria to receive some social work experience, helping mentally ill patients.

A withering Leroy was one of her patients. He'd lost his cherished wife in the Twin Towers' collapse. And with her death, lost his will to live.

Leroy's wife, Doreen, had worked as a cook at Windows on the World in the North Tower. When the passenger jet struck, there was no escape for Doreen. She was trapped on the 107th floor. A cameraman videotaped her jumping, following her flailing body until it bounced off a canopy. Leroy, anxiously waiting for news about his loving wife, had seen the video several times on TV. When he learned the woman in the video was Doreen, he fell into a deep, deep depression.

Leroy became a special project for Maria. Single-handedly, she worked to lift him from the depths of his sadness. She comforted and encouraged him, showing him pictures of his sons and grandchildren, conveying the purpose and value of his life.

Slowly, Maria healed his broken spirit, convincing him Doreen wanted him to live and continue the family they started.

Commuting from her temporary residence at the Merchant Marine Retirement Center, Maria rode Leroy's bus every day after he healed. Like clockwork, he picked her up at the bus stop at bottom of the hill, near the entry gate. He had a profound respect for Maria, loving her like a daughter and wishing he had a fourth son to marry Maria, so she would give him the most grandchildren of all his sons.

Privately, Leroy felt it was best for Maria to marry, so she could experience the love he had with Doreen. Hoping to plant a seed of discontent, he told her, "Loving another person and the joy of children is God's gift to us."

The day finally arrived for Leroy, too. His young friend was leaving. He was sad, though, because Maria wasn't wise to the ways of the world. He worried that her unfamiliarity with the often unforgiving world left her vulnerable, blaming the nuns that controlled nearly every aspect of her life, making her naïve and shortsighted.

Last night Leroy stopped at the church to visit Doreen's grave. Lighting a candle, he prayed Maria's travel would bestow the life experiences necessary to enlighten her. He asked God to grant her the ability to take control, praying the direction forced upon her by Sister Florence would soon change.

He wanted Maria to find love, to be happy her entire life, just as he had.

He owed her his life and wished to return the favor.

~ ~ ~

Stepping onto the bus, Maria greeted Leroy with an enormous hug, a gentle kiss, and a warm smile. She held onto him longer than usual this time, knowing it was the last. Lifting a photo from her blouse pocket, she inserted it on the dash, next to the pictures of his sons, Doreen, and grandchildren.

"Here, Leroy, a picture of me!" Maria said in a perky voice. "So you don't miss me. I'll ride with you every day."

Leroy's tired eyes watered.

Maria sat in her usual seat across the aisle, where Leroy didn't have to turn his head to talk. She wore a denim skirt that covered well below the knee—long enough so men couldn't see beyond the upper portion of her calves when she crossed her legs.

She typically wore plain, simple clothing, often dressing in the same outfit because it was comfortable. She felt people were less critical when she put on certain outfits. Clogs were her shoes of choice.

Whenever a handsome man was nearby, Maria unconsciously flirted with her clogs, flipping them around. She wasn't aware of this subtlety, but Leroy certainly was. If Leroy learned anything from thirty-five years of driving a bus, it was the flirtatious habits of women. He was the always-observant bus driver, spying in his mirror the enticing presentations of the feminine lure. It's how he passed time, filling the many years of endlessly driving the same route each day.

All women flirted through their shoes, Leroy observed, flipping them on and off, tossing them in an advancing manner, conveying subtle, sexual messages of interest. Maria was no exception. She flirted, too.

Leroy found it amusing and ironic.

However, there were other days, Leroy noticed, when Maria went to meet Sister Florence. She didn't wear the clogs. And whenever, a priest rode on the bus, her clogs were dead silent.

But when an older, handsome businessman sat across from her, her feet danced an Irish jig.

The bus ride along Bay Front Parkway took only a few minutes. A black, ornate wrought-iron archway marked the entrance of the Retirement Center. Leroy turned left onto the property. Passengers familiar with the route looked puzzled. But Leroy didn't care. Out of respect for his friend, he was not going to allow Maria to make the long walk up the steep hill today.

The bus pulled to the porch. Maria touched his hand and smiled. "Leroy, I will always remember you. I will pray for you, asking God to bring you another friend," she said warmly, as she stepped off the bus.

"Thank you, Maria," responded Leroy, his age prevalent in the roughness of his voice. He hoped to see her when she returned, to know if God or his beloved Doreen had answered his prayers for Maria.

Leroy drove off to the next regular stop two blocks away. As he opened the door to let a passenger board, the wind whisked in. A familiar perfume, a perfume his wife had loved to wear, surrounded him. A half-Spanish, half-African American woman with plenty of exposed cleavage gracefully stepped onto the bus.

Leroy smiled. The woman reminded him of Doreen.

Chapter 16

On the stripped mattress of her first-floor bedroom sat her open suitcase. Maria placed the box with her painting in the center of neatly folded clothes. And when she flipped the suitcase lid closed, her canary-yellow bikini was lying underneath.

"Oh, crap," she said, realizing she hadn't hidden it yet. "Thank God Sister Florence isn't here yet."

The bathing suit was entirely too revealing for Sister Florence's approval. The trip to the airport would've been sheer hell. "Flo would be yelling the whole way if she knew I had this."

On the wooden dresser sat her pet monkey, a light brown stuffed animal with a thin piece of thread that served as a mouth. An elderly nun she had confided in while working summers at Our Lady by the Sea in Cape May gave her the monkey as a gift.

Each day, according to her mood, Maria altered the thread that formed the monkey's mouth to show either a smile or a frown. Today, the black thread displayed a big grin.

Only two people were aware of Maria's subtle communication of her mood—her mother and Sister Florence. Neither ever commented on it.

Lifting the monkey, she turned it face down. Sewn into the napped fabric was a small flap that concealed a tiny zipper. She unzipped it and stuffed the bikini inside, then tugged the fabric to smooth out the noticeable lumps.

"Keep an eye on my painting, Monkey."

Adjusting the thread once again to a smile, she tucked her soft friend next to the box that protected her painting. After spreading a towel and covering Monkey, Maria shut the suitcase, intentionally not zippering it. Several years ago, she'd caught Sister Florence rummaging through her personal belongings, finding a picture of a naked male friend. As a practical joke, he had slipped it into her backpack.

Flo went berserk when she discovered the photo, chastising Maria, lecturing her about her duty to God, making her feel extremely guilty about her association with the opposite sex. "Men are liars," Flo often lamented. "They'll steal your virginity and move on," Sister said bitterly. "Don't be tempted, Maria. Men are only interested in one thing, and lie to get it."

On that depressing day, Monkey became Maria's crutch, never smiling when Flo was nearby.

A holy card with embossed gold leaf edges was wedged in the bottom right corner of the dresser mirror. A picture of Saint Anthony was on front. Unwedging the card, she turned it and read the prayer on the back.

The card announced the passing of Sister Oliver, a nun Maria loved and respected for many years. The kind of person she aspired to be. Sister Oliver always seemed happy, positive, enthusiastic, with tons of energy. Oliver told her that as we grow older, our lifelong disposition etches permanently to our faces. "That's why it's important to smile all the time."

"I don't want to look like Sister Florence," Oliver would jokingly say to lift Maria's spirits when Flo had been difficult.

Maria opened her backpack and placed the holy card with her contact information should she have a problem, and laptop—a present from Flo—inside.

It surprised Maria that Flo would provide a laptop as a going-away gift, which included floppy disks containing inspirational readings about becoming a postulant—stories in the form of prayers asking for strength, forgiveness, and guidance. Flo said those readings would help her prepare for when she returned from Golfito to enter the convent.

Flo always conveyed her assumption that Maria was expected to enter the convent. When Flo spoke like that, Maria, who had a penchant to curse, would mutter underneath her breath, "I haven't made my decision yet, Flo. That's why I am going on this friggin' trip to Golfito."

It infuriated her any time Sister Florence implied her path in life was already set.

But Flo didn't care.

Maria sat on the bed, bounced her knee, and tapped the wooden sole of her clog. "Flo better not be late."

While she waited, her mind drifted back to her yellow bikini, when she formulated her plan to wear the bikini on Pavones. It would be the day she made her decision to join the convent final. Her good friend Sister Oliver had actually suggested the idea.

~ ~ ~

Our Lady by the Sea Retirement Center for aging nuns was where, Maria, working as a volunteer, had met Sister Oliver. During her college years, at the end of each spring semester, Maria traveled to Massachusetts to visit her mother then headed south to the center at Cape May Point.

The four-story Victorian retirement center was once owned by a railroad baron who had willed the beachfront property to the church. The rather ornate building sat on a spit of land where the Atlantic Ocean filled in the Delaware Bay. Maria's room was on the top floor, in an attic. From her window, she could see the entire town, including people walking on the boardwalk, but not the beach. Maria had to crawl onto the fire escape to view the ocean.

She worked long hours, washed loads of laundry, scrubbed bathrooms, and helped the elderly nuns climb the narrow stairwells. If she had free time, she kept the lonely nuns company, where they forced upon her lengthy conversation about their vocation, and why they chose to be nuns.

The most unconventional nun was Sister Oliver. She lived below Maria, on the third floor. One night, Oliver found Maria on the fire escape. And at the feisty age of eighty-four, she crawled out and sat with her.

They talked for hours. Oliver told Maria her sexual desires wouldn't wither with the passage of time, as Sister Florence stated. "The secret is to embrace your femininity, appreciate your sexuality, recognizing your wants as a reminder you are very much alive and uniquely whole.

"Learn how to release yourself from the physical confusion and angst that lives within. Find a way to satisfy yourself that doesn't break your vow of chastity, Maria. Seek out fantasies, and use them often," Oliver advised her.

But there were times when Maria was driven to the brink of leaving the church—a point even Oliver thought she couldn't bring her back from. Maria struggled with her sexuality, and theorized she compromised her biology. It was an intense feeling.

Sometimes, Maria expressed a need to date male friends, who showed a genuine interest. Periodically, she did date, and would have an okay time—and on rare occasions, a better-than-okay time. She didn't know what to do about male friends' deeper interest. There was nothing inside to draw upon, feeling an emptiness that she didn't understand.

Regarding a male suitor, Flo would simply say, "And you know how I feel about that, Maria!"

It wasn't the words that got the point across, it was the way Flo expressed it. With a shifty tone, while holding an emboldened glare, rounding her beady eyes in tandem with the words she wanted to emphasize.

Oliver reminded Maria there was no gender loss when you become a nun. It was a misconception, rooted within the fear that circulated amongst the women who sought an excuse to leave the convent.

"Your biology isn't altered," Oliver told Maria one night during an intense conversation on the fire escape. "I, too, have gotten deeply depressed. It's inevitable and stems from the often confusing internal argument linked to a lifetime of celibacy. If you don't debate with yourself, you can't properly work through the issues haunting your soul. It's a necessary evil.

"The problem isn't the sadness you feel, Maria, but how you effectively deal with your penitence."

Oliver attempted to get Maria to view her problem from a guiltless perspective.

"I truly believe you must overcome your depression, using it as a stepping stone, a launching point, not as a crutch. Find a device to break yourself free from the lasting sadness that often feeds upon itself within you.

"When I was young like you, needing to break free from the dread, I'd take long walks on the beach. And I did it in an adventurous way," Oliver told Maria.

"I figured God wouldn't mind a deviation, if it helped me remove my angst. I justified my daring acts by rationalizing they were necessary to gain a better understanding of how the other side lived . . . How can we, as teachers of church doctrine, give counsel if we haven't a clue what people feel inside?"

"What do you mean, Sister?"

"Well!" Oliver said with an adventurous, encouraging tone to her voice. "Before Our Lady by the Sea became a retirement home, it was a retreat. When I was feeling low, doubting my choice to become a nun, I came here to meditate. Sometimes, I wandered along the boardwalk shops, admiring the bathing suits. Then suddenly, I had a premonition, an idea to buy the skimpiest suit I could find. It took me hours to decide, because the thought of wearing it made me nervous.

"But finally, I'd purchase it, muster the courage to put it on, and walk the beach—all the way to the spit at the far end of the point. I'd stand there for hours, letting the sea breeze caress my body and ruffle my hair. I'd yell into the surf as loud as I could, 'I am Mary Francis Oliver,' over and over again. Then proudly, I'd dance, singing the Helen Ready song 'I Am Woman.'

"And when I returned and walked along the boardwalk, men admired me. I'd smile at them, thinking how surprised they would be if they knew they were flirting with a nun.

"It felt good. Then I went back doing nun stuff," Oliver said.

The memory of Oliver, who had a penchant for storytelling, often settled Maria's uncertainty, giving her the confidence to continue with her consideration to become a nun.

Maria surmised there must be two types of nuns. In one group were the beautiful sisters, attractive like Oliver, who could marry the richest man in the neighborhood. Have a perfect family, with perfect children, in the perfect home, with perfect love until they died at the perfect moment. These beautiful nuns possessed a sense of self-confidence, self-reliance, strength, and fearlessness—staunchly believing their vocation was a more valuable role for them.

In the other group were the Sister Florence types, domineering, controlling, and downright miserable. They found what they needed within the confines of the convent, an opportunity to exercise their thirst for control, particularly over children, adolescents, men, and sometimes more attractive women, whom they loathed for the natural beauty they possessed.

Maria looked at Sister Oliver's holy card one last time before she put it away. It reminded her of the promise made to Olivier—she was going to Golfito for Sister Oliver—and that she could have a good life as a nun, just as Sister Oliver did.

Outside, there was the familiar engine knock of Sister Florence's Lincoln Continental making its way uphill. Maria reminded herself not to get too depressed. "Soon, Flo will be far away."

† † † †
Sister Elizabeth Florence

Chapter 17

Sister Elizabeth Florence was German in ethnicity and temperament, with a discontented face that harbored a bold and eternal scowl. Buried behind puckered brows were belligerent, beady eyes. Beneath her peach fuzz cheekbones hung jowls that flapped each time she struggled to move her massive, genderless frame forward.

The car rose three inches as Sister Florence struggled to get out. Her black shoes, with square heels, elevated her hefty body an extra inch when she stood. Swollen ankles, from a lifetime of obesity, lipped the finely stitched shoe leather.

Her distinct walk could never be duplicated. Clenching her hands into fists, she pointed her thumbs outward to start each forward step. As her momentum built, she rotated her wrists and forearm, inside, then out, waddling from side to side. When she encountered a staircase, Flo bent her elbows outward, as a cantilever, then pursed her lips and pressed out her thumbs, clenching her fingers tighter, because the effort was more difficult.

Sister Florence made her way up the porch steps, across the complaining floorboards, opened the screen door, and boldly let herself in, unannounced.

Watching her arrive in her black linen nun outfit, Maria recalled how difficult it was to measure Sister's mood. She could barely see the pair of hazel eyes that peered through her tight squint. She didn't know Flo's exact age, except that her mother was a close, childhood friend.

Flo insisted on a receiving her greetings with a kiss and a hug, an act Maria despised, because Flo's skin was coarse with porcupine hairs that pinched. There was an odor that no words could describe.

Bang!

The screen door slammed shut behind Sister Florence.

"Hello, Maria," Flo said, wheezing, her massive chest lifting, as if she were going to drop dead of a heart attack. "Aren't you excited? Today is your big day."

"Yes, Sister," Maria answered in a sheepish voice. "Thank you for asking."

Sister Florence finally caught her breath.

"Here, I brought you more disks for your computer. They have interesting articles about the changes that are happening at the Vatican to stay current with modern times. Also, there's an article about Sister Oliver. The Bishop published her life story in the diocese newspaper. I thought you would like to read it. I know you were fond of her."

"Thank you, Sister." A smile lifted to Maria's face at the mention of Oliver.

"I'll read it on the plane. Thank you, Sister," Maria said softly, looking down.

Sister Florence walked over with the fistful of 3.5 floppy disks wrapped with a rubber band. She lifted the lid of Maria's suitcase and pushed aside the clothing, inspecting, pretending she was looking for a good spot to stick the disks. "I see you are bringing the painting your mother gave you. That's nice.

"It should remind you of your mother, who has high expectations of you while you are on retreat," Sister said, emphasizing the middle part of her sentence.

Flo cleared her throat, a habit Maria had observed that indicated an order was about to be given. "Err . . . Hm! Wouldn't it be nice if you gave your painting to Carlos? He would like that."

Flo referred to the custodian who cared for the Golfito retreat—Maria's contact once she arrived. "I bet Carlos' daughter would love the painting."

Maria sat silent, not caring to discuss what she planned to do with the painting. It was a gift from her mother, given to her before she left for college. It was sacred. Flo knew that, and could not order Maria to rid the treasured artwork.

The zipper on her suitcase chattered when Maria walked over and closed it.

Sister Florence still held the floppies. Without asking permission, she picked up Maria's backpack, unzipped it, and looked inside. She placed the disks in the bottom after moving everything aside, inspecting again.

"The flight is long. I hope you'll take the time to load them onto your computer and read the articles I'm giving you. It'll make the flight go faster, Maria. By the way, where are the disks I gave you last week?"

"They're on my desk," Maria answered.

Maria lugged the heavy suitcase off the bed. She hoisted the backpack to her shoulder and went outside to the car.

Wielding a congratulatory grin, Sister Florence followed. She'd single-handedly gotten Maria this far, and for the first time in many years, someone would actually attend the Fatima Center.

Florence was pleased it was Maria.

This was just the beginning, Flo thought to herself. Maria would be her showpiece. Many more would attend next summer.

The heavy suitcase scratched along the ground as Maria slung it into the trunk. She held her backpack close so Sister wouldn't scold her for fidgeting during the ride to the airport.

Sinking into the cracked leather seat, Maria watched Sister Florence work her way to the driver side. The car squashed down as Flo pulled the door shut, slamming it with an angry *oomph*!

In a gentle, soft-spoken voice, Maria looked out the window and said, "Goodbye, home. Goodbye, Staten Island. Goodbye, my little white house and the big oak trees that never let the grass grow."

The car circled the perimeter of the park where many vacant residences stood. Maria didn't say another word as they left.

Chapter 18

Sister Florence was familiar with Maria's many moods, particularly when she drove her anywhere. It was difficult to get Maria to carry on a conversation. She'd stare straight out the window, not saying a word. If Florence asked a question, Maria's answer was often a one-word response, or a slight nod. Many times, Maria would not say anything for the entire trip.

Lately, Maria seemed more withdrawn, a bit troubled. "Probably mulling over her final decision to enter the convent," Florence thought.

Even though the withdrawals were a concern, Sister Florence often disregarded them. She'd seen this disorder in other girls that went on to become nuns. It was common.

If there was a psychological problem with Maria, that would be just as good. Becoming a nun would be what Maria needed.

The big Lincoln swayed left then turned onto the ramp that led to the Verrazano Bridge and JFK airport. As Flo mindlessly drove in city traffic, she reminisced about her own special day, more than twenty years ago. The day she left for Golfito with her best friend, Jane, Maria's mother.

As Maria sat silent, Flo's memory drifted back to her childhood and the life journey that led her to become a nun.

~ ~ ~

Florence's well-off family was from Lowell, Massachusetts. They were in the printing business. Her parents, a heavyset couple, were devout Catholics. And naturally, Flo had inherited her parents' genetic characteristics. The boys made fun of her weight and so did adults with off-color comments.

Her busy, business-minded parents weren't terribly interested in raising Florence. They expected the private schools, the church, and substantial donations to substitute for their lack of nurturing.

Initially, Florence had no desire to become a nun. Her parochial school teachers were the ones who suggested it. Her inattentive parents, agreeing with anything they wanted, simply went along.

Portly Florence tended to be lazy. If she had a passion, it was literature. Flo loved to write. It passed time, occupied her loneliness, and quelled any sexual desire. Florence hoped someday a man would take a liking to her, but no one did.

While in college, Sister Bernadine, the Mother Superior, contacted Florence and asked if she would be kind enough to write stories about her friends, tell about their lives and what they were doing. Bernadine said it would be helpful to the church if they could understand what the next generation of young adults were thinking. Her work would improve church doctrine, so the youth of the world were better served by the Catholic religion.

Mother Superior's request made Florence feel special. It gave her a purpose and a sense of self-worth.

Excited, Flo regularly sent letters to Bernadine that conveyed observations of her classmates who were contemplating the vocation.

Sister Bernadine complimented Flo on the quality of her writing, asking if she would travel to Costa Rica and send letters from the Fatima Center. Sister asked to keep her writing a secret, because she wanted raw observations. The girls would react differently if they knew they were monitored.

As an enticement, Sister Bernadine said she would reward her for her efforts, promising to make her principal of the parochial grade school in her hometown.

This promise appealed to Florence, should she join the convent. She loved the New England climate, comforts of home, good food, and the stature she would have in her community. Flo could look forward to the day when she would meet the grown-up version of the people that ridiculed her as a fat child—harboring the day they'd arrive at her school as parents, to discuss their children's poor performances.

As children, Jane, Maria's mother, and Sister Florence lived in the same neighborhood. Best friends, they attended the same all-girl parochial high school and college. Jane was warm, beautiful, and kind-hearted, exactly the type the church sought.

Years later, Jane married Maria's father, Luke. Florence observed that Maria never truly bonded with him. He came across as superficial and somewhat feminine. Flo also knew it was partly her fault, letting it slip that Jane had become pregnant with Maria out of wedlock. Saying the pregnancy brought shame upon both families, because each set of parents expected Luke and Jane to become priest and nun.

Florence, who had good reason, had no use for Luke and avoided him whenever he was nearby.

~ ~ ~

As they drove through Coney Island, following a school bus with the bright sunshine rising to their east, Flo recalled the day she headed to Costa Rica. How dreadfully hot, as though someone opened an oven. And when it rained, it came as a deluge, every gully turning into muddy, blood-orange rivers.

A priest, Monsignor Perish, met them at the airport in an old school bus and drove them to La Puntarenas eighty kilometers away. Monsignor entertained the weary travelers with stories about his life work throughout Southeast Asia, and his devotion to God. About his work on the Burma Road, how he survived malaria and the thousands that did not. How he cared for wounded soldiers during World War II.

"Living in the jungle of Costa Rica will be good practice," Monsignor said to the sweltering young girls. "Consider it boot camp for those of you looking to do mission work in remote parts of the Pacific."

Florence could still taste the fine dust that sucked into the bus from the unpaved roads. Could still feel the horrid lack of relief when the grimy bus pulled to the steel-hulled sailboat docked at La Puntarenas pier. The ocean breeze through the windows did not cool them. She felt miserable and couldn't wait to go home.

She'd gone on this trip because she did not want to disappoint her parents and best friend, Jane, who'd made it clear her life would be as God's servant.

When Florence and Jane boarded the ship, Jane went below deck to play with the children that boarded.

Tired, Flo, needing a way to cool off, found a comfortable spot near the bow and stretched out in a mesh hammock, sturdy enough to hold her weight.

It was 4 p.m. when the ninety-four-foot steel-hulled vessel raised its sails, catching the wind to beat the arriving low tide. All the girls heading to Fatima had boarded and made themselves comfortable for the overnight voyage to Golfito. Inside the ship, Jane led the children in song. The soothing, beautiful sound of Jane's voice comforted everyone onboard.

Chapter 19

The year Flo attended Fatima, a summer school for children had been started as a way to offset operating costs. Wealthy Costa Rican families of coffee growers, at the invitation of Sister Bernadine, sent their children to be schooled. Also, due to the thinning number of girls, a limited number of men contemplating the priesthood were permitted to attend and meditate, provided they remain separate from the girls.

A young man named Luke managed to miss his vessel the day before and boarded Florence's ship. Other than the captain and two deckhands, Luke was the only other male onboard.

A short, feminine man with a Napoleon complex, Luke loathed his lack of height. He often fidgeted and shuffled his feet when standing next to taller women. Also, he despised physically superior men and wanted them to feel smaller than him.

One thing that Luke had learned was that he could woo women using the gentle tones of his talented tongue. Posing as a shy, delightful, noble lad considering priesthood was the perfect ruse—a fox in disguise who sought out vulnerability. He used his deliciously paralyzing gift to coax the surrounding hens into bed.

For Luke, there was no greater field of play than gaming young women contemplating the permanency of their virginity.

Insecure, Luke wanted to be perceived as an alpha male—tall, broad-shouldered, adventurous, genetically superior. He wanted women to lust for him, as they did the dominate males he despised.

Whenever he was in the company of one of these men, Luke sought to verbally dissect them, slowly, with patience and care. If a woman was present, he worked harder, cutting deep to embarrass the male, gaining the upper hand when his opponent stuttered and wilted.

Occasionally, Luke met his match, an Everest of a male he could not destroy—one who intellectually called his bluff. When that happened, Luke went to work on the other man's girlfriend, using his command of language to lure her away, eventually bedding her after many patient months of effort.

It was no accident Luke landed onboard a ship full of young girls that day. He had talked his way aboard the vessel of future postulants by assuring a sympathetic nun overseeing the girls that had he been born a woman he would have become a nun.

~ ~ ~

Florence watched Luke step off the gangplank and roam the deck, making small talk with some of the girls. He sat next to them smiling, chuckling, and trying to look cute. Flo studied him. And when Luke noticed her observing, he walked over and sat with her.

"You know, cats always select the most comfortable spot in a house to rest," Luke said, lifting his brow with a flirtatious glance, smiling, showing his perfectly aligned, snow-white teeth.

"Indeed, I did know," Flo responded, arching to reveal her robust chest. Florence saw his eyes drop. A warm, comforting feeling suddenly overcame her.

Getting comfortable, Luke engaged her in an intellectual conversation. Well-read, he seemed gentle and sensitive, and spoke with a soothing, slightly flirtatious tongue. Each of his sentences ended with a little smile, which made Flo feel good.

He complimented her knowledge of literature, elevating her self-esteem. He told her she had a beautiful complexion, that her skin was baby soft.

At sunset, the air grew cooler and Flo became chilled. Luke suggested she leave her hammock and sit beside him.

Florence looked about the ship suspiciously. Everybody had fallen asleep. Even the rustling of the children in the hull had stopped.

Her new friend helped as she rolled from the hammock.

Luke produced a wool blanket, stealing it from a bunk below deck. Kindly, he wrapped Florence. And where her body made contact with the ship, he tucked the edges.

Together, they sat leaning against the concave hull. Florence rested her head on Luke's shoulder and whispered, "Thank you," saying she was cozy and that he was kind and she appreciated his friendship.

A nearly full moon had risen three-quarters into the sky. A soft ocean breeze filled the sails as the tossing ship quietly progressed toward Golfito. She wished the ship would continue and sail around the world.

Flo fought back her sleepiness, reminding herself she was not yet a nun, and he not yet a priest. If something happened, that would be good. Her only fear was Sister Bernadine, how disappointed she would be should this man become her suitor. Her parents couldn't care less.

The couple gazed at the stars and drifting clouds that sometimes blocked the bright moon. Angling his glance to meet her eyes, Luke kissed her. Their lips locked. He probed and she trembled as the unfamiliar sensation inside her mouth continued.

His mouth briefly withdrew to reposition for another deep, wet, exploring kiss. As Luke guided his hand around the roll of her waist, an electrifying tingle traveled her spine. Tenderly, he kissed her neck, then lightly blew across her skin. Nibbling her earlobe, he gently gripped and suckled, then thrust his tongue deep into her ear, rendering her defenseless.

She wanted more. His tease was overpowering.

Guiding his hand underneath her blouse, Luke softly massaged the soft underside of her breast. It was the first time a man fondled them. And it felt good.

Luke groaned, excited that he had achieved his goal of caressing her enormous breasts. Florence shivered with a sexual bliss she had only imagined—Luke walking his fingers, searching to add to her pleasure. He freed her caged cleavage, unbuttoned her blouse then lowered his head underneath the blanket. With both hands, he lifted them from confinement.

She felt her breasts release and spring free. Luke's small, soft, womanly hands caressing—his warm lips, softly kissing within her fullness. He continued with gentle kisses, everywhere.

She wanted him to suckle her like an infant, experiencing the sensation she had suppressed her entire life. And when she thought he was going to finally draw on her, he teased once more, positioning as if he were going to extract the nectar inside.

As Luke worked his tease, she craved, elevating her chest, lifting them with her hand, guiding toward his lips, inviting him to complete her need.

His lips finally descended onto her bare, fully engorged nipple. The touch was hot, firm, wet. His tongue wrapped around. He drew hard and suckled the solid bud. The sensation was incredible as he repeatedly nibbled and pinched with his teeth, drawing each deep into the fold of his tongue. From the depths of her inner thighs, Flo quivered, rhythmically responding to the milking pulsations coming from inside her breasts.

She exploded and moaned loudly—Luke sliding his hand over her mouth, Flo replacing his with hers. Her lasting orgasm continued and she enjoyed every sensation, relieved that this might be the end of her lonely, celibate life and the beginning of her sexually satisfying new world.

Chapter 20

Golfito, a natural deepwater port, was shielded from the rough expanse of the Pacific by the Osa Peninsula to its west. The jungle peninsula reached around from the north, forming a bay forty miles across. Often, the bay was perfectly clear, with a turquoise hue. To the east of the quaint village was another jungle—the landscape rising steeply behind it.

An incredible variety of palm trees lined the thoroughfares, to where it seemed the jungle had swallowed the town. Most buildings were two stories, with corrugated tin roofs that covered the wooden structures like sombreros. Much of the design of Golfito buildings was to shed the tropical rains when they came.

To the south of town sprawled a date palm plantation with neatly aligned trees, stretching endlessly along a fluvial plain.

~ ~ ~

As the morning sun warmed Florence's face, Jane shook her shoulder. "Flo, Flo," the soft voice called. "Are you awake? The ship docked."

Florence opened her eyes to see the familiar smile of her brown-haired friend. Droplets of dew dotted the woolen fabric of the blanket still wrapped around her.

"You were sound asleep," Jane said. "I thought about waking you when the ship sailed through the Osa Peninsula, so you could see the beautiful bay at sunrise. But you were sound asleep. I didn't want to disturb you.

Realizing her chest was exposed Flo clutched the blanket and said, "Give me a few minutes. Yesterday was a long day. My sleep was deep. It's been years since I slept like that."

"They're unloading the ship," Jane said enthusiastically. "I'm going to help the children sort their things. See you at the retreat, Flo. Oh, this is such a beautiful place." Jane skipped off.

When the woolen fabric pressed against her, it hurt— reminding her of Luke. Flo didn't know how to feel about what happened last night, and needed time to think.

When Florence stood, the air felt a bit fresher. However, the humidity was still present.

Jane had run down the gangplank to the dock. She sorted the children's luggage, turning the task into a game they enjoyed. From the pier, Jane waved and pointed at the bus that would take them to the retreat.

Craning, scanning the activity at the pier, Flo searched for Luke. He was nowhere in sight.

Nervous, Flo descended the wobbly gangway, the humidity rapidly collecting beneath her clothes. She made her way to the bus and sat in the first seat, hoping Luke would arrive and sit with her.

There were colorful tassels, dangling beads, holy cards, and religious figurines in the front window. A smiling Costa Rican with a thick mustache started the engine. It took only five minutes to travel the unpaved streets to the retreat. The bus turned left and ascended a shallow grade, passing a church, Our Lady of the Angels. There were more turns. Then the bus finally ascended to a small plateau, where several rectangular dormitories sat perched on concrete pillars two feet high. A mixture of people busily moved about the buildings; many were girls from the ship.

Ticos arrived in little pickups and unloaded luggage. But they were not permitted inside, so they left the luggage on the small porches at the entrances.

The squeaky door of the bus opened. Flo was the first one off.

Before she went inside, she surveyed the property, looking for Luke. He was nowhere in sight.

Inside the dormitory, long rows of bunk beds lined both sides, forming an aisle down the center. An older nun, the one who was in charge, greeted her.

"I bet you are Florence," the elderly nun said, recognizing her. "Sister Bernadine likes to reward those who've been helpful. She asked that you get the private room in the back."

The nun smiled and directed Flo down the aisle past the metal frame bunks.

"Thank you," Florence said, relieved to see she had a marginal degree of privacy.

The door didn't open when the latch lifted; the humidity had swelled the wood. Forcing with her shoulder, Florence entered the spacious room.

The plank walls were painted lime green, matching the vaulted ceiling. Conduit wiring ran along studs to each outlet. A light hung from a truss in the middle of the room. A freshly made bed, twice the size of a regular bunk, had neatly tucked sheets. A private bath sat to the right of the doorway.

A small envelope leaned against the base of an oscillating fan on top a wooden desk. Flo went over and stood in front of the rotating fan. Her luggage had already arrived and was neatly stacked next to the dresser.

Flo read the letter.

Dear Florence:

I hope your journey was not difficult for you. I am ever so grateful for all of your correspondences over the years. You will make a topnotch English teacher once you return home and become a nun. I have talked to Father Michael from your parish. He said he would welcome your assignment with open arms.

I sincerely hope you will write me on a daily basis. Please find in the drawer plenty of pens, writing paper, and envelopes. Give your correspondences to the courier. He will dispatch your letters to me.

I am anxious to hear from you. Please keep me fully abreast of the happenings at the Fatima retreat.

Enjoy the fan. It's my gift to you.

May God bless you.

Sister Bernadine, Mother Superior

Placing the letter in the drawer, she went to her bed and rested.

Across the room the fan whirled, and outside the door she heard the scuffling feet of young girls, giddy with excitement.

But, where was Luke?

~ ~ ~

The next several days were an adjustment for the girls. Acclimating, they kept moderately busy. Jane took charge of the small school, organizing the classroom. Flo mainly slept with the fan blowing on her, a private shower making living conditions slightly bearable.

On Sunday morning, she'd finally located Luke at mass. He was sitting on the opposite side of the church with a group of girls from another dorm.

After mass ended, Flo made her way over before he disappeared. She wanted to say hello and tell him about her private quarters, with the hope he'd visit.

"How are you, Luke?" Flo asked, the pitch of her voice projecting a solicit octave. She stood straight so her pronounced bust filled the front of her blouse.

"I'm fine," Luke said with a puzzled look, as several of the girls stood nearby awaiting his attention.

"I've been looking for you since I got off the ship." Flo elevated her voice and lifted her chest again.

"The ship?" Luke questioned, pretending to be confused, glancing back toward the girls.

Flo's face grew flushed. *Did I actually dream what happened on the ship?*

"Are you sure it was me?" Luke turned to the other girls for affirmation in his statement. "After all, no one doubts a priest," he chuckled.

Backing away, Flo realized he was lying, refusing to admit to their night together in front of the girls—probably because he bedded one of them already.

"I'm sorry, I must be mistaken. It's been the long day," Flo said, lowering her voice.

The attractive girls accompanying Luke nodded.

"That's okay, we priests tend to look alike. You're absolved, Sister."

The encounter enraged Florence. Sister Bernadine had warned her about men like Luke. She said they prey on young, inexperienced, naive girls attending church functions, pretending to become priests someday.

"Stupid," Flo said. "How stupid could I be?"

The encounter made her bitter. She was hurt and deeply embarrassed, her self-esteem destroyed. She didn't know where to turn.

Back in her room, Flo collapsed onto her bed, but didn't allow herself to cry. Staring at the ceiling with her jaw punched forward, she pondered, solidifying her deepening belief there would be no more warmth in her heart for men who came into her world.

The first letter delivered to Bernadine from Flo requested a way to isolate the men. Two weeks later, two priests arrived, keeping the men occupied and away from the girls.

Flo wrote extensively to Sister Bernadine. She made a promise to Sister every girl attending would decide to enter the sisterhood. She would personally see to it the retreat received a score of one hundred percent.

As weeks passed, Flo took charge of all three dorms, assigning underlings to help with the tasks of preparing for the day they would announce their decision. Focused, she didn't speak to Jane much.

One day, Jane came into Flo's room while she was writing to Bernadine.

"Hello, Flo. Are you busy?"

"No!" Flo quickly removed the papers, shoving them into the desk drawer.

"It's been awhile since we talked. I didn't want you to think I was avoiding you. The children have kept me so, so busy. I didn't know there was so much to do."

Jane sat on the neatly made bed.

"That's fine, Jane. I'm feeling the same way. Mother Superior put me charge of planning the daily agenda and spiritual lectures. I'm worn out. Sorry, I haven't had much time, either. What's new with you? How are you coming along with your decision?" Flo asked, probing.

"Frankly, I haven't had time to think about it," Jane said. "That's why I want to talk. I need some quiet time to contemplate, and was wondering if someone at the school can replace me for just one day, so I can go to a secluded place to pray about my final decision. I was under the impression we would have more time to do that."

"Certainly, but I can't commit just yet," Flo said. "You've done a great job with the children. I must find someone as good as you. That may take some time."

"Oh, I would appreciate anything you can do. I promised myself I would spend an entire day thinking about my commitment to God. And by the end of the day, my decision would be official and absolute."

"What day would you like to take?" Flo suddenly changed her mind.

"A water taxi delivers supplies to small towns on the Osa. Every day the boat leaves at dawn to pick up plants from the rainforest that are shipped as medicines from Golfito. One of my students' father drives the water taxi. He spoke about a beautiful, isolated beach south of here called Pavones. He said the waves are beautiful when the wind blows from the south.

"When he described it, I knew I had to go, Flo," Jane said enthusiastically. "The captain said a south wind will come in a few days. If I can go then, I would appreciate it."

"Let me know when the winds are perfect, and I'll see to it you can go on a moment's notice."

Flo was anxious to get Jane on her list of confirmations, because the girls respected Jane.

"Oh, thank you." Jane gave Florence a kiss and a hug. "You're a great friend."

Two days later, a strong south wind arrived. The next morning, Jane hopped aboard the water taxi.

The captain warned the ride across the bay would be choppy, but the trip was worth it. "The long waves of Pavones go on forever," he said, pushing the throttle forward.

Chapter 21

As evening came, Flo waited anxiously for Jane to arrive from Pavones, hoping Jane would announce her intention to join the convent. To Flo, it was a given that Jane would commit, and she couldn't wait to dispatch the good news to Bernadine.

When nighttime came, Jane hadn't returned from Pavones.

Worried, Flo sent a Spanish-speaking assistant to the dock. "Go to the government office at the pier. Find where the water taxi is," she said to her assistant with a degree of deep concern.

The assistant went and located the docked water taxi. The captain was cleaning the wooden deck. When asked where Jane was, he told the assistant he had dropped the young girl off at Pavones early in the morning. Then he tried to retrieve her in the evening, but the surf was too rough to berth.

"My precious boat, *Angelina*, she is small," the captain said. "It was not safe to traverse the swells nearest the beach. She will swamp. The young girl, she is safer on the shore," he told the assistant. "The south swell was unusually big this time. I cannot sail until it goes away. There is a cabana with provisions. It's not the first time this has happened."

The young girl went back and reported to Flo.

Immediately, Flo feared that if Jane did not return safely, Bernadine might blame her for the poor decision of allowing her to leave Golfito. And maybe she wouldn't assign her to the school in her hometown as promised and would end up stranded at a mission in ant infested Africa.

Flo thought about Luke, and wondered if he really liked her. "Did he regret lying?" She wanted to run off with him, if he'd take her back.

~ ~ ~

For several days, the south swell continued. No ships arrived. Tethered fishing boats remained in their slips. Everyone at the retreat worried for their missing friend. An old rumor that circulated in town about another young girl, an artist, surfaced—she'd committed suicide. Her body was found on the rocky beach, half-eaten by hermit crabs.

The townspeople gossiped amongst themselves about the retreat and the pressure upon the girls, particularly when Bernadine arrived. They suspected Jane met the same fate as the artist.

Flo believed Jane could survive three days alone—she was resourceful. But Jane had been absent for five days. So Flo went to the government office and asked if there was a road into Pavones.

The supervisor said, "Yes, but there is a river to cross. And the ferry has broken loose and run aground downstream."

On the seventh morning, a gloom had set throughout Fatima retreat. The girls gathered at church to pray. Flo had to report the incident, making several drafts of a letter to dispatch to Bernadine.

Just before noon, as they all somberly assembled for lunch, a metallic, royal blue, jeep-like truck—a Scout—made its way down the narrow road that clung to the mountainside outside of town. It disappeared into the date palm grove and emerged minutes later into the streets of Golfito.

Strapped to the roll bar were two red kayaks. A man with long blond hair tied into a ponytail busily worked the steering wheel. He wore no shirt, just nylon shorts and sneakers with the backs cut open so he could easily slip them on and off.

Jane sat next to him with one hand grasping the top of the muddy windshield, the other gripping the shaft of the wooden kayak paddle strapped to the roll bar. Wind swept her hair across her face as the four-wheel drive vehicle bounced through the muddy ruts.

The Scout made its way to the plateau where the Fatima retreat sat. The girls came running to greet Jane. Church bells celebrated the good news.

Tires kicking the gravel, the Scout came to a sliding stop. Jane and the driver were laughing like children.

Leaping from the vehicle, Jane ran into the crowd of girls, hugging each of them. Overwhelmed with emotion, many cried.

The driver inspected his vehicle. His blue 1973 International was covered with mud. He inspected his paddle, making sure it hadn't come loose. Then went about tending to the details of his vehicle, kayaks, and camping gear in back.

Jane greeted everyone, saying she had an adventure like none other, and couldn't wait to tell about it.

Pumping her fists, forearms flipping outwards, Flo struggled to catch up with the gathering. The girls admired the shirtless, handsome man bending over to dig mud from inside the tires. Flo glanced at the man, observed his physique, and became tense. She greeted Jane, who came to hug her.

"Thank God, you are okay!" Flo said dramatically, though annoyed by the man's presence.

"I'm okay, thanks to my new friend, Mark," Jane said.

The other girls waited patiently, anxious to hear of her adventure, and about the handsome man with the broad chest, thick arms, and muscular thighs.

Jane turned and pointed to Mark, as he continued to pretend to check the condition of his truck.

"Mark, come here," Jane called. "Let me introduce you to my lifelong friend, Elizabeth Florence."

All heads turned to Mark, as if the girls had received permission to give him their full attention. Flo and Jane stood in the middle of the group. Mark walked to the edge.

Fully acclimated to the jungle, Mark wore light clothing. His bleached blond hair had grown to shoulder length. He was thin, with a washboard stomach. His face was tanned, weathered, and rugged—the product of living in the rainforest for a considerable period.

The yearning eyes of the girls traced the definitions of his muscles and stopped at his shorts to admire his buttocks. One girl observed his cutout sneakers and giggled.

He walked through the group to greet Flo, standing next to Jane. Many of the girls grew flushed as he brushed by.

Flo continued to be tense.

"I am the soon to be Sister Elizabeth Florence," Flo said with a subtle reminder to the girls regarding their purpose in Golfito.

Smiles dropped from their faces.

"We are about to gather for lunch, would you like to join us before you leave?"

Flo hoped he wouldn't stay for the noon meal, but knew it was unlikely.

"Thank you," Mark said politely. "It would be nice to have a decent meal before I leave. I'm sure Jane is hungry. She's been living off rice, beans, and papaya for the past several days."

Flo whispered into Jane's ear for her to ask Mark to put on a shirt.

Mark overheard, saying that would not be a problem.

~ ~ ~

The dining hall looked like every other building at Fatima—rectangular, freshly painted light green with an overhanging corrugated steel roof to shed the rain. Long rows of dining tables lined the front half. Golfito women cooked in the back kitchen.

Mark walked into the hall wearing a T-shirt. The front had a silkscreen print of a raft blasting through a wave. On back, printed words said, "Hell & High Water River Outfitters, *a hell of a ride.*"

As he walked past, the girls read his shirt and were aghast. If Flo saw it, she'd throw him from the building.

Two shielded his T-shirt as they escorted Mark past Flo to his seat at the head of the table.

To Flo, Jane's deep affection for Mark was obvious. Comfortable smiles indicated they'd bonded.

As they ate, Flo asked the question that needed to be asked.

"So, Jane, tell us how Mark found you."

Flo didn't care to know the answer, but felt she had to ask the obvious question out loud, so everyone could hear the story and forestall rumors that might arise.

She asked Jane, not Mark, hoping Jane would portray how they met in a palatable manner.

Flo wasn't sure what Jane was going to say, because they'd never discussed their deepest secrets about men. Jane, a bit reserved, never expressed her feelings on the men topic. All Jane ever said was that she was a very private person.

The girls at the table, admiring Mark's appetite, clearly enjoyed his physique.

"I didn't meet Mark until yesterday," Jane said.

Mark rolled his eyes toward her.

Flo caught Mark's subtle expression. *Did Jane just lie to us?*

"It was my day of meditation as you all know, D-day, decision day. The nice captain dropped me off at an old pier near a river that spilled into the ocean. He said he would be back before dark. But before he left, he instructed that I shouldn't panic if he failed to return. 'Sometimes the seas are too rough for my little *Angelina*, and I must wait a few days to return,' the captain told me. He said, 'Enjoy, it is rare that anyone sees the waves of Pavones. They only appear during a strong south swell.'

"My first day on the beach was terrific. The waves were very beautiful. Each was shaped perfectly, like identical twins. They rolled and rolled and rolled, one after another, for a very long distance.

"I expected a sandy beach. Instead, it was rocky, full of cobblestones and hard to walk. Inland, the jungle was thick and stopped right at the edge of the beach.

"My day of meditation was perfect. I found a comfortable spot underneath a palm tree where one of the waves lifted, fanned like a peacock and crashed hard onto the beach. I prayed to God, thanking him for this moment, asking to make the day last longer."

The girls giggled and whispered about Jane's good fortune of it lasting several days.

Flo attempted to quell their giddiness by adjusting her height in the seat, getting their attention by walking a glaring stare across their young faces.

The room drew quiet.

"I walked the beach most of the day and checked out the little shelter nearby. I had some food and water to last me and finished it by dark. I thought about my life, where it would lead, and prayed for guidance from God. And when the boat did not return, I spent the first night in a beach hut made from palms. It was stocked with some canned food and a cot with no mattress, just springs. I found it hard to sleep.

"When I woke the next day, the waves were even bigger. They were huge! I couldn't see the Osa across the bay.

"What was amazing was how perfect they remained. They grew longer, rolling much faster than the previous day. I couldn't see where they began and understood why the captain did not come."

One of the girls sitting at the middle of the table asked, "Did you get scared?"

"Yes and no," Jane answered. "I recalled when the missionaries talked to us about their experiences in Africa, how they got stuck in the Congo for days, and how important it was to keep your wits to survive.

"I kept thinking I needed to have faith and confidence that someone would find me. Fortunately, there was plenty of food in the shelter, even matches. I became a real camper, just like a Girl Scout," Jane said.

Flo let Jane talk. She could see the girl's perspective shift when Jane mentioned the missionaries. It portrayed a sense of singularity—a kind of "Unsinkable Molly Brown."

Flo recalled how Mother Superior explained that if the church could instill a sense of purpose within their postulants, the girls were less likely to draw into relationships with men. "Women with purpose tend to be independent, not submissive. However, men prefer a needy woman, which conflicts with the message of purpose and devotion to God."

Of course, there were men who were exceptions. They desired independent women. Self-governing and adventurous men, like Mark, didn't want a passive mate. They sought self-reliant females who'd go on explorations with them. These women would let their spouse freely wander the world in his infinite search for senseless, self-fulfilling adrenaline thrills.

"You have to be careful when you come across one of these alpha males," Bernadine warned in one of her letters to Flo.

Flo could hear Bernadine's voice inside her head. "When these adventurers arrive, they will have the pick of the litter. We are rendered powerless by the forces of biology and natural selection. They're worse than those who pretend to be on their way to becoming priests, because those young men will eventually marry and become good providers and loyal members of the church."

Mark ate while listening to Jane's version of their story. He stopped eating when Jane talked about how proud she was about surviving alone, particularly the part about how fearless she felt.

"By day four I was a real trouper. I explored, looking for a road. I walked an hour in the direction of Golfito, but was obstructed by a river that came into the ocean," Jane explained.

"Pavones was so remote, all I could do was hunker and wait."

"When did Mark arrive?" one of the girls asked.

"On the fifth day," Jane said, making eye contact with Mark.

"I walked up the hillside to see if I could see Golfito. When I got back to the shelter, I looked out into the waves and saw the strangest thing. It was Mark in his kayak."

"Surfyak," Mark interrupted, finishing his meal.

"I was surprised to see another person besides me. He was surfing the waves . . . Many times I saw him fly off the wave and into the air, landing upside down."

While Jane continued her story, Flo was busily working in the back of her mind a way to get rid of Mark. "The sooner the better," she thought. His mere presence was arousing many of the girls.

"I hadn't seen a soul in five days. I was anxious to get back to let you all know I was okay, but couldn't get his attention. Mark was surfing the waves; he must have been out there for six hours before he came to the beach. That's probably why he is eating so much."

Jane looked at Mark with a warm smile.

The girls bobbed their heads yes, including the listening cafeteria staff, amazed at Mark's appetite.

Flo forced a grin.

"He finally came to the beach. It was almost dark. I didn't realize how much time had elapsed, because it was interesting watching him surf those really long waves."

Mark finally spoke. "I was shocked to find someone sitting on the beach."

"Mark stared at me, as if I were an aberration," Jane said.

"I've been traveling Costa Rica for almost a year," Mark said, his voice lower. "You don't find a young American woman sitting on a beach in the jungle. I thought my guardian angel had appeared to keep me company."

Everyone chuckled at the remark, except Flo.

"Once we both got over the shock, he introduced himself, saying Golfito was a two-hour ride, but the ferry boat to cross the river would not be operable until morning."

Flo thought she'd caught Jane lying. How had Mark gotten across the river if the ferry was not operating?

"Mark caught a really big fish, a grouper, and cooked it. I stayed in the shelter. Mark slept on the beach in his pup tent."

Flo finally decided it was time to end this.

"Well," she said, "God answered our prayers, and we have Mark to thank for bringing Jane back safely. Where is your next adventure, Mark? I'll bet it is death defying." Flo looked at the girls with an expression that said, "Is this what you want to fantasize about? He's no good if he makes you a widow, or leaves to climb Mount Everest one more time, while you raise his children, alone and broke."

Flo, having allowed the girls their enticement, slammed the door shut by appealing to a deeper need, their sense of purpose.

Mark spoke. "I appreciate the meal, and everyone's warm hospitality, especially yours, Sister Elizabeth Florence."

"Mark, she's not a nun yet," Jane corrected.

With a volley of pleasantries, Flo said, "Our prayers are with you as you pursue your earthly adventures. Thank you for helping Jane. I hope God keeps you safe and close to his heart."

Flo stood, indicating it was time to leave.

"We have class this afternoon and mass tonight. Do you want to stay and attend mass, Mark?"

Flo gambled that attending church was the last thing he wanted to do.

Heads turned toward Mark in unison. They hoped he would say yes.

"I'm heading to San Isidro and must leave here to make it by dark. A river called the Rio Chirripo has never been run in a kayak. I've waited a year for conditions to be perfect for an attempt at a first descent of its rapids."

Leaving the table, Mark complimented the women that prepared the meal, speaking to them in fluent Spanish.

In a few moments, everything would return to normal, thought Flo. She'd allow Jane time to say good-bye to Mark.

Flo complimented herself on how well she handled this. The correct questions were put forth to snuff any growing dissention in the ranks. She had conquered the alpha male. And perhaps did a better job than Sister Bernadine, if she were in her shoes.

At that moment, Flo became certain she was going to become a nun. The decision was right for her. She planned to rise to a position of great stature, perhaps replace Bernadine.

Flo could feel the power of control, and relished it.

~ ~ ~

As Jane walked Mark back to the Scout, Flo positioned herself near a window so she could observe Mark's permanent departure.

Slowly, the couple walked along. They conversed until Mark remembered something. Turning, he went to his truck and dug. Just then, Flo saw the saying on the back of the offensive T-shirt—*a hell of a ride*. Biting her lip, she tapped her black leather shoe, upset because no one told her about the words on the shirt. She would have demanded he change into a more appropriate attire to dine with daughters of God.

Reaching into his duffel, Mark withdrew a weathered cardboard box. He opened it and handed Jane the painting of Pavones with its unusually carved frame.

After admiring the painting, Jane set it on the Scout's hood. She kissed Mark on the cheek and held him tightly. Tears streamed down her face. "I wish you didn't have to go," Jane said. "I'm confused. I don't know what to think, or what to say, Mark."

"Come with me now! Leave everything behind," Mark said.

He lifted her off the ground and hugged her.

Every girl in the compound stopped to watch, wishing it were them.

The couple stood there, stalling, anxiously kicking the gravel. Neither wanted to leave, their body language revealing a much more intense relationship. Mark bent over and kissed Jane on the lips. Jane gazed into his eyes as their lips slowly departed.

One last time they hugged.

Mark climbed into his Scout, put the truck into gear, and drove off.

Jane stood silent, watching the Scout disappear down the hill.

Cradling the painting, Jane went to her dorm and crawled into her bunk. She could still smell Mark and his travels. In the distance, she heard the faint, familiar rattle of the Scout—the fading echo of the engine, grinding gears as it climbed the hillside, kicking stones on its way to another adventure. Minutes later, she heard the far-off sound of the horn—a parting good-bye as he headed into the jungle.

"Mark is gone forever," thought Jane, regretting her decision. Had she said yes, she'd be sitting next to him at this very moment, heading toward unfamiliar waters with the man God had sent her.

"God answered my prayers at Pavones, and I didn't heed his calling," she thought—a decision impossible to correct.

With the frame tucked under her chin, Jane wept, her tears flowing along the crevices of the crucifixes, along the bodies of Jesus and the naked woman.

Tilting the frame to allow her tears to run free, she observed the detail of the carvings and wondered who the woman was.

~ ~ ~

That evening, Flo led a discussion group on the topic of marriage and family—the importance of selecting a responsible, committed husband. "A nun's role is to educate children so they become good citizens and lifelong church patrons," Flo lectured. "A husband must be supportive."

The picture she portrayed of the perfect spouse was a far cry from the adventurous nature Mark displayed.

Following the meeting, they gathered for mass. That night, three girls confirmed intentions to join the sisterhood. Flo thought it would be nice if Jane would be the first. But Jane did not show for the lecture, or church that evening.

"What would happen if Jane changes her mind?" she thought.

Jane wasn't the same after Mark's departure. Despondent, she withdrew. Flo had seen this kind of behavior from her good friend before, and hoped it would pass, as it had in the past. Many times, Jane traveled deep within herself. And when she returned, she apologized to Flo.

This time, Jane's depression went very deep. She seemed marginally functional, participating in some retreat activities; however, during downtime, Jane wasn't socially responsive, spending her days lying in bed holding her painting.

Flo realized she had a problem and did not know what to do about it.

Chapter 22

Other than the lingering problem with Jane, everything proceeded as planned at Fatima. Each night, more girls affirmed their intention to join the Sisterhood. The girls gathered into small groups, chitchatted about their futures, and supposed what responsibilities and assignments lay ahead.

Now that their decisions were final, everyone wanted to return home and celebrate the good news with their families.

The final ceremony was on Sunday. It was a major event for the village. A bishop flew in to serve mass and bless the prospective postulants and the Golfito children.

Flo and Jane were to announce at the final mass.

A rumor circulated that Sister Bernadine had heard the largest class in the retreat's recent history would confirm at one hundred percent, and wanted to see firsthand this terrific group of devoted Catholic women.

The following morning, a plane arrived. Several people got off, including the bishop, two altar boys, and Mother Superior, Sister Bernadine. Monsignor Perish had driven from his parish in San Jose.

A photographer accompanied them.

"Hello, Florence," Bernadine said, walking from the small passenger plane.

"Good morning, Mother Superior." Florence knelt to kiss her ring. "What a pleasant surprise. The girls are excited to see you." Florence rose to her feet. Secretly, she prayed Jane would not let her down tomorrow.

They stepped into a waiting bus and headed toward the retreat.

Touring the compound, Bernadine met with several of the girls and congratulated them.

"I hear we have one hundred percent so far," Bernadine said, walking toward the building where Florence stayed.

"So far," Florence answered, a bit nervous about Jane's mental state. "Everyone announced. It's down to Jane and me."

"Sandbagging, aren't you, Florence—that's not fair." Bernadine let a hefty chuckle. "An entire class of postulants, what a blessing. I am proud of you. You can join my staff, instead of the assignment I promised," Bernadine said, completing her tour.

Her suggestion thrilled Florence. Lately, she'd been thinking how she enjoyed being in charge of her Fatima classmates. The authority made her feel superior. Instead of making fun of her, the girls feared her.

"I need to freshen up. Can I use your shower?" Bernadine asked.

"Absolutely, Mother Superior!" Florence directed her toward her dormitory.

"How did you like your accommodation, particularly the fan?" Bernadine asked as they walked.

"It really helped, Mother Superior, thank you."

"I wanted to reward you for your input over the years by making your Fatima stay more comfortable. It can get dreadfully hot in Golfito. And based on what I see, more rewards will come to you, Florence."

The pair climbed creaking steps that bowed under their weight. No one was inside the dorm. The girls were at rehearsal for tonight's special mass.

Abruptly, Bernadine stopped and looked to her left. Hanging on the wall, above Jane's bed, was the painting of Pavones.

"What an interesting picture," Bernadine said, observing, curiously cocking her head, taking a closer look.

"What an unusual frame. The intricate woodwork is almost as good as the picture. I like the religious theme, but don't get its point. Who carved it?"

Scrutinizing the frame more than the artistry of the scenery, she asked, "Are those bloodstains?"

Mother Superior stood silent for a moment.

Speechless, Florence worried that Jane wasn't around.

"Those must be the waves of Pavones. I've heard of that beach. One of our girls drowned there many years ago. It was a sad day. I wanted the Fatima retreat to purchase the land and use it for meditation. But the bishop denied my request," Bernadine said.

"Whose painting is this?" she asked.

"The water taxi driver gave it to Jane. It was in his family for years—a gift for teaching his child." Fearful, Florence lied to Bernadine.

"Jane's a sweet person. Everyone falls in love with her because she's kind, as did the water taxi captain," Florence said, hoping the source, Mark, and his visit, would never get disclosed.

"You should get freshened." Florence directed Bernadine to her bedroom.

Bernadine lifted the latch on the wainscoting door. It stuck. She nudged her shoulder against it. It swung inward . . . An expression of utter shock came to her face. On the bed was Jane, naked, with Luke buried between her thighs—his hips responding, thrusting.

Locked like dogs, they couldn't uncouple. Jane refusing to release, working him until assured the deed was done.

And, as if Jane had timed it for the celibates, Luke moaned with an excited sigh of release, then collapsed to the bed.

Florence and Bernadine stood frozen; time had stopped, forcing them to stand as eyewitness until the mating completed.

Rattled, Florence finally mustered the courage to swing the door closed.

Bernadine was shocked, but only for a second. She saw it as an opportunity—something she could hold over Florence her entire career—an event that would pay dividends for years to come.

That evening, Bernadine summoned Monsignor Perish. He had a way with these things. Monsignor drove Jane to San Jose the next day.

Bernadine cornered Luke in private and threatened him, telling him she would publicly humiliate his socially entrenched, status-conscious, Catholic parents, exposing his antics, if he didn't do the right thing and marry Jane, should she become pregnant.

That night, Florence announced her intention to enter the convent.

Bernadine was pleasantly pleased.

Before everyone left, a rumor circulated that Jane had fallen into a deep depression, and that she was truly a troubled child with a hereditary disorder. Florence confirmed to those who doubted, saying she knew of Jane's disorder and concealed it for a long time.

A month later, the church newspaper ran a full-page article with photos about the wonderful things that happened at the Fatima Vocational Retreat in Costa Rica that year. A record number of young girls were now postulants.

Chapter 23

After returning to her hometown, Jane found she was pregnant. Her Catholic parents, concerned about the embarrassment of being bastard-child grandparents, strongly suggested Jane marry Luke.

Flo returned and took her vows, and as promised, Bernadine assigned her to the parochial school in her hometown of Lowell, Massachusetts.

Luke, marrying Jane, never apologized to Flo. Nor did he acknowledge the fact they met on the ship. It hurt Flo deeply. Though often cordial whenever in each other's company, she loathed him, deemed him a coward, and had no use for the man.

When Maria was born, Jane asked if Flo would be her godmother.

Maria attended Flo's parochial school, and on occasion spent a night at the convent. The nuns loved having Maria around, and as expected, naturally accepted the expectation that she, too, would join the sisterhood.

Maria matured into a beautiful young woman. In many ways, she was much like her mother, and nothing like her father.

It was Flo who educated Maria about her womanly biology.

As Maria became an adolescent, the temperament amongst the sisters surrounding her slowly changed. They seemed stricter and guarded in their conversations with her. She was no longer privy to the informal discussion about cute priests and handsome altar boys.

Flo completely avoided talking about men in front of her, and disrupted conversations she didn't approve of when Maria was present.

"Men cannot be trusted," she often communicated to Maria. "They are useless, dirty, and don't tell the truth."

Sister Florence clipped newspaper articles and tactfully left them about for Maria to read. The articles reported about women who'd been badly beaten by their husbands, or some other sinister act.

As she matured, Maria heeded Flo advice, believing men were inferior creatures, to be avoided at all costs. She spent summers at various retreats maintained by the church, or with Sister Florence helping prepare for the next school year.

One week after Maria graduated high school, Sister Bernadine died from a massive heart attack. Maria heard the Fatima vocational retreat had been mothballed, and was saddened because it was expected she would travel to the retreat when her time came.

Flo hoped, after Bernadine's death, the church would promote her to Mother Superior. But the promotion never came. Instead, there was a reorganization and Flo ended up in New York City.

Maria, attached at the hip to Flo, followed her to Manhattan.

Flo told Maria many stories about Golfito, saying, "Someday the church will reopen Fatima. And when it happens, Maria, you will attend."

While in college, Maria's relationship with Sister Florence grew stressed. Sister became more controlling, directive, inflicting varying degrees of guilt and criticisms. Flo became intrusive, investigating her personal affairs.

As Flo increased her scrutiny of Maria, *The Waves of Pavones* became her escape. Whenever she felt depressed and at odds with her mentor, she pulled up a chair and admired the details in the picture, tracing her fingers along the intricate cuts of the hand-carved frame.

It seemed to have a story, a story of a woman and her attachment to Jesus. Many of her friends said, "The frame was carved by a deeply disturbed person."

The Decision

Chapter 24

When the big Lincoln pulled to the departure terminal at JFK airport, Maria turned to Sister Florence. They'd not spoken since crossing the Verrazano Bridge. Flo was daydreaming, off in a world of her own.

Excited about leaving for Golfito, Maria reached and shook Flo by grabbing her flabby triceps. "Flo, Flo, is everything all right?"

A river of tears ran down Sister Florence's sagging cheeks, soaking her blouse.

"She must've been crying for some time," Maria thought.

"I'm sorry," Maria said to her, assuming Flo was crying about their separation. She felt guilty about leaving. But this was the direction they both set a long time ago.

"No, you shouldn't be, Maria. It's your time." Flo collected herself. "It's a shame I cannot come inside the terminal to see you off. They won't let even a nun into the gate area these days. I was looking forward to spending those last few moments with you."

Flo dried her tears.

"I guess it is for the good of our country," she said, referring to the airport security rules in place since 9/11.

Maria leaned over and gave Florence one of her patented Maria hugs. She wrapped both arms around Sister Florence and affectionately squeezed. Her hands were unable to meet around Flo's back.

A shiver went to Flo's heart. It was a feeling that couldn't be duplicated. God had blessed Maria in a manner that indicated she was one of his special children, with rare qualities no one else possessed. Her natural qualities of love, support, and affection indicated to Flo that she must see to it Maria became one of them.

The trunk flipped open. Maria stepped from the car. She lugged her suitcase like a sailor who'd just arrived at port, ready to ship out, then waved goodbye to Sister Florence.

A jet roared overhead.

She greeted the waiting skycap with a smile, assuring it had a penetrating effect, then said, "Take care of that suitcase, there's important stuff inside."

The Italian skycap took a close look at her ticket, smiled, and said, "I'll put a special tag on it, if you give me one of those big smiles again, sweetheart."

Maria consented, then, swinging the backpack to her shoulder, she waved goodbye to Flo again and went into the terminal.

~ ~ ~

JFK airport was hectic, busy with people hurrying in random directions. Her plane was on time, and twenty minutes later, she boarded and sat in a window seat.

The jet raced down the runway. It was exciting, more exciting than the amusement park rides at Cape May, thought Maria.

Pressing back, she thought, "how cool" as the plane lifted from the runway. She peered out the window, watching as homes became dollhouses with toy cars buzzing about. People looked like ants. It was all so surreal, until her vision obscured as the jet climbed and banked into the clouds.

Suddenly, a blinding sunlight burst into her window and warmed her face. Puffy, cumulous clouds floated like mountains of gathered cotton bales. "I wonder how close to heaven I am," Maria thought, admiring the incredible contrasting beauty.

The flight to Miami was smooth—the landing as exciting as the takeoff. Palm trees were everywhere.

Her excitement continued to build. "Costa Rica must look like this," Maria thought.

It took thirty minutes to traverse the terminal to the gate where her Lacsa flight was scheduled to depart to San Jose. Feeling slightly fatigued, Maria sat down. The excitement had caught up with her.

The backpack sat on the seat next to her. There were several Spanish-speaking people talking in their native tongue. She tried to make out what they were saying, but they talked too fast.

Thump!

A hollow sound from behind drew her attention. Three young men arrived. Two held surfboards, a third gripped a double-blade kayak paddle. The two surfers giggled, chiding each other, pushing about. The third stood taller. He had bleached blond hair and bronzed skin.

Instinctively, Maria bit her lower lip. The activity was disruptive. The young men behaved like adolescent lions, pawing each other, playfully testing who was superior.

She turned her attention to the taller man, wearing loose-fitting, yellow nylon shorts, and a T-shirt with a tropical design that said, "Costa Rica River Expeditions." His thighs were thick and muscular, his teeth white and perfectly aligned. Sunglasses hung from his shirt collar.

He seemed concerned.

"An alpha male," Maria thought. The kind she only saw in magazines—magazines she peeked at while studying at the college library. She'd never seen one up close, and couldn't deny he was attractive.

His muscles were round and solid, obviously from plenty of exercise. It was his time.

Maria noticed two women nearby observing, tracing his buttocks with their stare, pleasantly smiling.

"How disgusting," she thought. "Women lower themselves when they stare like that, to admire this so-called 'perfect specimen.'"

She blamed the man for his good looks, assuming his personality was trash, incapable of matching her nearly perfect righteous demeanor. "I'm too good for him in every way," she thought.

Plunk!

Plunk!

Surfboards plopped to the floor. The men started playfully shoving each other.

"Oh, how annoying and childish," she thought. "They are disturbing everyone in the seating area."

Just then, the gate attendant announced they would board shortly.

The handsome alpha male, still gripping his paddle, brushed past her and approached the attendant. Maria could feel his commanding presence as he breezed by. It annoyed her. She didn't know why.

The man started talking to the attendant in Spanish.

"He speaks Spanish? Well, that's a surprise! He doesn't look like the kind that is smart enough to speak another language."

The conversation seemed tense. The man pleaded, pointing to his paddle. All Maria understood was "*nueve, uno, uno.*"

She surmised the attendant wouldn't let his paddle onboard because of the 9/11 rules.

But he didn't give up. Pulling out a fifty-dollar bill, he offered it to the attendant. The woman adamantly refused.

She picked up the phone and spoke in Spanish.

Moments later, the steel door opened and a ground crew member came in. He went to the alpha male and conversed in Spanish.

"*Un momento*," the alpha male said.

Listening, Maria determined he wanted to add some protection to the paddle before the ground crew took it to the cargo hold.

"Hey, bozos, get over here. There're going to load everything through this door, including your surfboards. Both of you go into the bathroom and get me rolls of toilet paper," he said assertively.

His friends ran across the hallway chuckling, and barged into the men's bathroom. Moments later, they appeared and started throwing rolls of toilet paper.

"Hey, Chris!" they called. "Here's your toilet paper. Catch!"

Immediately, four rolls launched across the hallway.

"Guys, cut it out!" Chris said, laughing.

The rolls flew through the air, unraveling. Three clobbered him. A fourth roll bounced off the window, unrolled, and stopped at Maria's feet.

"How ill-mannered," she thought. "Childish!" She snickered. "I should report them."

The alpha male didn't pay attention to the roll that bumped into Maria's stationary clog. Instead, he started wrapping the tissue around his paddle blades. His hands worked fast. From his backpack, he pulled a roll of gray duct tape and started peeling off long strips.

Rip—the tape made a sharp tearing sound. Everyone sitting nearby watched as the entire paddle turned into a cast.

Chris handed the paddle to the waiting attendant and pleaded with him to be careful, thanking him several times in Spanish for waiting.

Turning, he looked for a seat.

Kicking away the toilet paper, Maria turned her head and looked away.

Chris walked toward Maria, lifted her backpack, and said playfully. "Hey, baby cakes, do you mind if I sit here?"

The hair on Maria's neck rose. She grew angry and reacted instinctively.

"I have a real name, you know."

"What is it?" he asked.

Maria refused to answer.

Just then, the gate attendant announced they were to board.

Standing, Maria quickly went to the gate to wait for her seat to be called. Moments later, she boarded, but this time, she didn't have a window seat. She hoped no one would sit next to the window so she could look out.

Just then, Chris came onboard. Maria peeked over the back of the seat in front of her. The pilot greeted him and so did the attendants, as if they were friends.

When he came down the aisle searching for his seat, she pretended to look away, making sure she didn't make eye contact as he passed.

Thump!

A wisp of cologne-scented air blew by her. Chris had sat next to her on the aisle.

Oh! How awful!

Looking down, avoiding eye contact, she squeezed her backpack, digging her fingers into the canvas. Trying not to notice the man's hairy legs, she turned her head and looked out the window. He crossed them, trying to get comfortable in a space too small for him to fit.

Maria was in a panic.

Chris twisted, bounced, and continued to fidget, then leaned across Maria to see outside.

"Do you mind if I look out the window, girl without a name?" Chris asked.

Maria nervously sat still, trying to avoid eye contact.

"Yes, I do mind." Her knees squared, her feet flat to the floor.

Leaning anyway, Chris placed his palm on the window and stretched across.

He had no body odor. His cologne was subtle. She saw his muscles up close. They were large, round, and firm. She could feel his warmth.

Chris pulled back into his seat.

"I am sorry for reaching across, but I wanted to make sure my paddle made it onto the plane."

"Why are you so obsessed with that thing?" Maria asked, her curiosity heightened.

"It's an Ashland paddle," Chris said. "Very few in the world are like it. It was a gift, custom-built and hard to replace. I travel to Costa Rica often, and plan on doing lots of whitewater kayaking. That paddle must make it in one piece.

"I'm sure none of this means anything to you," he then said, squirming, adjusting to the cramped conditions.

"No, it doesn't," Maria answered, remaining rigid.

The flight attendant pulled closed and sealed the door.

"Looks like you can move over to the window," Chris said, thinking her moving over would give him more leg space.

"You look squashed." Maria ended her sentence with a smirk, happy he wasn't comfortable.

"Why is it so special?" Maria asked, referring to his paddle as the jet pushed from the gate.

"This guy—his name is Keith—he builds them. They are the best in the world, superior in every way. They convert a river's energy . . . Oh, I'm sorry." Chris stopped in mid-sentence, realizing he would lose her if his detailed explanation continued.

"Where are you heading?" Chris asked.

"Golfito," Maria said, realizing she was finally on her way as they lifted into the air. She smiled, revealing her mouthful of teeth, not hiding them this time.

"Why Golfito?" Chris asked, adjusting his legs, trying to make more room by pushing under the seat.

Just then, the seatbelt sign went off and Maria moved to the window.

"Thanks," Chris said.

Excited that the final leg of her lifelong journey had begun, Maria loosened, becoming a bit talkative.

She told him about Golfito, the Fatima Vocational retreat, and that she planned to become a nun. She explained the church's staffing dilemma, that few girls wanted to become sisters these days. She proudly mentioned the retreat was filled to capacity years ago.

"Aren't you concerned?" Chris asked after Maria finished her explanation why she was heading to Costa Rica.

"Concerned about what?" Maria asked.

Fidgeting in his seat, he extended his legs into the aisle.

"About losing what is great in life—marriage, children, motherhood, family—all that kind of stuff? All you're going to do is pray all the time. I don't get it. Why would women sacrifice what they were made to do for something that may not be real?" Chris questioned.

Casually looking out the window, watching the blue ocean below, she pretended not to be provoked. It was a question she'd heard often. Though she had a very detailed and scripted response, Maria chose not to say anything. Instead she ignored him, pretending to be more interested in scenery outside the plane. "Are we flying over Cuba?"

"You know, lady without a name, those clothes are going to give you a hard time when you get to San Jose."

"He's trying to provoke me," she thought.

She reacted.

"It's Maria. I have a name, and it's Maria."

She bunched her brow.

"Okay, Marrrria." Chris made fun, emphasizing in Spanish. "When you arrive in San Jose, it's going to be like an oven door opened and blasted your face. The airport is not air conditioned, and ever since 9/11, the windows stay closed. It gets really uncomfortable standing in the customs line.

"You'll sweat like a pig. And if you're a Yankee, as your complexion reveals, with your thick blood, you could get sick, fast."

He reached into his backpack and placed several bottles of water on the seat between them.

Maria turned and looked at the bottles, then obstinately said, "I'm not thirsty."

"It doesn't matter, sweetheart."

Chris rolled the bottles closer. "Force yourself to drink."

"Advice taken, jungle man," Maria blurted, annoyed, not knowing where that comment suddenly came from.

"Okay, don't take my advice. You can't say I didn't warn you."

Chris pulled his feet in from the aisle and slid them underneath the seat again. Sitting straight, he stretched, releasing the tension in his back.

After considering, Maria unzipped her backpack, removed the laptop, then put all but one bottle inside. She twisted off the cap and started to drink without admitting he was right.

"What kind of laptop do you have?" Chris asked.

"It's a Mac," Maria said.

"Figures, school teachers go for Macs. I'm proud of you."

"It was given to me as a present last year."

"Can I take a look at it?" Chris reached for her computer.

"No, but I guess I have no choice."

Smelling his cologne again, she drew a breath through her nose and held it briefly.

"Dr. Jones," she thought. "He wore cologne."

"It's been a while since I played with the Mac's operating system," Chris said as the computer booted. "Holy shit! Who's snooping on you?"

A bit buoyant, Maria looked over, puzzled. "What do you mean?" she asked.

"When a computer boots, short lines of script tell what software it uses."

Chris typed. "Monitoring Mommies spyware has been installed. It tracks everything that goes on inside your box, especially the Internet. Here, take a gander."

The screen went black except for some lines and symbols that looked Greek to Maria. Chris pointed to the script that loaded the spyware. He typed a few commands and a whole bunch of lines showed.

"See, there's a file with information in it. The last time you used this computer was late last night. You were on the Internet and checked your flights. In fact, you checked your reservations like five times that day.

"What is the Inspirational Guide?" Chris asked.

"They are disks that Flo gives me."

"Wouldn't trust this Flo person, he is the one who is monitoring you."

"She," Maria corrected.

Chris explained in detail how spyware works; showing the websites she visited, and how the disks Flo gave her tracked her.

Maria was appalled. *Flo monitoring me?*

It was disturbing, because she thought she'd gotten around most of Flo's snooping. She didn't like her private thoughts revealed, especially the recent notes regarding her indecision to join the sisterhood.

Flo told her the disks contained prayers and educational information to read.

Chris was convincing and accurate about what web sites she visited. She had some limited computer knowledge, enough to know Chris was correct.

Disturbed, Maria drew back into her seat and folded her arms. Flo now knew her most intimate secrets. Florence had deceived her.

Would this affect her decision? She was not sure. This morning she was committed to go to Golfito, enjoy the retreat, and become a nun—like Oliver, not Sister Florence.

Maria stewed. The handsome man next to her looked a little more handsome. Maybe she would get even by flirting with him. She had written about her thoughts of flirting with Dr. Jones. And how she'd marry him if she could. Flo knew all this, and much, much more.

A blank expression came to her face as Chris continued to tinker with her laptop. Maria's memory drifted back to her childhood, when she could remember loving Flo like a mother, and the attention given. But there came a time when Flo became more dictatorial, opposing any self-expression. The change made her sad. She felt empty and wanted to be far away, as far away as the waves of Pavones.

Chapter 25

Maria felt a bump on her elbow. She didn't want to turn and look so Chris could see the sadness on her face.

He nudged her elbow again.

Maria looked at him.

"Here!" Chris handed her a piping hot wet washcloth. "Put this on your face and hold it there for a few minutes. Be careful, it's hot."

Feeling the relaxing warmth of the towel in her hands, she pressed it to her face. All the tension inside her poured out.

"Thank you, I really needed this," Maria mumbled through the steaming towel. "Where did you get the hot cloth?"

"Hot tea water," Chris said. "Latinos drink primarily coffee, not many order tea on Latin American flights. The tea water gets hot because it stands. I do this all the time."

"Here, eat these peanut butter crackers." Chris opened a pack of crackers he had carried in his backpack side pocket.

"What are you doing?" Maria asked.

"I am administering first-aid." Chris twisted off the cap of a water bottle and handed it to her.

"There's nothing wrong with me," Maria rebutted.

"Oh yes! If not now, later." Chris pushed the bottle to her hands and asked her to drink up.

Reluctant, she started to drink. Her big brown eyes fixed upon him like a nurturing baby. She gulped the liquid, eyes glued to Chris' face.

Captivated by her look, her simple and natural beauty overpowered him.

"So you think I need first-aid?" Maria asked with an undertone of cynicism.

"Yes, you do. You're pale, anxious, emotional. Chances are you haven't eaten at all today. If you don't take care of yourself, you could end in a Costa Rican hospital by nightfall."

"Preposterous," Maria uttered.

"When people get sick, it's usually a chain of events that puts them on a path toward illness." Chris opened another water and handed it to Maria.

"Drink, hydrate yourself."

This time he forced it upon her because he wanted to see that special look she gave him one more time.

Although she didn't want to admit it, Maria knew Chris was right. She hadn't eaten at all. She took the bottle and drank almost two-thirds—again, staring with her big brown eyes.

"I'm in the outdoor adventure business," Chris said. "Often, I deal with injuries in remote places. When someone is injured on a river, or catches hypothermia in the backcountry, a sequence of events occurred early on that led to the injury. It's how I stay safe, uninjured, and alive. By being cognizant, recognizing the critical paths that lead to injury, I avoid mishaps. Let's just call it a sixth sense . . . You are on one of those paths."

Maria listened. She was feeling better. The nourishment improved her mood. She set her face back into the washcloth.

"You may be right, but I don't think I was bad off," Maria mumbled from underneath the cloth.

"We never know what the future holds," Chris said. "By anticipating what may happen and taking action, it costs a lot less than the consequence. You never traveled overseas before?" he observed.

"Okay, Sherlock, make your point."

Maria lifted her head from the towel and once more set her captivating glance upon him.

Each time Maria looked at Chris, it was as if she kissed him gently, softly, several times. He melted. It took all his strength to contain himself, and to keep the conversation on track. Her need for affection was obvious. His need, to provide her that love, was overwhelming.

Chris continued. "You're wearing the wrong clothing for the tropics. When you get off this aircraft, that thick denim skirt that hangs to your calves will trap the heat that rises from the ground. Your complexion indicates you're from the north. Your blood is probably still thick. As your body tries to circulate blood to cool you, your heart will race, unable to keep up. Eventually, you'll get heat exhaustion, possibly heat stroke—the latter is more severe. The only thing you have going for you is that you are young, or it might be raining when we land."

Maria sat silent. Her nature didn't want to agree. Though she was reluctant to admit it, Chris made good sense.

"If the heat doesn't do you in, an infection will," Chris said.

"Infection?" Puzzled, Maria questioned the remark.

Chris took an apple from his backpack and handed it to her.

"Here, have some fruit. It's good for you. The natural glucose will give you energy."

She didn't question. Each time he handed her something, she felt better.

She bit into the apple, her wanting eyes staring.

"This guy is a nice guy," she thought. "Where did he come from?"

"Oops!" Her clog fell off.

Reaching, he lifted the clog and slowly slid it onto her slender foot.

"Thank you, Chris." Maria pressed the shoe against the back of the seat to make it snug.

"A serious cut can become septic in fifteen minutes."

"I'll be careful not to get scratched." She bounced her leg. The clog slid and dangled from her big toe.

"In the tropics, it's rare to find air-conditioned places, even airports. It's too expensive to keep a place cool. When we land, you'll wait at customs for over an hour. Once you pass through, you must walk a narrow walkway near a chain-link fence, where children beg for U.S. dollars. The fence is bowed and in a bad state. Tourists often cut themselves as they push against it.

"Costa Ricans know Americans aren't entirely familiar with the difference in the exchange rate of the Colónes. When an American gives a begging child a dollar bill, they're handing them the equivalent of twenty dollars in Costa Rican money.

"You clearly stand out as a vulnerable foreigner. The children know this. Your shyness makes you a target—they sense it. They will paw, whine, and shed false tears. Wanting your attention, they push hard on the fence. If one of them gets a hand on your skirt, it will get yanked off. Their hands are dirty—get cut and it'll become infected immediately. If you don't have good antibodies, your night will be spent in a poorly maintained hospital," Chris warned.

"Well, that might explain the priest," Maria said.

"The priest?"

"Yes, Sister Florence gave me specific orders to wait for the priest. He'll take me to where I'm to catch my plane to Golfito. I told her I could take a cab, but she insisted, and wouldn't hear of it. If the Golfito flight got canceled, the priest would be there to take me to the rectory."

Maria finished the apple, leaving practically nothing. She cradled the apple core in the fold of her skirt.

"What's with that paddle at the Miami airport?" Maria asked. "I noticed you were upset."

"True," Chris said. "I was concerned. That paddle always travels in the cabin with me. Today was the first time I had a problem getting it onto the plane. The pilots and attendants know me because I fly frequently to Costa Rica. I give them a few bucks for their trouble. But the security rules make traveling with equipment more difficult these days.

"I don't want it broken, or mishandled. It's an Ashland paddle. They are rare. It's priceless and impossible to replace."

"What makes an Ashland so special?" Maria asked, looking doubtful.

"Ashland paddles have an uncanny ability to capture the energy within moving water. I can leverage my maneuvers with less physical effort. In extremely difficult whitewater, the paddle is a godsend." Chris cleverly inserted the word *God* for Maria's sake.

"Amen," Maria laughed then turned her face directly toward him and smiled. "I didn't understand a word you said. I guess it has something to do with getting more of an adrenaline rush than the other guy."

"Nice to see you actually have a sense of humor. And yes, you do get it."

"What brings you to Costa Rica?" Maria asked.

"Rio Chirripo."

"I take it's some sort of adventure."

"Yes." Chris started to describe his next adventure. "The Chirripo headwaters are in the central mountains of Costa Rica. The river drops steeply and empties into the Atlantic Ocean. It's been navigated only once—as far as I know."

"Why weren't you the first?" Maria couldn't help the dig.

"The first was the guy who taught me to kayak—saved my life."

"How did he save your life? Was it in some treacherous rapid, where you almost died?" Renewed, Maria felt a sense of vigor by challenging the alpha male, sensing a weakness.

Wanting to avoid an in-depth conversation, he answered, "No."

"How then?"

She shoved past his evasiveness.

Chris didn't want to explain, but her big, beautiful eyes dissolved the resistance.

"His name is Mark Weston. He managed the whitewater rafting company I once worked at. But before I worked there, they had an educational program where they took troubled kids on whitewater trips. I was one of those kids.

"On my first trip down the river, I knew this was my destiny. Kind of like a man who meets his wife for the first time, and knows immediately he should marry her."

Her clog swayed by the strap at the tip of her big toe.

Chris explained how the outdoors helped him find himself.

"It drew me from the vicious circles troubled teens are so often trapped within. The social work system just wasn't doing it for me.

"I fell in love with running rivers. Mark became a mentor and worked me hard. He knew many people in the industry. And when I moved on, all I had to do was call someone who he knew, and I had a job.

"Like today, I need some money while I adjust to the tropical climate and prepare for my solo descent down the Chirripo. When we land, I must meet guests I'll guide down the Pacauri River. It pays well."

"Hey," he said, sending her a smile, "you should come rafting. You'll love it. It's an incredible experience for first-timers."

He hoped she'd say yes—most women did.

Not answering, Maria said instead, "Why are you critical of the social work system?" She redirected the conversation away from the curious invitation.

"I was too much for them to handle—always in trouble."

"You don't seem as bad as the individuals I've met in the system." Maria identified that she had worked with troubled teens.

"That's why guiding whitewater has been good for me. The interaction with people, the thousands of miles of rivers, and the guidance of Mark made me a better person. You see, there is hope," he said.

Chris lifted both arms and rotated his torso. Stretching, his skin drew tight. The muscle groups in his large shoulders and biceps bulged.

Maria nervously bounced her leg against the seat in front.

"Mark taught me a long time ago to make it a point not to let your troubles become you. Use your adversities as an example of what not to be. I hold onto that thought, closely, every day of my life," Chris confessed.

He lowered his arms then flexed his chest, tightening his muscles again.

Mesmerized by his physique, Maria managed a response. "How profound."

She was thinking this must be a sign. "He comes from nowhere to sit next to me, hours before I am isolated in the jungle. God must have something to do with this encounter."

"I was still in high school when I left home. I lived in the back of a car. Mark didn't know that until I graduated. Someone tipped him off."

Chris continued with his life story.

"He had this house in the country and let me live in the attached apartment. But the deal was, I had to go to college if I wanted to continue to live there. I went on to finish a four-year degree."

"Let me guess what you got your degree in—computers," Maria said, reaching to direct the air-conditioning vent toward her head.

The cool air flipped the brunette bangs that covered her high forehead. She combed them back over.

Chris observed how thick and shiny her hair was. He wanted to run his fingers through it.

"You got it—computer security. But I prefer to run rivers. Mark told me not to follow his footsteps, and not do what he did for a living. I disagree with him on that point."

Just then, the jet slowed and pitched. The time had passed quickly. Maria couldn't recall looking out the window. She turned away and peered out. Towering cumulus clouds surrounded the jet.

"Looks like we are going to have a classic Costa Rican landing," Chris said. Leaning over, he joined her.

"What's that?" Their shoulders touching, she felt his respirations on her neck. It felt good.

"Should I make my adventure more interesting by going on this trip to the Pacuari River?" she thought. "How would Flo react?" Then she said to herself, "No one can stop me."

"This is going be cool. The pilot cannot fly into those clouds. They rise 40,000 feet, as high as we are. The pilot must fly in between and down almost 30,000 feet. Watch the reaction of everyone on the plane when this happens," Chris said, his eyes wide with anticipation.

The captain announced they we are about to descend, and asked the flight attendant to prepare the cabin. Mark shifted back to his seat.

The jet banked steep left, far more than normal. Maria's stomach fluttered. Mark's eyes twinkled as they plunged through the convection. The Costa Ricans on the flight cheered. The rapid descent continued as the plane skirted a thunderhead, plummeting through the edge of the overcast.

As it came out of the cloud, the jet rolled, pitched, and then leveled. A cheer erupted. Maria saw mountains all around her. She was ecstatic. A sense of excitement overcame her. Her adventure had begun. The plane circled the perimeter of a giant valley. The city of San Jose passed underneath. Heads bobbed and craned to look out the window.

The captain came on the intercom to announce in Spanish that they'd arrived and were about to land. He asked how they liked the descent. Everyone applauded, including Maria and Chris.

Maria thought for a moment. "This isn't normal," she said to herself. "Aren't passengers supposed to be calm, reserved, non-celebratory and unenthusiastic, like in the United States? How nice to see such display of enthusiasm." To her, it wasn't ordinary and was against her reserved nature to have fun.

The jet banked steeply one last time, and landed—more applause.

Maria was elated. She'd arrived in an abnormal way.

Chris turned and said in a calm, relaxed voice, "That was cool, best landing yet. Here." He pulled a five-dollar bill from a pocket in his shorts. "Take this. You will need it."

Maria's look locked onto Chris, then the money. The bill was rolled like a cigarette.

"No, thank you!" She was puzzled and a bit perturbed. "I don't need money. And I can't understand why you would offer."

"You'll need it."

Chris tightened the roll and inserted it into the top pocket of her white blouse. The edge of the bill pushed against the inside fabric, scraping along and touching her skin.

Maria shivered. A tingling sensation traveled her spine. Once again, she looked at Chris with innocent eyes.

This time, Chris felt her reach inside and seize hold of his heart. He wasn't sure what to do about this feeling he was having.

"When you leave customs you'll walk along a narrow, outdoor corridor to get to your luggage—as I explained before. A chain-link fence holds back begging children. Be wary, they're much more astute than you think."

He wanted to explain why he handed her money.

"These children are forced to beg—put up to it by their parents. You can see the adults watching from underneath a tree in the distance. They dress their kids in shorts with no shirt or shoes. On the other side of the fence is a slimy, sloppy slope. The fence doesn't leave much room for the children to stand, so they press against it and constrict the walkway to where one passenger at a time can squeeze through. The children will look at you with big, sad eyes. You'll feel sorry for them," Chris said, trying to enlighten Maria.

"If you don't give them money, they'll yank your skirt, your blouse, or your backpack to get your attention. They'll spit, if you don't give them something.

"It's easy to cut yourself on the fence. And if you are cut, be careful not to let them touch your wound. Many of the kids urinate where they stand, because they don't want to lose their place. You could get sick," Chris warned.

"I had my shots." Maria reacted, but not as Chris had expected. Her mood changed. She became angry. "What a horrible thing."

She never heard of this. Her inclination was to try to help their plight—not add to it.

"I don't need your money and certainly won't add to their helplessness by giving them money. What the poor need is an organization like the church to help them."

"No one is willing, not even your church," Chris said. "Or your convent; they know better. Welcome to the third world and its harsh reality. Better lose that naïveté. A perspective like that will cost you dearly. Children are to provide for the family. They're not raised in the manner you think. It's different here."

The aircraft pulled to the gate. The air-conditioning shut off. It got warm.

Though Chris saw Maria had become defensive, he was compelled to inform her. "I don't have time to explain. I have to load a bus with equipment and drive it to the Pacauri campground before dark. What you should do when the time comes is take that five out of your pocket and raise it in the air. Yell loudly, '*Cinco dinero.*'

"It'll draw the children's attention. Toss the money over the fence, beyond them. They'll back away from the fence and race for the money. It will allow you enough time to pass the gauntlet."

"What a horrible thing to do. Take your money. I'll have none of this," Maria said harshly.

Refusing to take back this money, Chris stood in the aisle and repeated the provocation. "Time to lose that attitude of yours, baby cakes."

The aisle filled with passengers. Maria was stuck in her seat.

Chris offered her space. But Maria refused.

As beautiful and compelling as this girl was, Chris wasn't going change how he dealt with her. Familiar with situations where people ignored practical advice, he had learned to let them be. "She'll learn through her own ignorance," he thought.

Chris stalled the departing passengers to allow Maria to get out. She changed her mind and stepped into the aisle, but ignored Chris. Slinging her backpack loaded with water bottles and apples onto her shoulder, she moved forward.

A blast of heavy, hot, humid air hit her in the chest. It was overwhelming. She pushed along the ramp and into the gate area where the crowd thinned. A gathering sweat trickled down her back, soaking the center of her blouse. Winded, she became mindful that if Chris had not helped her, she would have collapsed.

Chris tugged on Maria's backpack. "Hey, do you want to join me on a raft trip?"

Again, he hoped she would say yes.

Still a bit perturbed by the offer of money to placate the begging children, Maria turned away and started to walk toward customs. "Should I talk to this guy? Am I overreacting? Am I so naïve, I don't understand other cultures?" she thought, following the Spanish and English signs that directed her.

Chris didn't want to leave things as they were. He hadn't expected to meet this beautiful woman on this trip, unearthing such feelings. Maria ignored him, and Chris couldn't stand for her to walk away. He wanted her not to reject him.

He stood quietly next to her while she waited in the slow-moving line.

Unnerved, she turned and looked at Chris with her consuming eyes. "Thank you for your help. I am not interested in going with you. I don't know you that well. Going to Golfito is what I came do."

She batted her eyes.

"I can get you through customs faster, if you'd like," he said.

"How? . . . Oh, let me guess, you'll bribe those guards over there holding machine guns. Perhaps if you threw five dollars into the air, they'll look the other way."

Maria folded her arms and stood stiff.

Frustrated, disappointed he couldn't make any progress with her, Chris vented. "Have it your way, baby cakes. I offered you help. That's all. Your righteousness knows what is good for those begging children from your so-called expertise in social work. You're out of your element. It's a shame, there may have been a connection between us. I feel sorry for you, Marrrria."

She lifted her nose and looked away.

Suddenly, one of the airport's ground crew appeared and interrupted Chris. He handed him the Ashland paddle.

"Shit, I almost forgot it. Damn women. It's time to go to work," he said, leaving Maria, heading toward the security guard and greeting him. The guard set down his gun and hugged Chris. They spoke Spanish.

Puzzled, Maria watched as Chris opened his backpack and lifted out a plastic rod about two feet in length. Attached to the end by a sliding ring was a braided loop. He showed the security guard how it worked, sliding the ring along the handle, opening and closing the braided loop.

Waiting in the slow moving line, the passengers watched.

Reaching into his backpack again, Chris produced a small plastic jar, unscrewed the lid, and grabbed a hold of the rod. The loop dropped into the jar and dunked several times.

Amused, the security guards looked on.

Chris lifted the rod and slowly slid the ring, opening the loop. A soapy film filled the opening. As he waved the wand, the air flowed through, forming an enormous bubble.

The eyes of the onlookers grew big. Children pointed, gasped, and clapped.

The security guard had a childlike grin.

Chris closed the loop. An oblong bubble wobbled into a symmetrical, four-foot sphere. It floated, drifting toward the waiting passengers.

Amazed, Maria admired the rainbow of colors as it passed overhead.

Snap!

The bubble's life abruptly ended, raining soapy water onto Maria's hair.

Chris looked at Maria, smiled, and said, "Oops."

The passengers in the terminal laughed.

The security guard, shaking Chris's hand, graciously accepted the giant bubble maker as gift. He told Chris his children would love this toy and invited him to dinner when he came back to San Jose.

Chris walked out, bypassing customs.

~ ~ ~

It took Maria an hour to get through. She drank two of the three waters Chris gave her. When she passed customs, she found herself standing in another line. This time a chain-link fence on her left didn't permit ample room to continue.

Slowly, the passengers shuffled along. Suddenly, the fence leaned and collapsed inward. A dozen sad-eyed children chocked off the flow of passengers. Their dirty, tiny hands poked through holes and begged.

The humidity, combined with the stench of urine, nauseated her.

People handed the children money. Each child lucky enough to get hold of the currency passed it to a runner, who raced back to a group of adults waiting beneath a cluster palm trees.

The crowd slowed to a standstill. Maria squashed against the fence. An emaciated child with sad eyes tugged on her denim skirt and nearly jerked it off her waist. They pawed her blouse, screaming, "One dollar, one dollar, please, hungry."

A taller boy with longer arms pulled on her blouse and tore it; another reached for the dangling zipper on her backpack.

Maria was trapped and not moving. She was unprepared.

"The rolled money in my blouse pocket," she thought.

Quickly, she reached in her pocket and waved the five-dollar bill into the air, yelling, "*Cinco dinero, cinco dinero.*"

The children pulled back from the fence as she threw the money over, beyond where they stood. The beggars scurried down the embankment. A fight broke out. The pathway opened and the crowed shuffled through.

Moments later, Maria found herself on the sidewalk outside the building. Her luggage, with special tags, had been mysteriously placed at curbside.

Her blouse torn and smudged from pawing hands, Maria limped over and sat on a bench near the luggage.

The sky darkened. It started to rain, quickly becoming a deluge.

She needed to get the suitcase out of the rain.

Frantic, she started to drag it toward a canopy about 100 feet away. She worried her painting would get wet.

"Monkey, keep my precious painting dry. Oh, please, monkey!" she prayed.

Suddenly, her suitcase was ripped from her grasp. Someone was running off with it.

"Oh, my God!" Maria panicked. "Someone's stealing everything I own."

The thief stopped under the canopy, put the suitcase down and abruptly left. It was Chris.

Dripping wet, Maria ran underneath the canopy. The curl in her thick hair lay straight. Her drooping denim dress barely clung to her waist; her clinging blouse smudged with mud.

Maria squinted to see where Chris went.

The rain obscured a white minibus loaded with people and equipment. On top were kayaks, deflated rafts, waterproof containers, and lifejackets sealed in clear plastic bags. Chris crawled on top of it all, securing equipment. He was shirtless and wore sneakers with the backs cut out. The downpour hadn't fazed him.

His head lifted and he looked over at her. He smiled, jumped from the bus, and trotted over.

"This is your last chance to join me. You are missing a real adventure."

It was a final attempt to get her to come.

In her mind, Maria tried to work it out. She hadn't anticipated the encounter. It threw her. Her adventurous spirit wanted to race for the bus and experience a world she'd never known. But her indoctrination fought the urge to break and run. It argued and scolded her. She needed to think. There was no more time. Soon, he would be gone.

"No thank you, perhaps another time," she said, finally listening to the scolding voice inside that said it was foolhardy—her adventurous nature losing an argument that raged within her.

Chris' expression turned sad. "It's been a pleasure meeting you. Perhaps in the future, we can meet again. Maybe I will come to Golfito to visit."

After walking his first few steps backwards, he turned toward the bus, jumped into the driver's seat, and pulled the door closed.

Chris rolled down the window and spoke above the muffling sound of the letting rain. "See you later, baby cakes."

He waved and drove off.

This time, she didn't take his words as an insult. Though she met Chris for a brief period, she'd lived considerably, realizing that she was entirely too judgmental. It was her weakness, judging people by the way they looked and how they acted.

Chris had been kind to her. She failed to treat him the same.

"What just transpired?" she questioned.

All her life she'd been under the influence of Sister Florence and the Catholic Church. Her response to Chris was reactive, instinctive. But something inside wanted to surface.

"Was Chris the man I'm supposed to marry?"

Maria was not sure.

"Was this God's doing to get me to seriously think about the permanence of my celibacy? Or was it just 'chance' with no meaning whatsoever?"

Closing her eyes, she imagined Chris standing in front of her, smiling; his wet muscles, the confident person he was. He came across as able, honest, and intelligent.

Chapter 26

A battered, bronze Cadillac splashed along the potholed road that led to the airport terminal.

"Could this be the priest who is supposed greet me?"

Maria was accustomed to seeing priests and nuns drive big, older-model vehicles—often donated, and American made. She had ridden in them many times. They all looked alike.

Monsignor Perish rolled to the curb, struck an overturned garbage can, and ran over the trash before coming to a stop. He lowered the window, but his severe arthritis did not permit him to turn his head. He wanted to look directly at the young girl, but his war wounds and the remnants of malaria he'd contracted limited his range of motion.

He had received a letter from the diocese saying they were reactivating the Fatima retreat at Golfito. The diocese asked if he could help as he did in the early years, making sure Maria arrived safely.

Monsignor never denied a request, even though he was barely capable of performing it. His task today was simple. Pick up Maria and drive her to another location, near the airport, where puddle jumpers departed to the smaller countryside towns.

Maria's final connection to Golfito would be on a propeller-driven plane. The flight would last only forty minutes, arriving just before sunset.

~ ~ ~

"Oh, my God, an old and decrepit priest," Maria thought. "He must be ninety. How can he drive?"

Standing, Maria adjusted her damp skirt so it wouldn't fall.

"He's the kind who has nothing to say. He'll not talk, just mumble as he probably does during mass."

Older priests annoyed Maria. They were the old guard. She held them responsible for the submissive rules nuns were forced to abide—treating them as second-class citizens. "Nuns deserve an equal footing, allowed to say mass." And if Maria joined the sisterhood, she would work diligently to end this discrimination.

She lugged her suitcase toward the car. The trunk popped open. Maria lifted her soggy bags into the cavernous space.

"It's getting late. I hope my plane is there and will get off on time, so I don't have to go back to the rectory with this old geezer," Maria said to herself.

As quickly as the storm came, it cleared. The aging afternoon sun slipped beneath the cloud line. The rain had provided no relief from the oppressive heat. The stubble on her legs itched. Her small waist struggled to hold the skirt. It was a disgusting feeling.

"Good afternoon, Father." Maria greeted the priest, failing to see the red collar that indicated he was a monsignor. Sister Florence would have reprimanded her for that lapse of respect.

Monsignor responded with a nod. He couldn't hear out of his right ear. He saw Maria mouth the greeting, but his back was too stiff to turn toward her.

"Just as I expected," she thought. "He's upset because he has to come here in the rain to deal with me. I'll keep my mouth shut and let him take me where I need to be. Flo said it's a short distance—she'd better be right."

The ride lasted five minutes. The Cadillac came to the long side of a metal building that housed the airline. Several older planes were parked nearby. The condition of the planes concerned her.

"Thank you, Father," Maria said, lifting the door handle. She waited for him to offer a blessing as was customary.

Slowly, he turned. "Looks like God is with you today, Maria. Your plane is over there, where the luggage is stacked."

Monsignor surprised her. He called her by name.

Getting out, she stopped at the window to thank the priest one more time—she didn't want him telling Flo she was disrespectful.

Monsignor turned his head slightly to acknowledge Maria.

"You're as beautiful as your mother was the day I drove her from Golfito. It was a long drive, almost eight hours. I remember the beautiful painting she carried with her. She held it in her lap the entire trip, not letting anyone touch it.

"Your mother was sad that day. I tried to comfort her, telling her God had a different plan. I am an old man. Life has made me wise. One of the greatest gifts God gives to me each day of my fading life is the ability to see he has an agenda for all his children. A plan we don't know.

"Today, he speaks with your presence," Monsignor said softly. "Before me stands the child of that fateful day. God again, touches me with his reason. A life has come to live, to grow, and give. Follow your heart, young lady, and know God will love you no matter what your decision may be."

Monsignor's arthritic hand waved goodbye as he drove away.

"What was that all about?" Maria thought. Her mother had never spoken of Monsignor Perish.

Bewildered, she dragged her suitcases to the plane. The voice of the priest inside her head, repeated, "Follow your heart."

Again, she'd misjudged.

What profound words of encouragement. Had she followed her heart, would she be on the bus, right now with Chris, as they headed off on a great new adventure?

Maria dropped her luggage and climbed into the tiny cabin.

A weathered pilot greeted her. "Golfito, señorita?"

Maria smiled and nodded. "*Sí, por favor.*"

"Monsignor said I wasn't allowed to depart until you boarded. I need his prayers," the pilot said, who looked American.

"Thank you."

Maria sat in the cramped seat behind the pilot. Too tired to be nervous, she contemplated Monsignor's words as she looked out the window at the steamy countryside. Much of the jungle appeared cleared from the hillsides.

It was humid. She heard Chris' confident voice. "Drink lots of water."

She thanked the voice for reminding her to drink the water he'd slipped in her pack.

The pilot didn't waste any time. The propellers turned and chopped. The buzzing plane taxied, traveled just a few feet, and lifted like a kite. As she leaned her weary head against the window, San Jose came into view as the plane banked and headed for the Pacific.

The pilot announced, "Next stop, the beautiful village of Golfito. How about some cool air."

As the small plane increased in altitude, the cabin chilled. The lightweight aircraft tossed about in the convection, skirting the billowing thunderclouds, chugging across the mountain range that ran the spine of Costa Rica. Below, patches of rainforest and grasslands topped the mountainous terrain.

"How interesting, I expected Costa Rica to be an entire jungle."

The cabin got cold. Goose bumps covered her arms and itchy legs. Maria reminded herself to persevere. The flight was short.

As the plane lifted over the highest mountain, the clouds gave way to a setting sun. On the horizon, the Pacific Ocean spanned and sparkled like an emerald blanket. The bent elbow of the Osa Peninsula came into view.

"Oh, how beautiful," she said, as the view consumed her. The incredible scenery, turquoise water, and gorgeous landscape made her forget she was chilled and tired. "It's all that I expected."

A thick rug of plush rainforest sprawled beneath. She felt like she could touch the trees.

The plane descended, leveling just above the tree canopy. The pilot flew away from land and over the ocean, circling off the edge of the town, Golfito. Maria was fixated. Southward, an infinity of waves bathed an endless strand of white sand beach.

"Are those the waves of Pavones?" she wondered silently.

Golfito came back into view. Elevated two-story houses lined dirt streets. Enormous coconut palms easily outnumbered buildings. A date palm orchard, with its endless braid of thick, mature trees, spanned south along the narrowing coastal flatland.

The plane banked one more time, avoiding the approaching steep hillside to the east. The pilot skillfully aligned with the runway and landed on a grass field. The aircraft spun around at the end. The engines revved and shutoff. The propellers chopped and halted.

Without warning, the thick humidity returned. The airplane quickly became a sauna.

Smiling, blessing herself, Maria gave thanks to God for arriving safely.

Chapter 27

A miniature Toyota pickup approached the plane. A short Spanish man with a little girl stepped out to greet Maria.

"Good afternoon, or should I say, evening," Carlos, the Fatima caretaker, said in broken English. His copper-complexioned daughter looked to be about nine years old.

"My name is Carlos. It is my job to see you get settled. We have been anxiously awaiting your arrival. You must be tired, Maria."

Carlos placed her suitcase into the back of the pickup. "It's been a long time since we had a future postulant stay at the retreat. Welcome!"

"Thank you, Carlos." Maria brushed back the hair stuck to her forehead. "It's been an interesting day, to say the least. I am excited. Golfito, from the air, looked to be everything I dreamed about."

"*Sí, es muy bonita.*" Carlos forgot to speak English.

"What's your daughter's name?" Maria asked.

"Alexandria," Carlos replied.

"Hi, how are you, sweetheart?"

The shy little girl with coal-black hair and thick eyelashes hid behind her father's leg. She was hesitant. Her charcoal eyes studied the light-skinned woman—her young and innocent facial features as stunning as Maria's.

"You have a beautiful name, the name of the artist who painted my picture. Could you be her?" Maria directed her question to Alexandria.

Alex came from behind her father and answered, "I was named by my mother. She died when I was born."

Carlos interjected, explaining her mother died shortly after childbirth. Before she died, Alex's mother asked her daughter be named in memory of the young artist Maria spoke of.

"What an incredible coincidence. I am sorry to hear her mother died."

Maria went around to the other side of the truck and climbed in. Carlos raced ahead and opened the door. Little Alex, as she liked to be called, jumped into the back with Maria's luggage.

A thick jungle ascended the hillside next to the runway. The village couldn't be seen from the cleared area of the airport. When they got beyond the tree line, the rainforest that encapsulated the buildings and dirt thoroughfares appeared in front of them.

It was humid, hot, and sticky.

Pointing out the village shops, Carlos told Maria not to worry about shopping for food. The retreat was well stocked. He told her most of the town's commerce took place at the docks, several blocks below Fatima.

Carlos turned right and drove toward the port. The long, unusually high pier, built to accommodate larger vessels, ran parallel to the muck shoreline.

"Bananas and dates grown in southern Costa Rica are processed through this port," Carlos described. "The residents live on the east side of this avenue."

He turned left into a residential neighborhood. They traveled about three blocks and came upon a grassy square. At the far end, a magnificent stone church stood as sentinel to the village.

"The church is named after the patron saint of Costa Rica, Our Lady of the Angels. Isn't she *bonita*?" Unable to find the correct English word, Carlos kept the Spanish word to describe his church.

Continuing alongside the town square, the little pickup traveled past the church and back into the shade.

"Boy, it gets dark fast," Maria noted.

"The retreat is ahead, Maria."

He turned on the headlights as they arrived.

There was not much vegetation on the higher ground. Several rectangular buildings butted against the hillside. A small, lit porch marked the entrance to one of the buildings.

"Here you are." Carlos said, stopping at the porch.

Exhausted, Maria noted with a sigh of relief her journey had ended safely. She blessed herself. Little Alex ran ahead into the building and flipped on all the lights.

"She's excited to see you. And hoping to get schooled, and to be around a girl," Carlos said.

"I'll be glad to teach her," Maria volunteered.

They entered the impeccably clean dormitory. Several rows of steel bunk beds with no mattresses lined the perimeter. Exposed electrical conduit mapped the outlets, switches, and lights.

Alexandria led the way, running energetically down the center to the back. She jumped and landed at a door.

"This is your room." Lifting the latch, she shoved the stuck door open, but didn't walk inside.

"I'll go get your bags," Carlos said.

Maria thanked him and went into the room.

Alex ran in and jumped onto Maria's bed.

"I made the bed for you." Alex spoke in perfect English.

"Why, thank you," Maria said, thinking Alex must've had some additional schooling to speak English so well.

The room was simple. A small cot sat against the back wall. To the left of the cot, on top of a dresser, a fan labored to circulate the stagnant air. A small entryway on the right led to the bathroom.

Alexandria jumped off the bed, ran into the bathroom, and flipped the light switch.

"You are so sweet and helpful. Thank you, Alex."

The child blushed and ran back to the bed to bounce some more.

Tired, grimy, and ready to collapse, Maria couldn't wait to take a shower.

Carlos brought her luggage, gathered Alex, who was reluctant to leave, and told Maria he would check on her in the morning. He said he would come late, so she could sleep.

It was dark outside when Carlos left.

Maria wanted to check the painting to make sure it wasn't damaged. Unzipping the damp suitcase, she first lifted out her monkey. "Hi, Monkey. Did you look after my painting?"

The smile on the monkey's face was flat. Maria repositioned it so it would smile again. She placed her monkey on the dresser next to the fan. "I bet you need to be cooled off, too. You feel damp."

The thick cardboard box protecting the painting was dry. The waxy exterior of the container that protected it from the humidity and moisture had held up. She removed the painting and saw it was intact. Maria was relieved.

A nail on the wall over the desk looked like a good place to hang *The Waves of Pavones*.

"Welcome home, my friend." Maria hung the painting.

She slid the suitcase beneath the bed, lay down, and gazed at the painting. The events of today passed through her head. She visualized Chris, standing on the bus roof, fastening his precious paddle, smiling at her, mouthing the words, "See ya, baby cakes."

Maria fell into a deep sleep.

Chapter 28

The echo of pattering feet outside her bedroom door woke Maria.

Though not fully conscious, she reasoned it was little Alex, running about. She rubbed her eyes. The lime green walls came into focus. The painting of Pavones—its wooden frame had tilted and to the left. She crawled to the end of the cot and straightened the frame.

A bit woozy, Maria remembered Flo telling her to take it easy for a least a week, until she acclimated.

"This place is nothing like Miami. It's much hotter and more humid," she thought.

Maria cracked the door to see what Alexandria was doing. Alex was in a bunk bed, pushing on the springs with her feet. Carlos was in the far corner, painting the sash on one of the many windows.

Neither saw Maria. She went back into her room to shower.

The hot water faucet was missing. "I guess, since it is always hot here, you don't need hot water. A little detail Flo failed to mention," she thought.

To stay cool, she put on her favorite dark-blue gym shorts with the NYU logo. Her slender, snow-white legs poked through the bottom. A plain white T-shirt was tucked into her waistband.

The door to her room jammed. Maria pulled hard to open it.

She walked into the cavernous hall and greeted Carlos. Alexandria sprung to her feet and ran over.

"Good morning, little Alex," Maria greeted her with a warm smile. "How are you today?"

"I am well, but it is afternoon," Alex said—again in perfect English.

Once again, Maria was taken by the clarity of her speech, and that she corrected her about the time of day.

Carlos put the lid on the paint can, came over, and asked if she was ready for a tour.

Together, they toured the kitchen and adjacent buildings. He told her the rainy season had started. The town regularly lost its power. Therefore, her refrigeration was limited.

He advised Maria to be back before two o'clock each day. "It rains exactly at two p.m. almost every day."

"*Dos, gracias.*" Maria practiced her Spanish.

"Stay away from Main Street at that hour. The men in town go to the cantinas to wait out the downpours, because their wives don't want them home yet."

Carlos told Maria about himself.

"My family worked the banana plantation for many years before the blight came. Many residents left Golfito, but our family was fortunate, because the church asked us to take care of the retreat. I'm the only caretaker left, and grateful for the job. Also, I drive the water taxi to earn money."

They strolled from the compound, down an unpaved street toward the well-kept Spanish-style church two blocks away.

"We are excited Our Lady of Fatima will get busy again. I have a daughter and don't want to marry her off to one of the men at the cantina when she reaches age fourteen. I want to send her for more schooling," Carlos said, expressing his concern.

"Little Alex speaks remarkably well. Where did she learn such good English?" Maria asked, surmising it didn't come from Carlos, because his English was poor.

"An American that lives alone on the other side of town, near the hospital, watches Alex when I run my route in the water taxi. I don't want her on my boat, she's too busy and could easily fall overboard. The American teaches Alexandria English. I clean his property and maintain it when he is away. Alex likes him a lot. He is nice to her, but I prefer she have a woman's influence."

"You have a boat?" Maria asked, as they approached the street where the church entry was.

"*Sí*, señora." Carlos lapsed back to his native tongue. He, as the other people in town, were advised in years past, to refer to Fatima postulants as señoras and not señoritas. It was more proper.

"*Sí*, a water taxi. It's at the dock." He pointed straight ahead where the street sloped toward the bay. The large wooden pier that dominated was visible.

"Once a week, I travel to the villages on the Osa to deliver supplies and retrieve harvested plants for delivery to pharmaceutical companies," Carlos said.

They walked the marble staircase and rested on the last step at the edge of the stone terrace that marked the church's main entry.

Unaccustomed to the humidity, climbing the stairs winded her. Maria caught her breath.

"Have you ever …" she paused to fill her lungs, "heard of a beach called Pavones?"

"*Sí*," responded Carlos, as they both sat, enjoying the view of the bay.

Scaling a stone wall on the side of the terrace, Alex squeezed through a gap in the metal railing to join them. She crawled between them and nuzzled against her father.

Carlos put his arm around his daughter and pulled her close.

"*Es very bonita.*" Carlos struggled to speak English. "Pavones is less than an hour by boat—two hours by truck on a muddy road, but only if the unreliable ferry is operating. Not many people live in Pavones. There is a cantina that grills food.

"Sometimes, I go with the American to watch him surf the waves when the ferry is not working. But getting there during a swell can be *muy dificil*."

"Is it true what they say about the waves? That they're the longest in the world, every wave perfect?" Maria asked, envisioning what it might look like.

"Yes, it is true. But you must wait for a storm to bring in a south swell. The swell is rare, but it comes."

"Will you take me to that beach someday?" Maria looked directly at Carlos with her undeniable, asking eyes.

"*Sí*, señora," Carlos answered, blushing.

"Oh, thank you!" Maria said, excited.

"I will take you during a swell, when the waves are the most beautiful."

Maria was excited to hear first-hand the beautiful waves of Pavones actually existed.

It took two hands to swing open the heavy, wooden church door. Entering Our Lady of the Angels, the threesome genuflected and blessed themselves.

Maria whispered, "Sister Oliver told me whenever you enter a church for the first time you should make a wish. She said God granted her wish every time."

Bowing her head, Maria prayed God would enlighten and show her the way to her final decision.

Carlos whispered, "Only the postulants are permitted in the first three rows. To this day, as a gesture of reverence, no patron sits in those pews."

He shared a memory. "When I was Alex's age, my mother took me to church on the day the postulants announced. I remember them going to the altar and facing us. They dressed as nuns. Each one made a pledge of obedience to the church.

"When they walked about Golfito, we were told not to talk to the girls. 'They must meditate and pray for God's calling.' The nuns who oversaw the postulants warned if we disturbed the girls, the retreat would relocate to another town."

"Odd," Maria said. "I don't recall Flo telling me I must dress as a nun for mass."

They walked back to the retreat. It started to rain. Though the pounding rain made an awful racket on the metal roof, in seconds she fell asleep.

~ ~ ~

The next day at 2 p.m. the rains came. A laterite goo washed from the mountainside, raced along the pitch and ruts of the Golfito streets, and emptied into the bay, spoiling its turquoise hue. The sun returned, forcing steam to rise from the landscape.

Once again, Maria heard Alexandria running around inside the dorm. She'd tracked in red mud.

Maria opened the door just as Alex was ready to knock.

Waiting in his pickup, Carlos had agreed to give Maria a tour of Golfito to familiarize her with the surroundings.

Quickly, she hoped in and headed with him to the south side of town.

The only road leaving Golfito ran through the date palm orchard that spanned the coastal flats. At halfway, the road abruptly turned left, exiting the orchard, switchbacking the mountainside toward the Pan-American Highway to San Isidro.

At the entrance to the orchard, a small hospital sat by itself. Carlos told Maria an American woman doctor worked there, but left the country for several weeks, training.

"She is a kind doctor. Perhaps when she returns you can volunteer at the hospital, as did the other postulants." Carlos referred to a retreat tradition, where Fatima girls volunteered to care for the Ticos.

"Where is the archeological site? Are college students working the dig?" Maria was shopping for information about Dr. Jones, knowing he once worked the Golfito dig. The idea was far-fetched, but she hoped Carlos would tell her about Dr. Jones and that he expected him to return.

"I'll show you," Carlos said. "The university students came for many years. But I haven't seen anyone at the site in three years. It's all washed in. You can't see much."

"Then let's not go." Maria was disappointed and didn't want to deal with the emotions that stirred. She would go when she could draw time for herself.

The municipal dock was a short distance from the hospital. The tiny white pickup, making its way along the widest street, parked at the pier. Alexandria leapt from the back and chased a pelican to the end of the pier, finally cornering it. Carlos pointed toward his moored water taxi.

"At one time, Golfito was a busy port," he said. "Bushels of bananas and barrels of dates waited for ships. But the business has gone away. They say the palm oil is unhealthy and bananas sold for less in Guatemala.

"In the winter, a few sport fishermen come. Other than that, we barely survive on our earnings. I am blessed to have the income from the retreat. If I lost this job, I would have to send Alex away to family in San Isidro to raise her."

He wanted to convey to Maria how important it was he kept his job.

"Let's eat. A small restaurant is over there."

Carlos called for Alex and invited Maria to cross the street.

"The Osa is west, across the bay."

Carlos pointed across the bay at mountains that lifted from the water's edge. "Eight thousand plant species grow in the Osa. It is a special rainforest, one of the oldest in the world. Gold was mined once, and almost destroyed it. But the government now protects it."

He turned and pointed.

"Pavones is south, just outside the bay on the eastern shore. Many, many years ago, drug runners from Panama came to shore there and occupied Pavones. They built cabanas—small shacks. The cabanas make for a nice place to sit and watch the waves."

"In the rainy season, it is hard to drive to Pavones. The road is muddy, hilly, and washes out. That's why we go by boat," Carlos said.

He turned his attention to Main Street.

"Further down is a coffee shop. You can sit and drink Costa Rican coffee to pass the day, if you like, Maria. The family that operate the shop are friends. They'll be kind and treat you well."

He drove Maria back to the retreat and bid her good evening. She thanked him for the tour and filling her day.

Maria sat on the porch and listened to the sounds of the jungle. It grew dark. The birds called. Invisible frogs croaked. Lonely, she thought of Chris, and her mother and the unusual observation Monsignor made referring to her sadness.

Chapter 29

With each passing day, a steady diet of fresh fish and tropical fruits helped Maria acclimate. Each morning, she walked to the coffee shop and sat for hours, watching the Ticos busily work the pier.

To break the boredom she developed a routine. After breakfast, and several addicting cups of coffee, she wandered about town trying to make friends. It was difficult to communicate, so she took Alexandria along as her interpreter.

Maria loved the company of the industrious child who darted about. She reminded her of herself when she was that age.

Each afternoon, before the timely rains came, Maria was back inside her dormitory. The steady drumbeat of the deluge on the tin roof made her drowsy. And regardless of the number of coffees she drank, she napped.

Often her seclusion involved reflections of her life, the finality of her decision. The commitment she would soon make.

Other times she fantasized, but not of Dr. Jones this time. She dreamt of Chris, wondering where he was. Would she see him again? Would he come visit? Did God want her to marry him?

She envisioned the last moment she saw Chris—an honest smile, no shirt, the incredible definition of his muscles. Maria recalled their conversation, imagining what would happen if she said this or that? If she went with him when he asked? Would she still be a virgin? When and where would she have lost her virginity? Deciding the loss should wait until they visited Pavones, making love at the exact spot *The Waves of Pavones* were painted.

It was on weekends that Maria felt loneliest, because Carlos and Alex did not visit.

On Sunday, a priest came from San Isidro to say mass. Maria sat in front, in the empty pews—the staring eyes of the curious Golfito residents watching. They didn't dare sit near her, especially the young girls, fearing they may get the calling from God if they sat too close.

As each day passed, Maria loneliness deepened. The routine became boring. Her monkey, the thin thread of its mouth, stopped smiling. To pass time she cleaned the dormitory. And when she asked Carlos to take her to Pavones, he insisted she wait for a south swell.

~ ~ ~

On Monday of the seventh week, Maria determined it was time to consider her decision—the choice to become a nun or not. Like a sandspur in her sock, her inability to decide irritated her.

The time drew near. Maria remembered what Sister Oliver said. "Picture the life you want to live. List how you honestly feel about the church, your family, and future. Somewhere during the process, your answer will arrive from God."

It rained mostly all the time, making it impossible to leave the dormitory to walk about town. Maria paced the long building to chase away the claustrophobia. In the dormitory, she walked in circles and argued with the walls about the pros and cons of marriage. She did the same with her choice of celibacy and complained to the bunk beds—her audience.

When the rain subsided and the walls could finally listen, Maria was no further along.

That evening she opened her laptop for the first time. The presence of Sister Florence's spyware made her reluctant to use it. It angered her that Flo had invaded her privacy in such an underhanded way.

Maria plugged in the computer and booted it.

"The humidity may have damaged it," she thought.

Sitting at the desk, she pondered the painting's ability to become crooked each night. Several times, she tried to stay up late as possible, to see exactly when it slipped sideways on the nail, but each time fell asleep. When she woke, it was cockeyed again.

The computer booted. Chris said he deleted Sister Florence's spyware but she was suspicious, and warily watched each line of script as it passed.

Suddenly, the screen went black for several seconds.

"Shit, this isn't normal."

A cluster of tiny, colorful dots flickered in the center of the screen. The cluster bounced to the right, then the left.

"Weird, that's not supposed to happen," she said. "Damn, what did Chris do!"

The colorful dots spiraled and gathered to form a tiny shape. It was too small to focus her eyes upon it. The figure danced in a circle.

Maria leaned close—her nose almost touching the screen.

The figure pulsed, smaller, bigger, smaller.

"It looks like a set of lips," she said, puzzled.

The image rapidly expanded, growing larger, filling the entire screen.

"Oh!"

Maria jumped back.

"It's a set of lips. I was right."

Smack went the lips, as if they were trying to kiss her.

The word "SMACK" appeared in flame-red lettering, smooching.

Maria was confounded, as the set of lips repeated itself, this time ending with the word "KISS," followed by "XO XO."

"Hello, Baby Cakes!" flashed on the screen. The red lips spoke, ending with another kiss.

Overjoyed by the practical joke Chris had played, Maria laughed hysterically.

"Thank you, Chris," she chuckled. "I needed that."

She shut down the computer and rebooted it. It went through the same sequence. Again, Maria laughed, happy her friend had arrived to be with her when she was feeling low.

But her laughter soon turned into tears. The anguish she harbored had unleashed itself. Maria recalled her distant and withdrawn mother. She rarely showed her affection. Her mother, often staring at the painting of Pavones for hours as if she were reliving a memory—a story she'd kept secret, alluded to by Monsignor Perish.

She cried for a loving father, because Maria felt she had no father. Luke was cold, distant, and acted more like a stepfather.

Finally, she cried about her life, blaming the church for the indoctrination that caused her to react to men in a manner that drove them away. She was not prepared to deal with encounters such as the one with Chris. And she may have missed her only opportunity for everlasting love.

Maria was confused, unable to cope with the emotions that flooded her.

And when her tears ran dry, she fell into a deep sleep.

Chapter 30

When Maria woke up, it was raining. Carlos banged on the bedroom door.

"Maria, Maria, are you okay?"

"I am fine, Carlos."

"I have mail for you. I wanted to give it to you yesterday, but I did not see you."

"Come in." She'd slept in her clothes.

"I thought the mail didn't come on Sunday," Maria said.

"*Es no Domingo*, Señora, it's Monday."

Maria realized she must have slept through the night and the entire next day. "My goodness, I missed mass!"

"It has been raining for two days. When it rains like this, many Ticos sleep very long. Some say it's good for you. Others say it passes the time more quickly. We are having a big storm, much bigger than I can remember," Carlos explained while reaching into his satchel.

"These letters came."

Respectful not to enter Maria's bedroom, Carlos stood outside the doorway.

"Where's Alex?" Maria asked.

"She is with the American. He is back in town and hadn't seen her and offered to take her while I complete my chores."

Carlos handed Maria the letters, told her he was happy to find her okay, and would check in a few more days. Carlos warned it could rain for several more days. He said, "Be patient, the storm will soon move out to sea."

Then he said something to lift her spirits. "When this storm departs, a south swell will come. You will go to Pavones then. The waves will be there for you to see."

Maria was excited. The long sleep must have done some good. It was a defense mechanism to combat an onset of severe depression.

Maria looked over at *The Waves of Pavones.* The frame was crooked again. Her monkey was sitting just beneath it with a frown.

Crawling off the cot, she went and lifted a smile on Monkey's face.

"Painting, you win. I won't straighten you this time. You'll have to do it all by yourself."

The letters that came were from Flo and her mother. She didn't know what to think. Neither wrote much. Flo's letter looked more like a greeting card. She wondered why Flo had failed to tell her about the endless days of rain. She wasn't prepared for the isolation and boredom of Golfito.

"Perhaps Golfito is so beautiful you forget the bad things," she thought. Flo should have told her anyway.

Maria opened Flo's card. It was a religious card with a picture of a young nun holding her hands in prayer, with Jesus in the clouds above her head, smiling. There were no preprinted words, just handwritten sentences.

Hello Maria,

I hope you are enjoying your stay, and that Carlos is taking good care of you. By now, you should have had plenty of time to contemplate.

I sincerely pray God calls you to our order. You are such a perfect person.

All of my love and prayers,

Sister Elizabeth Florence

P.S. I forgot to mention at times it can rain a lot, sometimes for several days. Please forgive me for not telling you before you left. I'm sure it would not have affected your decision to go.

"Too frigging late, Flo," Maria almost cursed.

Curious about what her mother had to say, she opened the second letter.

Written in longhand, it filled the front and back of each page. Her mother's handwriting was beautiful, but curly. The circular letters made it hard for her to make out some of the longer words.

She read slowly.

Dear Maria:

I hope you are doing well. I am so sorry I have not been faithful in writing you. However, your absence made me realize all these years that I am a pathetic mother.

I am sorry, Maria—Forgive me.

The words came as a sudden shock. Maria went to the desk and sat straight.

The letter went on to be a confession by her mother, who kept asking forgiveness.

Her mother wanted to spend time with her, making up for the years she left her with Flo. And that her final decision would be supported, for whatever direction she chose, as long as it was what she wanted and led to eternal happiness.

Maria felt her mother wanted to confess something.

She didn't want to have high hopes, because in the past her mother had been incapable of sustaining the openness and emotion expressed in the letter. There was a sadness to her mother; something Monsignor Perish alluded.

Perhaps someday soon she would learn the story of her sadness.

Chapter 31

It rained all week. The electricity often went out for several hours. The end of Maria's stay neared. She decided to be productive by formalizing an approach to finalizing her decision. Maria considered using the laptop to keep notes, but Chris' practical joke was too distracting.

There was an old composition book with a black and white cover inside the desk. Maria opened it and started writing. In the front half, she wrote the reasons why she should be a nun. In the back, beginning with the last page, the reasons why not.

She mulled over the day that Flo told her in sixth grade that God had given her the calling to become a nun. How her mother faded from her life then. She remembered high school and considered how she had changed from an outgoing adolescent to a shy, insecure woman. And even though she excelled in sports, particularly basketball and track, she was so different now—a recluse.

Lengthier entries listed the influence of Sister Oliver, and reasons why she should become a sister.

The list took shape, reading like a virtual book of her life.

Maria tallied the contradictions. The greatest number pointed to Sister Florence. She noted the times she caught Flo rummaging through her belongings, and the guilt Flo laid upon her when she discovered improprieties.

"Becoming a nun requires a constant denial of her physical freedoms—a lie to her body," Maria thought, contemplating her biology.

She thought of marriage and of friends who had made the natural choice. They seemed happy. Could she buy into the notion that the sacrifice of physical pleasures would be rewarded to her in heaven?

The answer eluded her.

~ ~ ~

The storm that brewed was relentless. The monsoon continued to pound the metal roof.

Tired of writing, recalling and measuring her past, she paced the dormitory. Antsy, on edge, she had to leave before she went stir crazy. Finding a poncho inside the kitchen supply cabinet, she draped it over herself, tucked her composition book underneath her arm, and headed to the coffee shop.

As she walked the side street that ran the length of Our Lady of the Angels, the rain started to taper. Plodding across the soggy park that marked the town square, she headed down the shallow grade toward the pier and the widest street.

At the coffee shop, Maria ordered breakfast and a bowl of diced tomatoes and peppers to kill the odd taste of the eggs.

The dripping poncho draped a rickety wooden chair with legs that failed to meet the concrete floor all at the same time. Opening her book, she began to review her list.

Glad to be outside amongst the Golfito citizens, who seemed not mind the rain, she sipped her coffee and ate. Her mood improved.

Outside the large plate glass window, a dark blue Scout with a ragtop roof arrived and parked across the street, near the pier. Two kayaks were lashed on top. A wooden kayak paddle secured next to the boats looked like an Ashland.

It caught Maria's immediate attention.

Her heart raced.

"Chris!"

Jumping from the table without her poncho, she ran into the pouring rain looking for the driver. The rain beat on her. Oddly, the driver had disappeared. She went back inside, asked for another cup of coffee, and waited for him to return.

A fog rolled in. It grew gray and started to rain heavily. The dark blue Scout blended with the grayness. From where she sat, Maria could barely make out the outline of the kayaks.

Then suddenly, a tall figure wearing a khaki poncho appeared in the window, trotted across the flooding street, and hurried into the vehicle. It was a sudden surprise.

Maria raced out the door.

Not thinking, she carried her notebook. Just as she reached the center of the street, the Scout drove off. The driver apparently didn't see Maria through the cloudy plastic windows.

"Chris!" Maria yelled, chasing the vehicle down the street.

Her knee bumped the notebook. Slipping from her hand, it landed in the gutter. The rushing water carried it off—the inked pages quickly dissolving. In those short seconds, her written thoughts were gone.

The Scout turned left and traveled toward the retreat.

She gave chase, her muddy tennis sneakers splashing the puddles. When she got to the open park, she saw the Scout had parked next to the terrace in front of the church. A ponchoed figure was leaving from a side door.

"Chris!" Maria screamed. But her feminine voice couldn't be heard beyond the driving rain. The tall figure got in the vehicle and left.

Sprinting straight across the park, she raced up the church steps and tripped on a piece of heaved marble. Soaking wet, she tumbled and split her knee. Bleeding, she limped to the massive wooden doors, tugged on the handle, and squeezed inside.

On the tile floor wet footprints tracked to a rack of candles on the other side of the confessional, next to the statue of the Blessed Mother. Someone had lit three candles. A wick, dowsed in the sand tray, still smoldered. There was a puddle of water beneath the statue.

"Chris must've lit the candles and stopped to pray," Maria thought. "But why did he light three candles? What was the significance? Who did he pray for?"

Suddenly, she realized it might not have been Chris. She couldn't envision him in a church. But then again, he'd surprised her before.

Maria stood dead center in the cavernous house of God looking at the large painting of Jesus hanging on the cross behind the altar. Wooden trusses that supported the roof crossed high above. The rain that struck made a muffled noise.

Her knee hurt. Blood ran down her leg. She hobbled into the corner of the last pew and began to pray.

"Please, help me, Jesus! Oh, please, help me, dear Jesus!"

Tears streamed her face. The intensity of her sadness, the loneliness and confusion deepened.

"I don't know what to do, God. I have nowhere to go and no one to love me."

She recited the Lord's Prayer.

"Our father, who art in heaven . . ."

Her voice ached in pain. ". . . deliver us from evil. Amen."

Blessing herself, she set her head in her hands and wept.

Finally, gathering strength, she stood and staggered back over to the candles and warmed her hands.

"Lord Jesus, stop this wretched rain. Permit me to see my way in life."

Maria pulled the stick from the sand and dipped it into a lit candle. A small flame ignited. A puff of white smoke swirled. She touched the flame to the wick of a fourth candle. It came alive.

Just then, the rain hushed. The echo that drummed above ceased. Our Lady of the Angels became quiet. The soothing sweet scent of the burning beeswax drifted her way.

Pushing open the tall wooden doors, Maria went outside and stood on the terrace. As quickly as the rain ended, the sun broke through the clouds. A mist rose from the jungle. The truck with the kayaks wasn't in sight.

~ ~ ~

When her composition book fell into the gutter, the effort to arrange her thoughts had been destroyed. Maria justified the loss, reasoning that perhaps its only purpose was to purge her emotions.

Her painting, *The Waves of Pavones,* still hung crooked. Angry, she cocked the frame further, letting it hang nearly sideways. On the dresser, the little thread on her monkey's face contorted in a manner that made it look angry.

She heard Carlos call her name. "Maria! Maria, are you there?"

"Yes, Carlos," Maria answered, stepping from her room into the spaciousness of the dormitory.

"I have some good news." Carlos put a smile on his face; his dark Latino brows lifted.

"Tomorrow, early in the morning, I'll take you to see the waves at Pavones. The storm that passed was very, very big. The waves should be beautiful and perfect."

Maria couldn't contain her enthusiasm. Running over, she gave Carlos a firm hug.

"Oh, thank you, Carlos. Thank you. I am excited." She kissed him on the cheek.

Red-faced and stepping away, Carlos asked her to meet him at the dock before sunrise.

"Finally, something's working out," she said to herself. She thought briefly of the church visit, the burning candles, and her prayer to Jesus.

"The Lord stopped the rain," she thought. "He listens."

Then she laughed.

"No, no! It was Sister Oliver. She must've run over and cursed at God to stop the rain."

Her laughter grew harder.

"I wonder what curse words she used and how God reacted."

The thought of Oliver made her think of the bikini zipped inside Monkey.

"It's time, time to be a free spirit. I'll wear it when I walk on Pavones tomorrow."

Chapter 32

A day when fate organizes in a manner to alter the route of someone's destiny can commence just as any other day. A chance encounter, at a unique moment, topples a domino—hurling the soul and others with it onto an utterly different life journey.

God works in funny ways. If Keith Ashland had not attended mass out of boredom that fateful day in Vietnam, he would have never met Sister Katherine, nor experienced the horror that drove him into a deep depression—a sadness that holed him in the Appalachians. Sister Katherine may have lived, realizing her dream to change the discriminating philosophies of her religion.

Had Keith lingered at Gleason's diner, his favorite place to eat, for a moment longer, a second piece of homemade pie, he may have never witnessed Mark's inconceivable descent of the Slides. He would have missed the enlightening conversation that revolutionized an industry—designs that improved dramatically the propulsion device used to challenge the most difficult whitewater in the world.

And young men like Mark and Chris, exploring their limits, may have never purchased Keith's paddles, giving them the confidence to explore their physical and mental limits at a time when men sow wild oats, so they can proceed to their next stage in life.

What selfish rejection turned the sweet nectar of a woman's want for love to poison? Such a thing that happened to Sister Bernadine and Sister Florence, an illness that delivered a festering, lifelong bitterness, because men broke their virgin hearts.

Fate, or perhaps the hand of God, binds all lives. Chris, homeless, fending for himself, was helped along by a compassionate man, Mark Weston—sympathetic because his past closely matched that of the abandoned boy.

All were toppling dominos, their life journeys tumbling toward Maria.

Finally, they arrived, knocking over her piece, a healing cog that God inserted to correct his mistake. Maria's mission in life was to bridge a gap, heal Mark's wound, so God's continuously unfolding tapestry of love would continue as planned.

~ ~ ~

Dawn came. The retreating storm took with it the relentless humidity.

Maria was buoyant, refreshed, overjoyed. Standing at her dresser, she altered the thread on Monkey's face to display a big smile.

Suddenly, she became puzzled. *The Waves of Pavones* hung perfectly level. Overnight, it corrected its angle.

"How unusual," she thought. It spooked her.

Last night, Maria had unzipped the secret compartment sewn into the back of her monkey and removed the bright yellow bathing suit. Putting it on now, she covered it with a long beach shirt that draped to her knees. After packing a lunch, she headed to the pier.

A medium chop lapped at the barnacle-encrusted wooden pillars of the municipal pier. The Golfito men were repairing their boat tethers. Others, with nothing to do, talked to sleepy government officials starting their day.

Excited, Maria was anxious to get underway. Today, the waves that were an uncertainty her entire life would prove Sister Florence wrong, she thought, recalling how Sister insisted the waves of Pavones were merely fiction, a figment of her imagination.

Carlos arrived, holding a broad brim hat in his left hand. A decorative, woven twine satchel hung from his right forearm. Greeting Maria, he invited her aboard the tossing boat, then prepared for the day's voyage.

The twenty-three-foot water taxi had fairly high gunwales, capable of handling the rough chop. Debris deposited by the storm drifted about. The often clear warm ocean water was cloudy.

Maria made herself comfortable on a storage locker that doubled as a bench.

Carlos placed the broad brim hat on her head, telling her to sit and enjoy the journey. First, he would stop at Pavones, then retrieve her in late afternoon, after he finished his deliveries to the Osa. He advised that if he didn't return, a cantina in the tiny village would board her for the night. "Tell the owners you know me, and they'll care for you like family until I arrive.

"When I drop you off at the inlet, you will find a cabana not far from the inlet. Use it to stay out of the sun and the gale," he instructed. "Also, you'll have privacy."

The reliable diesel engine stirred. Puffs of carbon swirled. He untied two ropes, taking care to coil them neatly. The idle increased. The modest vessel backed gently from its slip.

The drone of the engine was too loud for them to actively converse. Carlos kept busy navigating the annoying swell that buffeted his craft, staying as straight as possible to save fuel and time. His round-trip journey would consume the entire day.

"Where is little Alex?" Maria asked, loudly.

"She is staying with the woman doctor today. The doctor arrived in town last night. The American man who teaches her

English usually watches Alex. But he is gone, as he does sometimes."

Carlos tried to speak his broken English, but the engine noise made it difficult.

The panorama of Golfito came into view. The rainforest seemed to encase the quaint village—its only access to the outside world an airstrip and narrow mountainside road. Dr. Jones described the geology of the Osa Peninsula as a "Ria Coastline," she recalled. A coastline formed by a drowned mountain range.

Carlos pushed the throttle all the way forward. The slow trot became a gallop, oddly in sync with the rolling swells as they headed south toward Pavones. A stiff onshore breeze captured the dissipating black smoke that spewed from the starboard exhaust.

Maria leaned against Carlo's satchel supporting her back. The morning sun warmed her while she admired the grandeur of the tropical landscape.

Her thoughts wandered to Sister Florence and the overbearing expectation—the burdensome pressure to decide before she left. Her sudden isolation. Her indecision. The unbearable humidity.

"Why was Fatima retreat located in Golfito?" she wondered. "Was it a way of influencing our final decision?"

Contemplative, she hung her hand over the side to feel the water. It was warm—like bathwater. To her, the ocean was cold, like Cape May.

Maria prayed Hail Marys for her mother. "How gratifying for her to write," she thought. But what was her secret? The old priest, Monsignor Perish and the story he told—his vivid memory of the day her mother left the retreat, crying, holding tightly the painting. His message, "Follow your heart." The observation, an expectation, he'd waited a lifetime for Maria to arrive, answering his prayers.

Maria couldn't piece it together.

She pictured Sister Oliver walking the beach, confident, beautiful, immune from the cynicism of other nuns who criticized her unconventional ways. Her unique way dealing with celibacy, a waltz amongst staring men as a stealth. How they admired her physical form.

"Sister Oliver died happy," she thought. The person she intended.

The reliable water taxi chugged south toward the mouth of the Osa. Exactly where was Pavones?

Maria closed her eyes, imagining her painting with its perfect tumbling waves. She opened them. "We must be getting close," she thought. The passing shoreline looked much like the Pavones painting.

Time had passed quickly. The mouth of the peninsula grew wider. The chop had turned into surging ocean swells—the little boat timing each crest as if it were happy to play with the open sea.

Carlos steered toward the coastline.

Finally, the cycling diesel hushed. The rolling wake folded inward—pushing, lifting, and shoving the stern.

Carlos had been watching Maria, thinking, "This young girl always seemed tense, stressed. Today, though, she's different. Her forehead no longer furrowed. The anxiety that hung her face is gone."

But he kept his thoughts to himself, as he usually did any time someone from the church visited. The church's money clothed his child. It made for a comfortable life. He didn't want to upset the delicate balance of his livelihood, with even so much as a bad thought of the church and those who governed it.

"Pavones!" Carlos pointed to the shoreline off the port bow.

Standing, Maria struggled to hold her balance. She strained her eyes to see where Carlos pointed. All she saw was a mountain that dropped to the ocean, and waves that crashed onto the rocks.

"Come here and look from where I am standing," Carlos said.

He removed one hand from the weathered steering wheel and pointed. "Maria—*mira*, follow the shoreline until you see the rocks end. At the rocky point, a river empties into the ocean. On the other side is Pavones."

To stay steady, Carlos steered his craft into the wind.

"I see the point and a small inlet, Carlos. Finally, Pavones!" Maria beamed.

"The beach is hard to see from the ocean, that's why not many people visit."

Carlos pushed the throttle. The boat's speed quickened.

When the inlet was about two hundred yards away, Carlos slowed the craft, entering the mouth of a river. He maneuvered the water taxi, skillfully side slipping against the current, ferrying toward a dilapidated wooden dock that reached from the point.

Thrilled, Maria gathered her pack in preparation of her leap onto the dock. Carlos handed her the end of a coiled rope and gave her instruction how tie to the cleat.

The noisy engine cut off. There was a rapid and noticeable transition to the sounds of the jungle. Drifting quietly, the taxi nudged the dock that answered with a complaining creak.

"Now!" Carlos said.

Maria jumped onto the gunwale, then two feet higher and onto the dock. She wrapped the frayed rope around a cleat and cinched it.

Her neck craned to see the beach, but the rocky rise of the point obstructed her view.

There were no structures, no benches to sit on, just a lonely pier in need of repair. The rocky slope to the point protected the dock from the firm ocean-borne wind that lifted over their heads from the other side.

"Over that knoll the beach begins." Carlos' voice was much clearer. "It is a long beach. You'll see the waves halfway down. There is a cabana where the beach break finishes. I'll return late afternoon and meet you here, Maria."

Carlos untied from the cleat and set his craft adrift. He started the engine and ferried the bow into an oncoming current, allowing it to spin, pushing out to sea.

Waving goodbye, Maria turned away and trudged up the sandy knoll that obscured her view of Pavones.

Chapter 33

The Pavones sand was black brown, the color of mussel shells. Its texture was rough, not the fine silk Maria had hoped. As she reached the crest of the knoll that blocked her view, a concave beach, about fifty yards in width, appeared.

"Oh my God!" Maria said as several barreling whitecaps tumbled in from the deep blue horizon.

"The waves are beautiful, more beautiful than I imagined. Thank you, God! Thank you!"

The collapses were captivating, rolling in a continuous free fall, in pipeline-like fashion, unloading an endless energy—each wave meeting death at the exact spot its older twin did, seconds earlier, with a final push, the seawater exploding, rushing, thinning, dissolving into the cobblestones.

Astonished, Maria gazed in awe. All her emotion, good and bad, lifted to make room for her delight—a lifetime dream came true.

Her eyes panned the entire arc of Pavones beach. There wasn't much sand, just a narrow strip where the jungle ended and the high tide did not reach. In the distance, where the beach terminated, jutted a sheer cliff.

"I should find the spot where *The Waves of Pavones* was painted," she thought.

She sighed.

"But first, I must do what I've dreamt about for a long, long time. Be like Sister Oliver."

Reaching to her shins, Maria grasped her beach shirt and lifted it over her head. She draped the cotton shirt on a horizontal coconut tree that reclined toward the ocean. Slipping off her sandals, she set them with her satchel at the base of the palm.

Standing straight and proud, she took a deep breath. Her posture was perfect. The warm sand folded over her toes—the scant canary bikini barely covering her.

Looking down, she stepped onto the cobblestones. The stones were slippery, unstable, and hurt her feet. She stepped back onto the width of pumice and started to walk in the direction of the biggest breaks.

A gust of wind blew in from the ocean. She paused to watch the wind shear the barreling thunder. The firm wind grew stronger, lifting bits of sand. With her broad-brimmed hat, Maria covered her face as the bluster caressed her slender frame.

Not far off, her beach shirt lifted from its resting place. It flipped playfully within the squall, up and over the point, landing in the mixing ocean one hundred feet from the little dock, vanishing.

"Oh crap!" Maria cursed. "My shirt, it's gone. I have nothing to replace it. What's Carlos going to think when he sees me in this suit?"

She turned and leisurely walked the beach. In the short time since she arrived, the waves had increased in size. They were continuous, evenly spaced, rumbling, one after another, collapsing near a little cabana that came into view.

Nearly naked, she happily danced, singing the Helen Reddy song Sister Oliver often sang, "I Am Woman."

The daringly thin bikini failed to cover never-exposed body parts. It clung, gingerly, as if to tease the wind, the sun, and the sea, leaving little to imagine. The waves were at an incredible height, standing proud, peacocking, until the last conceivable moment. Flopping. Disintegrating.

The fragrances in the air shifted with each wave that rushed in. Maria detected the hardy, earthy scents snitched from the jungle soil of the Osa. Her brown eyes gazed to watch yet another perfect wave come to life. Far off, within the building crest, tiny oblong dots with flashy colors seemed to appear. Maria squinted and blinked to clear the dots from her vision. The odd shapes did not go away. Several kneaded into the swell then washed out the back.

"Seaweed?" she thought, not sure.

"Otters, perhaps?"

"Oh!" she said after a long pause. "Village children on surfboards, how cute. The Tico children must know how to surf."

Carlos mentioned she may see people at the south end, but if she stayed near the cabana, she would be alone.

A surfer managed to stand and continue atop the roll—the wave building, the tail of the board perilously racing ahead of the collapsing curl.

Maria watched as the surfer traced the glass face, easily outrunning the froth, then twisting, spinning into the tongue, pivoting at the last second, running away. The surfer, ahead of the break, repeated the maneuver with ease.

As the endless wave neared, the crouched surfer came closer. He appeared tanned. His hair bleach blond. Toned, lanky arms flapped with every motion.

Closer he came.

"He is not a native, but a young man," Maria thought. One who closely resembled the men she saw at the Miami airport. "Surfers!" Young men she'd seen many times, drunk beneath the Cape May boardwalk. Brazen men who'd heckled her often.

"Crap!"

Her pleasurable day seized to a halt—her lure fully exposed with nowhere to hide and nowhere to run.

"Crap! . . . Shit!" she cursed loudly, as each wave lifted another surfer sending him her way. One after another, they came. And as they neared the peacocking wave, each kicked out, to avoid being crushed onto the cobblestones.

Trapped like a cornered cat, she watched a towheaded man stand in knee-deep froth, gather his board, tuck it underneath his armpit, and wade toward the beach. His eyes opened wide, like a child on Christmas morning.

"Whoa—dude!"

Shaking his head in disbelief, he surveyed Maria with his glazed, blue eyes.

"What a fine piece of eye candy," he said to himself, shaking his head, seeming not to direct his words toward her.

"Got to be the pot, dude. Some wicked hallucinogenic shit grows here," he said again, while staring at Maria.

"You've got to be that ghost the Ticos bullshit us about." He cocked his head, brushed back his stringy hair, and turned away, as if another lover summoned.

One by one, the young men trudged from the surf, stopped, observed Maria, then moved on.

They seemed disinterested.

Standing there in her bright yellow bikini, Maria was taken by their lack of interest. It defied her teachings. They ignored her.

How could that be?

Many times, she'd felt the fondling stares of men who couldn't care less how she felt about their molesting gaze. Men who, if they found she was a virgin, would risk the deadliest of deed to change her status.

"Aye, young purist virgin," a raspy voice suddenly called from the cabana on the beach.

The voice startled Maria.

"Aye, sweetest of the virgins, what's wrong? You're naked to the sun and not a salty dog wants you."

Maria twisted to see where the voice came from.

Up the slant of the beach, just past a three-foot seawall, stood a small shelter made from bamboo poles and thatched with palm branches. Inside, a redheaded woman, wrinkled and weathered, watched her. The toothless woman wore a red cotton wrap with large flowered prints. Her facial features were strong, her skin, leather.

A stern stare came from the woman. Maria forced a friendly smile.

Her raspy voice called again.

"The man you must know and love. He plays with the sea lions. All on this beach sublet to him. You are the secret he must learn, and love."

"Huh?"

Confused, Maria tried to place in her mind the culture the woman reminded her of.

"I am the secret?" Maria was puzzled. "Whose secret?"

"Who are you?" she demanded.

Then it dawned on her. It was not of a tribe, nor a culture, or even a race, but the expression she'd witnessed a thousand times—of homeless women, schizophrenics who blurted senseless verbiage with no real meaning.

"You are dressed as a lure. Your scent will for sure invite the boys. Give them time, sweetie. You are too beautiful to deny. They'll not resist, once the sun sets and the waves sleep."

Maria panned across Pavones beach, watching the surfers hike back to where they'd started. Suddenly, they stopped and started pointing. She followed their stares toward a swell that grew, cresting farther out—building much sooner.

Quickly, Maria spun her head back to the shelter, to challenge the schizophrenic. But the woman was gone. She ran to the cabana expecting to find the woman hiding. It was empty.

Maria shook her head. "Was that my imagination?"

"Hey, dudes, here he goes again. Man, he kicks some ass in that thing," a voice yelled.

As the swell rose, Maria clearly made out the lone surfer, preparing to ride the largest wave. He wasn't on a surfboard. He seemed to be sitting in a red kayak, the wave lifting behind—a towering face building. The kayak raced down the swell. And with an effortless stroke, the boat spun 180 degrees and disappeared into the barreling curl.

A cheer erupted from the beach.

"All right, the submarine move again, very cool!"

Seconds later, the kayak, with its human, rocketed from within the wave, launching into the air, clearing the water by several feet.

With voices suspended in the sea breeze, Maria heard someone say, "How does he generate so much power to pull off that move?"

She watched them shake their heads in jealous disgust.

The kayak landed bow first, disappearing again. The maneuver seemed an amazing feat of acrobatics.

The young men erupted into a wild cheer as the giant wave rolled, its enormous curl collapsing several lengths.

The daredevil was not visible.

Then, suddenly, his finned hull reappeared inside the froth. The surf kayak shot from the barreling pipeline onto the open face of the wave again.

Maria stood there, perplexed. Her fantasy had turned to a nightmare and now a bizarre tale.

The lone surfer came closer, racing the break, spinning on top at the edge of the lip, then down the curl. His paddle appeared motionless. It seemed to work like a straw, sucking the energy of the powerful wave, using it to do as he pleased.

The kayaker repeated the move done earlier—disappearing then reappearing. All eyes locked on him as he reached the point of the steepest pitch, a peacocking wave that stood tall, ready to slam onto the rocks directly in front of Maria.

Reacting to the wave that suddenly grew enormous a short distance away from her, Maria yawed back. The wave lifted higher and opened much bigger than before. It had plenty of energy as it fanned. The surf kayak rode boldly into the collapse.

Barely thirty feet away, Maria was about to witness a certain tragedy.

Her jaw dropped. She saw the paddle. It looked like Chris' wooden Ashland. Her frozen mind didn't allow another thought, because the horror of his impending death was about to happen.

The Ashland knifed into the collapse and sliced the curl, splitting it like a ruptured peapod. The craft, with its occupant, disappeared just as the crest finished its crush onto the beach.

The water raced toward Maria. It came fast, consuming her legs, knocking her down. She tumbled within the whipping turbulence, clutching her bathing suit, spitting salty seawater.

Struggling to orient herself, she tried to sit, just as the froth reversed direction, sucking her toward the ocean. What sand there was washed over her.

She braced as second wave came. This time, the man in the red kayak was on its crest. She ducked. But the wave wasn't as strong, and gently pulled back, setting the kayak in the stony sand next to her.

Dumbfounded, she looked to see if it was Chris. It wasn't. His gray mustache said he was older. But the absence of his youth didn't detract from his handsome features. Like Chris, he was chiseled, with ripples and ridges along every muscle and brawny paws that fused to the shaft of his kayak paddle. His skin was tan. His narrow waist was belted within a neoprene skirt secured so tightly to the kayak; it looked like there was no way to escape from inside the boat should it flip upside down.

Searching for an expression, Maria locked onto his penetrating, deep blue eyes. His cheeks lifted, tripling the wrinkles that extended from the edges of his outer brow. Perfect white teeth shined as exhilaration came.

"Whoa!" he said. "Where did you come from?"

Bewildered, Maria stumbled to her feet. "I came from Golfito."

He studied her. Maria felt his stare, as if he was trying to activate a memory.

"You look familiar—like someone I knew a long, long time ago," he said.

Shocked by what transpired—events that had turned her pleasant stroll on Pavones into a carnival, Maria raced inside her mind to collect herself. She tried to cover her overexposed body with her thin arms.

"I'm Mark," the handsome man said. "Sorry for the scare and the awkward introduction. Here, can you hold this?"

He handed Maria his paddle just as another small wave rushed under his boat and slid him further onto the beach.

She studied the kayak paddle. It was featherlight. A lacquer coating accented the grains that ran in the direction of the intricately aligned wood laminates.

Mark pulled the spray skirt. The rubbery edge flipped off the fiberglass lip that kept it stretched and in place. The neoprene recoiled to a size much smaller than the cockpit.

He slid onto the back of the deck and lifted his muscular legs. Pressure lines on his thighs showed where his body made contact with the inside of the surf kayak. Standing, he flipped his boat upside down, then end-to-end, draining the water. A saturated sponge flopped out. He picked it up, wringed it, and placed it inside, then finally hoisted the fiberglass hull to his shoulder.

"How can this man, who looks beyond six feet tall, fit into such a small craft?" Maria thought.

The dripping wet figure that towered asked her name.

"It's Maria," she politely replied.

"You must be the girl they talk of in Golfito. The first of many who will come to cloister at the convent."

Smiling, he looked at Maria's bikini. "Hmm, unusual clothing for a nun."

Referring to the retreat as a convent, and her as a nun, agitated her. Wanting to lash out, she quickly realized she was in no position to argue.

"Let's go to the cabana," Mark said, chuckling. "I've got something inside my kayak that may help cover the missing parts of your bathing suit."

About ready to come undone, Maria followed him to the seawall that protected the cabana.

"It's got to be a real surprise for you to see all these men on this beach," he said.

"It's a shock. You men shouldn't be here." Maria didn't know if she should be upset or mad.

"Let me explain. There's a south swell, the biggest in twenty or so years. These surfers come from all over the world. Satellites linked to the Internet tell them many days in advance when this swell will arrive. This beach, Pavones, has the longest left-point breaks on the planet. The die-hard surfers, you see, spent their last dimes to get here, just to surf this once-in-a-lifetime swell."

"Lucky me," Maria said sarcastically. "I picked the wrong day to come for my walk."

She traced her toes in the sand. "I'm puzzled, though. Why do the surfers avoid me?"

"They're punch drunk from all the adrenaline." Mark chuckled. "Sometimes other things are far more important than a nearly naked woman walking the beach. They probably think you're not real."

After setting down his boat, Mark reached inside and pulled out a small, pale blue waterproof sack.

"They're focused," Mark said, referring to the behavior of the other surfers. "Because it takes a lot of nerve to ride those waves—competing to see who is best. The excitement, adventure, camaraderie, and challenge have them worked into a stupor. That's why they ignore you. They're distracted. This surf is going to get even bigger over the next few days. They're testing themselves, challenging personal limits in preparation for the much bigger, more dangerous waves to come. The last thing on their mind is tending to mating instincts."

Pulling a musty T-shirt out of his rubber sack, he shook it then presented it to Maria.

"Put this on. It's a little wet, but it'll make you feel more comfortable."

Graciously accepting the covering, Maria read the words on back.

"Hell and High Water? That's an unusual saying to put on a shirt." She pulled the faded shirt over her head. It drooped to her knees.

"Who was the woman calling to me from the cabana?" Maria asked.

"What woman?" Mark said.

"There was a woman with red hair, acting kind of crazy, calling out to me," Maria explained.

"That sounds odd," Mark said, thinking, trying to recall something.

"I once heard a story from the locals that the cabana was haunted by a young girl from the convent that died here. They say she walked into that large wave, the one that explodes at the very end. It snatched her away and drowned her. They say it was a suicide."

"Retreat!" Maria was tired of him calling Fatima a convent. "It's the Our Lady of Fatima Vocational Retreat, not a convent."

"Sorry about the miscue, but we all call it the convent. As far as I am concerned, anyone who goes there ends up a nun. Lots of stories float around Golfito about that place, especially the mean nuns. It's got history," said Mark, challenging Maria.

"It's not a convent. It's a place of mediation where we have the opportunity to consider our careers, with no pressure to decide yes or no. It's the modern church's way of allowing us free will to decide if we want to pursue a life with God."

Maria adjusted the T-shirt to stop it from clinging to her body.

"I can see you're already brainwashed," Mark said.

The provocation mounted, as if her entire being had been challenged. She had no choice but to defend her past.

Maria criticized him. "You're an arrogant man. You have no right to make that kind of assessment. What's an old man like you doing here anyway? Haven't you grown up yet?"

"I can see you're well trained, especially the criticism part. You got that down. It's unfortunate that you are already at the point of condemnation of another person's perspective. I simply made an observation different from yours. It doesn't give you the right to judge me, and then follow with a personal attack."

Mark became frustrated for allowing this to happen. Her innocent face reminded him of Jane, and unearthed his love for her. The nuns at the retreat took her away from him. He blamed the retreat for his emptiness. His life would have been different if they'd married.

Without saying any more, he hoisted his kayak onto his broad shoulder and reached for his kayak paddle.

"It was nice meeting you. You'll make a terrific nun." Mark turned to leave. "God help us and the children you influence," he murmured.

Mark deliberately trotted down the beach as fast as he could. He couldn't wait to get back into the surf to calm himself. Maria had speared his heart by calling him an arrogant, immature male. He'd heard those words before, and couldn't cope with unjust criticism.

The pain Maria's accusation exhumed overwhelmed him. The surf was his friend; he must go there to quell his anger, soothe his spirit, and quickly rid his memory, before its sadness returned.

Maria was upset too, after overhearing his parting comment. She reacted angrily with stinging criticism, and yelled into the wind. "How dare you insinuate I am pious and that my perspectives will have a negative influence upon children.

"Sister Florence was right. Look at them all on this beach, out here pursuing senseless adventures that give no meaning to their lives. Why would I ever want to get involved with a man?"

It was a long time since Maria felt that way. Perhaps it was the lesson learned, and the viewpoint she needed to finalize her decision. She'd done what she came to do. The progress of time ruined her dream of Pavones. It was time to move on.

"There is nothing here for me anymore," she said, looking out at the turbulent Pacific. Maria sighed. "It's time for me to head back home to be the next Sister Oliver."

Maria was ready to leave Golfito and join the convent. But there was a problem. To leave Pavones she had to wait for Carlos.

As she stood on the seawall, waiting for Carlos, the shirt she wore had dried and was blowing in the breeze. The sky, the mountains all around, the textures of the beach, Maria suddenly realized that this was the exact spot where her Pavones painting had come to life—in front of the cabana from the top of the seawall.

She'd spent a lifetime standing before her painting, imagining this spot. When she was troubled, she asked God to take her here, far away from the world and the people she hated.

Now, there was no comfort, because she was inside the painting, asking God to let her out—back to her troubled world.

A stiff onshore wind pushed back tears as they drained from the corners of her eyes. She looked to see Mark catch his first wave, dancing masterfully on the top of the curl with amazing skill. And in the short time it took for him to run the beach, the ocean waves had grown bigger. The surfers, afraid, had gathered at the cantina at the far end of the beach.

Mark appeared comfortable in the mayhem, in control, able to do as he pleased in the turbulent sea. He acted as if he was daring Mother Nature to bring on the fight.

"Who would win?" Maria pondered.

She stepped off and headed north, away from the surfers, toward the coconut palm near the point and the dock where Carlos would come.

Her experience at Pavones was anticlimactic. A day of meditation, realizing her dream, might have cleared her mind so she could decide. Sitting at the base of the coconut palm, Maria ate her lunch and thought of Chris.

With glazed eyes, she stared blankly out at the sea.

Chapter 34

As the afternoon turned early evening, the southerly wind blew stronger. The sun had started to set near the mouth of the Osa peninsula. The sky was blazing orange-red.

Maria sat with her knees crouched under the oversized T-shirt, forming a tent. She pulled the collar over her eyes to ward off the swirling sand. The ocean was too rough. "It's obvious Carlos is not coming," she thought. Would she have to act on his suggestion and head to the cantina to stay for the night, amongst the gauntlet of young men?

She worried it might not be safe if she spent the night.

Hungry, the sun setting, she decided to approach Mark.

Though they had fought, he was older and seemed nonthreatening. From what she could see, everyone on the beach respected him. He was the dominate male, and she determined she would be safe as long as he was nearby.

Mark finally finished surfing just as the sun sank below the horizon. He paddled in Maria's direction, his shoulders rotating like spinning windmills, each blade of his paddle digging into the water.

Maria watched him. "Doesn't this guy get tired? For an older man, his physical ability is amazing."

Mark ran his boat onto the cobblestone beach, released his spray skirt, and repeated the motion he had done before, emptying by rocking bow to stern. Again, the saturated sponge plopped out.

He smiled at her as if he'd forgotten the conversation that turned sour so quickly.

"Do you need a ride back to Golfito?" he asked, approaching, leaning against the horizontal trunk of the coconut palm.

Disconcerted, Maria nodded.

Mark could tell from the expression on Maria's face she had done some thinking, and may have had a change of heart. He was feeling better after considering his own conversation with her. He needed to temper his emotion. She was young, beautiful, and out of her element. He forgave her.

"Come on, I'll take you to Golfito. And if you can find it in your heart to forgive me, I'll cook you a decent meal." Mark pushed off the coconut palm and invited her to come with him.

"You're forgiven. And, thank you," Maria said, reaching for her backpack. "Do you want me to hold your paddle?"

"No, that's okay. Thanks for asking. It kind of keeps me balanced when I walk."

The surf kayak hung from the cockpit rim on Mark's right shoulder. He held his Ashland in his left hand and walked briskly toward the cantina.

"How long does it take to get back to Golfito?" Maria asked, jogging to keep pace with Mark's swift gait.

"Two hours, if we don't get stuck in the muck." Mark looked at the sky to gauge what time it may be. "We'd better hurry. I need to get across the river before dark. The family that operates the ferry goes to sleep early and I don't care to wake them."

It took five minutes for them to reach the cantina, where the surfers gathered. Many made suggestive comments about Maria. Mark reacted by badgering the young men, reminding them there was plenty of daylight to continue surfing—yet they'd chickened out and sat on the beach.

"If anyone wants to make smartass remarks regarding my companion, they'd better be prepared to join me in those waves tomorrow. Let's see who's around to surf with me in the morning," he chided.

"That'll shut them up," Mark whispered to Maria. "Tomorrow the waves will be triple-overhead. No one has ever surfed waves that big at Pavones. They're all nervous, and wondering who has the courage to surf them with me."

They walked around the back of the cantina where Mark had parked his truck. Maria was eager to leave this men-infested beach.

The truck, a Scout, was the one Maria saw in town. The one she chased to the church. Maria climbed into the passenger seat while Mark lashed the surf kayak and secured his Ashland. She considered inquiring about the day she'd seen him in town.

As she tossed her satchel into the back, her eyes fell onto the Dr. Seuss book *Oh, the Places You'll Go!*

"That's Alex's favorite book! You're the American who watches Carlos' daughter, aren't you?" Maria asked, surprised.

"Yes, she's a cutie. Carlos takes care of my home when I am not around. That's my favorite book too, and Alex enjoys it when I read it to her."

The Scout's engine started.

"Her English is good. You must be a good teacher," Maria complimented him.

"My major was geography in college. I planned on teaching at some point. But my life was diverted."

The road through the jungle was in poor condition. There were long stretches of mud pots to negotiate. Maria hung on as she bounced about. After many close calls and steep climbs, they arrived at the ferry.

Thinking the ride was exciting, she took to observing Mark, noting his concentration, and how the rough ride through the jungle was as much fun to him as surfing.

"Dr. Jones couldn't hold a candle to this guy. Here is a real adventurer," she thought, guessing him to be in his late forties.

The husband and wife team that operated the ferry were very warm to Mark. She was impressed with how well spoken and polite Mark was to them.

After they'd traversed the river, road conditions improved. Mark didn't need to concentrate as on the rougher terrain.

"Have you made your decision yet?" he asked, assuming she knew what he was talking about.

"No, I haven't. But on the beach today, you almost made it for me. It took some time to rethink, realizing I wasn't going to let anger cut my path in life," Maria said.

"Great, I am glad to hear that. We kind-of got sidetracked. I reacted poorly—sorry," Mark apologized a second time. "Went to a Catholic school and wore holes in my knees as an altar boy. I remember the priest reading the gospel one day. It was about how women should be obedient and subordinate to their husbands. I take it that's true with nuns, too."

The Scout crashed through a mud hole. Briefly, Mark cut his conversation.

"Obedient to God, not priests," Maria added.

"The Vatican holds to the literal translation of Ephesians 5:21. The part in the Bible that says a woman must obey her man."

"It's a disgusting thought. I must agree." She continued, "I take issue with that Bible verse. I'd like to think, as humans, we are all on equal footing with God and each other. All hearts beat as one. If I am created in God's image, why must I be subordinate? Every time that particular part of the Gospel is read at mass, I watch the women squirm in their pews."

Mark interjected with some fatherly advice. "I've learned you have to listen to that voice inside. If you don't, it will haunt you for the rest of your life."

"I haven't been able to make up my mind about joining the convent. Each time I think about it, it gets worse," Maria confessed.

"What's the voice deep down say?" he asked.

"Don't become a nun," Maria said, rather candidly.

"You have your answer," Mark replied.

"I wish it was that simple. People are counting on me, particularly the individuals who I can help. I feel like I cannot let them down. The nuns that raised me say it's selfish if I don't become one of them. I can't part with a guilt that's etched deeply within me."

~ ~ ~

Mark stopped by Carlos' house to let him know he didn't have to go in the morning to retrieve Maria and risk becoming swamped in the heavy seas.

Mark invited her to stay for dinner. She accepted.

The muddy Scout arrived at Mark's home in Golfito, near the hospital.

"You live here in town?" Maria was curious why he made Costa Rica his residence and not the United States.

"I find peace here. No one knows me. I won't be bothered. The Ticos are much nicer than Americans. They open their hearts and homes to you, much like Italians. I can't be bothered with what goes on in the States these days. Lawyers have ruined society up there."

"What's with the grudge against attorneys?" Curious, Maria decided to probe.

"They're in the business of perception. The more divergent they keep opposing perspectives, the greater the rift that exists.

As long as no common ground exists between two parties, the lawyers make loads of cash."

The whole time he talked, Mark's face twitched. It was obvious he harbored resentment. Something had happened.

"Why were you forced to relocate to Golfito?"

"Why are you forced to become a nun?" Evading the question, he turned it back at her.

Swiveling in her seat, she slapped her lap and almost blurted out, but restrained herself. The last time she overreacted, their conversation deteriorated. *He has his reason. I'll not push this.*

Mark lived in a two-story house on the south side of town near the date palm plantation. His living area was on the upper floor. The storage area downstairs was chock full of kayaks, fiberglass molds, climbing equipment, wetsuits, and two mountain bikes—every outdoor toy imaginable. The second floor was clean, intelligently decorated, and organized.

"Nice place for a single male," Maria observed, as they climbed steps, entering the living room.

"Make yourself at home. I've got to unpack the Scout, check the oil, and ready for tomorrow. There's a room in back where you can shower in private. Find yourself some clothes. I'm sure nothing will fit."

Mark went downstairs to repack his gear so he could head back to Pavones early in the morning.

Searching for the bathroom, she realized she'd gotten used to the primitive living and couldn't wait to get clean.

"Hot water, holy crap!" Maria shouted after turning the faucet.

Shedding her clothes, she stepped into the fresh, cleansing spray.

A half hour later Maria emerged wearing a long dress shirt, buttoned in the middle, and oversized slippers.

Uncomfortable about wearing someone else's undergarment, she wore her bikini underneath.

"I see you've made yourself comfortable," Mark said, standing in the kitchen preparing a grouper and fresh vegetables.

Maria roamed the cozy house while Mark cooked. There were no pictures of family members, just interesting photos on the wall of him involved in some sort of acrobatic kayak stunt.

Inside a smartly furnished, neatly kept den sat a sophisticated computer setup and radio transmitter. On the desk, a small gold-framed picture caught her eye. It was a picture of Mark standing on the beach at Pavones with the beautiful waves in the background.

In the photo, he seemed much younger with no mustache.

Walking into the living room, Maria recalled her mother had a similar photo, but of her. Her mother said the cantina owner took photos for anyone who bought a drink.

"It was nice to take a warm shower. Your home is well kept, with lots of gadgets." Maria was about to ask about the small picture, but got distracted by the smell of the food. She was starved.

"The house is a work in progress. We lose electricity a lot. I'm sure you're aware of that. I have a generator, Internet, and all the comforts necessary."

Mark invited her to sit and eat.

"I don't have warm and fuzzy feelings toward the retreat, you know."

Mark tried to explain why he had such a harsh reaction earlier.

"Stories surrounding the retreat have circulated about town for years. It was nice to see it closed."

"What were some of the bad stories?" Maria asked, curious.

Suddenly, his expression became twitchy. "How all the girls were so beautiful; most of them made the choice to become nuns. Rumor had it they were brainwashed. The decisions weren't their own.

"I went to a Catholic grade school and remember vividly the guilt—how we were literally forced to believe at least one person in class should become nun or priest. Like a quota system. It scared the hell out of me when I was in sixth grade. I didn't want to become a priest and felt guilty about it. I don't believe that's how you educate children, through fear and intimidation."

While they ate, Mark talked.

Devouring her meal, Maria allowed his explanations. She knew exactly what he was talking about, having experienced it.

"Would you like some wine?"

"Sure!" It had been a while since she drank wine, or any alcohol.

"I like the California Cabernets. I have a friend, or should I say 'adopted son,' who brings it when he arrives in country."

Mark pulled the cork and poured each of them a glass.

As the wine relaxed her, Maria began to feel a strange connection to the man who spoke so freely. Holding the glass, she went to the Ashland paddle that leaned against the wall. "I take it this never leaves your side."

"Correct."

He cleared the table and started to wash dishes. "It's the center of my universe, keeps me whole. It does something for me. Call it my crutch."

Setting down the glass, Maria lifted the paddle to get a feel as to how it felt to kayak with it. "It's featherlight and feels odd."

"Left-hand control," Mark said. "That's why it feels that way. The shape of the shaft in the left hand is different. You must be right-handed."

"What does that mean, left-hand control?"

"It means I use my left hand to rotate and control the blade angle."

Mark dried his hands, came over, and demonstrated how to hold it.

"A close friend made it for me. This is the best paddle in the world, and impossible to replace. The design loads a tremendous amount of energy."

A right-hander, Maria found gripping it awkward.

"The left-hand control is the secret as to why I am so effective in the surf here at Pavones," Mark said.

Maria noticed the changing expression on his face as he grasped the Ashland. It was his love. All his tension became subdued, as if he'd been greeted by a faithful, loyal pet.

"The waves on Pavones are left-point breaks. That means the waves always collapse left to right. Since I am left-handed, it affords me an advantage. My left hand—we call it the control hand—it's always on the inside of the wave break. I have more leverage and can easily pivot around its axis. My right-handed kayaking buddies don't know about this subtle difference."

Maria enjoyed listening to Mark, to the fine detail of his technical explanation. It was like sitting through Dr. Jones' class again.

She poured a second glass of wine.

Maria was never comfortable talking to men about other men. But she had to ask about Chris. The wine had relaxed her to where she worked the nerve. "You know, I met someone at the airport with a paddle just like that—an Ashland. He was obsessed with it, much the way you are."

"Which airport?" Mark questioned.

"Miami! We were on the same Lacsa flight."

"Did you meet him?"

"Yes, sat right next to him. His name was Chris," Maria said.

"Oh, damn! I forgot to contact Chris. Shit!" Mark hurried into the den. "I was supposed to get a hold of him. I can't believe I forgot to do that! Excuse me for a minute."

Mark turned on the transmitting equipment.

"What, you know him?" Maria followed him into the den with the Ashland in one hand and wine glass in the other.

"I have to let these radios warm up first," Mark said.

Maria wondered what was going on.

"I am sorry. I was supposed to get a hold of the guy you met at the airport. Our conversation reminded me I had to contact him over an hour ago. I forgot. Funny you met Chris. He's a great guy. Had a hard life and found a way to overcome his hardship through the river."

"We had a nice talk about that on the flight. And once we landed, I found how entertaining he can be."

Brushing her fingers through her thick hair, she recalled the bubble bursting over her head.

"That's the river guide in him."

The transmitter emitted static. Mark played with the dials.

"Chris has been in the country for a while. He's preparing for his lone descent down the Rio Chirripo. I've known him for quite some time. Reminds me of myself when I was his age. He has talent and intelligence. He hooked up all these computers, see."

Mark keyed the microphone. "Golfito Base, calling Chirripo Remote."

He repeated the call. "Chirripo?"

There was a prolonged squelch, then a clear voice blurted, "Where the hell were you? You're friggin' two hours late."

It was Chris—Maria clearly recognized his voice.

"Sorry, dude," Mark apologized. "Pavones was a double-overhead today. Had to stay."

"Cool. You probably pissed off those surfers with that surfyak of yours," the voice on the other side said.

Sitting, Maria crossed her legs and started to bounce her foot. She flipped the oversized slippers with her feet and nervously rolled the Ashland along her thighs. She was glad to hear Chris' voice.

"What's doing?" Mark asked, keying the microphone.

Chris talked. "Well, I hoofed it in from the Pacauri River Gorge, the next valley over. It took two days of hacking through the jungle with lots of damn rain." When I got here, the Rio Chirripo was bank-full, and I've only kayaked about a third of the river, so far. I'm here camped, waiting for your call."

Maria's slippers danced.

"So, you're at the falls. Give me the coordinates." Mark had booted the computer.

Chris called his location.

"Nine degrees, twenty-eight minutes, thirty-eight point nine seven north."

There was a pause.

"Eight-three degrees, twenty-three minutes, forty-nine point one west."

On the LCD screen, a slowly rotating globe grew larger, then zoomed his location. The blurred screen rendered, showing a 3D image of the Chirripo River Valley.

Maria peeked over Mark's shoulder. She wanted to interrupt their conversation, but felt they were talking about important stuff, so she held off.

"Okay, got it."

Mark looked closely at the flat screen. "You're at the top of the falls, Jacob's Ladder."

"Who named it that, you?" Chris didn't wait for a response. "The rain hasn't let up and the canyon walls are steep. I'm camped right at the fork."

Listening intently, Maria thought how afraid she would be if that was her, stuck in the jungle alone. She couldn't imagine men as daring as Chris and Mark.

"Mark, I got your laminated notes here. But I think they're useless because the river is too high."

"Chris, you may lose battery power."

"Good point," Chris said. "Run through those moves one more time, now that I'm at Jacob's."

"I named the Ladder after that nasty rapid on the North Fork of the Payette in Idaho," Mark said, before starting with his instructions on how to run the nearly vertical series of waterfalls.

"There should be a cliff on your left. Start your run river-left, against the cliff. Peel out and stay left until the current slows just before it drops over the falls," Mark instructed.

"I saw that eddy and the slowing current when I got here before dark." There was tension in Chris' voice. "I almost ran that rapid backwards because I didn't know it came so soon after the forks."

"Hey, deal with it! You shouldn't be doing this anyway," Mark said in a tone Maria determined as a scolding.

"Let's continue. Before the falls, start charging hard toward the right. Don't go directly over on the main flume; it smashes onto a flat rock at the bottom. It'll bust you up. You can't afford to swim, either. It'll kill you," Mark warned.

"Got that!" Chris responded.

Maria became concerned. She was uncomfortable listening to these two adventurers plan their conquest.

"Your first waterfall is eighteen feet high. You won't be able to see the bottom as you head over. Jagged rocks on your left, cutoff half the flow. Aim for the pothole on the bottom-right. Make sure you hit dead center. It's deep, you won't bottom out. The current will spin the bow while you are vertical and set you down flat," Mark said.

"Amazing," Chris said. "How the hell did you figure that move?"

"I didn't. I didn't care if I lived or died at the time. I was trying to kill myself," Mark said. "That's why no one wants to run the Chirripo with you, Chris. It's too dangerous and shouldn't be run alone."

Maria looked at Mark and wondered what his story was. She was alarmed and concerned for Chris. *What's going on here? Is Chris crazy?*

Maria stopped bouncing her leg and continued to listen to the instructions.

Chris' voice began to fade.

"We don't have much time. Your radio battery is almost shot," Mark said.

"Okay, talk . . . I'll just listen," Chris replied.

White-knuckled, Maria sat at the edge of her chair, clutching the Ashland.

Mark continued to map Chris' route. "Once your kayak lands flat, align the stern so that you can do a reverse peel-out. You need to be facing upstream. Then ferry river-left and eddy out."

"Got it!" Chris said quickly.

"The second waterfall is nine feet with an infinite eddy on the left. It's not a true vertical. But you should know that three-quarters of the river's current sucks into that eddy. It looks like a giant draining toilet bowl.

"You can't scout or portage it; the canyon walls are sheer, with no escape. The river level concerns me. It may be too high to run tomorrow," Mark warned.

"Do me a favor, Chris. Wait until the river level drops before you decide to make your run. You have nothing to prove. My advice would be, walk away."

"Why do young men do this?" Maria thought. "What's the sense in thrill seeking?"

Then she recalled a conversation in Cape May, when Oliver explained her view on the male species.

Oliver couldn't sleep one night and invited Maria to crawl through her window and onto the gable. They were four stories off the ground, overlooking the ocean. It was dangerous and exhilarating. That night, as their feet hung over the eave, they talked about men—why they seek adventure.

"It's innate—part of their make-up. Men seek adventure to learn who they are. Without risk takers, there'd be little quality to our lives," Oliver said.

Sister Oliver told her that males must sow their oats before they make good husbands. "Socially, it's a good thing, because these men no longer feel the need to run off with the boys for the weekend, leaving you alone with your children. Their divorce rate is less, because they are more your partner than the unsettled spouse, whose only conquest was his wife.

"Maria, if you choose not to become a nun, that's who you marry."

For Maria, Chris might fit that bill. But first, he must get off the river alive.

Fidgeting, she couldn't sit still.

Mark continued. "From inside the river-left eddy, peel out and charge hard right to left. The current will rocket you, and doesn't hesitate before it goes over the second waterfall. Your bow must be less than six feet from the right bank. Your angle must be forty-five degrees—not fifty or forty. Got that, Chris?"

"Got it—exactly forty-five," Chris responded calmly.

"Keep that angle into the drop and over the falls. Be prepared to get buried at the bottom, alongside the infinite eddy," Mark said, continuing his description. "You'll shoot out like a fire hose. Keep your center of gravity centerline-forward. The bow should nose up and pivot away from the toilet bowl. You'll submarine for about twenty feet and surface as you hit the third waterfall."

"Aw shit!" came over on the radio after Mark described the second drop.

"The third waterfall recycles onto itself and curls right to left. It shouldn't kill you, but you'll get trashed. If you flip or swim here, you can recover before the last waterfall. Which is nothing but a bunch of white foam and jagged rocks, not as vertical as the others. Just a bouncer down the middle," Mark described.

"If you make it through Jacob's Ladder alive, plenty of Class-V rapids have to be survived before you get to the end. I don't have to tell you about those rapids. You are good enough to figure how to run them. And I don't want to hear you drowned either. Got that?"

"Thanks … *shhhh…*" Chris' sentence became static, then returned. "You taught me that life was about making good decisions, not to doubt them once you made them. I can't believe I'm about to do this."

"You have all night to think," Mark replied. "There comes a time in life to step back. Only you know when that is."

"I think this may be it," Chris said. "After this run, I'm going to find that girl I met at the airport and marry her. She was the one for…*shhhh.*" The radio became static again.

Maria's eyes grew big and round. She couldn't believe the confession she overheard. She wanted to talk to Chris.

Surprised, Mark looked at Maria. He raised his eyebrow, as if to say, "It's up to you."

The key on the microphone clicked. "I have someone here you may want to propose to, Christopher."

Mark rarely called him by his formal name, only when he wanted to make an extremely serious point.

Maria jumped from her seat and ran to the transmitter. She wanted to beg and plead Chris not to run the waterfall, to hike out and come to Golfito so they could talk.

"Chris, are you there?" Mark called.

Maria stood next him.

"Chris, Chris!" Maria yelled. "Oh, please answer!"

Shh ... hhhh.

Only static; no response. After several attempts, Mark said, "His batteries must be dead. Sorry, Maria. He is a great guy. And you are a beautiful woman. I know little about you, but you seem a good person.

"Chris is trying to follow my footsteps. No one should go there," he explained. "It would be nice if he stopped. But if he doesn't make that decision on his own, he loses a part of himself, forever—never regaining it."

"I am tired and should head home," Maria said, yawning.

A long day; Maria had traveled the entire range of her emotion. Drained, there wasn't much left to think about.

"I'll take you to the conv—uh, I mean retreat."

They climbed into the Scout for the ride through Golfito. The wind was blowing hard. Debris tumbled across the littered roads. Maria's mind was on Chris and the conversation she overheard.

"Will he return to marry me?" she silently wondered. "Do I want to marry? Will he live?"

The Scout squeaked and rattled.

"The storm off the coast must've grown into a hurricane. The Pavones waves are going to be extremely big tomorrow, possibly thirty-footers," Mark said, maneuvering the steering wheel.

"If Chris makes it down the Chirripo, he'll come to stay with me. I'll tell him where to find you."

Barely keeping her eyes open, Maria wasn't listening.

Chapter 35

When the battery died on the satellite phone, Chris placed it in an ammo box to keep it dry. He read Mark's handwritten laminated notes, written after his successful run of Jacob's Ladder, studying them one last time.

Locating a high ledge to avoid the rising river, Chris lugged his gear and secured it in a tree. He tied a rope sling so he wouldn't fall off when he fell asleep.

Soaking wet, tired, he rethought this insane attempt of the Rio Chirripo. He measured how difficult the rapids were, prior to this point. Mark received credit for this first decent, and no one would care, or remember, who ran it after him.

"It's barely navigable." The more Chris thought, the more he questioned his ability to traverse the waterfalls and the remaining canyon rapids.

"What a tragedy it would be if I died," he thought. "There are many more places on earth to see and explore. I've much to live for.

"Have I miscalculated? Am I following a man who had a death wish, and threw caution to the wind?"

Chris contemplated his life agenda. The cute girl in the airport, how beautiful—her wanting look, tugging his heart. He wished she had accepted his invitation to travel with him, so she'd get to know him.

"Somewhere out there in the world is the woman I will eventually marry," he thought. "Where does she live? What is she doing right now?

"Is Maria the one?"

~ ~ ~

In the morning, Chris woke to a dense fog and the rush of the flooded river below. He was chilled and tired, and smelled like growing moss.

Opening his mess kit, he made coffee on his tiny stove. A half hour passed as Chris watched the swift current disappear over the falls. He tried to imagine what was below by studying the rising mist that rose from the unseen rapid. The canyon walls were entirely too steep to climb and portage. He must run Jacob's Ladder blind, without ever seeing its obstacles. It's something he'd never done before.

One, two, three hours ticked away; Chris couldn't gather the courage. The sun came out briefly. He tried to justify a reason why he should, or should not, continue. He recalled an enlightening moment when Mark and he were trapped at the top of an impossible rapid on the upper section of the Blackwater River in West Virginia.

"Chris, they call this the step-back point, a point, where you stop testing your personal limits. If you time it perfectly, it'll be where your next decision ends in death. Once a young man steps back, he can go no further. It is time to start a more meaningful life journey."

How funny and mushy that comment sounded at the time, and the contrast as to how appropriate it was at this moment. Chris admired Mark, finding him to be wise. But it confused him as to why Mark had never stepped back.

"This is insane," he thought. "What do I have to prove by surviving the Chirripo? Jacob's can only be navigated with an attitude of complete confidence." A confidence he couldn't find within. Chris had reached his step-back point and didn't need to continue on.

It was a two-day hike out of the canyon, through the thick, dense jungle—a task much easier to complete than what may have laid ahead.

Although it was a blow to his ego, Chris was comfortable with his decision not to continue. Mark would not fault him for turning back.

"It was a mature decision," Mark would tell him.

Chapter 36

It was nine o'clock when Maria woke to the sound of an airplane crossing the treetops. The passenger plane throttled down and landed not far from the retreat. Realizing she'd slept in her bikini beneath Mark's button-down shirt, she undressed and tossed the flimsy swimsuit to the bottom of her bed, then fell back to sleep still in the shirt.

~ ~ ~

"Maria, Maria," a familiar voice called. "It's me, Sister Florence."

A firm, heavy hand rocked her shoulder.

Maria lifted her eyelids to see Sister Florence peering upon her. Not wanting to participate in the dream, she rolled and buried her head in the flat pillow.

Suddenly, her thoughts cleared. "The Flo odor, it's not a dream!" she thought wildly.

Sister Florence was for real and stood at her bedside. Alarms went off inside.

"Sis-sister Florence," Maria uttered. "Wha . . . what are you doing here?"

Flo seemed elated. However, the permanent scowl that perpetually dominated her facial expression was still present.

"Good morning," Flo said, as her full figure cast a shadow. "I bet you are surprised. Today is going to be exciting for you. It's time to start your postulancy."

"What!"

Bleary-eyed, bewildered, Maria was in total disbelief. "I thought it didn't start until I went home."

"No, no, sweetheart, all the girls who attend Fatima begin their postulancy before they leave. Didn't you read the computer disk I gave you?"

Flo grabbed the nearby desk chair and slid it to the side of Maria's bed. The chair quivered and creaked as it tried to hold together under the load.

"I'm sorry, Sister. I . . . ah . . . I didn't."

"Oh, Maria, I am disappointed. It's all on those disks, exactly what will happen—particularly today. But I forgive you. You are the first of many to come. I'll walk you through the ceremony."

Pausing, Flo caught her breath. She panned the simple room, recalling the moment when she found Maria's mother in bed with Luke.

Maria was a little perturbed about the information she was supposed to have read on the diskettes. She hadn't dared look at them because Chris had convinced her Flo was spying on her.

Thank goodness, Flo didn't ask to boot the computer. She would have a coronary if she saw the joke Chris played.

Maria watched Sister's eyes walk toward the foot of the bed.

Oh my God, the bikini!

Too late—Sister Florence leaned across and lifted the scant garment, examining the revealing canary yellow suit. Flo's barely pleasurable expression morphed into an angry scowl.

"I smell alcohol, Maria. And is that a man's shirt I see on you?"

Flo went into intimidation mode.

Cringing, Maria started to wilt.

Furious, Flo's blood boiled. Her vendetta against Jane, a lifelong effort to script and control Maria's destiny, might have come undone. The horror was, "Maybe Maria lost her virginity in the exact spot her mother lost hers."

Racing through her memory was Luke's betrayal, and the event that ruined any hope of marriage and freedom from the church.

"I don't know what happened on the church's property, Maria, but it better not happen again."

Flo balled the bright yellow bikini and stuffed it into the pocket of her black skirt. "We will not speak of this. Get up! I've arranged a special mass for you today. It was to be a surprise. Instead, I end up the surprised one.

"On the dresser are your garments for mass. Put them on!" Flo demanded. Still not in complete control of her anger, Flo left the room, affording Maria a few moments to pull herself together.

Outside the doorway, Flo pondered where Maria had gotten the bathing suit. "Where did she buy it? Carlos was supposed to be my eyes in Golfito and report such deviations immediately. I gave him specific instructions to call. He never did."

Flo balled her fists.

"Humph! I'll get hold of Carlos and find out the story of the bathing suit and the man's shirt. Then destroy whoever she's seeing.

"Carlos depends on me for his comfortable living. He pilfers food from the kitchen storage, and siphons diesel from the backup generator for his water taxi. He'll do anything to protect Alex."

Sister Florence walked the empty dormitory, thinking how she had enjoyed clearing the hall on Sunday afternoons, turning it into a bowling alley. Each time she peered back at the door to Maria's room, she relived the moment Sister Bernadine walked into her old bedroom; finding Jane and Luke entangled—locked like dogs, the graphic scene vividly carved into her memory.

~ ~ ~

Maria turned the monkey's face into a frown by lowering the thread. A tear ran down her cheek. She felt alone, vulnerable, and wished there was someone in her life to help her—Sister Oliver, Chris, perhaps Mark.

Flo barged in without knocking.

"Maria, on the dresser!"

There was a pause as Flo caught her breath again.

She pointed. "The package. Open it and get dressed," Flo demanded, curling her fingers into tight ball with clenched thumbs.

Inside the sealed package were white and black linen garments, nuns clothing. Maria opened the plastic bag.

"What? This is a habit. I am not supposed to wear these until my investiture ceremony." A tightness came to her chest.

"You'll put them on," Flo commanded.

Standing at the dresser, Maria fumbled to separate each piece. Lifting the tunic, she became nauseous. This was much too difficult to deal with. Dropping the tunic, she collapsed to the bed.

Flo snatched the garments from the dresser, ripped them from the plastic, and threw them on top of Maria. She'd knocked over the monkey, which fell to the floor. The black thread that served as Monkey's mouth broke.

Maria's sad eyes fell upon the stuffed animal's broken expression, and she thought how ironic it represented her broken spirit.

"Get dressed," Flo demanded. "This was all on the CDs."

Flo knelt next to Maria and separated the pieces of clothing, laying the scapula and tunic at Maria's feet. She then draped the veil, wimple, and coif across her chubby forearm.

Maria's round eyes were swollen and sad.

Flo remained unfazed, determined to see this through, forcing Maria regardless of her objection. And if she resisted, she planned to unleash a gauntlet of guilt and criticism that assured her submission.

"Stand up!" Flo demanded, pulling Maria from the bed by her wrist. "Put these on. You're running out of time."

She handed Maria a pair of oversized, waist-high underwear.

Maria slid into them.

Flo quickly handed her black pantyhose that reached the upper part of her narrow waist. Next came a white blouse with many buttons. It draped to her thighs.

"Turn around," Flo ordered, lifting the tunic to drop it over Maria's head.

Claustrophobic, disappearing within the flowing linens, Maria stood silent as Flo adjusted each piece, holding a smug, selfish grin—the smirk of a controlling mother dressing her daughter on her wedding day—ignoring her daughter's underlying doubt.

"Si-Sister," Maria said, searching for words, working the nerve to utter something. "I thought . . . I was not allowed to wear these until my investiture."

"True, Maria. But it's been decided, since this is such a special occasion, the reopening of the retreat should be symbolic, honoring the traditions of Mother Superior."

Flo recalled Sister Bernadine broke the rules all the time. She had so much dirt on priests, they dared not object.

Anxious to get Maria into her habit, Flo wanted to gauge her discomfort—beginning the processes of acclimating her to the wardrobe of a nun. The first time was difficult for them all.

"The sooner you get comfortable, the faster you'll adapt, Maria," Flo said, thinking she wouldn't turn back once she grew accustomed to her garb.

"Maria, this will feel a little confining." Flo raised the coif. "It was for me. But I got used to it—so will you."

It took two hands to open the broad collar. After setting it on Maria's head, Flo pulled the tails around her neck and buttoned it down the side. It covered her ears.

Maria didn't like this at all. A dog collar was around her neck.

"There, that's not so bad, Maria. Sister Oliver looked as beautiful as you," Flo said, patronizing her. "No, let me correct myself. You look as beautiful as Sister Oliver."

Oliver was always vocal about wearing bulky nun clothing.

"How ridiculous it looked," Maria recalled Oliver saying, calling it her uniform, using explicitly foul language while getting dressed.

The crown and black veil fit perfectly around her head.

Finishing dressing Maria, Flo, with sweaty palms, patted flat the wrinkles. The bulges that didn't disappear were eliminated when Flo tugged at them until they complied.

Sister Florence stepped back to admire Maria. She smiled and rubbed her palms on the side of her skirt, which meant she was satisfied.

"You won't have to wear this often," Flo said, pleased, feeling she still had control of Maria and her emotions.

~ ~ ~

Little Alex ran into the dormitory and raced past the bunks, halting just inside the doorway of Maria's bedroom.

Alex saw Flo, then Maria dressed in the nun outfit. She cocked her head in confusion. With a child's curiosity, she examined Maria's costume. Then she saw Maria was upset.

"Maria, I have a letter for you," Alex said, excited, hoping Maria would allow her to read it to her. Extending her tiny arm, Alex offered the envelope.

Flo came between her and Maria.

"Hello, little girl."

Flo knelt to be at eye level. "You must be the most beautiful, precious Alex God placed on this earth. Will God call you to be a nun one day, sweetheart?"

Stepping back, Alex stared at Florence with her large brown eyes.

"God called Maria when she was your age."

Alex didn't understand what Flo meant. To her, the fat woman was another costumed person from the outside world that had something to do with the retreat . . . Something different always happened when they arrived, usually involving a party with cake and sometimes ice cream.

Gingerly, Alex moved past the big woman to complete her delivery. Handing the letter to Maria, she waited for the warm, loving response only Maria could convey.

As Maria knelt to greet Alex, her flowing wardrobe gathered around the olive-skinned child. "Why, thank you, Alex. You are such a good girl." Maria invited Alex into her open arms.

The linens expanded all around. Alex didn't know where to hug as Maria pulled her close and held her tight, burying her face in Alex's head of hair.

Alex sensed Maria was in need of some extra affection and wrapped her arms around Maria's neck and squeezed as hard as she could.

Maria looked at the return address on the letter. It was from her mother. She shoved the thick letter into a pocket behind her tunic. There was no way she was going to open it in front of Flo. The last letter her mother sent showed an unusual shift in her sentiment.

The bathroom door was open. Flo went to wash her face and to snoop. Maria had hung the long-sleeve shirt Mark gave her on the towel rack. Curious, Flo inspected the shirt and sniffed it to see if there was a man's odor. There was a hint of cologne.

"Let's go, Maria," Flo said suddenly, racing from the bathroom. "I flew in with Father Peter. You remember him. He agreed to come all this way to say a special mass for you.

"And guess what? He told me they're assigning a parish priest at Our Lady of the Angels. Not since the retreat was mothballed has there been a priest in Golfito. This morning he's going to announce it at your mass.

"We have to hurry," Flo said, guiding Maria by her elbow. "We're running late."

Chapter 37

The stiff onshore wind that pushed through Golfito and amongst the towering coconut palms pinned their skirts against their legs, mirroring the shape.

Maria didn't know what part of her wardrobe to hold down.

As they walked in silence, Maria tried to regain her composure. Even though she looked the part, she had yet to confirm her intention to become a nun. And she didn't know when exactly it was required, but had believed it wasn't until the last Sunday of her stay.

Flo tried to engage her in conversation, baiting the idea that it might be possible to stay in Golfito, assisting Father Peter with getting the retreat fully operational.

"Golfito could use a parochial grade school. And you could tell Alex, she has the calling from God, and see your dream come to fruition, too."

But remaining in Golfito was conditional, only possible once the mystery of the skimpy bathing suit and man's shirt was disclosed. If there was a temptation, Maria wouldn't be allowed to remain, or ever visit.

The church bells started to ring. Sister Florence's sagging jowls lifted upwards. Her dream to bring Maria into the sisterhood would soon be reality.

~ ~ ~

The congregation had already gathered at Our Lady of the Angels as Flo and Maria entered from a side door.

"Maria," Flo said, holding her back. "You must wait in back until Father Peter starts mass."

Having met Father Peter many times, Maria didn't care for him. He was too pompous, dictatorial, and overly opinionated. His conversations were always one-sided.

The mostly female congregation filled the pews. Nearly every seat was occupied, except for the first three pews, reserved for the Fatima girls, as tradition dictated.

"What'd happen if they ran out of room? Would anyone sit there?" Maria thought, waiting for the priest to arrive. "Probably not, they'd stand in back."

In the fourth pew, directly on the aisle, Flo sat as sentinel. Somehow, she'd corralled Alex, forcing her to sit next to her.

Maria smiled, knowing Alex's busyness would annoy Flo the entire mass.

A guitarist played a religious Spanish song. Everyone rose. Father Peter stepped from the vestibule.

Instinctively, Maria lowered her head, folded her hands in prayer and progressed up the aisle. Every head turned. Father Peter, standing at the altar, waited patiently. Flo sat proud.

Keeping her head low, Maria genuflected then sidestepped to the center of the first pew.

Father started mass with a sermon about Maria, the important decision she must make. He announced that Fatima would fully open next year, ushering in more future nuns. "They too, will need your prayers."

When he proclaimed the assignment of a fulltime parish priest, the congregation politely applauded.

As the mass continued, Maria sat silent with her head low to appease all who observed. She reran in her memory the many lonely weeks here in Golfito. Her personal journal to help make the decision—its rain-soaked contents, destroyed. She daydreamed about Sister Oliver, the flight from Miami with Chris, yesterday's encounter with Mark.

Father Peter started his homily. Maria pretended to listen. The sermon was about vocations—his, Flo's, and now Maria's sacrifice. Peter spoke of the need for men and women to enter the priesthood and sisterhood—how their Catholic religion was in crisis; short-staffed, forcing the Vatican to combine and close parishes.

"Fewer and fewer of our sons and daughters answer God's calling," Peter said. He faulted the community for not encouraging their children, and prayed every day their selfishness would soon change. He reminded them that two slots to attend the Fatima Center were always reserved for the daughters of Golfito.

Peter's homily made Maria think of her mother, and the question no one ever asked—the reason why Jane didn't enter the sisterhood.

The thought reminded her of the letter stuffed in her pocket, and the mystery that surrounded her. Pulpit Peter, as Maria often called him, would ramble for another half hour. It would be a good time to sneak the letter and read it, to know why she wrote so suddenly.

"Flo is far enough back," she thought, "and won't be able to see, as long as she keeps her head bowed."

Sneaking her hand into the skirt pocket, she worked the envelope to where she could remove the letter. It contained several pages.

As the loose-fitting garments concealed the papers in her lap, she began to read.

Dear Maria:

With you so far away, experiencing what I experienced at your age, I could not help but try to feel the discord you are struggling with.

Maria read on; this wasn't typical of her mother.

Tonight, I looked at the wall in the reading room and noticed the discolored area where our painting of Pavones once hung. I never told you the true story behind the painting. And for many years, I have felt guilty for misleading you.

I know we talked only briefly about my time in Golfito, and how it's supposed to be a place for reflection. We talked of my desire to walk on a lonely beach, where I would make my final decision regarding my commitment to God, and how you would like to do the same.

But we never talked about why I didn't enter the sisterhood.

My confession to you is that a man gave me the painting. I met him while walking alone on Pavones.

On that fateful day, I was pretty much resolved to become a nun. There was nothing further from my mind than falling in love.

When I arrived for my day of contemplation on Pavones, I never expected anyone to be there. I was enjoying the rolling waves, thinking how great my life was and about the journey ahead.

Apparently, I had failed to notice a man, about my age, out in the waves on a very odd-looking surfboard. He was very good, and played in the waves for hours.

When the man I watched for hours finally finished riding the waves, he beached his craft in front of me. I guess it was a surprise to find me there.

As the first words of hello left his lips, and as our eyes met, there was an attraction, a friendship. A new world instantly opened, as if God placed us on this beach together to meet. As if we were heaven's soul mates meeting on earth for the first time.

I was taught to believe men such as him, handsome adventurers, were not good people. He proved that wrong.

We talked into the night about our lives, sharing our deepest secrets next to a fire on the beach.

Maria couldn't believe what she read. She'd already determined it was Mark her mother had met.

She read on.

Sometime before dawn, I fell asleep in his arms, warm, comfortable, and solemnly happy. We spent several days together and learned everything there was to know of each other.

But in the end, we agreed that perhaps we were too young to marry. I was not ready to terminate my commitment to become a nun.

His name was Mark. And what brought him to Pavones was the painting you have. Curiously enough, it made its way back to where it was painted. He said he searched for weeks in an effort to find this beach, and had almost given up when he stumbled upon it the day before I met him.

I told him I must go back to Golfito, that my time with him was terrific.

What neither he nor I realized was that we'd fallen in love. We were driven by our ambitions, agreeing to go separate ways.

To this day, I deeply regret that decision.

Mark gave me the painting of Pavones as a memory of our time together. After we departed, I realized that I had made the wrong choice. We were destined to marry.

The point of this letter is to tell you this secret. To let you know that you should pursue what you feel is in your heart, not what I or Sister Florence may have said to influence you.

You probably wonder how I ended up with who you believe is your father.

Maria, I am so sorry to tell you this, so late in your life.

Soon after Pavones, I found I was pregnant with you. With nowhere to turn, and no way to reach Mark, what I did know was that no one would approve if I married Mark, or if I had his illegitimate child.

Luke—he's not your father. I committed the ultimate sin, tricking Luke and Sister Florence. It was wrong of me to keep this secret from you all these years.

Maria's hands trembled as she read the final portion. Life, as she knew it, was now entirely different. In a blink, everything changed.

I have no idea where Mark is, or how his life turned out.

I often wonder. Many days of my life have been consumed thinking of him, and the opportunity I missed. I hope you don't make the mistake I made.
God Bless You,
Jane

Maria started to hyperventilate. Her heart raced. She looked at Father Peter, then turned. Sister Florence seemed smug, proud of her success, no doubt contemplating plans to fully activate the retreat next year.

An urgency came upon her. Her biological father, Mark, needed to know he had a daughter.

I have to get to Mark and show him the letter, right away!

Nothing can be more important. He's at Pavones, surfing the giant waves left by the storm. What if he gets hurt or, even worse, drowns before he receives the news?

Maria rose to her feet.

Sister Florence, dealing with a fidgeting Alex, failed to see Maria slide along the pew and step into the center aisle.

Suddenly, Father Peter glared at her.

Maria turned and panned the congregation, who were smiling, nodding their heads. Her eyes were full and ready to burst like a tropical downpour. She motioned her lips to say, "I'm sorry. I'm so sorry for disappointing all of you."

Alex had climbed under the pew.

Distracted, Flo grabbed Alex by the forearm and gave her a yank, hard enough to let Alex know it would hurt even more next time.

When Flo finally saw Maria standing, Maria was looking directly at her. As their eyes met, Maria ran and raced past Sister Florence, who reached and tried to snatch her arm. She burst through the heavy wooden doors of the church and raced down the terrace steps and across the village square.

For a brief moment, Father Peter stuttered, but regrouped and continued with the mass.

Uumph!

Flo jumped from the pew and waddled down the aisle, giving chase, rotating her wrists inwards and outwards, fists clenched.

By the time Sister Florence made it outside to the terrace, Maria was gone.

~ ~ ~

A strong onshore gust suddenly plucked the veil off Maria's head, whisked it skyward, pinning it in the prickly branches of a tall palm. Turning the corner where the street opened to the pier, Maria ran to the dock and to Carlos' boat.

The bay whipped into a frenzy, testing the moorings, slapping the barnacle-encrusted piers.

"Carlo, Carlos!" Maria yelled to get his attention.

The short Costa Rican busily worked the ropes that fought with his tossing boat within its slip. He heard Maria yell and turned to see her running toward him, her black and white clothing flapping in the gale.

"Oh, Carlos, take me to Pavones. I am desperate. I have urgent information to tell the American. He's my father!" Maria burst out crying.

"My God!" Carlos said. "You are dressed as a nun. Maria, the seas are rough. The gale, it is strong, and blows from the south. The headwind is too much. My engine is tired. It will not get you there," Carlos said sorrowfully.

She looked at him. His expression said it all. The wind blew steady and strong; nearby palms leaned and fought the wind.

Carlos thought of a way to help. Though he didn't like to travel the rough roads to Pavones and risk damage to his pickup, he understood a father's love for his daughter.

"I will drive you," Carlos said, securing a tether to its cleat.

"Thank you, thank you, Carlos!" Maria hugged him and ran to his pickup, parked near the pier. She unsnapped her headpiece and wedged it behind the seat.

Carlos threw his travel satchel in the back and turned the key to start the engine. He wasn't concerned about Alex, because he had arranged for another family to take her home after mass. Golfitons often looked out for each other. The jungle can be a harsh environment; an engine could break down, or a mudslide could close a road for several days. Ticos living in the Costa Rican jungle regularly adjusted their lives accordingly.

"Please don't drive by the church!" Maria begged.

"Maria, I must pass. It's the only way out of town." Carlos wondered what all the commotion was.

"Hide!" Carlos said.

The little Toyota raced along the side street, next to the church. Maria ducked under the dash. Music came from the stained glass windows as they raced by. Two blocks away, Sister Florence waddled up a side street, her arms swinging, pumping in an odd manner, heading toward the dormitory to find Maria.

Chapter 38

Carlos drove aggressively through the plantation, up the switchback and toward the ferry. He worried he'd get stuck.

With the urgency on Maria's face, he did his best to get her quickly to Pavones, so she could greet the American as her father for the first time.

After crossing with the ferry, the pickup weaved its way, did its best to avoid the lengthy mud ruts. At the crest of the hill, the expanse of the Pacific Ocean came into view. The road from the mountainside flattened before it ended at the beach.

Near the cantina, coconuts littered the ground. Thundering waves pounded the shoreline. Maria and Carlos looked in awe. The sea was in a fury. Whitecap swells extended well beyond the ocean-filled horizon.

"My God!" Carlos said, amazed. "*Es muy, muy grande!*"

Maria gasped.

Many surfers squatted on a seawall that barely protected the cantina. Their broken surfboards were heaped on the dry side. The thatch on the cantina roof flipped in the wind, the thunderous, crashing waves a short distance away.

Maria had only one thought. Get to Mark and tell him about her mother. Show him the letter. Give her father a hug for the first time.

Anxious to spend time with him, she knew her father could help solve the confusion in her head. Perhaps her mother would finally be happy, after she learned they had a child together.

She imagined what it would be like to see them meet. *Do they still love each other?*

She searched for Mark. He wasn't amongst the surfers. He wasn't sitting at the cantina bar, either. Maria peered toward the ocean. The waves were high—too high to surf, she thought.

The surfers took notice of her black and white outfit, but quickly turned their attention to the waves. They were searching for something.

"Surely he wouldn't be out there," she thought. "It is suicidal, physically impossible."

Maria considered briefly that Mark might have a death wish. What events in his life drove him to act in such an irrational manner, with no regard for his soul?

Carlos didn't follow her to the seawall. Instead, he went into the cantina kitchen to find the owners. They told him the waves were the largest in a generation—ten meters. The owners were concerned. The beach wash came dangerously close.

"Have you seen the American?" Carlos asked in his native tongue.

"Yes," the cantina owner replied. His nervous wife stood next to him. "He's in the waves. He has been out there for hours. Occasionally, they see him. The surfers want to climb onto my roof to watch him surf the large waves. I won't let them. I am afraid it will collapse."

The owner pointed to the cliff at the end of the beach. "On the cliff are surfers watching. They see the American and signal when he gets close."

Maria stood on the seawall, her outfit whipping in the wind.

"Hey!" a voice alerted. "He's coming."

Everyone stood to get a glimpse. They strained their eyes to find him.

"Cool," a voice called from the top of a coconut tree. "In the third wave, he just pulled that ender move—caught a glimpse of the hull when it launched into the air. Now I can't find him."

Two tanned men shimmied a nearby palm.

"Found him," the observer called.

Everyone turned to look at the perched surfers pointing at the crashing sea.

All Maria could see was the bedlam of the collapsing ocean.

The reports continued. "Here comes another set. Some really nice barrels have set up further out. He's surfing them for about one hundred fifty meters, then peeling off before they closeout. The guy's fuckin nuts."

Heads shook in disbelief.

Pacing the seawall, there was nothing Maria could do. "How long will it be before he comes in?"

Carlos grabbed Maria by the shoulder.

"Let's go down the beach. I'll sneak you onto the roof of the abandoned cabana. Maybe you can signal him from there."

Walking the dirt road that paralleled the shoreline, Carlos led Maria through the brush, along a sandy trail to the back of the cabana. He lifted a small ladder used to fix the thatch. After climbing to the peak, they lay along the roofline.

A heavy gale blew in from the ocean; towering, steamrolling waves rumbled. The salty froth from the pounding surf showered them.

"Look, in the middle of those waves." Carlos pointed.

Squinting, she saw Mark's paddle penciling along the bottom of a trough. As the wave broke, his boat flung into the air, landed, tossed, then zigzagged the wave face, outmaneuvering the deathly jaws that closed behind.

"Why is he doing this? No one else is," she said to Carlos.

It was hard for her to understand. She hoped he would stay safe, and felt she needed to scold him, as a daughter to a father who does risky things.

Mark spun from the enormous wave just as it began its final, crushing grind onto the cobblestones of Pavones. A massive rooster tail lifted high, like a giant hand, then slammed, making a thunderous swoosh, its remnants racing up the beach, breaching the seawall, washing across the road.

She watched Mark catch yet another wave.

"There must be a way to get his attention," she thought. Get him to stop and tell him about the dramatic juncture in their lives. That conversation needed to begin. But for now, it was a nightmare that failed to end.

"I must get down to the beach," Maria told Carlos. She started to climb from the roof. "I must get his attention."

A nail snagged and tore her linen skirt. Maria yanked until the fabric shredded and pulled free. Racing to the water's edge, she waved her arms frantically.

"He's got to come in sometime soon. That has to be exhausting."

Just then, Maria spotted Mark. Again, she frantically flapped her arms, signaling.

Coming closer, he didn't abandon the wave. The bright red surfyak completed a 360-degree pirouette. It disappeared into the funnel, riding inside the rolling pipeline; then blasted through, ahead of a burst of spray, pushing from behind.

Several surfers jogged over to watch Mark finish his ride.

Holding her shredded skirt to keep it from dragging in the gritty sand, Maria ran, stopping short of the beach wash.

He came closer. The swallowing white foam tossed Mark's surfyak upside down, then right side up.

Maria waded in and waited for the ocean to pull back so she could move forward some more.

Directly in front was the peacocking wave that sucked the stones. Maria saw his face, his concentration, the focus in his eyes as he prepared to deal with the exploding wave that concluded itself.

Frantically, she signaled. "Mark, Mark . . . Dad!"

The surfyak journeyed into the swallowing trough. The Ashland jammed the rip. Mark absorbed the energy and pivoted, allowing the energy to build. The surfers hurried to get a glimpse of the dramatic maneuver he was about to make to escape the massive wave moments before it crushed the beach.

As the kayak slingshot up the wave face directly in front of her, Maria waved her arms.

Mark, preparing for his exit, saw Maria and her expression.

Suddenly, he realized the festering memory that plagued him since they met. She was Jane's child, the woman he longed to love.

Their eyes locked, their souls joined. She saw the realization and love on her father's face, as if time halted long enough for them to say, "Hello."

Though fleeting, it was too late. Mark's concentration stalled long enough to prevent him from making the maneuver needed to escape the crushing collapse. When he looked from the wave top, he saw only rocks. There was no time to roll underneath to escape the fury.

The hull lifted behind him and sucked upwards into a vertical position. The bow arrowed and raced downward, impacting the abrupt, rocky upslope that formed the immense beach break. As the full force of the ocean came crashing, the Ashland snapped like a toothpick, splintering. Releasing his grip on the useless paddle, Mark leaned forward, changing his center of gravity. Fanning his fingers, he clutched the side of his kayak—the full weight of the ocean pursuing. Tons of water pressure hammered from more than thirty feet high—all at once.

There was nothing Mark could do.

The nose of the surfyak ruptured. The bow disintegrated. The gel coat broke away as the once ridged layers of fiberglass and Kevlar returned to their original fabric form. The seams that married the deck and the hull split. The dense Ethafoam support pillars broke free.

First to fracture were his ankles. Tightened tendons ripped from the bone. The tibia and fibula in both legs snapped cleanly.

Like a ramming piston, the heaviest and most forceful part of the collapse rushed over Mark's head. His senses shut down. He couldn't hear, and didn't feel the pain when the splintered shaft of the Ashland penetrated the thick meat of his right thigh, lodging against the femur and holding firm.

The maximum force of the wave was upon him. The weight of the water crushed his ribcage. His sternum separated where the cartilage held it together. As he tumbled in the froth, a broken rib punctured his lung, then retracted. The beach wash twisted his body sideways and rolled him along.

Mark's lucid head floated in the froth, miraculously untouched—an errant backwash acting as a pillow, setting his head gently in the draining sand.

A final flush deposited him at Maria's feet.

Instinctively, she grabbed hold of his body before he rolled back toward the ocean.

A second surge caught them both and washed them higher, onto the beach. Maria tumbled and scraped across the stones. She dug her feet and gripped the stones to keep from getting sucked into the ocean.

She held Mark's body the best she could, as the retreating wave tried one more time to slurp him back to the sea.

His body was jelly.

Chapter 39

"Nelson, get me a surfboard," yelled the first surfer arriving to help Mark.

"Go to my hut and get the triage bag next to my cot," ordered a shirtless young man with a thick black mustache, who happened to be an emergency medical technician.

Carlos came running to a dazed Maria.

She sat there, shocked and bleeding from her kneecaps.

"Take that dress off of her," someone ordered. "Start shredding it into strips to make cravats for splints."

Carlos wanted to object but the surfer said those rags weren't going to do her any good, they must come off anyway.

They stripped Maria to her undergarments.

Carlos left to get his satchel with a towel inside to cover her.

"The girl, she's going into shock. Someone pay attention to her," the in-charge EMT barked.

Maria stared at Mark's lifeless body. Two men had already reduced her garments to strips of cloth.

Carlos came with the pickup and drove it close to the beach. He dried her off and tried to move her, but Maria was reluctant to leave.

The men tending to Mark worked methodically, each with a task, taking directions from the EMT.

The impaled shaft that protruded from Mark's thigh was immobilized. A surfboard, turned into a backboard, lay alongside him. The strips of cloth from Maria's black skirt were set underneath and readied.

"Okay, on the count of three—one, two, three, lift." The surfboard slid underneath. They strapped him down to immobilize his body.

Though unconscious, Mark was breathing.

"Put the nun in the back of Tico's truck," a firm, confident voice commanded. The EMT didn't know Carlos' name, saying the first thing that came to mind.

"Let's go."

A procession of fit men slid Mark's limp body, lashed atop the makeshift backboard, into the bed of Carlo's pickup.

"He has a flailed chest—sandbag, hurry," a voice yelled.

Immediately, a bystander ran to a portion of the beach where there was wet sand. Filling a sock, he packed it full.

"He has a punctured lung. Rotate the backboard on a forty-five-degree angle, so the blood will drain to one side of the chest cavity. Hand me two more cravats." The in-charge held out his hand.

"Place the bag of sand over the sternum. Wait! Hold off, too much sand—take some out!" A quarter of the sand poured from the bag.

"Enough."

The EMT snatched the stuffed sock, placed it over Mark's sternum, and fastened it with the cravats while four men held Mark in position.

Someone arrived with the triage bag and tossed it into the back of the truck.

"Keep the board rotated at a forty-five-degree angle, guys. Stuff whatever you can under the board so his body doesn't lay flat. He has internal injuries. If we have a fighting chance to save him, we must let the blood pool to one side."

Crouching in the corner of the truck bed, Maria ran her fingers through Mark's hair.

A small crowd had gathered. Someone put the broken half of Mark's paddle beside him.

Maria saw the inscription burnt into the blade. It simply read, *Tombstone.* She flipped the blade to hide the inscription.

"Ticoman, drive, *vamos.* But take it easy, *muchacho.*"

Carlos let off the clutch and drove cautiously toward Golfito.

~ ~ ~

It took three hours to travel the rough road to the small hospital on the south side of Golfito. A female doctor met the team of men. Immediately, she recognized Mark and shook her head, saying, "Sooner or later this was bound to happen."

Maria saw the doctor was upset and wondered how intimate the relationship with her father was.

During the ride, she discovered that sprinkled amongst the surfers were professionals. Some were in the medical field, others, engineers. They came from all over the world to surf the south swell at Pavones. They respected her father, revealing what they knew. That he was an adventure, an innovator who had no real job.

They said he was barely alive.

~ ~ ~

Several hours passed. Napping on a hallway bench, Maria awoke to the voice of the doctor outside Mark's hospital room. Carlos had gone to the dormitory to get Maria clothes.

Mark lay quietly in a hospital bed. He was on a respirator.

Heartbroken, Maria tried to summon the inner strength she deployed from years of dealing with the sick and bereaved. She went inside the room and found a chair next to his bed and nearest the doorway.

The woman doctor came into the room.

"Hello, I'm Gail," the doctor introduced herself. "Carlos filled me in on you. You're the young girl everyone in town talks about. The one who opened the Fatima retreat."

The doctor went to Mark and looked at him affectionately. She checked his bandages and repositioned the respirator tubing. Gail yawned. She'd been in surgery with him for many hours.

Maria noticed Gail's fondness.

"He is my father," Maria said.

The doctor heard her but didn't turn to look. A clicking noise, the mechanical sound of the air rushing through the respirator tube, filled the silence in the room.

After a pause, the doctor spoke. "His condition is critical. Personally, I don't think he will survive. If you have special favors to collect from God, now is the time to use them—all of them.

"Your surfing friends on the beach are responsible for getting him here alive. If he is really your father, you have them to thank."

Resting her head against the wall, Gail yawned again.

"Doctor, how did you come to know Mark? And what's an American doctor doing in such a remote place?" Maria sensed the doctor's attachment. Her second question surprised Gail.

Gail answered the second question. "Many of us Americans who reside in Costa Rica came here on our search for youthful adventure. Costa Rica is beautiful. If you love nature, this is the place to be.

"When you have turmoil in your life, you think of an escape. You want to run away. Those who actually do, end up in remote places like Golfito. I'm here because I want to practice medicine the traditional way—in a small-town setting with honest people who love and appreciate you."

Gail examined Mark.

"I know very little of Mark. The only thing we had in common was that we took care of Alex for Carlos. He is handsome. His body is a hell of a specimen for his age. We hooked up from time to time, but never dated seriously. Though it would have been nice."

Gail sighed, affectionately stroking the soft hair on his forearm.

"What I do know is that there's an emptiness within Mark. Something happened back in the States that brought him here. He tries to fill that void with adventurous exploits. I was never able to get inside his head to discover his secret. There's a past out there, a pain that keeps him distant," the doctor said. "That's all I know.

"Are there next of kin you know of?" The doctor mulled over how long it would be before he died.

"I'm not sure. I just found out today he might be my father," Maria said.

Twisting her head, Gail looked at Maria then back at Mark. "There's a resemblance. You have the same high cheekbones, and the nose, for sure. If you locate his family, let me know ASAP."

Tired, the doctor departed.

Maria sat there watching Mark. She thought of the doctor's comments. If he had family, someone should notify them. Maria was an only child, and always imagined what it would be like to have brothers or sisters.

"This man has a past," she thought. "He has a mother who would be my grandmother."

The more Maria thought, the more she realized people related to her had no idea she existed. Finding them would go a long way to understanding who she was, answering her many burning questions.

"It's funny how God works in such mysterious ways," she thought. If she had decided early on not to be a nun, she may have never known this secret.

Maria prayed. She asked God to spare Mark's life so she could selfishly reunite with him; so he would know he had a daughter who wanted to love him.

Before her was a man she knew nothing about, except for the one night they spent together, unknowingly as father and daughter. For that, she was thankful.

A soft, little hand came to rest on top of hers. She turned to see Alex smiling at her. Her innocent expression disappeared when she saw Mark.

Alex climbed into Maria's lap, curled into a ball, and started sucking her thumb.

Standing nearby, Carlos blessed himself and prayed. It'd been a long day.

Chapter 40

The double doors to the hospital ward swung open. Sister Florence, unable to fit through one door, boldly entered and confidently passed the nurse's station, where Gail was busily making notes. Florence moved with such assertiveness, the nurse assumed she had business on the floor.

Flo spent the entire day looking for Maria, finally tracking her down at the hospital.

"Carlos, Maria," Flo said, taking a deep breath. "I think there's an explanation owed."

Each had an anxious look; neither expected to see her here.

"I want an explanation," Flo demanded, setting her hands on her bulky hips.

Overwhelmed, surprised by her intrusion, neither Maria nor Carlos knew what to say.

A foul, sweaty odor followed Flo as she moved further into the hospital room. As her eyes came upon Mark's lifeless body, she became ridged, tense. There was silence as several minutes passed, as if she forgot why she came to the hospital.

Flo couldn't believe Mark had suddenly arrived back into her life to haunt her like this.

Regaining her composure, Flo threw a furious look at Carlos, then Maria.

"He is my father," sad-eyed Maria said.

The words shot through Flo like a spear. Sister snapped back angrily, "I'll hear none of this, Maria. You are going home with me in the morning."

Both women turned to Carlos for assistance.

"Carlos! Go pack Maria's things and bring them to the rectory. She'll stay with me and Father Peter tonight," Flo ordered. Suddenly, without explanation, she left the hospital room.

Outside, the doctor could be heard arguing with Sister Florence.

Carlos looked at Maria with a sorrowful sigh. He had to follow Sister Florence's orders.

Coaxing Alex from Maria's lap, Carlos left.

Flo burst back into the room. "If you don't come with me, Maria, I will terminate Carlos' employment. He and Alex will be living on his boat by sunrise. I provide him with a home and plenty of food. He lives comfortably. You don't want to take that away, do you?"

"No, Sister," Maria said.

She glanced over at Mark, wishing for his advice. She didn't know what to do.

"He isn't your father," Flo said assertively. "The church has records. We will clear up this mess when we talk to your mother."

Flo had no clue what her mother might say. She was trying to assemble the thoughts that would break Maria from this man.

"I told the doctor there was no verification you were next of kin, and that the church funds this primitive hospital handsomely. I'll see to it that their funding is pulled if the doctor permits you information, or access to decisions involving this man's medical condition."

That angered Maria. She found Gail to be sympathetic, caring—genuine. Her father would be dead had the doctor not been here to patch him up.

Grabbing Maria by the wrist, Flo commenced to drag her from the room. She had such a strong grip, Maria couldn't break free.

"Come with me now, or Carlos and Alex will be evicted. If I leave the hospital without you, I'll put them both on the street."

Torn, Maria stopped resisting. But before she left, she stretched over and kissed her father on the forehead.

Flo didn't release her death grip until they left the hospital.

Maria couldn't get it out of her mind how incredibly cruel Flo was. She didn't want to go to the rectory and listen to hours of criticism. For sure, Father Peter would scold her for disrupting his mass, laying a line of guilt, saying, "She's not good enough the join the convent."

Maria's arm hurt. But the sudden separation from her father hurt even more. The only thing stopping her from running to Mark's bedside was the eviction of Carlos and Alex, and the financial threat to the hospital.

As she got into Flo's Cadillac, Maria had an idea. "Mark has a home. Why can't Carlos stay there? I will offer him Mark's home.

"I'm not going!" Maria said, working the nerve, looking Flo stubbornly in the face. "I am not going, and you can't do anything about it."

Struggling, Flo waddled around the car. She raised her hand as a warning, preparing to slap Maria.

"How dare you defy me?" Flo said angrily. "How dare you, after all I have done for you."

Reaching, she grasped Maria's forearm before she could pull away. Her left hand reeled and swung, striking Maria squarely on the face.

A stinging white flash blinded her—another slap, and another blinding flash. The last blow tore the soft skin on Maria's right cheek. It began to bleed.

Twisting her arm, Maria broke free from her grip.

Flo tried to grab her so she could shove her into the car.

Maria became enraged as venomous hate filled her. Years of psychological and emotional control exploded within. She turned and ran into the date palm orchard as fast as she could, hiding amongst the ancient palms.

When it got dark, Maria snuck from the orchard. She made her way along the unpaved backstreets and narrow alleys and arrived at Mark's home. She didn't think Flo knew where he lived and believed she was safe there.

~ ~ ~

It had been an exhausting day. Tired, Flo headed to the rectory to discuss how to handle Maria with Father Peter.

Regretting striking Maria, she wished her frustration had not gotten the best of her. She wished it wasn't too late to correct her lapse in judgment.

After talking to Peter, they determined that Maria might flee the country, perhaps head to her mother, telling her the news of Mark. The only way back to San Jose was by bus or plane. They agreed that Father Peter would stake out the bus depot and Flo would see to it no plane flew with Maria on it.

The idea to evict Carlos was delayed. It might make matters worse—possibly to a point where Flo may never get Maria back under her control.

Deep in thought, Flo laid in her uncomfortable cot. Had she pushed Maria too hard? Was Maria's life in such disarray that she was capable of drastic measures?

"I'll evict Carlos when Maria's left Golfito," she grumbled. "Everything's turned inside out. Maria is now defiant, vulnerable, and unpredictable. This time next year, I'll personally see to it Pavones is solely owned by me," she said bitterly. "No one, not even those lawyer surfers, will be permitted to walk on it again, as punishment for ruining my mission in life."

As night came upon the quaint tropical town of Golfito, Flo agonized about how she was going to get Maria back under her control.

Chapter 41

Mark's residence was dark. It seemed abandoned. Entering, Maria didn't turn on the lights. Instead, she hid until she thought it was safe to move about. Peeking outside, she noticed Sister Florence's Cadillac pass several times.

Maria rummaged through Mark's belongings and personal files, searching for information on his relatives. With the house still dark, she searched on his computer, then online, looking for threads that could trace Mark to a previous life.

The Google search page illuminated the screen. Maria looked in Mark's favorites menu and found no indication of family. She scrolled the mouse to the dropdown menu. Every airline in the world was on it.

"Interesting," she thought. "He must travel a lot."

The spelling of Mark's last name was unique enough to consider dropping it into the search engine. "Perhaps his family members have some sort of Internet presence."

She typed his name, "Mark Weston."

There were too many hits.

She clicked the images icon and scrolled through the photos.

One such image caught her attention. A blond man with a beer belly stood holding a wooden kayak paddle. Next to him was a short balding man. Behind them was an old stone building and signpost with Mark's name on it.

"He owns some sort of business in that building," she thought.

Maria clicked on the photo, enlarging it to read the business name. Mark Weston, Tax Preparation, 10-5 Main St., White Haven, PA.

"No way, this couldn't be him," Maria thought. She couldn't picture her father as an accountant. He was too adventurous.

She quickly disregarded the notion and went to the satellite phone to see if she could reach Chris.

There was no response.

Maria wandered the comfortable home, looking at its decor. On his desk was a small framed picture she hadn't seen before. It wasn't there last night. Mark must have taken it out of a drawer and been looking at it.

It was a picture of a young girl standing with a big smile on Pavones beach, the perfect waves in the background.

"Perhaps it's a relative," she thought.

To get a closer look, she lifted the small photo preserved in a gold frame.

"This looks like Mom!" she said loudly in the empty house. "Holy shit—it is! It's a duplicate of the photo on Mom's desk at home."

Maria suddenly filled with hope, and a determination to locate her father's family members.

Returning to the computer, she looked at the image again.

"White Haven—Chris mentioned that town to me on the plane. There might be a link."

The mouse rolled to span the name White Haven. Maria pasted the name into a new search box and clicked enter.

Several references appeared, many related to bed and breakfast inns. She clicked the images icon to see if pictures of the town revealed information. There were several historical photos of trains in what looked to be a quaint, little town. The last photo had a raft blasting through whitewater.

"Yes, whitewater rafting—got to be Mark," she said.

Maria drilled through the photo and found a website for a rafting company called Ted's Outdoor Center. Continuing to search Mark's name, she found a newspaper caption, "Three children suffocated. Father found . . ."

"Huh?" There were no more words. Mark's name was not mentioned. She quickly clicked on the link to take her to the article. But the article wouldn't load. She tried several more times to no avail.

"That's spooky," she said. Maria pondered the implications of the caption. "Someone in town must know of him."

Desperate to find someone who knew her father, she considered traveling to White Haven but struggled with the guilt of abandoning him while he lay in a hospital bed clinging to life.

"Should I leave Golfito on the off chance I can find someone in White Haven?" she considered. "If I go to the hospital in the morning, Flo and probably Father Peter will be there. Who knows what powers they wield in this country?"

Maria considered the scenarios that could put her under the control of Sister Florence and Father Peter.

"I must leave Golfito and find someone who can help me. If I spend a day in White Haven asking questions about Dad, I may get answers, perhaps finding someone who can certify that I am his daughter. The round-trip will take three days."

Using an American Express card found in Mark's desk, Maria booked a round-trip flight from San Jose leaving in the early morning.

"Sneaking out of Golfito on the 8:10 a.m. flight without being detected by Sister Florence could be a problem," she thought.

~ ~ ~

By morning, the persistent onshore wind had finally subsided. The thick humidity returned. The Ticos worked busily clearing debris left by the storm.

Arriving at the rectory in his pickup, Carlos leapt out, ran along the overgrown walkway, and knocked furiously on the rectory door. A maid answered, and he asked if Father Peter was there. The maid left to summon the priest.

Carlos told Father, Maria was at the hospital. He said to tell Sister Florence that she had agreed to leave with them.

After thanking Carlos, Father Peter went inside to notify Flo.

Immediately after leaving the rectory, Carlos sped to the dormitory and packed Maria's belongings, including the monkey. But the painting of Pavones was gone. He looked behind the dresser to see if it had fallen. It wasn't there.

Returning to the bungalow housing provided by the church, Carlos packed his and Alex's possessions and left to move into Mark's home.

Sister Florence arrived at the hospital twenty minutes after Carlos left the rectory.

"Maria must have reconsidered," thought Flo. "That slap on the face must have knocked some sense into her. Now I must get her out of Golfito."

Sister Florence climbed the short stairs that lifted the hospital off the jungle floor. Clenching her fists, she pointed her thumbs outwards, laboring to lift her frame the final two steps.

Shoving the double doors, she went to Mark's room, expecting to see Maria sitting at his bedside.

But when she entered, Maria wasn't there.

"Perhaps she went to the restroom," Flo thought, while staring at Mark's barely alive body.

With each click of the respirator, Mark's chest mechanically rose then fell. Flo stood there watching, waiting for Maria. Hoping Mark would die.

Several more minutes passed. "Maria's not here," Flo finally realized.

Overhead, the straining sound of the twin-prop engines of the 8:10 a.m. flight as it climbed over the jungle canopy, passed.

"She's on that plane!"

Duped, Sister Florence leaned over Mark's body, looked him angrily in the face, and said, "Never, never, again!"

The heavyset nun, after switching off the alarm on the respirator, reached under the unit and removed the wall plug.

Mark's chest stopped moving. His face turned blue, cyanotic.

Flo quickly exited the hospital.

~ ~ ~

When Chris arrived in Pavones and learned of Mark's injury, he immediately headed for Golfito. Arriving at the hospital, Chris noticed a Cadillac blocking the front entry.

"That shouldn't be parked there," he said.

Anxious to see how Mark was doing, he jumped from his van loaded with kayaks and started up the steps. The double doors burst open. A heavyset nun hurried his way.

Briefly, neither knew whether to go left or right.

Phew, she smells awful.

Chris stepped aside to let her pass, then raced up the hall, poking his head into three rooms before finding Mark's.

"Holy shit!"

Chris saw Mark gagging. His face was purple, his throat chocking on the respirator tube, arms flailing.

Quickly, he yanked out the tube, opened Mark's airway, and inflated his lungs, giving mouth-to-mouth until his color came back.

"Help, someone help!"

Doctor Gail, who had just come to the unit, heard Chris' cry for assistance. She raced to the room.

After working on Mark for several minutes, she finally stabilized him.

"He was breathing on his own," she said. "It's incredible that he doesn't need the respirator. I think he'll live." She looked over the machine, frowning. "Looks like it somehow got unplugged accidentally."

That afternoon, Mark's condition improved enough for them to move him by ambulance to a bigger hospital a hundred miles away in the town of San Isidro.

Late that evening, Sister Florence returned to the hospital. Walking along the hallway, she passed Mark's room and, without slowing, took a quick glance inside. The bed was stripped, its equipment removed.

Florence smiled and exited through the back door.

Chapter 42

Bang! Bang! A loud hammering sound disturbed Maria's sleep. As she lay reclined in her rental car, a cold chill came upon her.

She collected her thoughts. Yesterday's flights went well, but she had difficulty negotiating the winding, nighttime country roads leading to this quiet river town.

Her eyes were bloodshot. She had a slight headache.

"This town seems as remote as Pavones," Maria thought, peering through the windshield and pea-soup fog, trying to identify where she was.

She wasn't ready and went back to sleep.

An hour passed.

Screeeech. The sound metal makes when dragged across a concrete floor woke Maria. Flipping the car seat lever, she launched herself upright. The fog had partially lifted, and the lower half of the surrounding buildings was visible. Directly in front was an old, two-story, stone building. Behind her, where the noise came, was a foundry.

Across the street, a lit sign read "Family Diner."

"Civilization! Coffee!" she said. "I need a pick-me-up."

She opened the car door and rotated her knees. Goosebumps jumped to her legs as the damp air came across them. Stretching her arms, then her legs, Maria loosened her muscles.

"My blood must have thinned," she thought; her body was not ready for the change in latitude.

She looked around. A signpost built from creosote railroad ties stood at the corner of the stone building. On top it read "Lehigh Depot, 10 Main St."

"What luck! It's the street address I am looking for."

Her curiosity heightened, she opted not to get coffee, but to search for clues.

"This is the place," she said in a hoarse voice, approaching the stone building.

She peered into a large plate-glass window. Inside was a cluttered office with random stacks of papers and files strewn about.

"Looks disorganized. What a mess."

Her eyes fell upon a life-size skeleton hanging next to a messy, wooden bookcase made from rough-cut pine.

"Gross! Must be a country doctor's office."

But Maria's eyes didn't stay fixed on the skeleton. Leaning next to it was a kayak paddle.

"An Ashland. Someone must know Mark."

Stepping away, she read the signpost again. "Danny Dougherty, Chiropractor."

"Someone's gotta know Dad, perhaps across the street at the diner."

The fog continued to lift. Rooftops were now visible. A maroon pickup with a gun rack in the cab's rear window traveled along Main Street and parked to the side of the art deco diner where an active railroad track ran behind.

Maria wondered how a train could pass without ever hitting the diner.

She entered the diner, where the strong smell of cigarette smoke hung in the air. There was the clink of porcelain coffee cups. A busy waitress burst through a swinging door with an armload of breakfast plates. Snatching a coffee pot, she raced around the Formica counter, toward a booth, setting the entire meal in front of an older couple.

The cashier outed her cigarette when she saw Maria.

"Can I help you, deary?" she asked, exhaling a smoky cloud.

"Coffee, please," Maria asked.

The woman walked from behind the register and over to the counter, where several freshly brewed pots sat.

"Here, or to go?" the cashier asked.

"Uh, oh . . . for here," Maria responded, not knowing where to go or what to do next.

In the background, someone's continuous cough turned into a wheeze, then a hacking. It went unnoticed by everyone except for Maria.

The older couple, eating breakfast, lifted their heads to scrutinize the young, thin stranger.

As Maria sat at the counter, the cashier poured her a steaming cup. Next to her, a bearded, heavyset man quietly slid over a stainless steel milk dispenser.

"Milk, deary?"

"Yes, thank you," Maria said politely.

"Breakfast?"

The wrinkled woman who poured the coffee pulled a menu from its holder and set it in front.

"Yes, thank you," Maria said again.

Maria wrapped her hands around the warm cup. "How many times my father must've frequented this place," she mused.

The hacking sound at the far end of the diner continued. This time it lasted several minutes.

"Emphysema, a smoker's cough, I feel sorry for that person," Maria thought.

She turned to find where the coughing came from. A heavyset woman sat in a booth, alone, facing her. Their eyes met briefly.

Darting her glance away from the woman, Maria swiveled her stool to address the cashier.

"Ma'am, can you help me? I am looking for information about someone across the street."

The cashier nervously lit another cigarette. A thick trail of smoke coiled off, blending with the haze that floated above their heads. The couple eating breakfast paused to overhear. The burly man cocked his head so he wouldn't miss the pronunciation. The waitress delayed her retreat into the kitchen so she could listen.

"What is the name, deary?" the cashier asked before lipping her cigarette.

"Mark Weston."

The woman's expression turned to stone. The restaurant's chatter instantly ceased. The couple eating breakfast looked at each other, aghast. The waitress turned pale. The burly man sat straight, stunned to hear the controversial name. But the lady in the back booth continued her cough.

The first words she spoke in this quiet town had struck terror with the ordinary people who inhabited it. Maria waited for an answer.

Relaxing her expression ever so slightly, the cashier affixed her eyes toward the coughing woman, and then back to Maria.

"You best talk to Gerti." The cashier motioned with her eyes toward the wheezing.

Although she didn't hear what was said, the coughing woman caught on that something happened. She saw Maria and the cashier looking at her. Her bold German eyes grew cold.

Carrying her coffee, Maria walked the aisle to the booth where Gerti sat. All eyes followed, their faces clearly confirming the cashier provided the correct answer by directing her to Gertrude.

Gerti's glare stalked the girl to where she stood. Maria looked familiar. She sensed it had something to do with the whitewater boys she was fond of. The boys were always in trouble with women near and far—and here came another story.

"The kind lady at the register told me to talk to you about someone I know," Maria said, a bit nervous. "Can I sit?"

"You can." Gerti curtly opened her hand and pointed to the seat across from her. "Who is it you want?" Each of her words gurgled.

Maria hesitated to say Mark's name again.

"M-m-mark Weston," Maria blurted, expecting a reaction.

Though Gerti's stomach tumbled, she didn't flinch when she heard Mark's name. Overreacting would have sent her into an uncontrollable coughing spell, and it would take her several minutes to regain her composure—entirely too long for her to wait. She wanted to know what brought this girl here, and where Mark, a man she loved like a son, had disappeared to.

"Who's he to you?" Protective, Gerti directed her words to get to the point.

"He's my father."

Maria studied Gerti's full face, waiting for a response.

Curiously staring, Gerti studied Maria's physical features, looking for similarities.

The waitress conveniently came to refill Maria's coffee and to deliver Gerti's breakfast, with the hope of overhearing and reporting to the other people in the diner. She set breakfast on the table—two sunny-side eggs with a double side of bacon on a separate plate. Then she slowly filled Maria's coffee, stalling.

Gerti's stern eyes confronted the snooping waitress with a displeased glare that said, "I know what you are doing. Now scram!"

Tossing a snub, the waitress left.

"Yes, I see him in you," Gerti said.

"You know my father then?" Maria asked, anxiously.

"Yes, very well, nice man. I worked for him."

Gerti's hands trembled. For her to call up his memory, and the fun she had working with him, was a struggle. Her rich German temperament wanted to vent. It took all she had to force out her simple sentences without exploding into a tirade about the raw deal Mark got.

"Why the shock when I mention his name?" Maria asked.

"I'm not going to answer that—shouldn't. Not my place." Unable to bring it upon herself to reveal Mark's life story, Gerti directed her to his good friend Danny Dougherty. He should tell her.

Gerti began to cough. It was several minutes before she caught her breath again.

"Err-hmm." She cleared the phlegm.

"You must talk to the chiropractor across the street. He'll tell you the story." Gerti broke the yoke of her eggs with the pointed edge of the dry toast.

Maria contemplated pushing the issue but decided not to. There was too much of a negative reaction to probe deeper. She had an answer that put her in the right spot, and she hoped to know soon the mystery that surrounded her father.

The clouds outside had parted and grown puffy. Sipping her coffee, she peered out the large plate-glass window. A school bus bounced over the railroad tracks, past the foundry, and onto a bridge that crossed the Lehigh River. The sun broke through, shined into the window, and thickened the heavy haze of smoke.

Gerti reached and drew the verticals.

"Doc usually comes in about 10 a.m., if he's on time—which is never," Gerti said with some cynicism. "He has patients today. Wait in his office. He'll be late."

Gerti dunked her teabag.

"Who exactly is Danny Dougherty?" Maria asked.

Gerti snickered, laughed, and then coughed several times.

"He's Mark's closest friend, and before he will reveal any information, he will try to provoke you. It's his way of testing you, measuring your character. Show him you are tough, and he'll be kind.

"This is a small, odd town. No one will talk to you about someone's business unless you approach the right person. Unfortunately for you, sweetie, Danny is that person."

She smiled, relishing the fact that, even though Danny would act in his usually provocative manner, Maria's presence would shock the shit out of him. It pleased her to learn about Maria before Danny did.

" 'Odd' is right," Maria thought. She learned in Dr. Jones' cultural geography class that remote towns in the Wild West had evolved this way, where a stranger needed to talk to the right person to get information. She didn't think such a culture existed today.

The curious waitress came to the booth to clear Gerti's plate and to ask Maria if she wanted breakfast. Maria ordered an egg and cheese sandwich to go.

The robust lady and the young girl talked a bit more. Maria probed for more information, but Gertrude was too smart, directing her questions to Danny for answers about her father.

Gerti's mood soon changed. Her demeanor became sympathetic, friendly, and warm. Maria could tell the lonely woman missed her father. There must have been an understanding and a strong working relationship between them. She appreciated the pleasant modification in Gertrude's disposition.

The egg sandwich waited for Maria at the cash register—the cashier refusing to take her money.

"It's on me, deary."

Chapter 43

Danny Dougherty's office was cool, and as raw as a dripping mine tunnel. In the far corner, a woodstove sat dangerously close to a pile of newspapers. The chilled stove had set a reverse draft that drew into the cavernous waiting room a sour odor of creosote. Hands on a plastic barroom clock mounted to a hemlock support pillar pointed an entirely different time.

Patients waited in a sitting area that seemed a bit cleaner. A couch paired with wicker chairs gathered around a glass-top coffee table stacked with gun and fishing magazines.

Maria decided to sit in the lone chair farthest away, by the woodstove. She ate the greasy, cheesy, oversized egg sandwich.

Sleigh bells attached to a wooden door jingled with each new arrival. As the room filled, patients made room for each other. The waiting room remained quiet—their flat expressions never changing.

An hour passed.

"How odd," Maria thought. "The doctor is late and no one gets upset."

At five minutes to eleven, a pickup with an oversized camper turned the corner at the signpost, the truck almost rolling over from the top-heavy camper.

The patients in the nearly full room smiled and adjusted themselves in their seats.

"This must be the doctor," Maria surmised, noticing everyone's expression brighten.

Moments later, the bells chattered. The entryway door swung open and slammed the wall. A short, balding man in heavy leather hiking boots hurriedly walked in. Halfway up his muscular biceps, the sleeves of his red flannel shirt were scissored off. If it wasn't for his outdoor attire, a leprechaun could easily be confused as his twin brother.

Refusing to acknowledge the patients, the chiropractor unlocked his office and disappeared. Moments later, the sliding door to his adjusting room opened.

"Clara," he called.

A patient sitting on the wicker couch stood and happily went inside. Minutes later, Clara reappeared, smiling, laughing, thanking the doctor, slipping him cash.

This process repeated itself many times, lasting about forty minutes, until all the patients were gone.

Maria observed the doctor talked to each patient personably. He asked about their spouses, their pets, and discussed their politics. Each was pleased to engage in a conversation with the doctor. No one scolded him for being late.

After telling a dirty joke to his last patient, the doctor bid her good day then turned to Maria.

"Next," he said, greeting Maria with a warm smile, rubbing his hands, keeping them warm. "I don't know you," he said, looking at her oddly. "Get on the table."

Danny pointed to his adjusting table in a weakly lit room.

"I'm not here as a patient," Maria said, politely.

"Okay, fine. Now get on the table."

Walking into his room and around to the back of the adjusting table, Danny changed the paper on the headrest.

Maria crossed the floor and stopped at the corner of the sliding door. "But I'm not here to get adjusted," she repeated.

"Fine, but how am I going to know who you are without adjusting you first?"

This doctor wasn't going to take no for an answer, she realized. She went into the room and laid facedown on his low table.

Danny came around to her side and felt along her spine for several minutes. His hands were warm.

"Man, you're a mess," he said, probing her tense back muscles.

Maria jumped each time he pressed.

He walked to the base of the table, gripped her ankles, and paired her heels, lifting her feet to where her knees bent ninety degrees. Setting her feet down, he began his adjustment.

Crunch—the tension and dull pain she had since boarding the plane in Costa Rica instantly disappeared. He worked her spine, applying pressure; then a sudden jolt—another crunch. Asking her to roll over, the chiropractor cradled her head and applied traction, then manipulated until all the vertebrae were in line. He cocked Maria's head with a sharp twist, snapping her neck. Maria heard all sorts of popping and crackling sounds. He repeated the process, this time in the opposite direction— *crunch*.

"Lay there a few minutes while I get a new patient folder. Let my work finish." Danny got off his stool and walked into his messy office.

Maria felt much better. Her headache was gone, and her sinuses cleared. The creosote smell stopped annoying her. Less tense, she lay there, listening to the doctor rummage through the debris in his office.

"I didn't think Mark had any more children," Danny said, suddenly.

Maria flinched; the tension returned.

From his office, the chiropractor paused and watched her tense up.

"Yep, I was right!" he said, grinning, proud of his assessment and the fact he shocked her.

"How'd ya know that?" Maria demanded—the taint in her New England accent surfacing.

"I am a good chiropractor," he said. "Often, family members, and sometimes relatives, have mirroring ailments. Their muscles sometimes knot the same way. Spines are as unique as thumbprints. What's really cool is, if I mapped the adjustments of family members, they'd be nearly identical. I adjusted you just as I adjusted Mark many, many times.

"Plus, Mark had this incredibly straight spine. It's part of the reason why he kicked my ass all the time when we competed on the river. Your spine is identical. Your hips, though, aren't his, or his wife's."

"Wife?" Maria considered the chiropractor's words.

Danny walked into the adjusting room. Asking her to lie down, he set his hands firmly around her pelvis. He checked her again, reaffirming his observation.

"I adjusted your father often. In fact, he used to get the same sinus headaches. It can be only one person—Mark."

Danny went back to his desk and sat in an antique teacher's chair. The skeleton Maria saw earlier hung behind him.

Reaching into a stack of files, he pulled Mark's chart. Then he pulled a second chart, studied it, and swiveled around. He studied Maria more closely.

Though a thousand questions went through her head, she didn't want to jeopardize the limited flow of information that was coming.

"You're not the daughter of his wife," Danny reasserted.

Leaning back, he set his feet on a stack of files.

"I didn't know he was married." Maria entered his office.

"This is entirely bizarre. I show up in this town looking for answers about my father and end up with many more questions."

Next to the suspended skeleton was Danny's Ashland. Gripping the kayak paddle, Maria lifted it from its spot and walked from the office, spinning the shaft.

Danny glared at her like a sportsman whose wife just took his hunting rifle.

"Dad's paddle was a left-hand control paddle. Yours is right-hand control," she said, growing a bit frustrated, weary of his stultified manner. He was her father's best friend and seemed to withhold something.

Danny sat straight. Maria had gotten his attention.

"How come your Ashland has no inscription on the blade?" Maria said, again demonstrating she knew a bit more about his sport.

The swivel from the chair squeaked loudly. Danny pulled a long bamboo tube from behind his desk. From the drawer, he produced an eight-inch dart and inserted it into the tube. Lifting the blowgun to his mouth, he pointed it at Maria.

Pssst. A sound came from the tube, launching the dart. It whizzed past at eye level, striking the poster pinned to the post in the middle of the waiting room. Her eyes chased the dart and caught up with it as it embedded into a picture of Hillary Clinton. Several other darts already decorated the political poster.

"This guy is all about shock value," she thought. "Like a dog whose bark is worse than his bite. I'll play his game, if he'll tell me about my father."

Danny measured Maria's reactions. He was testing her—he tested everyone. If she didn't overreact to his tasteless humor, he could respect her and tell her everything. If she reacted with a volley of insults, he would lie about her father, knowing she couldn't handle the truth.

"You don't intimidate me," Maria said. She thumped the paddle blade against the pine floor.

Leaving his chair, Danny came into the waiting room and snatched his Ashland. He smiled as if his long-lost love had returned into his arms.

Maria had seen the same expression on her father's and Chris' face each time they cradled their Ashlands.

"Have a seat. I'll tell you something about your father.

"Your father owns what is known as a Tombstone stick. Keith Ashland didn't start naming his paddles until your father plucked him off Tombstone Rock on the Upper Youghiogheny River. It's rumored Keith had some sort of out-of-body experience that day, and the few paddles he now carves are considered to be very special.

"A Tombstone Ashland harnesses much more energy. And there's something else that's unique. Tombstones have holograms embedded in each of the blades. It's now the rage.

"I'm still waiting for a stick I ordered from Keith years ago. They're cool and I want one." He sounded discouraged, and she detected a note of jealousy in his voice.

The Ashland suddenly flew through the air, across the room toward Maria. Reacting, she caught it—another test by Danny to determine her toughness.

Maria threw him a conceited smile that said, "I am on to your little game."

Reaching for his portable phone, he went to the couch where his patients once sat. As he propped his hiking boots on the coffee table, several magazines slid onto the dusty plank flooring.

The conversation with Maria continued. "You wouldn't be here if Mark wasn't in some sort of serious trouble. My guess, he's either dead, or near death."

"Yes, Doctor. He's not dead, but close," Maria said, sadly.

"Where?"

"In Costa Rica."

"Got to be Pavones, that's where I figured he went."

Uncrossing his boots, Danny set them on the floor. Rubbing his baldhead, he leaned forward and started talking.

"We met while registering for college—a week late. Your father and I didn't care for waiting in long lines. He said it was inefficient. It didn't make much sense to me, either. So we attended the classes we thought we liked, and if the teacher was not boring, we went and registered for it—after the rush was over.

"The day I met Mark he was trying to convince some beautiful babe in the registrar's office to admit him to a closed geomorphology class. He schmoozed her, convincing the girl to let me in, too. In class, we competed to see who got the better grade. Then, one day, he leaned over and said he got this cool job guiding whitewater rafting trips, saying I should check it out during spring break."

The portable phone rang. Danny answered. "What's up, Oms?"

Someone talked on the other end.

"Oms, when you finish with the shuttle, come to my office. Someone here wants to meet you." Danny pressed the end call button.

"Oms," Maria said. "What an odd name."

Danny smiled, then grinned wider, knowing he was about to shock her. "That's your uncle, Mark's brother, Omar."

Maria's jaw dropped. "Mark has family nearby?"

"Yes, and he's coming over. He'll tell you more about your family. I'm sure you are anxious to know," Danny said. "Oms is going to shit when he sees you."

"Why do you call him Oms?" Maria asked.

"His nickname is Omar the Tent Maker. The river guides named him because he refused to tell us his real name," Danny said, laughing about a prank that had outlasted a decade.

"Us river rats have a culture of our own. It's that efficiency kind of thing that's innate to our lifestyle," Danny explained. "We shortened his name to Oms, because it's easier to say."

"So I have learned." Maria thought how Mark and Chris explained their concept of conserving energy through motion. The surfers on the beach talked about the same concepts to describe their different maneuvers. And when they worked on her father at Pavones, their effort to save his life was swift, efficient, and focused.

"Oms and I are paddling the river this afternoon. If you want to know more about your father, I can think of no better place than on the river. Mark loved the Lehigh," Danny said.

"Why did he leave?"

"I'll tell you his story when we get to a spot on the river where Mark loved to spend his time. You'll need a wetsuit."

Danny went into a closet and produced a stylish purple wetsuit.

"I'll tell you the entire story. First, it's best you understand why we live here." Danny threw Maria the wetsuit. "Here, put this on. It'll fit."

Trying to get information on her father in this town was like pulling teeth. Danny took his time, drooling morsels of information as if there were some sort of barrier he needed to penetrate. "Perhaps this Omar guy will be more compliant."

After inspecting the spongy Neoprene suit, Maria went into the bathroom and squeezed into it.

When she exited the bathroom waddling like a duck, Danny had disappeared.

Leaving the coolness of the building to search for him, she stopped suddenly in the hallway—a mail slot displayed her father's name.

"It is hard to believe he lived here. What was the mystery? Why is it so hard for people to talk about him?"

The chiropractor annoyed Maria. He probably annoyed plenty of other people, but it was clear the doctor didn't care.

"Danny is Danny," Maria recalled, remembering the voice of the coughing woman. "Gerti was right. He's his own person. It seems to be a pattern with these thrill seekers," she considered. They lived a culture outside the norm—with a set of rules and comradeship that spoke its own language.

Maria felt a lingering sadness. The effects of yesterday's long flight, the sudden climate change, and the ongoing tease had affected her, physically. Her conversation with Danny took work.

It was emotionally draining dealing with the standoffishly friendly people of this little hamlet.

As she sat outside on a flagstone stoop, the sunshine that burned off the morning fog warmed her wetsuit. The radiance penetrated the thickness of her glistening brunette hair. Maria wondered what was to become of her life.

What if her father died? Where would she go?

Should she join the convent? She questioned herself for not trying to reason with Flo. She could have worked it out.

Crouching, she bunched her knees to rest her chin. "At least I have my relationship with God. Why is he making this so hard?"

Then she considered, "Maybe it's God who led me here. It was certainly God's decision I found my father."

Maria closed her eyes and silently prayed.

Suddenly, there was the sound of a grinding bicycle chain and crunching stones. It came closer.

Weary, she didn't lift her head to see who it was.

"Hey, baby cakes!" a voice called.

The words jolted her. Abruptly, she raised her head to the familiar phrase. She couldn't believe she was hearing those words again.

"Chris!"

A medium-size man with pudgy cheeks and messy blond hair stopped his mountain bike a few feet away. He propped one foot on the flagstone decking where Maria sat.

The young man smiled affectionately, pleased he'd gotten the expected response from his "baby cakes" comment.

"No, not Chris, I am Omar. Where is Doc?" he asked.

Just then, Doc emerged from the basement of his building carrying a battered kayak.

"Here, Oms, this pig is yours. You need to lose some fat from around your belly, Santa. Paddle Patches and work up a sweat."

Maria guessed Patches was the name of the kayak.

Danny tossed the heavy kayak to the ground.

Wooomph.

"No problem, mon," Omar mimicked.

Danny set his hand on Maria's shoulder. "By the way, meet your niece."

There was a pause.

"No way!" Omar said, surprised.

Maria told Omar her story, including the Retreat, Sister Florence, and how she discovered her father.

"I'm familiar with some of that stuff," Omar told Maria. "A nun in Catholic grade school told me I had the calling to become a priest. I seriously considered it.

"Doc, let's get our asses in gear," Omar said. "The dam keeper shuts off the damn whitewater at noon today."

Grunting, Omar lifted Patches. "Hey, didn't Keith Ashland own this boat?"

He opened the back of Danny's camper and heaved Patches inside. Maria glimpsed inside the camper. It was a mess, just like his office.

Traveling the river wasn't something Maria wanted to do. But if the secret of her father was to be revealed soon, she must.

"Surf's up, let's go, niece," Omar said warmly as they all crammed into the truck cab.

"How odd this town is. Especially these two men," Maria thought, squashed between them. Omar and Danny seemed educated. In fact, it seemed the case with all the adventurers she'd met the past few weeks. She'd misjudged them. Many surfers at Pavones were not bums, but professionals. If it wasn't for their skills, her father wouldn't be alive.

"What a contrast their lives are from mine," she thought. On each side sat men who viewed ego as a good thing. They seemed close friends, respectful. And though their dialogue was odd, it was playful, yet serious when necessary.

Her father was that way with Chris on the radio, when he was instructing how to run the Rio Chirripo. Their communication flowed with a sense of comradeship, humor, and respect. On the other hand, communication amongst nuns seemed strained, lacking candor.

The pickup and its oversized camper left the macadam and rumbled along an abandoned railroad grade, stopping at a metal building in front of the state park entrance. Several inflated rafts sat on the sparse grass outside the building.

As they unloaded, Omar complained to Danny about how heavy Patches was. He grunted, then lifted the heavy boat to his shoulder. Grabbing his helmet, he chanted, "Boat, paddle, lifejacket, spray skirt, brain bucket—and niece. Very cool."

Omar broke into a song as he headed down the path to the Lehigh River. "I'm off to see the river, the wonderful, wonderful river of Oz ..."

A man slightly taller than Danny suddenly appeared from behind a stack of inflated rafts.

"Maria!" Danny said. "I want you to meet someone."

"Ted, meet Maria." Danny smiled. He liked this game of shocking his friends by introducing Maria. And couldn't wait to taunt Gertrude with the news.

"Purple wetsuit," Ted said.

Purple wetsuits were cut as a perfect size six.

"Yes," Danny said, admiring Maria. "Purple."

Maria stepped boldly forward to shake his hand. "I take it you knew my father, Mark Weston."

Maria beat Danny to the surprise.

"Father?" Ted looked to Danny for affirmation.

Danny nodded. "Yes, I'll explain on the river. We got to get going."

"He has no children left. You must be an illegitimate child," Ted said.

"Children!" Maria seized. What did he mean by that?

Chapter 44

Balancing the heavy inflatable over his head, Danny lugged it through a cluster of low-hanging birch trees, and along a narrow trail that led to the river.

"How does Ted know my father, and when were you going to tell me about his children?"

Whipsawed, Maria dogged Danny, chasing him. The branches that scraped the sides of the turtled raft flipped back. Using her forearm, she blocked the swinging branches.

Danny talked from beneath the raft he carried. "Be patient, young lady."

Arriving at the river's edge, he flipped the raft halfway into the water, then straddled the outside tube.

"Come on, jump in! Treat it like a giant waterbed." Danny bounced.

Frustrated, Maria climbed in. The floor was unstable. Water sloshed beneath her feet.

Danny quickly shoved into the river and immediately they picked up the current and headed downstream. Lifting his paddle, he skillfully negotiated to the center of the river.

Overhead, Maria heard the rumbling of cars and trucks as they floated underneath a towering interstate bridge. Small waves lapped at the bow. A refreshing headwind came from downstream.

On each side of her, a deep-green mix of beech, birch, and maples lined the riverbank. The current held a Polaroid transparency that filtered the sunlight as it tried to penetrate the choppy surface. Just ahead, a sturdy railroad bridge spanned, as a blackened sentinel with massive I-beams that rested on towering stone pillars.

The bridge signaled the start of the Lehigh Gorge and "Initiation," the first major rapid.

"You're a son of a bitch, doctor," Maria said, challenging him, tired of his tease. "Why didn't you tell me Mark has children?"

"Had," Danny said. "Didn't you hear Ted? He said 'left.' His children are no longer alive. And you're right, I'm a son of a bitch," he said proudly.

"Shit, sorry!" She was taken aback, as it suddenly became clear. Danny had been trying to summon the courage to tell her whatever tragedy she needed to know. Now Maria understood why she must be patient, and why Danny took his time. He was feeling her out, to see if she could handle whatever he was about to disclose.

"The people in the diner freaked out when I mentioned his name. Is that why?"

"Mostly," Danny said. "I promise you'll hear the whole story when we get a little farther downriver. Now pay attention. Do you notice anything different?"

"Yes, it's peaceful, relaxing—pleasant," she observed.

"True," Danny said. "But that's not what I meant. When you were standing on the riverbank, the water was flowing by you. Now you're riding along with the current. The shoreline is moving. It's the opposite effect—the current is stationary," Danny instructed.

"That's the first thing you need to know about navigating a river. Few people realize this, subtle, but important fluid dynamic."

They drifted under the railroad bridge and over a ledge that created a series of rolling waves. The raft lifted, behaving like a rollercoaster. Enthused, Maria began to understand why these men were drawn to this addiction.

Entering a boulder garden, Danny let the inflatable watercraft wander. With subtle corrections, he allowed them to pass playfully around the larger sandstone obstructions. The scenery, the sounds of the river, mesmerized Maria. For one of the few times in her life, she set aside her guilt and allowed herself to feel pleasure.

Danny studied Maria's expressions. A teacher at heart, he loved to see his students experience new things. They couldn't resist the aphrodisiac qualities of the waters that flowed beneath them. He was pleased to see this tense girl begin to relax and feel free.

The first rapid ended with another series of rolling waves. Briefly forgetting her concerns, Maria laughed hysterically as Danny maneuvered the craft at an angle that maximized the effect.

They drifted lazily. A quiet pool allowed Maria's mood to evolve. It was peaceful. A soft breeze brushed past her as the rapid echoed good-bye. All she could hear was the dipping of Danny's paddle.

For one of the few moments in her life, Maria felt euphoric.

"I guess it's time to tell you about your father." Danny interrupted the peacefulness.

Maria didn't turn to look. She heard him. It was time.

"Many years ago, when Mark returned from his first journey to Costa Rica, he was noticeably different. He never talked about what happened, except to say he found a really neat beach that Keith Ashland had turned him on to.

"Mark loved to surfyak. That's surfing ocean waves," Danny explained. "It's relatively difficult, because unlike river waves, ocean waves aren't stationary. They roll toward shore. I don't want to take the entire trip explaining the dynamics as to why surf kayaking is much more difficult. But when Mark discovered ocean surfing, he pursued mastering it with a vengeance."

As they drifted between a series of miniature islands, the current quickened, but not fast enough to create waves. Maria stared into the water, watching the moss-covered cobbles race beneath them.

"Back then, all of us were at pivotal points in our lives, sowing our oats—searching for our purpose, and often experimenting with love. I went to chiropractic school. Ted went off to claim many first river descents. Mark stayed behind to work full time on the river.

"On weekends, I came from school to guide river trips with him. Mark was always happy to see me. We'd drink beers and chase women until the sun came up. Many weekends, we didn't sleep." Danny thought fondly of the good memories.

"As you know, your father was fearless. Many of us who went on river trips with him stopped following him through the more difficult rapids. The drops he ran were just too damn difficult, and entirely too dangerous."

Maria listened while Danny talked about her daredevil father.

She reflected on Golfito, how the shades of tropical green on the hillside behind the retreat were similar to the evergreens towering around her. She envisioned her father—he must have kayaked by here hundreds of times—his smiling face. She wished he'd paddle by at any moment, saying hello—perhaps calling her baby cakes, drawing her attention.

The raft floated underneath another bridge, its decking made of hemlock. As the steel bridge disappeared, another quiet pool came beneath them.

Danny continued. "I barely survived half the drops I followed him through."

Their raft entered a narrow chute near the left riverbank.

"This rapid is called Triple-Drop," Danny said, cutting off the conversation. "Hang on. This will be fun!"

The once calm river was suddenly narrow and steep—the vessel bobbing violently. Confident, Danny sat high on the back tube, smiling.

When Maria turned forward, all she saw was a wall of white, swirling turbulence coming straight at her. Before she could react, the boat crashed into the chaos. She lurched ahead. The water was chilly. And as quickly as the surprise came upon her, it ended.

Danny was laughing in the background. "That was Triple-Drop," he said. "It's almost as good as sex."

Repositioning herself, tucking her feet beneath a crosstube, Maria thought about the comparison and wondered what sex must feel like. Would she ever come to experience the pleasure he referred?

"It was here in Triple-Drop that I had the rare occasion of rescuing your father's sorry ass. He would have drowned if I hadn't saved him," Danny said proudly, telling the story of the rescue.

"The Lehigh was way above flood stage, at a level we rarely get to paddle. Stubsy, the dam keeper, opened the gates of the flood control dam all the way. That little wave you went through is called a hole—a wave that never stops breaking upon itself. If you get trapped, it's hard to escape. Everyone was afraid to surf it at super flood stage, except your father.

"Mark decided to set the record for surfing Triple-Drop. When he dropped in, it flipped him many times, dislocating both shoulders. And because he couldn't move either arm, he couldn't grab his spray skirt to release from the kayak. I jumped into the flooded river upstream and swam into the hole, snagged his body, and drug his sorry ass out.

"That's the day he coined the term *The Cathedral Syndrome*. He told me how peaceful and calm the experience was. He said, 'If someone wants to commit suicide that would be the way to do it. You won't even know when you die, because it's a pleasant experience.'"

Danny scratched his chin then rubbed his cheek. "Sometimes I think he really was trying to kill himself."

"Why do you think that?" Maria asked.

They rounded a bend where the river became wide and shallow. A whiff of jasmine scented the air.

"Honestly, when I really think about it, your father wasn't trying to kill himself. He was finding himself. Not many people out there think the way I do. You'll have to decide for yourself, Maria."

Danny continued. "I remember this set of rapids on the Rouge River in Canada, Seven Sisters. It's a series of waterfalls that'd never been run in a kayak before. Mark ran the first five waterfalls, cleanly. He got hammered in the sixth, and went around and around at the bottom, like in a washing machine. We couldn't rescue him because of the cliffs on both sides. All we could do was watch for what seemed an eternity.

"Eventually, Mark's kayak spit out, then drifted upside down for a while. We thought he'd drowned. But suddenly, Mark rolled and ran the last waterfall, cleanly.

"He should've drowned, but miraculously survived. Sometimes I think he's alive solely by the hand of God."

"Funny you mentioned God," Maria said. "I don't take you for a religious person."

"It's the only explanation that makes sense," Danny replied.

"Here comes Omar." Danny pointed his paddle upstream.

Omar's arms pinwheeled as each blade of his Ashland dug like a steamboat paddlewheel. Seconds later, he arrived and glided alongside. He smiled at Maria and draped his dripping arms around the tube to rest.

"Hey, niece," Omar said with a broadening grin. This time he took care not to call her baby cakes again.

"Hey," Maria said warmly, thinking how addictively friendly he seemed.

"Oms," Danny said, "I was talking with Maria about something you and I discussed many times. The debate whether your brother had a death wish or not."

Omar looked at Danny, not saying anything for several seconds. They were communicating nonverbally. Omar manifested an expression that asked if he told Maria about the event in Mark's life that forced him to abandon his life and isolate himself in Costa Rica.

Maria, cueing in on their silent conversation, said, "That doesn't explain the reaction in the diner. This town knows something."

Letting go of the tube, Omar allowed his kayak to drift from the raft. Danny sat back and silently contemplated. He felt Omar should tell the story.

The threesome drifted through a small rapid until they hit another quiet pool. The canyon walls had increased in height.

Wanting to break the silent stalemate, Maria finally demanded they tell what happened to her father. "It's time, guys! I've waited long enough."

"Yes, more is to this story." Danny broke the silence and decided to get to the point.

"When Mark returned from Costa Rica, he told us about the first descent he claimed of the Rio Chirripo, a river deemed unnavigable. Mark was the first and only one to run the river."

Maria interrupted. "I know all about that."

Danny raised his eyebrows and wondered what she knew about the rapids on the Chirripo.

He continued. "He told us about Pavones and this unusual place, where young women cloistered and decided to become nuns.

"Many of us didn't believe the story, because sometimes he joked while holding a straight face. But it looks like you're living proof," Danny said.

"After returning there was a noticeable change. Mark spent most of his time at Rockport, surfing his favorite wave for hours. 'It's where I like to do my thinking,' he used to say. He said it 'centered' him.

"Mark always had this thing about getting centered. I guess it is how he dealt with whatever internal debate was raging within him."

Danny looked downriver. Omar had paddled off, darting in and out between smaller and larger boulders.

"Then, one day, Mark meets this girl on the river and out of the blue he marries her. Her name was Lucy. We were all shocked," Danny said.

Leaning back, Danny slid his paddle into the water and pulled like a rudder. The raft nudged a jagged rock, deflected, and accelerated into a spin.

Maria looked up to see the sky spiraling around.

"We just passed Wilhoyt's Rock," Danny said. "That's my little move to add some excitement."

Danny continued with his story.

"Mark met Lucy while she was skinny dipping at Rockport. Lucky bastard," Danny said, envious that Mark had stolen one of his longtime dreams—rescuing a naked woman in the Lehigh.

"It turns out Lucy was the daughter of one of the most prominent Catholic families in the county. They lived on a farm, on Peat Moss Road. We'd never seen Lucy before because she attended a small all-girls college somewhere in Vermont. She'd just graduated and returned home to visit.

"Mark found out where she lived and hunted her down for a date. But Lucy refused to date him. She was concerned how dating an adventurer looked to her parents. They wouldn't approve. Plus, Lucy was heading to the convent—your convent in Golfito, believe it or not. Mark was a nice guy and needed someone in his life. Lucy was a good catch. She had lots of spunk.

"Lucy finally went out with him. They fell in love. And within a year, married. Her family didn't approve. In fact, they tried to block the marriage by bringing in longtime family friends, a priest and nun, to try to split them up."

Danny had to stop his story so he could negotiate "No-Way," one of the more technical rapids on the Lehigh. Meanwhile, Omar popped from behind a large rock directly in front of the raft, startling Maria.

Danny grinned and aimed for Omar, trying to run him over. Maria closed her eyes, thinking he was going to hit and crush her newly found uncle.

Suddenly, Omar rolled upside down at the last second. The raft passed right over. Danny smiled.

Maria laughed, realizing they played a practical joke.

With ease, Danny skillfully negotiated No-Way rapids. At the bottom, Ted caught them. Omar joined Ted. Both hung onto each side of the raft to engage in the conversation.

Maria observed how comfortable these three men were with each other—true friends, with no barriers amongst them. It was apparent each had a profound respect for the other—a rare quality.

"I guess you have an understanding of your father, us, and the river by now?" Omar asked.

"Yes," Maria answered. "It's interesting that all of you, including Dad, ended up here."

"We could have gone off into the world and made careers, but decided enjoying each day like this was much more important," Omar explained.

"Please finish. Tell me what happened to his children," Maria urged.

The raft drifted around a bend and into another calm pool. Tall white pines mixed with hemlocks towered above, shading the hillsides, allowing only enough sun to warm the peaceful current.

The train track that ran the entire length of the river gorge had disappeared into a tunnel.

"This is your father's favorite spot," Danny said.

Omar and Ted nodded, confirming the observation.

"I can see why," Maria replied. "It's tranquil, perfect place for meditation."

"At the end of this pool is that funny-looking wave I was telling you about. I wanted to wait until we got to this spot to tell you about him," Danny said apologetically.

"We liked Lucy," Omar interrupted. "She was attractive, athletic, and intelligent—like me," he joked.

"It didn't take her long to get pregnant," Ted said, smiling, winking at Maria.

Danny and Omar chuckled. The raft drifted slowly along. The story continued.

"There were two other children right after that, too," Ted added. He lifted away from the raft and adjusted himself inside his kayak.

"After the third child, Mark stopped hanging out with us. He was always tending to his kids," Omar said.

The three men were now telling the story.

"We saw little of him or his wife. And when we stopped by to see our friend, she got annoyed.

"It was customary when we got off the river to down a few beers together. But Mark made excuses and went home immediately. He wouldn't even stop at Latchette's Bar to have just one beer with us.

"When we asked him to hang out like the good old days, he cut us off, saying Lucy would make him pay if he came home ten minutes late. Apparently, she turned out to be a controlling person, often using the children as a tool to manipulate Mark," Danny said.

Omar and Ted both nodded, while Danny told the story.

"After the birth of his third child, Mark had isolated himself altogether. We later learned, at the trial, that his family situation had completely broken down."

"Trial," Maria blurted.

Danny didn't react. "I'll get to that in a moment. One day, Mark suddenly quits working at the rafting company. Turned out, Lucy didn't care for his profession of working on the river—something he loved. She told him he needed a more responsible occupation."

"Trial?" Maria repeated. The thought was still stuck in her head.

"I'm getting to it," he said.

The raft had stopped moving downstream, and was circling in a large eddy. Omar and Ted were no longer hanging onto the inflatable. They were sitting back in their kayaks, drifting within the eddy, intently listening, contemplating their own thoughts.

"After Mark quit his job, he tended to his children full time. But he couldn't find another job because this area is known as the Rust Belt. There aren't many jobs for people with his kind of education.

"So Mark decided to go back to school and become an accountant—a profession counter to his nature. He told us he became an accountant because that's what the most number of ads for jobs in the classifieds were for. He figured he could find employment his wife approved of, so she would be happier, less difficult," Danny said.

"That explains the accounting practice," Maria observed.

"Plus, he figured his wife's family would finally accept him—they didn't."

"Anytime we saw Mark, he was with his children or doing something for his children. He was a good father. Many people in town thought that too.

"One day, when his youngest daughter was just eleven months old, something tragic happened."

Danny paused; Ted and Omar came close and held onto the raft, as support for Danny, who became emotional. His eyes filled. "We loved his children.

"According to Mark's testimony, he was sitting on the couch, while Lucy was in the kitchen. He was studying for the business classes he was taking. Mark couldn't remember what she was doing in the kitchen, but said he noticed his daughter was crying an unusually long time.

"Mark said Lucy had tended to his youngest daughter, then disappeared upstairs, where his two older children were in the bathtub, getting ready for bed. He thought it was unusual his daughter had stopped crying so suddenly. So he went over to check."

Danny paused for a moment. Omar and Ted's eyes focused upon Maria.

"His daughter was dead, suffocated. Mark tried to revive the child, but it was too late. Mark ran upstairs and found his wife sitting on the floor, holding her other two children in her arms, rocking. They were dead, too. She'd drowned them in the bathtub."

"Wow!" Maria was in awe—speechless.

"Did they arrest her?" she asked after a considerable pause.

"Lucy told the police Mark killed them. Said she had nothing to do with it."

"Oh my God!" Shocked, she listened as the story unfolded.

"No one knew who to believe," Omar said, adding to the story. "Mark's wife was from a family with deep ties to the county courthouse. Everyone perceived the deeply religious family to be noble and reputable. No one in town could remotely believe it was her."

"Except for us," Ted added.

Omar nodded.

"The police arrested Mark and charged him with killing his children. The trial portrayed his wife in a positive light. Her attorney brought out how she worked so hard to earn a living, while her irresponsible, outdoor husband had quit his job and sponged off her.

"Lucy's family was related to the district attorney, who was a nasty son of a bitch. He tried to destroy Mark," Omar said.

For the first time, Maria saw Omar serious, not jovial, as he tended to be.

"When it came time for Mark to present his case, we thought he didn't have a prayer. Mark testified his wife had killed the children as I described. But Mark told a story none of us heard before. It explained why he spent more and more time at home, taking care of his children."

Omar rested his back against Patches' bulky cockpit rim. He tried to get comfortable as he continued to describe what had happened.

"Mark said soon after he married Lucy, he witnessed periods of deep and severe withdrawals. The episodes became more frequent, and more sustained, after the birth of each child. Finally, she'd slipped completely into this alternate personality. Mark said he was dealing with a Jekyll and Hyde situation almost on a weekly basis."

"Didn't Mark point this out to anyone?" Maria asked.

"No, he never told anyone—not even me, his brother," Omar said. "Mark did state he inquired to her family about her odd behavior. But the family treated him like he was making some sort of accusation. They got defensive and ignored him.

"He said he just dealt with it, and tried to protect his children, because when she was in this alternate mood, she severely criticized her children, especially the son."

"Sounds like some sort of complicated disorder. Perhaps Bipolar II behavior, possibly cyclothymic," Maria indicated.

"Hmm," grunted Ted and Danny, who seemed to be digesting the memory.

His back hurting a bit, Omar leaned forward, away from his cockpit rim.

"Mark had many, many witnesses who testified on his behalf. Everyone testified he was a great guy, and couldn't conceive him killing his children."

"What was Mark's wife testimony?" Maria asked.

"Lucy said she was outside gardening. When she came inside, she found them dead. Told the jury Mark was on the couch, watching TV like a couch potato. Claimed he was depressed about not finding work, and lately, was having a hard time dealing with it. She feared he would flip out and beat her and her children."

"So what happened? Was Dad found guilty?"

"Hung jury," Omar said. "They deliberated for many days. The trial headlined the newspapers for many weeks. Mark felt disgraced."

"It all becomes clear now," Maria said. "Everyone in town is split, just like the jury. Dad is forever under suspicion he killed his children, so he splits to a place where he can hide from the hardships of his life."

"Pavones," Danny said.

Ted and Omar exhaled. Maria saw their tension as the story was retold.

"Mark just suddenly disappeared, not telling anyone. We figured we'd hear someday he'd died on some river," Omar said. "How sad—looks like he's almost done it."

Danny spun the raft and directed it out of the eddy into the current.

"What happened to Mark's wife?" Maria asked.

"Oh, forgot to tell you," Danny answered. "Shortly after the trial, the family sold the farm on Peat Moss Road and moved away. Years later a rumor starts circulating in town that Lucy was committed to an institution. The family said it was the result of her losing her children. A year later, her father dies and some of the sisters and brothers finally open up, revealing their sister, Lucy, was severely bipolar. They said it ran in the family genes. Their dominating father was obsessed with ridding his lineage of the disease. When a severe case of it showed in Lucy, he didn't want anyone to know about it.

"See, Lucy was supposed to join the convent—not have children. But Mark ruined that plan. That's why her parents treated the both of them poorly. Their daughter passed her guilt onto Mark and his children. Each time she had a child, her condition worsened, exacerbated by the changes in her body chemistry, and the guilt laid upon her for possibly continuing the bad family gene.

"Finally, one of the sisters confesses that Lucy's controlling father had laid a level of guilt so great on Lucy after the third child, she snapped, killing her children. It turns out that hours before the children were murdered, her father had told Lucy she should have been the last in the bloodline to have the disease, blaming her for passing it along, demanding she stop having babies."

Maria interrupted and explained to the men she knew about this topic.

"Families, particularly wealthy families, will attempt to purge bad genes from their bloodline, forcing children who exhibit mental disorders into the priesthood or convent. The Catholic Church understood this and gladly took them in. The families were indebted, and remained faithful contributors as a means of protecting the family secret.

"I know this story all too well," Maria said. "I feel for Dad. No one but his good friends believed him. He certainly wasn't going to get help from the church."

Danny, Omar, and Ted nodded. Maria had put them at ease.

Omar paddled toward the raft, nudging with the nose of his kayak. It pushed into the current, drifting.

Everyone was quiet, contemplative.

Maria thought about her father's raw deal. Why had God dealt him such a bad hand?

"Mark's favorite spot is downstream on the right." Danny pointed. He saw Maria was obviously upset.

She peered downstream at the glass-like stretch of river. The horizon dropped, water leapt, slapping the air, then folded over and disappeared. Seconds later, as they floated closer, the dancing water repeated.

"This is Dad's spot," Maria observed. "It's simple, yet beautiful. I like things simple and beautiful. I can see why he liked it here. It is peaceful, solitary—the perfect place to meditate to center yourself."

Danny nodded. Omar and Ted had drifted away.

The raft rolled into the faster current. Danny spun them so Maria could see the dancing wave as they passed.

Maria thought of her father lying in Golfito hospital. She should go back. She missed him and suddenly felt an urgency to return, so she could comfort and heal him—make the rest of his life happy. She was his only remaining child and wanted him to love her. She refused to consider he might not live.

Danny pulled the raft to the take-out. A small stream came into the river just above the takeout steps. "Be careful, Maria," he warned. "You've been riding on a waterbed for the past few hours. Your legs aren't used to standing on the dry land."

The water was shallow. Stepping onto the rounded river stones, Maria transferred her weight. Immediately, she fell. Chilling, cold water rushed into her wetsuit.

"Damn—brrrr." Maria sat on the rocky bottom up to her waist in icy water. "Why is the river so, so cold?"

"Welcome to Rockport," Danny announced. "It's cold because the tributary flows from the Buck Mountain coal mine—forty-three degrees year-round."

Soggy, Maria climbed the steep, homemade steps to the railroad grade. Omar and Ted had already loaded their kayaks and stowed their gear.

Maria turned to find Danny with the entire raft on top of his head.

She chuckled; he looked like a turtle running by.

Wooommmp!

Danny flipped the raft and it crashed to the ground.

Pissshhh!

The valves opened to deflate it.

All three men kept busy, attending to the task of loading and securing equipment. They worked in harmony, like tidy ants preparing their mound.

Maria took a few moments to take in the natural surroundings. The cold creek made a ruckus as it tumbled over bleached rocks.

"Come on, Maria, get in the van," Omar said, removing the top half of his wetsuit, releasing the tension on his Santa belly.

Ted jumped into the driver's side and started the engine.

"That was fast," Maria said, observing how they processed and packed their equipment so quickly.

No one responded—it was routine.

In the short time Maria knew these unique men, she had developed a profound respect. She admired their nonconformity and the deliberate way they fashioned their lives.

Now she understood how important it was for her father to live as he did. She envisioned him here, in the van with his close friends.

"Rockport is the perfect place to collect and sort things out. Pavones has the same qualities," Maria thought.

"How my father must've loved this river, and his little surfing wave. He must've been here often, praying to God, seeking help in dealing with his troubles—an earthly therapy."

The rickety, light blue van groaned as it made its way, ascending a steep, single-lane road. Ted beeped the horn that echoed a warning to oncoming cars as he rounded the blind curve. The van pushed against a berm, where the embankment dropped to the cold creek below. The kayaks held fast as the van bounced and rocked anxiously side to side.

Maria looked at Danny sprawled on the seat behind her. He was fast asleep. Omar sat in the passenger side, calm, quiet, contemplative—obviously thinking of his brother.

A canopy of ancient pines shaded the road. The van rounded a corner where a small church sat on the right. Two beautiful waterfalls spilled over on the left.

"What a beautiful spot—a perfect place for a church."

Maria envisioned living here, sitting on the church steps, listening to the waterfalls, smelling the cool fresh air stirred by the creek, inhaling the scents from the summer pines. She dreamed of her father coming from the river in his Scout loaded with kayaks, stopping to chat—talking for hours. She envisioned them happy, father and daughter, and imagined her mother meeting her father again.

Did God want her here today to learn about her father's adventurous lifestyle? Was God trying to correct a mistake, or tell her something? Was she sent here to do just that?

Maria wondered what God's plan was.

The lumpy road gave way to a rolling landscape and freshly harvested farmlands. The sun shined brightly. Maria could feel its warmth. Ted turned the van onto the main road.

It took about twenty minutes to make their way back to town. The mood was somber. Maria's thoughts turned to Golfito, Sister Florence, and Chris. "What am I to do? Is it my mission to carry on Sister Oliver's dream to change the church's discriminating ways? None of this could have come to be without God's guiding hand," she thought.

"What about Chris? Did God put him in my life because I am to be a mother, to give my father grandchildren?"

The van bounced over the railroad tracks. The kayaks held fast.

Danny finished his nap. Omar took his gritty feet off the dashboard. They passed the diner and turned into the lot where Maria's rental car was parked. Tired, Maria thought about the flight to Costa Rica in the morning and was anxious to go.

~ ~ ~

The shower refreshed Maria. Her new friends were sitting on the flagstone patio outside the depot building, waiting to talk with her.

Danny opened a beer and handed it to her. "We must toast your father," he said, barefoot, still in his wetsuit. "We wish Mark well and hope to see him soon."

All four people clanked their glass bottles in tribute.

"You can stay at my place tonight if you want, Maria," Omar offered.

"If you can stand the mess and the cooties," Ted joked.

They all laughed.

Chapter 45

The Comair flight leaving Wilkes-Barre, Pennsylvania, departed on time. When she boarded, Maria's thoughts were of her life, how it had changed. She came to this beautiful, rural hill country to learn about her father. She departed knowing him and a bit more about herself.

Omar and Maria talked at length before she went to bed last night. He reaffirmed her father was a good man, undeserving of the misfortunes of love. She shared her life with Omar, the people in it—Sister Florence, Oliver, and even Dr. Jones. Omar was an interesting person, capable of discussing or debating virtually any topic. Maria saw her introspective nature in him. She shared with Omar her mother's letter, the story about the chance encounter on Pavones that resulted in her birth. Omar assured Maria he would contact the hospital in Golfito and give her permission to act on his family's behalf. He told her to hurry back and give a full report on his brother's condition.

The return flight could not progress fast enough. Maria reconsidered her hasty departure from Golfito. Abandoning Mark's bedside wasn't rational. She concluded her decision might have been her only way back as an increasing anxiety grew. She yearned to be at his bedside and prayed to God to make him well, so he could help her resolve the issues of her own life.

On the surface, Mark appeared to be a complete, competent person. Yet she'd missed underlying signs of a troubled soul. Leroy, the bus driver, lost his wife and became a broken man. Mark lost his children. And unlike Leroy, he exhibited no outward signs of sorrow. Mark abandoned his home, his friends, and his life. Maria didn't know of his anguish until she visited his hometown.

Was Mark an emotional wreck like Leroy, in need of an angel to heal his heart, save his soul? Was Mark trying to find a peaceful way of killing himself, to get closure—evaporate the pain that embedded itself deep inside him?

"It's hard to separate," Maria thought. Mark chased the natural cycle of life. As a young man, he searched for his purpose, sought adventure, and then marriage and children. But with life, no guarantees exist. His mate, Lucy, had her own misfortune. And after the tragedy, Mark returned to the part of his life that made him whole again.

A strong man, Mark survived by barricading his sorrow beyond his thoughts. He purged the horrific tragedy that dogged him through sport—on a razor's edge. An absolute focus stayed his sadness—numbed his pain. And when he was at the edge of mayhem, an instant came to set him free. If he could pass that pain into another realm, lift it to the next heavenly step, his sadness would be cauterized—the anguish removed permanently—so he could love one last time.

He must've been waiting a lifetime for the Pavones storm—waves so high not even the surest of daredevils sought the dare. And when Mark got beyond the beach break, it must have been clear that this was his biggest challenge. Like an addicted gambler, maybe he'd cash in big this time, recoup losses, step away from the table even, his sorrow erased, washed away with the tide. Maria had pieced it all together.

On that long flight, it became clear. It made sense.

Maria closed her eyes and summoned her father's final moment on Pavones. High on the wave, his deep-blue eyes—their gazes reunited from a prior eternity.

Through his expression, she heard his confession, his thoughts. "All this time I've searched in the wrong place. Standing on the beach, an arm's reach away, is my answer, a daughter, Maria. Her kiss of love can easily heal my gaping wound—a love so powerful, her slightest smudge could scrub the sadness calcified to my troubled heart."

~ ~ ~

The San Jose flight landed. Anxious, Maria wanted to get to Golfito fast. She needed to know her father's condition.

While waiting in customs, Maria pictured Chris, tall and handsome, beating the system with a smile and a child's toy. She reflected upon her attitude, her negative thoughts about Chris. Where had they come from?

Maria took a cab to the hangar for the short hop to Golfito— the final leg, her journey's end. This time she remembered to drink plenty of water.

The little propeller-driven plane lifted like a butterfly on a windy day. It bounced, rapidly rising within the afternoon convection. Maria was not afraid of the turbulence. If the plane crashed, she'd confront God for the answers to dizzying questions that swirled like the plane.

The sky above the Osa's ocean was cloudless and blue. To the east, where the sea breeze fought with the land, venting thunderheads had erupted, the inland jungle receiving a drenching—Golfito escaping the storm.

Maria couldn't wait for the plane to land. The richness and beauty of the landscape below didn't register this time. She prayed her father would be conscious, so she could tell him she was his daughter, and hear for the first time his love for her.

The plane banked left, then right, and dropped onto the runway. Maria raced to beat everyone to the waiting taxi.

Moisture hung in the air like a wet sponge ready to ooze at the slightest disturbance. Beads, then streams ran along the inside of her white blouse. Empty water bottles bounced in her backpack, as she made her way, quickly.

Maria stuck her head into the taxi's window and said. "*La hospital, por favor*—please, *muy rápido.*"

The middle-aged Tico nodded and motioned for her to get in. Within five minutes, the aged taxi rolled to the hospital doors.

The sun had slipped below the horizon. The lights inside the small hospital flickered. Much of the staff had left for the evening. Racing up the steps, she burst through the doors and into the ward. She arrived at Mark's doorway, overshot, and grabbed the frame to stop.

She looked inside the room, expecting to see her father, conscious and smiling. The room was empty—the bed stripped.

Her first thought was this was all a bad dream. Her lasting thought was he died. Maria's stomach churned. She stood still and stared at the empty bed, hoping Mark would reappear in the condition she'd left him—respirator working, clinging to life.

A hushed, compassionate voice from behind her said, "Maria, Maria, he is gone."

When she heard those words, she thought her father had gone to Pavones to go surfing. But the voice cut off the wish by saying, "I am sorry, Maria. Mark has passed."

Maria collapsed to the floor and cried hysterically. She wanted to make it to the bed where he died, to feel his presence, but her body was too weak. She cried heavy and hard . . . Sister Florence, the voice that delivered the lie, combed her meaty fingers through the thickness of Maria's hair.

She grieved for several minutes. Flo tried to lift her several times, but she was not ready. Maria was guilt-ridden. She wasn't at Mark's bedside when he died. She'd abandoned him. Mark died alone, deserted by the joy he would've known had he met his only living child.

Sister Florence towered over Maria. She stood stoic, falsely sympathetic and determined. Flo had to remove her from the building, fast, before anyone told her Mark was at the San Isidro hospital, alive.

Maria's heart was filled with the deepest sorrow. There was no more emotion or strength inside to deal with Flo's presence.

As consolatory as she could muster, Flo said, "Come on, Maria, you should leave." Hoisting her by the waist, Sister Florence limped Maria out of the building.

Weak and groggy, Maria continued to cry. Vulnerable, she wasn't thinking clearly and allowed herself to go with Florence.

"Where are we going?" she asked, tears streaming.

Sister Florence said, "Maria, we are leaving Golfito. We are going to drive to San Jose and stay there for the night. You're not right. I can understand and forgive you. Father Peter and I are taking you back to the United States."

"But what about the funeral?" Maria stood straight and gathered herself.

Flo thought fast. The lie deepened. "Mark was cremated. He died the morning you abandoned him. The climate of the jungle requires all remains to be disposed of immediately, to prevent the spread of disease. He's gone."

"What?" A lump stuck in Maria's throat. She shook her head. "My painting, I want to hold onto my painting."

"I gave it to Alex. It's been too much of a crutch for you. You don't need that painting, Maria." Flo escorted her to the passenger side of the Cadillac.

What Flo didn't know was little Alex helped Carlos pack Flo's car with Maria's belongings before they left to stay at Mark's house. Alex, discovering where Flo had hid the painting, secretly returned the painting by slipping it under the passenger-side seat. During the ride to the hospital, unseen by Flo, the painting of Pavones had slid from under.

Getting into the Cadillac, Maria kicked the painting. It caught her eye.

"What are you doing with my painting? No, you didn't give it to Alex." Maria opened the passenger door and unwedged *The Waves of Pavones*.

She held the painting to Flo's face. "You lied to me, Flo."

Caught, Flo couldn't defend herself and struggled to react. Bitter and red-faced, Flo yelled back, "Maria, you lied to me, too."

Angered, Maria slid across to the driver's side and pressed the button that locked all the doors.

"Maria, Maria, open the door . . . Now!"

Turning the key, she drove off.

Chapter 46

Four blocks away, next to the church, sat the rectory. Without transportation, Flo needed to summon Father Peter for his assistance. With clenched fists, thumbs curled and punched outward, she started toward the rectory. When she hit the grade of the last street, she strained, her forearms bent and pumped outward at sixty degrees. Flo waddled as fast as she could, uphill, toward Our Lady of the Angels.

Drenched, Flo pushed on. Her chest tightened and she couldn't take in a full breath. At the base of the steps leading to the church terrace, she leaned against the rail and pulled herself along the staircase.

On the terrace, her left ankle gave way. The black leather shoe with its boxed heel had twisted in a crack. The shoe leather dug into the gap of her swollen ankle and bent it at a torturous angle. A sharp, stinging pain shot through her thick leg.

Florence hobbled across the terrace. Her lungs were heavy, her breathing more constricted. A piercing, severe, crushing pain slammed the center of her chest. She could no longer draw air. Her eyes rolled and she looked at the cross that towered over the steeple. Flo's massive frame twisted on the heel of her shoe. Her knee buckled. Her ankle snapped from the uneven distribution of weight, and Flo tumbled to the marble decking.

Bearing the weight of the fall, her forearm had snapped. Flo lay flat on her back. Her eyes rolled into her head.

She convulsed, choking; her heart seized.

Sister Elizabeth Florence died.

Chapter 47

Maria had driven the Cadillac only a short distance into the date palm orchard. Hunched over and choking on tears, she was unable to come to terms with her father's death. The brief encounter with him and the lives he had touched; she had come to love him as a father.

There was nowhere for her to go. She had stolen Flo's car and feared she'd be arrested. Maria decided to drive to Pavones, the end of the road for her.

Somehow, Maria made it to the ferry before it shut down for the night. In the dark and along the rutty road, she drove the Cadillac to Pavones.

She parked behind the cabana and cried herself to sleep.

~ ~ ~

The mid-morning sun struck Maria's face. She had slept curled in the lumpy front seat. Her sad eyes roamed the Cadillac, finally fixing upon the painting of Pavones on the floor.

Recalling yesterday's grief, she didn't care to move.

"What do I do now?" she thought. "Where do I go?"

The emptiness inside returned; her depression deepened. She looked at *The Waves of Pavones*—the painting no longer a friend.

A compulsion overcame her. "Run into the ocean with the painting and drown it. Keep walking until I can no longer touch bottom. I want to die, so I can be with my father. God will forgive me. Mom will cry and Dad will love me."

Wanting to rid her pain, she seized this idea that came as the answer—take her life, end it here at Pavones. A new life would begin in heaven, beside her father, joining Sister Oliver.

A melancholy overcame her. The sadness, the grief, and a lifetime of angst suddenly lifted. Soon, she would be with her father; all she had to do was walk into the ocean and drown herself.

With the painting underneath her arm, Maria crawled from the mud-covered vehicle, bypassed the cabana, and stepped off the seawall. The spectacular view, the beautiful day, afforded no pleasure.

Maria was lethargic—in a stupor. The surf had subsided, the perfectly shaped waves gone. Maria had cried out her tears. The well in her soul ran dry. Holding the painting prisoner against her chest, she stared out at the expanse of the placid ocean.

Progressing, she winced as the cobblestones pinched her bare feet. Determined to follow this through to its end, Maria waded into the gently lapping waters. She wanted to be with her father, to join him at the spot that took his life.

She continued her steady pace, deeper and deeper. The seawater came to her calves, then her knees. The warmth of the ocean encircled her waist.

"Keep going," she repeated, the water rising. "Keep going, I can do this. It will soon be over."

Then she thought, "How do I keep from floating?"

The frame of the oil painting pressed firmly against her chest.

"Hold my breath, sit on the bottom, and pile rocks onto my legs. That'll work."

"I'm coming, Dad. I love you," she said as the ocean covered her shoulders.

"Please help me, Dad. I want to be with you. Let me die."

The increasing depth slowed her progress.

It came to her neck. Maria tiptoed until her feet could not touch the rocky bottom.

Deliberately, she forced the air from her lungs and started to sink.

There was silence.

Then she heard, "Hey, baby cakes!"

"Dad is calling me. How peaceful."

An arm wrapped around her waist.

"Hi, Dad, you have come to get me."

"Yes, drowning is peaceful."

Her eyes closed.

~ ~ ~

After Chris accompanied Mark in the ambulance to San Isidro, he planned to return by bus to Golfito. Mark was conscious and asked Chris to go to Pavones and get the Scout. He also told Chris the girl he said he planned to marry was still around.

Chris returned to search for Maria in Golfito. He even approached Sister Florence at the rectory. That's when Flo learned Mark was alive.

After Flo told him Maria had left to an undisclosed location to start her postulancy, she monitored the hospital, guessing Maria might return.

In Pavones to retrieve the Scout, Chris stopped at the cantina to say hello to the owners, and to hear more of the story of the giant waves.

With the ocean calm and the storm long gone, all the surfers had left. Pavones was quiet. The wife of the cantina owner was outside, hanging tablecloths on the line. At quite a distance up the beach, she noticed a Cadillac parked behind the cabana, and thought its presence odd. When Maria emerged from the car and walked into the water, the wife ran into the cantina and alerted Chris.

Chris sprinted toward Maria, calling her. By the time he arrived, Maria had disappeared beneath the surface.

Marking the spot where she submerged, he raced into the ocean and swam the short distance. Diving under, Chris found Maria and wrapped his arms around her body.

~ ~ ~

"Ouch, that hurts!" Maria felt someone's arms wrap her waist and squeeze hard.

Releasing the painting, she opened her eyes underwater.

"What's Mark doing?" she thought, feeling herself pulled upwards. "Who's this?"

As she broke the surface, a voice said, "I'm not going to let you drown, so you better stop trying!"

"Chris?" Maria said, startled, recognizing him. "It's really you!"

Chris lifted Maria and carried her to shore.

"Maria, I've been searching for you," he said. "I love you."

Suspended in his muscular arms, she looked into his deep-blue eyes. "I love you, too," Maria said, her heart racing. "I want to be with you forever."

As they kissed, Maria felt the love of her father within him.

God had given her his greatest gift—eternal love.

♥ The End ♥

Epilogue

Later that afternoon, after almost making love inside the cabana, Maria and Chris headed to San Isidro to visit Mark. They took the Scout.

Maria was elated when she saw Mark conscious and recovering.

Father and daughter exchanged histories and bonded. Their spirits healed.

Jane packed her bags, abandoned her New England lifestyle, and settled in Golfito. Sister Florence's will read that Maria inherited her entire estate—worth several million dollars.

Maria and Chris married.

With Florence's money, they persuaded the church to sell them the old banana plantation. Together with Jane, Mark, and Carlos, they turned Our Lady of Fatima into an environmental education center. Named in honor of Sister Oliver, it became so popular they had to expand within a year.

Danny, Omar, and Ted came to Costa Rica to visit and explore the countryside. Danny lost his edge enough that they asked him to teach full time at the center. However, everyone kept a watchful eye.

Danny wanted to name the latrines after Sister Florence. Maria, Chris, Jane, and Mark balked at that suggestion. They forgave Sister Florence for her weakness, and created a charity that would properly assist those seeking a vocation with God.

Maria gave birth to twin girls. Jane and Mark remained friends and involved themselves with helping to raise their grandchildren. Carlos raised little Alex, who went off to college, returning as a doctor.

www.ingramcontent.com/pod-product-compliance
Lightning Source LLC
Chambersburg PA
CBHW062008170626
46813CB00001B/71